# WHAT OTHERS ARE SAYING

*What others are saying . . .*

"A fascinating story . . . through well-written fiction, *Messengers* captures the essence of the ongoing reality."

Robert Bauval, author of a dozen books, including co-author of *The Orion Mystery, Message of the Sphinx.*

"Julie Loar has given us a magical tour through a world of fascinating ancient mysteries. We are invited to explore the unknown crevices of the past though the spiritual eye of a perceptive heroine, Alex, as she takes us around the globe on her heart's quest."

Rose Flem-Ath, co-author of *When The Sky Fell: In Search of Atlantis*

"An inspiring and insightful deep romp through time and space and the human journey of discovery. Julie Loar's experience through dream-work and transcendence gave me a good read that kept the light on late at night."

Sue Lion, Author-Illustrator

"This book dramatizes the inner search that thousands of people feel themselves to be embarked upon when they understand the mysteries of the Great Pyramid and Sphinx. This shamanic quest is personalized vividly in the characters Ms. Loar has created. To the author's credit, this book credibly conveys the challenge facing anyone who wishes to restore knowledge of our lost cultural heritage. *Messengers: Two with a Guide* creates a vision of ultimate success in attaining the knowledge we need to become our full selves."

Ed Conroy, author of *Report on Communion*

"Julie Loar gives us a thrilling adventure with this novel. She takes us deep into the temples and teachings of the Maya, Egypt, and Atlantis, all the while entertaining us. Her descriptions of the sites are breath-taking. She captures the oppressive heat of touring Palenque, the exhaustion of climbing the Grand Gallery in the Great Pyramid, as well as the relief of delicious meals, the colors, sounds, and merchandise of the markets. Her descriptions of Atlantis are so vivid one would think they come from her memory. The soaring visions and revelations of the characters inspire us, keeping us reading way past bedtime. Loar shows us these countries, their cultures and indigenous teachings as only one who has traveled well and studied deeply can—a *tour de force*."

Theresa Crater, author of *Three Awakenings* and the *Power Places Series.*

"Julie Loar has written an exciting novel, rich in the mystical tradition of Dion Fortune, Joan Grant, and Moyra Caldecott but with her own distinct and unique style. I found *Two with a Guide* particularly engrossing, being personally involved in the same research concerning the Hall of Records in Egypt. I recommend it highly to all those interested in a timely and fascinating story."

Stephen S. Mehler, M.A., Director, The Kinnaman Foundation

This novel is a well written and engaging mystery. But, beyond that, it gives insight into what shamans and people who remember their dreams experience, something I have always wondered about. Plus, it explains some of the theories proposed regarding ancient mysteries that still remain enigmatic today. A good read by any measure, I highly recommend it.

Judy Cole, retired Organizational Development consultant.

Julie Loar's intriguing conspiracy of entrained characters appears here in a new enhanced edition ... and on a very personal mission to decode a legendary network of interlocking clues from an ancient world still existing in as contemporary a context as you will ever find. *Messengers* continually tips the scales with far more than a dreamcatcher of feathers, offering knowledgeable insights and well-groomed style while highlighting adventure, suspense and amazement that is guaranteed to leave you in thoughtful wonder ...

Ted Denmark, PhD, author of *Winged Messengers* and *Masters of Space and Time.*

# MESSENGERS

## TWO WITH A GUIDE

JULIE LOAR

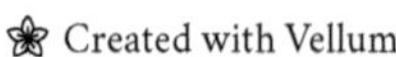 Created with Vellum

*For Seshat*
*The Great One, Lady of Letters and Builders,*
*Mistress of the House of Books.*

Among the stars, stones, and legends
the ancient wisdom dwells.

# TABLE OF CONTENTS

# PROLOG

Gray light faded in the winter afternoon. Outside the leaded-glass windows of the study huge snowflakes fell, blanketing the Philadelphia neighborhood in white. Christmas lights sparkled on the eight-foot Scottish pine, standing proud between the fireplace and the window.

Alexandria Mackenzie Stuart looked at the tree in delight. Tinsel and glass ornaments reflected colored lights, and the scent of pine and tobacco from her grandfather's pipe filled the room. He held a lighted match to the bowl of tobacco to relight his ornate wooden pipe, inhaling and turning the tobacco red hot. A gold ring with an etched triangular symbol glinted on his finger as the match flared. Duncan Stuart's graying hair shone like silver in the reflected light of the crackling fire. Alex watched a curl of white smoke rise from the pipe in a spiral motion.

Every ornament she'd ever made by hand held a place of honor on the tall tree. No presents yet lay underneath the full branches to tempt curious eyes as family tradition dictated that gifts appeared like magic on Christmas morning.

Alexandria turned intense blue-green eyes away from the dancing flames in the fireplace and focused her gaze on her grandfather, Duncan Stuart. Tall and still handsome, he sat in a wingback chair on one side of a large brick fireplace. Seated in an identical chair opposite him was Alexandria's father Philip, a younger version of his father with red-gold hair and striking features. Her mother and grandmother sat together on a couch. Alex sat on the floor with her arms folded around her knees as her devoted cocker spaniel Stanley slept at her feet.

"Did you have a nice birthday, Princess?" her father asked.

"Oh yes! It was perfect."

"I'm glad," her grandfather said, tapping his pipe on an ashtray that sat on an antique table next to his chair."

"What was your favorite gift, Alex? her mother, Blanche asked.

"I especially love the pearl necklace."

"I believe pearls represent how our characters are formed through the experiences of our lives," her grandmother Rose said.

"What begins as an irritating grain of sand inside the oyster becomes a beautiful pearl as the creature responds and adapts to the stimulation," Duncan added.

She smiled, touching the necklace. Her stomach was full of cake and ice cream, and she felt cozy and safe, nestled in the warm presence of her family. In another week it would be Christmas.

"Grandpa?" Alex asked.

"Yes, love?"

"I had another dream," she said quietly.

Duncan and Rose exchanged a quick glance.

"Tell us about it," Philip said, in an encouraging tone, opening his arms for her to climb onto his lap. She joined her father in his chair, and they all gave her their complete attention.

"This one scared me," Alex said.

"Then maybe you shouldn't dwell on it," her mother said, frowning.

"It's just a dream, Blanche, and it may help her to think about it, her father said, looking at his wife.

"It felt so real," Alex said, crossing her arms over her chest. "I was about the same age as I am now but in a different place that was like a fairy land with beautiful flowers and trees everywhere. In the first part of the dream, I was with other kids, going to school or learning. We wore long robes and sat under a huge tree. We listened as a woman talked to us—she was like an angel. I was so happy."

"What happened then?" her grandmother asked.

Alexandria pushed her curly red hair behind her ears and looked at each member of her family in turn. "Then the dream changed. I was still dressed in a robe, and in some place like a church, but also like a hospital. Somehow the people in the dream used crystals for healing and to talk with each other.

Does that sound weird?

I wasn't supposed to be there, so I hid in a dark corner and listened to men talk about danger. One of the men was you, Daddy. I think I had sneaked into the church to find you. I was really scared, then I woke up."

"I think you may have remembered something from long ago, Alex," her father said.

"You mean like past lives that you and Gran talk about?" she asked.

"Yes," Duncan said, standing and placing another log on the fire. He poked the embers and bright sparks exploded and logs popped and crackled. Her grandfather sat back down in his chair and relit his pipe. The sky had gone dark and the only light in the room came from the fire and Christmas lights.

"Alexandria, " Duncan began, "many thousands of years ago there was a great island civilization that was destroyed and disappeared into the ocean waters. I think your twelfth birthday is an auspicious time to hear the story of this ancient land."

Her mother started to object, but Philip raised his hand in a gesture of restraint. Blanche frowned but stayed quiet. Alex climbed back down to the floor and rested her back against her father's legs, drawing a crocheted blanket around her, waiting eagerly to hear what her grandfather would say.

Her father chuckled. "You have been fascinated with Egypt since you were three, pouring over Dad's *National Geographic* magazines until the pages were dogeared. You asked about pyramids and pharaohs, I guess it's time you learned about Atlantis."

Alex grinned.

Atlantis was a great island nation that had once been a larger continent," Duncan began. "From memories of psychics and other researchers the country looked very much like what you described in your dream. It's believed they had technology to match our own but of a very different kind."

"Really?" Alex asked.

"Over time the continent was broken up into islands through earthquakes and undersea volcanoes. The Atlanteans were a proud people and sadly their pride and lust for power corrupted many in leadership positions. Toward the end there was great division between those who wanted to follow higher principles and those who were consumed by greed. Sensing an ultimate confrontation, many who felt danger left the island and spread out and colonized what became the seven ancient centers of civilization—Egypt, India, Crete, Peru, Mayan Mexico, China, and Chaldea."

"Is that why I love Egypt even though I haven't been there yet?"

"I imagine so Princess, maybe you were a queen?" her father said. Alex giggled.

"There was a great plan to hide and protect what they knew along with the records of their history," Duncan continued. "The legend says that after a time a great cataclysm erupted and the entire island vanished under the waves of a giant tsunami. Everything was lost, but they had buried the treasure of their wisdom to safeguard the knowledge for future generations to find thousands of years later. What they left behind is more precious than gold."

"What is that?" Alex asked.

"Ancient wisdom," her grandmother said softly.

"That is why you are named after the ancient library that was destroyed," her father said.

"I wanted to name you Grace," her mother said.

"Truth cannot really be destroyed. Knowledge and wisdom have flowed through time, often hidden in plain sight through symbols or buried deep underground, but never really disappearing."

"Do you have this knowledge, Grandpa?"

"Maybe a little," he smiled, his gray eyes bright with humor. "Since the time of James II, the Stuarts have had a long legacy connected to hidden knowledge, and one day it will be up to you to carry the torch."

"That sounds hard," she said.

"Yes, it can be hard," Philip said with a twinkle in his eyes, "but I've learned that your grandfather is seldom wrong and it's wise to pay attention." He gave her shoulders an affectionate squeeze.

"But you'll be there with me," she said, looking at each of them in turn.

They sat in silence for a time. After a short while Emma, her grandmother's housekeeper and dear friend, appeared in the doorway.

"I'm sorry to be late for the birthday party. Happy birthday, Alexandria," Emma said.

"That's okay. Grandpa's been telling me about Atlantis."

"Tall tales," Blanche said, "filling her head with things she shouldn't be concerned with."

"After my dream I think I needed to know, Mom. You worry too much."

"It's my job, but it's time for bed in any case," Blanche smiled as she sat on the arm of Philip's chair and put her arm around him.

"Alex rose and kissed each one of them.

"Sweet dreams, Princess," Philip said.

"Happy birthday," Duncan said.

"Goodnight. I love you all," Alex said with a yawn and turned to leave with

Gran and Stanley taking up the rear, carrying the music box Gran had given her. They ascended the carved wooden staircase and walked down the hall to her room.

Gran gave her a hug and tucked her into the canopy bed in a room decorated in shades of purple and lavender. Stanley jumped up and settled into his favorite spot at the foot of the bed. "Try not to think too much about what you heard, Alexandria."

" . . . but Grandpa said . . ."

"Never mind. Just go to sleep, you've had a big day. Gran kissed her on the forehead and turned out the light on her way out of the room.

"Good night, dear."

"Good night, Gran, thanks for everything."

Alex wound the key and placed her music box and pearl necklace on the small table next to her before snuggling into the fluffy, pink and white covers. The music box played *Skater's Waltz*, and a ballerina twirled on top. The music gently slowed as Alexandria drifted off to sleep, feeling warm and content. Images from her grandfather's story drifted vaguely through her mind. She hoped she would dream about the beautiful angel lady again.

CHAPTER I

# REVELATION

A hat box seemed like an odd legacy. Alexandria frowned at the round, striped object as if a cobra might strike if she opened the lid. *She can't be dead. I'm supposed to be visiting and having fun this weekend. Gran said she had a surprise for me.*

There had been no warning. No illness. No goodbye. Only Emma's call in the early morning darkness, saying Gran had died in her sleep; even Doctor Balin had been surprised. Gran's attorney had made cryptic remarks about the hat box, insisting that Alex open the box in the privacy of Gran's library. Alex leaned forward and raked both hands through her curly mass of red hair.

"I guess it's now or never," she said, expelling a breath and easing the lid off the vintage box. Inside was a puffy manilla envelop with her named written on the outside in Gran's sweeping script. Alex sliced open the top of the envelope with a letter opener and let the contents spill onto the desk.

An old book fell open with photographs spreading out that had been inside the front cover. Most of the photos were black and white pictures of her family from earlier times. Two small keys on a ring, travel documents, and another letter-size envelope also fell onto the desk.

"Why the mystery?" Alex wondered aloud.

She opened the vellum stationery envelope her grandmother had loved and her hand trembled as she removed a single feathery sheet of paper.

*My dearest Alexandria,*

*If you are reading this letter I'm already dead. I am so sorry that I waited so long to tell you about Mexico. I'm even sorrier I kept other secrets from you and that I can't even now speak more plainly. I only meant to protect you, but I'm afraid I've put you in danger instead.*

*Your task will be harder now as you'll have to puzzle this out for yourself. I had only begun to suspect how serious things were and didn't have time to prepare you. Know that your grandfather had powerful enemies but also many allies. You'll find help in unexpected places and Mexico is important. I pray you will find it in your heart to forgive me.*

*Your loving Gran.*

Tears spilled from Alex's eyes as she battled both grief and anger. She wanted to crumple the letter and throw it across the room but couldn't bear to let go of the last piece of her beloved grandmother. *What the hell does she mean?*

Sniffing, and wiping tears from her face with the back of her hand, Alex picked up the old hard bound book and looked at the title, *The Promise of Nuclear Energy.* She took a closer look at the photos. The first image gave her chills. It was a black and white picture of the gigantic mushroom cloud that had formed when the atomic bomb was first tested in remote New Mexico. Grandpa had written TRINITY TEST, JULY 16, 1945, on the back in all caps. She recalled him showing her an old film of that test and remembered his sense of shame that minds like Oppenheimer, Fermi, and his own, had wrought such horror. He had been there that day and witnessed the detonation.

Next was another black and white photograph of Gran and Grandpa with a group of people. A shiver crawled up her spine. A younger version of the strange, Raven like man she had seen at the cemetery during Gran's funeral a week ago stared at her from the photo. He'd given her the creeps. Written at on the back of the picture, in Grandpas small precise print, again in all caps, was ALTERNATE ENERGY CONFERENCE, 1962, MANHATTAN PROJECT GROUP.

The next photo was a picture of her grandparents in front of the Great Pyramid. When had that been taken? They looked so young. Another captured them with her father in his Navy pilot's uniform, which must have been taken shortly before his fatal crash in 1974 when she was twelve. God he'd been handsome. More tears came.

She did not recognize the building behind them and wondered about the location. Her tears became sobs as she looked at a picture of her parents at the ocean, her mother smiling and holding Alex as a baby. They looked so happy. A tear fell on the picture and she gently wiped it away. Her mother had never recovered from his death.

With an aching heart Alex examined the travel documents, which included colorful Mexican brochures, itinerary, and airline tickets in her name. The destination was Palenque in the Mexican State of Chiapas. According to the literature, Palenque was the site of famous Mayan ruins. The departure date was just seven days away. Alex sat back in the chair and stared at the assembled items.

*What does all of this mean?*

She placed the articles back in the hat box and stood in the center of the large room and turned around slowly, absorbing the magnitude of the task ahead of her. Gran's will specified that the house and all of the contents should be sold except everything in the library and Gran's white Spitz Crystal, who was her dog now. Three walls of the library were floor-to-ceiling bookcases that overflowed their capacity. Gran's antique roll-top desk bulged with papers, books, notes, postcards and letters from her wide and eclectic circle of friends. The matching secretary was crammed with Knick knacks, newspaper clippings of Grandpa's discoveries and patents, vacation photographs, and the innumerable spiral notebooks that were Gran's journals.

Alex went to the window and turned the handles of the big leaded glass panes, opening them wide and breathing in fresh air. The library overlooked Gran's garden, which was at the back of the vintage Victorian house. Dew drops sparkled through her tears like precious gems on green velvet. Pear, apple, and cherry trees bloomed, adding the delicate grace of their beauty, and the rich scent of their blossoms, to hyacinths and lilacs. Purple irises framed a fountain next to a statue of Saint Francis of Assisi. Birds chirped and bathed in the little pool that was watched over by their patron saint. A Robin sang with such intensity that Alex thought its tiny breast might burst.

Alexandria's mood was a stark contrast to the glorious spring day. Funerals belonged in November when tears blended with icy rain, clinging like grief on tinted windows and dripping from black umbrellas.

The front doorbell rang, interrupting her dark reverie. Alex heard Crystal bark followed by the sound of the dog's paws speeding toward the front door. A few moments later Crystal appeared at the library door accompanied by Emma, Gran's housekeeper, who was eclipsed by an exquisite floral arrangement of lilies, white roses, and birds of paradise.

"That smells intoxicating—Gran's favorites. Who sent them?"

"Here's the card," Emma said, handing her the small envelope."

"The angels of heaven rejoice at her homecoming. Sorrow not," Alex read. "That's easy for them to say. I can't make out the name. Who on earth could they be from?"

"Who on earth indeed" Emma said, placing the flowers in a vase on a coffee table.

Alex checked the number on the florist's card and called.

"This is Alexandria Stuart. I just received flowers and I can't read the name on the card."

"Ah, Miss Stuart. I'm afraid I can't help you. We received the request from Mexico and did our best to reproduce the name."

"Thank you anyway." Alex hung up the phone. "The flowers came from Mexico but the florist couldn't read the name either."

"Don Miguel maybe," Emma said, a questioning expression on her face.
"Who?"

"Don Miguel Piedra, an old friend of your father and grandparents."

"Did you know about the hat box, Emma?"

Tears filled Emma's pale blue eyes. "Only that Rose was in a big hurry to get her will finalized with her friend Judge Trusdale a couple weeks ago."

"Crystal, I miss her so much already." Alex said as tears spilled from her eyes. The sensitive Spitz licked her face and whined.

Alexandria looked up to see tears streaming from Emma's pale-blue eyes.

"Your grandmother was not just my employer, she was my dearest friend," Emma said.

Alex stood and embraced her grandmother's dear friend and companion, and they clung to each other. Emma had been part of the family for thirty years. Alex sat back in the chair and rubbed Crystal's head. "None of this makes sense. The angels of heaven have some explaining to do."

"Can I get you something to eat, dear? If I know you, it's been hours since you've stopped, and you must be a bundle of raw nerves." Emma brushed gray hairs from her kind round face with the back of her hand. Removing a tissue from her apron pocket, she wiped her nose.

"That would be wonderful. I'm feeling like a stretched rubber band about to snap."

"Come into the kitchen, the kettle's hot. You have tea while I see what I can whip up." Once in the kitchen Emma turned on the gas burner, busying herself with the solace of familiar actions.

Alex sat in her regular chair at the big wooden table with Crystal beside her, chin on Alex's knee. Sensing her pain, the dog looked up into Alex's eyes, ears cocked. Her tail swept slowly back and forth on the floor. Alex stroked her head in a gesture that comforted both of them.

Emma poured steaming water over Chamomile tea bags in a porcelain tea pot. They were silent as the tea steeped. Alex poured the fragrant, yellow tea into a delicate China cup, adding a dollop of clover honey. She closed her eyes and sipped the hot sweet liquid.

"I thought I'd stay here this weekend and get started on the library," she said quietly. "Gran left me tickets to Mexico in the hat box. That makes the puzzle of the flowers even more mysterious. Did you know about the travel arrangements?"

"Rose didn't mention it." Emma frowned as she served a bowl of steaming, home-made vegetable soup, with freshly baked bread, chunks of cheese, and hazelnut brownies.

"Emma, this is fantastic." She ate in silence until she felt the soothing influence of the food calm her. "I think I'll lie down for a while. I can't think about Mexico or what that means yet."

"Good idea. If I know you, you haven't slept a wink these last few days, trying to take care of everything."

"First I'll phone Sheila and ask her to drive me to the airport and keep an eye on Mom while I'm away. She can back you up too."

"That sounds wise," Emma said.

Alex nodded and rubbed the place between her eyebrows. She stood and gave Emma a hug, then headed down the hall. Stomach full and bone weary, Alex collapsed in her clothes on the small single bed in her father's childhood room. This had been her room at Gran's since her father died when she abandoned the frilly, four-poster bed upstairs. She always felt closer to him here. Crystal positioned herself at the foot of the bed where she slept whenever Alex visited.

Despite that warm presence Alexandria felt alone. Hot tears traced rivulets down her cheeks and fell silently on the pillow. She closed her eyes and prayed for sleep.

CHAPTER 2
# VISITATION

Hours later Alex rolled over in bed in the dark room. She thought she heard someone calling her name. She sat up and listened, but there was no sound. She wondered what time it was. *I should probably get up and put on pajamas, but I'm just too tired.*

She pulled up the bedspread and covers, curled up in a ball underneath, and lay her head down on the pillow. A moment later she heard the sound again. Her heart pounded. The voice sounded like Gran's. *I have to be dreaming.*

"Alexandria, can you hear me? My dear, you must hear me."

"Gran? Is that you? I'm losing my mind. I must have fallen asleep."

"You were sleeping," the voice answered.

"I can't see you."

Gran's voice giggled in the darkness like a teenager at a slumber party. "Of course, you can't. Wait just a moment."

A doorway seemed to open and light poured into the room. Alex shielded her eyes from the brilliance. Gran took her hand, and they walked through the strange opening that led outside. The air was warm and smelled of the sea. Gulls and pelicans screeched and dove toward the water in search of food.

Alexandria gaped at her grandmother. Years had vanished from her appearance. She looked radiant in a long, blue robe that accentuated the color of her sparkling eyes. Silvery hair was pulled back into a bun at the nape of her neck, highlighting her fine features.

"Gran, you look beautiful."

"Why thank you, love," Rose Stuart replied, amused and beaming.

"Come along, Alexandria, we have much to accomplish. I didn't intend to leave you quite so soon and unfortunately several details were left unattended."

"What do you mean?" Alex asked, still staring at her grandmother.

Rose Stuart walked along a broad avenue lined on both sides with towering palm and fir trees. Alex followed, hurrying to catch up. Red and yellow hibiscus flowers spilled out of terracotta pots placed along the walkways. Sand-colored buildings lined one side of the avenue. The other side was bordered by a sparkling, turquoise ocean. A warm breeze rustled the palm fronds and Alexandria's mane of red hair.

They turned into the entrance of a large white building constructed of a stucco-like material. The grounds were lush with tropical foliage and the heady fragrance of brilliantly colored, orchids, lilies and plumeria birds of paradise flowers permeated the air.

A large green parrot perched on a palm branch. "What's your name?" the parrot squawked.

"Alice in Wonderland," she frowned. "And I'm getting curiouser and curiouser."

"Patience was never your strong suit, Alexandria,"

The two women entered an open doorway into a central courtyard where a sparkling fountain emptied musically into a meandering stream. Sunlight filtered through the lattice roof, creating patterns of light and dark green on potted plants.

"This looks like paradise," Alex exclaimed. "I'm glad I didn't put on my pajamas."

Gran's eyes twinkled with amusement. "And so, it should, Alexandria."

Alex turned and gasped, eyes suddenly wide. "Are we in heaven?"

"Oh my, Alexandria," Gran sighed. "Sometimes you do miss the obvious. Come on, there's someone waiting to see you."

In a room just off the courtyard, three men faced a window, deep in conversation.

"Please forgive the intrusion, gentlemen, but our guest has arrived."

The men turned to face them.

"Daddy!" Alex screamed. "Grandpa!"

Philip Stuart grinned and held his arms open wide to his daughter. The huge form of the handsome Scot beckoned to her. Curly, red-blond hair framed blue-green eyes the same color as his daughter's. The joyous sound of his laughter echoed in the open room.

Alexandria ran to him, and when he scooped her up in his arms, she felt twelve years old again with the same sense of warmth and love as when he had been alive. Joy flooded through her like the rush of strong wine and years of loss and grief melted away.

Alex stared at her father transfixed. "What kind of dream is this? You look exactly the same as I remember, but now we look close to the same age."

Her grandfather laughed and the sound echoed in the room.

"I still feel thirty-eight," he laughed. "And you, little Princess, have grown into a remarkably beautiful woman in the last twenty-three years." She blushed.

Duncan Stuart stood next to his darling Rose, smoking his pipe and grinning.

"Alexandria, I'd like you to meet an old friend, Miguel Piedra," her grandfather said, turning to the Indian man beside him. Black eyes shone from a regal face. Jet black hair, laced with streaks of gray and white at the temples, surrounded a chiseled countenance. He was dressed in western clothes, but Alex thought he looked like pictures she'd seen of Mayan Indians.

"It's a pleasure to meet you," she managed to say. "I think I saw your picture with those Gran left."

"The pleasure is certainly mine, Señorita," Miguel replied, bowing low. "So, this is the young lady who was named after the famous library huh, Felipe? Well, if she is as strong as she is beautiful, all will be well. Now, if you will please excuse me, I'm sure you have some catching up to do. We will meet again soon, I am sure."

Alexandria bobbed her head at him distractedly. "Yes, of course." She looked at her grandmother in disbelief. "I don't understand."

Pointing to three stuffed chairs which surrounded a glass table Gran said, "Let's sit down, shall we?"

A handsome young man, dressed in white linen, brought a tray of fresh fruit and a pitcher of sparkling golden-colored liquid. He placed the tray on the glass table, pouring shimmering liquid into three silver goblets. He flashed a warm smile at Alexandria, who flushed crimson.

"A toast, to old times and new adventures," Duncan Stuart said, raising his glass. He smiled and the ruddy complexion of his Celtic features was illuminated. Gran and Philip mirrored the gesture. Alex lifted her glass with difficulty. She was so overcome by their presence she was paralyzed by joy.

"Alexandria, we don't have much time," her father said. "You won't remember all the specifics of this encounter so it's important that . . ."

"Impossible," she interrupted, "I've never forgotten the way you used to visit me in my dreams. Why did you stop?"

Her father and grandparents exchanged glances, then smiled at her with love and compassion. "You closed your heart, Alex. It was your way of coping with the pain and loss after my death," her father said then reached over and took her hand. Gently squeezing her fingers in his own, he leaned over and kissed her cheek.

"I've missed you so much." Tears rolled down Alexandria's cheeks.

He smiled. "I have always been here, even when you couldn't feel my presence." He squeezed her hand.

"Alexandria, dear," Gran said, "it's all my fault. After your father died, I worried about your safety. I'm afraid I made a terrible mistake in not keeping you more informed."

"What do you mean?" Alex asked, sniffing, and wiping her eyes. Gran handed her a lace hanky and sent a pleading look toward her husband.

"To be brief, you know our Stuart name is linked to both the French and English thrones," her grandfather began.

"Yes," Alex said impatiently.

"There are some who believe that name is also linked to the legendary treasure of the Templars through the Scottish Rite."

"That's a stretch isn't it, Grandpa?"

'There is some truth to our role as guardians of priceless treasure, but it has nothing to do with material wealth. The treasure we guard is wisdom. Nonetheless, our role has made us a target."

"A target for what?" Alex asked.

"There are always forces of darkness who seek to destroy the light. This battle has raged for countless thousands of years, maybe forever, between those who would keep humanity imprisoned and those who would set us free. After my death your grandmother," he paused to look at Gran, who covered her mouth with a hand and looked ashamed, "thought she could fight this on her own."

"But now I'm alone," Alex said. "Why didn't you trust me?"

"We thought we were protecting you," Gran said.

"Besides the treasure business my scientific work was controversial. This has made us a twofold target, and truthfully, we underestimated the danger.

"Things will happen quickly, but we'll help you," her father said. "You're not alone. Events will unfold soon that were set in motion a long time ago.

When Atlantis sunk beneath the ocean waves great beings who had walked and taught openly in that epoch withdrew. Not until a long cycle of thousands of years had passed would conditions permit them to appear openly again. That time is at hand. You must get busy with the specific work you came to do, Alex, and it is high time your mother learned to take care of herself. I think you're ready."

"You can visit us here anytime you choose," Gran said, taking her hand. "It's a simple matter of doorways. You'll meet our dear Miguel again soon. He will help you remember. I meant to explain everything, Alexandria. I thought there would be time, but things changed, and sinister forces became a factor I didn't foresee. Perhaps it will be better this way."

As her grandmother spoke, Alex saw images of temples, stone pyramids, and white robed figures engaged in ceremonies.

"You must open your heart Princess, no matter how much it hurts," Philip almost whispered. "Listen to the voice of your heart; it's the gateway to your soul. Trust your feelings, and never forget how much you are loved."

Alex woke in darkness as the grandfather clock in the foyer struck three. Her heart beat as loudly as the clock. She stared out the window at the stars a long while.

# MEXICO

Sheila Goldman stopped her car at the curb and waited for Alex to come down the walk.

"Thanks for your help on such short notice," Alex said.

"I have the sense you have things to tell me," Sheila said.

Everything about her friend Sheila was round and expressive—mouth, eyes, hair, and figure, and her smile could light up a room. She fondly referred to her long time friend as the Queen of Hyperbole. Sheila's favorite color was black because she thought it was slimming. Sheila joked that she wanted to do a funeral motif for her upcoming fortieth birthday.

"I don't know where to begin." Alex said. "I mentioned the hat box and the Mexico trip on the phone when I asked if you could drive me to the airport. The other big item is a powerful dream or vision I had where I saw my dad and grandparents and met a man named Miguel Piedra. I had seen his picture with those Gran left."

"That sounds like more than a dream, Allie."

"It's too much to process right now, but I have a strong feeling more puzzle pieces could emerge in Mexico, although I don't know how. Apparently my grandparents were involved in some drama related to his research that has disturbing aspects."

"You've been through a lot, Alex. Try to enjoy yourself and don't worry about your Mom. I'll keep an on her."

"You're the best."

~

ALEX FELT a conflicting mixture of guilt and excitement as she walked down the jet bridge to board the plane to Mexico City. The mystery of the tickets left a curious trail she felt compelled to follow. She still smarted from the conversation with her mother. Emma and Sheila would have their hands full for the next ten days.

Alex had digested some of the reference material in Gran's library, and the Mayan civilization had captured her imagination. She knew her grandmother's interests were eclectic, but she had not known the extent of her interest in archeology and ancient civilizations. Grandpa always seemed like such a conservative physicist. Now she wondered what else those two had explored together and the implications of their warning. *Why didn't Gran tell me?*

Exhausted from hectic travel preparations she fell asleep and didn't waken until the jet touched down in Mexico City. The airport teemed with a diverse populace as Mexican aristocrats and peasants jostled for luggage carts and vied for position at the baggage claim. An undercurrent of tension pervaded the crowd. Recent uprisings in San Cristobal de las Casas were an ongoing concern for tourists as the rebel base was only thirty miles away. Her mother had been terrified that she decided to travel to Palenque.

Alex changed planes and boarded a smaller aircraft bound for the city of Villahermosa in the northern part of the state of Tabasco. The calmer mood inside the smaller jet was a welcome relief from the crowded airport. She relaxed and read in the travel guide how rich oil deposits brought a boom economy to the city of Villahermosa. Sudden prosperity spawned satellite antennas, luxury hotels, museums, art galleries, shiny new shopping malls and traffic jams.

An hour and a half later, the pilot banked the plane to descend. Alex stared down at swampy plains dotted with palm trees, stretching from Tabasco to the jagged, northern slope of the Chiapas Sierra. Ducks and grebes moved through winding streams, and graceful snowy egrets flew over small lakes and swamps, casting long, afternoon shadows on the water.

Chartreuse vegetation covered the flat landscape like a thick textured carpet. Rivers snaked across the terrain like mammoth, brown Anacondas and arching bridges spanned the waterways at frequent intervals. Two lane, white roads took their course from the geography, rather than their destination. Alex felt a shift, a slowing down, a movement into another way of measuring importance.

Outside the airport, forty people stood in the sun, waiting to board a bus. Diesel fumes stung her nostrils, and engine heat radiated from the bus. Once inside the air-conditioned bus to Santo Domingo de Palenque, Alex felt another winding down in pace. The driver spoke into a static-filled microphone; he spoke first in Spanish, then English.

"Welcome to Tabasco. We will be in Palenque in a couple of hours. Don't worry, it is perfectly safe there. Revolutionaries are not terrorists."

A young couple sat across the aisle from Alex. The woman looked doubtful and frowned at Alex. "I hope he is correct."

"I'm sure we'll be safe," Alex said, praying she was right. She stared at the landscape through the tinted glass of the bus window. Indians worked crops of corn and tobacco in the fields along the two-lane road, setting fires in their *milpas* in the timeless way of their forebears. Pungent clouds of smoke hung in the air as the earth was prepared to receive the sacred maize seeds.

Tiny dwellings of gray cement blocks and wooden huts with thatched roofs dotted the fields. Carefully hung laundry, stretched on clothes lines, baked in the sun. The small, poverty-stricken village of Santo Domingo had grown haphazardly to twenty-five thousand as flocks of curious American and European tourists came to see the remarkable ruins.

*Now I'm another tourist, trampling the sacred ground in designer hiking boots. Why did you send me here, Gran?*

After three hours, the bus pulled off the paved road onto a gravel drive. Dense jungle vegetation enveloped the narrow drive like a green tunnel. A fragile truce existed between civilization and the jungle. Any lapse in vigilance and the forest would eagerly wrap its green tentacles around the meager human structures. This seemed less true where huge, tree-eating machines cut wide gashes in the ancient forest to feed an increasing appetite for mahogany and Ceiba wood in developed areas.

The bus stopped in front of a large wooden building with a thatched roof that was enveloped by jungle foliage. The central building housed a restaurant and meeting rooms. Ceiling fans circled slowly overhead. After checking into the hotel, she received her keys from an attractive woman who spoke no English and followed a young boy outside.

"*Mi nombre es Pablo,*" he said. "Paul, in English."

"*Mucho gusto, Pablo,*" Alex replied with a smile and a small bow. "*Soy Alejandria.* I am called Alex."

"Mucho gusto, Alex," he said, carefully forming the unfamiliar sound of her name. "Please follow me."

Pablo proudly struggled with her suitcase as they wound through a curving stone path deeper into the hotel complex. Wood and stone cabins with thatched roofs were barely visible through dense tropical foliage. The structures looked as if they had grown up inside the jungle. The guest casitas had been built several hundred feet apart in small, isolated groups, over-looking a stream running through the grounds.

Waterfalls cascaded musically throughout the grounds. Philodendron plants, with leaves as large as dinner plates, climbed up tall trees as parasites around the stone path. Inviting banana plants hung within easy reach. Six-inch butterflies, in brilliant hues of fluorescent yellow, blue, orange, and black, floated as though suspended in hot, thick air. Insects hummed and buzzed as parrots and macaws screeched from the tops of tall trees. Pablo stopped at the door of a charming casita that stood by the steam in a group of four buildings.

"Su casita, Alex. La charca piscina," Pablo said, pointing toward the swim-ming pool. Alex didn't understand the words, and a questioning expression formed on her face. She turned to look in the direction he pointed as Pablo placed her bag on the stone walk and moved his arms over his head like someone swimming.

"Ah," she said, "swimming pool. Como se dice?"

"La charca piscina," Pablo repeated slowly.

"Bueno."

Pablo unlocked the wooden door to the stone cottage, pulled her luggage inside, and handed her the key. Alex followed. The room was large, furnished with two double beds and furniture made from mahogany. Pablo switched on a single ceiling fan overhead; there was no air-conditioning unit. Alex walked through the room and out the back onto a screened porch, over-looking the stream and a waterfall.

After giving Pablo a generous tip, she decided to investigate *la charca piscina* and cool off before dinner. The swimming area was cleverly fashioned from stones of different sizes, creating the inviting illusion of a tropical lagoon. Stone bridges spanned pools of various sizes. Small rock islands provided humans and lizards with a place to bask in the sun. Tall date and coconut palms grew close together, creating a small forest around the pool.

Alex dove into the water and swam under the surface to the other side. She emerged refreshed and pushed herself up on the edge. She approached a counter with a large, thatched roof. Large, yellow hibiscus flowers grew from the thatch and tumbled over the edges. The handsome Indian man behind the outdoor bar had high broad cheekbones, almond-shaped, ebony eyes, and skin the color of burnt sienna.

"Que desea, Senorita?" He smiled. "What would you like to drink?"

"Cerveza, por favor," Alex replied, returning his smile.

He pulled a bottle of Carta Blanca beer from a cooler. Ice crystals clung to the brown bottle.

"Muchas gracias!"

He nodded and grinned. Alex turned and collided with a fortyish, tall and muscular blond man. She looked up into the most compelling gray eyes she had ever seen.

"I'm sorry," she said, trying not to stare.

"No harm done," he said, pushing hair off his forehead, "I'm more concerned with your beer. It's nectar of the gods in this climate."

"You're right," she said, lifting her bottle in a salute.

"Arrive today?"

Alex nodded.

"I'll see you at the slide show this evening then," he said, turning to leave.

Alex took a generous swallow of nectar and admired the tall form of the retreating Olympian.

CHAPTER 4

# CONUNDRUM

The hotel provided an orientation lecture each evening. The meeting room was a larger version of the bungalows, built of mahogany, Ceiba wood and stone with a thatched roof of palm leaves. Ceiling fans circulated the warm, humid air.

An eclectic group of European tourists sat at round tables. Alex heard French, German, Italian and Spanish. The presenter was a local Latino, a genetic blend of Spanish and Indian blood. He arranged his slides in a carousel, which he projected on the wall. Dressed in blue jeans and dirty, black boots with pointed toes, his short-sleeved, mint-green shirt was held in place inside his jeans by a leather belt that boasted a large silver buckle. The ornate oval buckle was barely visible underneath a protruding stomach. Alex thought he'd lost his soul to progress.

A Styrofoam cooler, filled with Coca Cola, Orange Crush, and beer, beckoned from back of the room. As she leaned over the cooler to pull an Orange Crush from the ice, the speaker glanced at the sterling silver necklace she wore. The stylized cross was one of her favorite creations, and she had never duplicated the design.

The top three arms of the cross curved inward, like backward letter Cs. She had inlaid them with semi-precious stones. His eyes narrowed, and his probing stare made her skin crawl. She sat at one of the tables and met his gaze.

"Buenas noches, Senores y Senoras, my name is Pepe Paniagua. Welcome to Palenque."

Alex thought his presentation seemed forced, a condescending caricature, created for the foolish tourists. She found his tone ingratiating, almost obsequious.

The attractive blond man she had encountered at the pool came in and sat next to her. Not a single, blond hair was out of place. His shirt and shorts looked starched and ironed, and he smelled of a pleasant aftershave. Alexandria's heartbeat faster and her palms were sticky. She felt like an idiot. *This guy's probably an anal-retentive bore. What's the matter with me?*

"As you can see from this aerial view," Senor Paniagua continued, "even today Palenque sits in grandeur." The slide projector hummed as small insects circled in the light and the fan blew dancing dust particles in the hot air.

"She is the jewel, the emerald, most beautiful of all Mayan centers. Palenque rests at the foot of a chain of hills, which are covered with the tall trees of the rain forest, just above the flood plain of the Usumacinta River. A small stream runs through the site and flows underneath the Palace complex through a vaulted aqueduct.

"Santo Domingo was founded in 1564, on the savanna of Tumbala, by a Dominican padre. The mission received the addition of de Palenque, or palisade, when the Spaniards ordered high walls built to protect themselves from the unfriendly natives resistant to conversion."

Pepe smiled, but no hint of humor reached his eyes. The projector clicked as he advanced the slides, pointing to pictures of stone temples and describing buildings nestled in the green forest.

"The last temple is the Temple of the Cross of Palenque," he said, and looked directly at Alex. "When it was uncovered, three beautiful carved panels were discovered. In the center was the image of the World Tree of the Mayas. Two human figures are on each side, and many glyphs, which tell a great story."

He paused, then advanced the slide. When the projector clicked, Alex was shocked to see a strikingly similar cross to the one she wore around her neck carved into the wall of a temple. Despite the heat, she shivered. She had created the design herself and had never seen anything else like it. Another layer of mystery.

Echoing her thoughts, Pepe said in a flat tone, "This is the only cross that is called the World Tree is the only one of its kind in the world." Pepe stared at her necklace, then paused, turned off the slide projector and switched on the lights.

Alex felt a strange sense of *déjà vu* and discomfort.

"Tomorrow you may see brilliant parrots and macaws flying above the trees," Pepe said. "If you are lucky, the gods may give you a feather. It is a special sign. If it rains, you will hear the roar of the howler monkeys."

"Wear insect repellent; otherwise, you will be lunch for the bugs. And you, lovely Senorita," he said, looking at Alex and pushing his greasy hair off his forehead, "wear much sun lotion to protect your fair skin."

Alex did not like Pepe Paniagua. He barely concealed his resentment for the *touristas*, but he seemed happy to take their money.

"You are fortunate; tomorrow you have a special guide. His name is Francisco Trujillo. He grew up here but is studying archeology at the University in Mexico City. Ask him anything about Palenque. Rise early and eat breakfast before the heat. After site-seeing, you can siesta. Sleep well, amigos. Buenas noches."

The group filed outside. A cacophony of insect sounds filled the humid darkness. The acrid smell of smoke from the thatched huts of hotel workers and the sweet fragrance of flowers permeated the night air.

"We haven't been properly introduced," the blond man said to Alex. He was almost a head taller, and she looked up in response. "I'm Erik Anderson. I couldn't help noticing the exchange that took place inside." His brow was furrowed, and the remark was phrased as a question.

Alex stopped and looked at him. "I'm Alexandria Stuart. Most people call me Alex. What exactly did you see?"

"You have something he thinks has value, and he's curious how you got it. Frankly, so am I. Your necklace looks remarkably like the cross in that temple."

Alex frowned and resumed walking. "Not that it's really any of your business, Mr. Anderson."

"Erik," he said, bending down to take a closer look at her necklace.

"I design jewelry for a living. I was stunned to see my cross in that slide." Alex covered her necklace in a reflexive gesture.

"No offense, but it appears that cross was someone else's before it was yours. I didn't like that guy's attitude one bit. Are you traveling alone?"

Alex snorted. "And you're going to protect me, right? Why should I trust you any more than him?"

They reached her bungalow. "Nevertheless, Princess, I plan to keep an eye on you, and conveniently, it seems I'm right next door."

A chill ran down her back to hear him call her Princess, only her father had called her that. Before she could object further, he strode off toward his own quarters in the adjacent casita.  She went inside and slammed the door. Alex found the man annoying but had the irrational thought that he didn't even try to kiss her.

# CHAPTER 5
# PALENQUE

The travel alarm beeped at six and Alex groaned. She punched the snooze button, and considered abandoning the early breakfast idea. Ten minutes later, the alarm beeped again. She swung her legs over the side of the bed and stared at the bathroom, willing herself there. She struggled to the shower, turned on the water, and stepped inside onto cool white tile. Alex closed her eyes while lukewarm water poured over her, dreaming of siesta.

She dried off her body but left her copper ringlets wet. Turning to throw the towel over the curtain rod, she almost stepped on the largest spider she had ever seen. The dark brown arachnid was larger than her hand. She screamed, dropped the towel, and ran from the bathroom. This was the stuff of nightmares. Summoning all her courage, she covered the spider with a plastic glass and slid a brochure beneath. Heart pounding, she carried the glass outside on the deck and released the spider in the greenery below.

Feeling victorious, Alex quickly buttoned a cotton shirt and pulled on long pants. Lacing up hiking boots purchased for the trip, she grabbed her camera, sun hat and insect repellent and hurried to breakfast. She was ready to consider the next bus back to the airport but entered the dining room and joined other guests at a large round table. Shy young girls, in westernized clothes, brought pitchers of milk and coffee to the tables. Frijoles, rice, eggs, and tortillas were served family style, in big bowls and platters. Smaller bowls of tomatoes, peppers, onions, salt, lemon, and butter provided spice and seasoning. Honey and cinnamon seasoned the coffee.

Alex asked for a Coca Cola. "I can't imagine drinking coffee in this heat," she said, then noticed that everyone else at the table had mugs of coffee. She blushed at her thoughtlessness.

Erik Anderson walked in a few minutes later and sat next to her. Alex thought he looked like an Eagle Scout dressed in khaki shirt and shorts with numerous pockets and pouches. *He probably has a Swiss Army knife stashed somewhere along with a flashlight, compass, and magnifying glass—maybe even a cell phone.*

Her heart raced. She decided this was lunacy as she had nothing in common with this man. She was glad she could blame her red face on heat and the monster spider.

"Morning," said, with a broad smile. "Feeling all right? You look a little flushed."

Alex, mouth full of beans and tortillas, glared at him. *Figures he'd be a morning person.*

Erik ate enthusiastically, speculating aloud on preparation and ingredients. Alex ate in silence, wishing golden boy would take the hint.

"Mind if I join you on the van?"

"Suit yourself," she shrugged.

"Excellent," he said, undaunted.

After breakfast Alex walked outside to wait for the van. The air was already steamy. Cicadas buzzed and hummed, and butterflies and dragonflies seemed to float in slow motion in the heavy air. A breeze blew through the open porch and felt like silk against her moist skin.

Eight people piled into the van, and the driver exited the hotel complex and headed toward the archeological site. Tall trees and thick vegetation grew to the edge of the narrow and paved road, which curved steadily upward around steep turns. The heaviest rains in Mexico created a rich tropical forest between the ruins and the mountains.

The van entered the archeological area and parked the vehicle. He led them down a dirt path toward the entrance of the ceremonial complex. Countless earthen mounds, covered with dense green vegetation, showed how much of the ruins' story lay uncovered.

The eclectic group of tourists walked a short distance and stopped in an open area at the entrance to the archeological site. A group of Mayan Indians, dressed in traditional long white robes with shoulder-length, raven black hair, stood to one side.

"They are Lacandones," the driver said, nodding toward the Mayan Indians, "one of two indigenous tribes who resist immersion into the modern world."

Hand-made arrows, ceramic pots, colorful dolls, bead necklaces and bright woven belts lay on blankets on the ground. Alex sensed an intrinsic dignity and poise in these people and felt drawn to them. Dark eyes radiated power and strength that seem to come from living close to the magic of the earth.

A light early morning rain blew in over the mountains, creating a green mist, which enhanced the other-worldly feel of the place. Gray stone buildings looked stark against the background of soft green foliage. Alexandria was moved by Palenque, even in its ruined state the site possessed a timeless and haunting beauty. She closed her eyes for a moment, trying to envision its original grandeur. She felt a mounting curiosity fueled by her grandmother's actions.

"It is my pleasure to introduce your guide, don Francisco Trujillo," the driver said with a flourish.

"Good morning," Francisco said with a trace of an accent. He was slight of build with nut-brown skin. Kind black eyes were creased at the corners, promising frequent laughter. He wore blue jeans, running shoes, a plaid cotton shirt and a red baseball cap. Alex liked him at once and thought Francisco was a delightful contrast to Pepe Paniagua.

"The ceremonial center of Palenque is not the largest Mayan center," Francisco said, "but it is beautiful even now. At this time of day, in the mist," he smiled, and circumscribed the surroundings with his arm, "Palenque is magical."

"Palenque was a western Maya center, and as you can see, beautifully situated at the foot of a chain of low hills that are covered with rain forest and just above the green flood plain of the Usumacinta River. One of its ancient names was 'City of the Sun's Daily Death.' Implied in the symbolism of daily death of the Sun is a daily resurrection. The Sun was reborn each day at the eastern city of Tulum.

"We are standing roughly in the center of the site, which covers twenty-four square kilometers," Francisco said. "More than four-hundred temples and buildings are buried within this area. Only a few have been excavated.

"The architecture was well suited to the humid climate. Tall roofs, with double vaulted ceilings, porticoes, and doorways, helped to keep the rooms cool. The ingenious use of small windows, shaped like an inverted letter T, symbol of Hurakan, the Wind God, brought in the god's cooling breath."

The group followed Francisco across a grassy area and stood in the welcome shade of a temple.

"The stucco decoration at Palenque is the most delicate and sophisticated of any Mayan area. The violence and sacrifice seen at other centers is not reflected in the frescoes here. Whatever its true Mayan name, Palenque seems to have been a place where tranquility prevailed, at least on the walls.

"Directly ahead is a complex of buildings, which covers about an acre, known as The Palace, a stone labyrinth of vaulted galleries, courtyards, porticoes and underground chambers. The Palace went through many changes during its long history. Interior features include a steam bath, urinals fed by water ducts from running streams under the floor and air vents. High vaulted ceilings helped to keep the rooms cool.

"The four-story square tower is an interesting feature and is unique in Maya architecture. There is a stairway inside, and the glyph for Venus painted on one of the landings suggests that the tower was used as an observatory.

"To the right you see the famous limestone Temple of the Inscriptions, where the fabulous tomb of the ruler Pakal was discovered inside. Pakal's accession to the throne is recorded as 615 CE, during what archeologists call the Classic Period, which began around the time of the birth of Christ. Please follow me."

The group trudged to the base of the pyramid, following quietly in a line behind Francisco, and looked up from the base.

ALEX FELT a strange and haunting sense of familiarity that she could not explain. She had never been to Mexico and the shocking similarity of her necklace, that she's brought along on impulse, was confusing. There had been other such puzzles in her life. Her reverie was interrupted as Fransisco spoke again.

"This structure is similar to a four-sided Egyptian pyramid, even the Great Pyramid, in terms of difficulty of access to the inside. Unlike the Great Pyramid, this structure contained a tomb and rich treasures. In fact, the crypt seems to have been built first and the whole outer structure them assembled around the tomb.

This pyramid, with a temple at the top, is the highest structure at Palenque," Francisco said, "perhaps thirteen stories tall. Nine courses of masonry, each with as many steps, ascend to the sanctuary of the temple, and there are more steps at the top. A secret internal stairway, which leads deep into the pyramid where the burial chamber of Pakal and its treasures was found, was discovered inside the temple area by the archeologist Alberto Ruz in 1948, It took four additional digging seasons to make their way to the royal burial at the heart of the pyramid.

"Until recently, this burial was thought to be unique in the Americas, but archeologists discovered a new tomb in 1994 in an adjacent pyramid still covered with earth. This new discovery is one hundred years older and just as fabulous as the ruler-priest Pakal's. We believe that his grandfather is buried there. What other fantastic surprises might still be sleeping in the jungle?"

Alex felt a mixture of excitement and vertigo as she contemplated the steep stairway of more than seventy narrow steps. The stairway was about twenty feet wide, but the steps were too shallow for her feet to fit. She noticed that Francisco, who was leading the ascent of the Temple of the Inscriptions, walked in a zig zag pattern, which allowed his feet more room sideways on the narrow steps.

Mimicking his technique, Alex carefully climbed the steep stone steps. Perspiring, and reminding herself to breathe, she took her time. The rest of the group was silent and intense and proceeded in the same manner. When they reached the top, they were breathless. Bottled water came out of day packs like champagne corks at a wedding. Francisco, who looked unphased, gave them time to rest before the downward climb deep into Pakal's tomb inside the pyramid.

Alex stood outside the small temple at the top of the pyramid, her chest heaving from the exertion in the forbidding climate. Stucco frescoes, long devoid of color, stood out from the front pillars. Her senses reeled with a combination of vertigo and haunting ancient images that stirred deep in her awareness. This was accompanied by an inexplicable feeling of grief.

She turned around and was stunned by the vision which met her eyes. The elevated position from the top of the pyramid provided a commanding view of jagged, gray mountains and the surrounding rain forest. No other visible structures interrupted the roll of the great plains that stretched like an unbroken emerald sea of waving grasses between the ruins and the mountains.

Francisco's tone was reverent when he spoke again.

"The Maya believed the universe was created when First Father raised the sky from the earth to form a cross, forming the World Tree. The center is called the heart of the world and the arms of the cross are the four directions. A god resides at each corner.

"Ready to enter the tomb?" Francisco smiled. "Please, do not touch the walls as the designs and glyphs are fragile."

Erik positioned himself next to Alexandria as they entered the inside of the pyramid through a rectangular opening in the stone floor roughly five feet by six feet. The opening revealed steps that had been hewn from large pieces of stone, some rounded, others jagged. Most of the steps were covered with slippery moss that flourished in the damp darkness. The ceiling of the staircase was vaulted in a typical corbeled Mayan arch, sloping inward with each layer of stones, and coming to a nearly triangular shape at the top.

Steep, damp steps inside the stairway, made slick from mold, inclined straight down for eighty feet inside a narrow passage built inside the pyramid. A pungent, earthy smell filled the dank space that was dimly lit by a few artificial bulbs. The stone stairway made a sharp right turn on a small landing, another right turn for twenty steps, and ended in a stone anteroom outside the burial chamber. The funerary crypt was small with an arched doorway.

Stalactites, grown from centuries of darkness and moisture, sparkled like jewels over the massive sarcophagus of the former ruler of Palenque. Pakal's body, his jade funerary mask, and other rich treasures had long since been moved to the safety of the museum in Mexico City. The mythical nine lords of the Maya underworld encircled the walls and were surrounded by the hieroglyphic inscriptions that gave the temple its name.

"When they discovered Pakal's tomb," Francisco said, "the floor outside the burial chamber was covered with cinnabar. Red is the color of the rising sun and symbolized resurrection. The ancient Chinese had a similar custom to help the spirit gain access to eternal life. The Spanish named their mission Santo Domingo. Domingo means Sunday but also Easter and Resurrection.

"Red represents east and south is yellow. The setting sun in the west is black, and north is white. The center of the wheel of directions is green, for the great World Tree and the earth. We know the directions were important to our ancestors, as they still are to Indians today," he continued.

"Much of the true meaning of these symbols is hidden, but there are Mayan shamans today who still know the old counsels." Francisco and most of the group started back up. Alex and remained, gazing at the remarkable tomb. She wanted to touch the walls, but honored Francisco's request. She studied the intricate design on the huge lid of Pakal's tomb. The figure of the ruler was at the bottom, looking almost as if he were gazing through the lens of a giant telescope and working the controls with his hands. If she soft focused her eyes, she could almost imagine the original colors.

The Cross of Palenque was carved here and had waited in darkness for fourteen centuries to be discovered. *How could I have designed such a similar cross? Did I live here once?* She sighed and stepped back to take a picture.

"Penny for your thoughts," Erik said.

"I can't take it all in. Thoughts. Feelings. Maybe ancient memories. What about you?"

"I came to get a firsthand look at some Mexican pyramids," he said, removing his hat and wiping perspiration from his forehead with his sleeve. "I think there has to be a relationship among the different cultures who built massive pyramids. I'm searching for a common origin in the distant past."

"You mean Atlantis as a mother culture?"

"Exactly," he said, looking pleased. "It's a tragedy how much knowledge has been lost or purposely destroyed through ignorance and greed."

"I read somewhere there are also huge pyramids in China, but the government won't let researchers have access," Alex said. "I saw photos, and they looked as large as those in Egypt. Francisco just said the Chinese used cinnabar."

"I hope to check that out at some point, although the Chinese want to suppress that knowledge. I wasn't supposed to come here until next month, but my team leader had an emergency. I'm glad I'm here now," he said, smiling at her.

"What kind of team?" Alex asked.

"I'm working in Egypt with a group of scientists from multiple disciplines. I'm the computer guy on our team. We're following the trail of an earlier scholar, author John Anthony West, who believes the Sphinx was weathered around its lower half by water, not wind and sand based on the earlier work of Schwaller d Lubicz. We're looking for further justification for the theory. Turns out geology is a major clue."

"In a desert?"

"West's colleague, geologist Robert Schock, covered up the head of the Sphinx and showed a photograph of the body to some geologist colleagues, asking them to identify the pattern of weathering. The geologists all agreed, classic water weathering. Then he uncovered the Sphinx's head and the geologists groaned. Turns out there hasn't been that much water in Egypt for thirteen thousand years."

Alex's eyes widened as the implication registered. "That's the same timeframe as Atlantis, right?  That's strong evidence to place Egypt's antiquity in the same ballpark."

Erik smiled and nodded.  "Bingo. Major disturbance in the archeological force."

She looked at him.  "My family believed in ancient civilizations that have disappeared, leaving legends but no proof.  It's part of why I'm here, although I don't yet know my real purpose.  Maybe it seems silly, but I feel some larger purpose unfolding in my life."

"I'm just trying to follow the science and the data.  I'll leave rewriting the history books to someone else, but all my life I've felt compelled to understand ancient civilizations.  It's like something always at the edge of my vision, just barely out of reach, but tugging at me.  I started studying Egyptian hieroglyphs in grade school.  Sometimes it makes me crazy, but I feel driven to find answers."

"That's funny," she said.  "My father used to tell me I couldn't get enough of my grandfather's National Geographic magazines about Egypt.  This place stirs up feelings of familiarity and loss.  Now I want to know everything about the Maya."

"Tall order," he said and laughed.

They climbed the slippery stone stairs in silence.  When they reached the top, Alex's breathing was labored.  Her head ached, and her clothes were soaked with perspiration.   They rested for a few moments to catch their breath.  Alex's heart thundered as she stared down the narrow stone steps on the outside of the pyramid.  The descent was treacherous, and a misstep could prove fatal.

They descended the steps of the pyramid with care and joined the group, following Francisco to the next temples. He stopped in a grassy area where three temples formed three arms of a cross around a plaza on the eastern side of the Palenque site.  Each temple rested on a stepped platform with a stairway leading to the front. Similar in design each displayed a mansard style roof with a comb and outer and inner vaulted rooms.  A massive hill, covered with foliage, filled the fourth point.

Alex felt overheated and exhausted.  She sat on a stone bench that circled banana trees and listened to Francisco.

"Although Pakal seems to have built the fabulous temple that housed his tomb, these three temples were constructed during the reign of his two sons, and they have a similar construction with decorated roof combs made of stone. " Francisco said, moving his arm to encompass the three structures.

"Archeologists believe these temples were used for ceremonial purposes.

As you can see, they seem to be seated on small hills. The pyramids beneath the temples have not been uncovered, so the climb is not as steep. When Palenque was found everything was covered with jungle vegetation. The structures looked like green hills. Even if they were restored it is doubtful they would seem as grand as the Temple of Inscriptions where Pakal was buried.

"Some of the most exquisite murals were found that tell the story of creation on a cosmic scale; how First Father joined with First Mother to bring the worlds into being. In some cases, the Bas Relief murals also relate the personal history of the accession of the throne of Chan Balam, son of Pakal. The temples were named for the sculptured panels found inside. The information on these murals is a rare treasure because it survived destruction by the Spanish friars.

"What you will see on the inside walls today are reconstructions. The originals are now in museums. The archeologist Merle Greene Robertson found a color code. For one thing, exposed human skin was painted red, but the skin of the gods was blue, similar to Egyptian temples and tombs. The temple facing west is called the Temple of the Foliated Cross.

"The Temple of the Sun faces east. Inside are the head and body of a great serpent and a large war shield. The Maya perceived the path of the sun as a serpent. The double-headed serpent was a symbol of kingship, like the Egyptian uraeus, the cobra that appears on the brow of the Pharaoh. The one in the north, looking south at the forest, is known as the Temple of the Cross of Palenque, which contained the beautiful carving of the World Tree.

"Climb the pyramid you choose and look inside the small temples at the top," Francisco said. "From the top of the Foliated Cross Temple you can see all of Palenque and for miles in any direction. I will wait here in the center to answer any questions. you "have after.

The Temple of the Foliated Cross was nestled in the surrounding hill, looking more like a small church than a Mayan temple. The two-story stone structure was enfolded on three sides by emerald-green trees. Flanking both sides of the upper level of the temple were two large openings, looking like enormous key holes. The doorway opened almost to the top of the building, culminating in a triangular arch. The roof comb was no longer visible, and the underlying pyramid was still covered by earth. Instead of the sharp ascent of the Temple of Inscriptions, the approach was a gently curving stone path.

Alexandria marshaled her flagging strength and stepped on the path toward the Temple of the Foliated Cross. After seeing the slide last night, and recognizing the design on her necklace, she felt compelled to see the reconstruction of the reliefs inside the small temple. She looked up as she climbed and a potent sense of *déjà vu* poured through her. She felt dizzy and stopped to catch her breath.

She closed her eyes and experienced a sudden, unbidden memory from her childhood that flashed before her mind with sharp intensity. She could see the stone wall that surrounded Our Lady of Peace church. She remembered the strange sensations she always felt when that wall was covered by spring and summer vegetation. That wall made her think of something, but she could never remember what. There were times she thought she could go through the wall, just like Alice and the looking glass.

"Are you okay?" Erik asked, startling her back to ordinary awareness. "You've been standing there for several minutes. I didn't want to disturb you, but there's a line forming behind us."

She looked at him in surprise. "I'm having a hard time with the climate and a sense of the surreal. I'll need to rest soon but I don't want to miss anything." She turned to continue the climb. Erik followed her as she ascended the terraced stone steps.

The temple had been painstakingly reconstructed by archeologists after nearly two thousand years of jungle growth had been cleared. A small rectangular building stood on a stone platform, and Alex entered the temple at the top of the pyramid. Inside the air was cooler, and she felt the lingering sacred energy like a fragrance of incense carried on a breeze. Open to the elements, there was an anteroom and a sanctuary. Inside a replica of the three-part mural, called The Foliated Cross, depicted the Mayan World Tree had been recreated on the wall. She felt glad the original was safe in a museum in Mexico City.

She gazed at the marvelous, sculpted reliefs and tried to probe their meaning. The edges of the mural were covered in Mayan glyphs. Two Mayan men stood on either side of a tall cross that climbed through the center of the sculpture like a tree. Francisco had called it the Foliated Cross, like a living thing. A strange bird perched at the apex.

Alex tried to imagine what the murals had looked like in color. She felt amazed that she had created something so similar in shape. She had thought the curved ends of the arms of her design were unique. She placed her hand over her necklace and thought of Gran. *What a strange and humbling synchronicity.*

She walked back outside and turned to look at the stone buildings of the ceremonial center of Palenque and the horizon in the distance. She was lost in contemplation of the green landscape and the hundreds of green mounds which were structures yet to be uncovered.  She stared across the cleared grassy area at the temple of the Sun and felt a quiver of recognition.  Palenque had a haunting familiarity.

"It's so beautiful," she whispered.

"And so compelling," Erik said softly.  "May I look at your necklace again?"

Erik's voice startled Alex from her reverie.  She took her necklace off and handed it to him.  She watched his sensitive, intelligent eyes, seeming to probe the details of the cross pendant.

"Do you feel like you lived here in another life?" he asked suddenly.

"I'm wondering about that.  Something keeps tugging at the edges of my memory."

"This center was abandoned six-hundred years before the Spanish arrived," he said.  "Why did they leave and return to a simple life in the jungle?  Did the people just stop following corrupt leaders?"

"Their origin seems curious too," she agreed.  "From what I've read, it's as if their civilization sprang to life fully developed, like Egypt and Sumeria.  The beginning and ending aren't connected to anything. Like what you said about these pyramids and those in Egypt.  Do you think the two cultures were related?"

"That's why I'm here.  The similarity of the pyramids seems too much of a coincidence."  Erik sighed.  "Ready to climb down?"

"I guess," Alex said.  She didn't want the moment to end.  She felt a powerful affinity with these temples and was also feeling slightly intoxicated by Erik's proximity. As they descended the stone steps, Alex mourned their faded majesty.

CHAPTER 6

# RECOGNITION

When they reached the ground, Alexandria noticed a distinguished Indian man talking to Francisco. He wore dark slacks, a white shirt, and a straw hat, like a Panama. Except for his Maya features, he looked like a European tourist.

Francisco waved and walked toward them. "I'd like to introduce my grandfather, don Miguel Piedra. He's visiting from Mexico City."

Alex froze, her eyes wide in shock.

"What's wrong?" Erik asked, his shoulders tensed.

"I recognize you."

The man smiled and riveted powerful dark eyes, like sparkling obsidian, on Alexandria's blue-green ones. "Strange, since we have not yet met. But I am not surprised. He bowed. "It is indeed my pleasure to finally meet the daughter and granddaughter of my friends. My name is don Miguel Balam Piedra. Alexandria, such a beautiful name, like the city of learning in ancient Egypt."

"What's going on?" Erik asked, stepping forward.

Alex tried to speak but found she had trouble breathing. She grabbed Erik's arm to anchor herself, but with the combination of unfamiliar heat and shock she collapsed.

Alex wakened to see two concerned Maya faces with hawk-like noses looking down at her. Brown muscular bodies were framed by bright sunlight and the background of the forest. Multi-colored fabric ties circled their

41

waists. Bracelets of woven leaves circled their brown wrists and ankles, and ornate necklaces covered their chests. Brilliantly colored feathered head-pieces crowned their heads.

She looked into the fierce, almond-shaped eyes of the young man who supported her. Alex felt incredible longing and a sense of recognition. She breathed deeply, closed her eyes a moment, and the vision passed.

"Are you all, right?" Erik asked, frowning.

Her vision cleared and she sat up. "I've never fainted before. This is beyond embarrassing."

"Allow me to assist," don Miguel said, and before Alex could object, he moved behind her. He placed his right arm under hers and his left arm held her left elbow. With a strength that startled her, he lifted her to her feet. Erik's astonishment over Miguel's feat showed in his open-mouthed stare.

Alexandria brushed herself off and looked from one to the other. She was confused and a little frightened. She wanted to be angry, but Erik's startled face made her laugh instead. His expression changed from surprise to a scowl.

"Why don't we have something cool to drink and sort out our confusion?" Miguel asked.

"I think that's an excellent idea. I need some answers," Alex said.

"You need to rest, Alex. You're shaking," Erik said. We need to get you out of the sun before you pass out again."

Alex's struggle with conflicting emotions about the situation manifested as annoyance. "We'll talk in the shade then," she said, marching off in the direction of the trees.

Don Miguel followed, his mouth twitching to conceal a grin, brought up the rear. Erik brought up the rear, clenching his fists.

Alex stopped in an inviting rest area behind the Palace complex, beside a stream. Water cascaded over rocks, creating a musical sound. Stone benches circled the trunks of a huge Ceiba tree, and a slight breeze moved the thick air.

Don Miguel handed Alex a cool bottle of water. She tilted her head and drank the contents without a breath. The water tasted like a divine elixir, but she saved some to splash on her hands and face. Breathing to calm herself, Alex glanced around to see if anyone else was in the area as she didn't want this strange conversation to be overheard. As if by magic other tourists had left and they seemed to be alone. She looked directly into Miguel Piedra's eyes.

"I've seen you before," she said.

Erik leaped to his feet. "Hold on here. I don't know who you think this *senor* is, but I think the heat's made you batty."

Miguel gave him a piercing stare, then his face softened, and he smiled.

Alex spun around and glared at Erik, "I may be batty, but it's no concern of yours. Back off."

Erik's eyes looked hurt, then the scowl returned. He opened his mouth to speak, but don Miguel raised his hand in the Indian gesture of silence before speaking.

"You are right, young man. My apology since you do not have the benefit of Alexandria's previous knowledge. But I am also curious how you recognized me," Miguel said, turning to her.

Erik crossed his arms, and his scowl deepened.

She stared at the hill, and the stone steps that curved up and around the back. When she turned to face them, her face was pale, and her eyes were moist.

"My grandmother died suddenly about a week ago."

"I'm sorry," Erik said, his scowl softening.

"The night of her funeral I saw her in a dream," she began, looking first at Miguel then at Erik. "My father, who died when I was twelve, and my grandfather were with her."

Miguel looked at her expectantly.

Alex was composed as she spoke, but tears spilled out of her eyes. She absently wiped them from her face with the backs of her hands. "There were beautiful temples in that dream too. They seemed to be made from sand and stucco and overlooked an ocean. I was introduced to you in that dream, don Miguel, and you looked exactly as you do now. My father said it was time to do the work I had specifically come to do, and that you would guide me.

"Earlier that day I had found an envelope with the tickets for this trip that my grandmother had arranged. I think she meant to surprise me, but she died unexpectedly before she could explain. There's also this." Alex pulled the silver chain and cross from her shirt. "I made it myself and believed it to be an original design."

Miguel's eyebrows raised and his black eyes sparkled with intelligence and curiosity. "May I?" he asked. She removed the necklace and handed it to him.

"Most intriguing," he said, looking at her pendant. "Alexandria, I did indeed know your father and grandparents; they were dear friends. Your grandmother's long silence was her way of protecting you. Recently, she began to worry that she had waited too long and the timing of her death was indeed unfortunate."

Alexandria's tilted her head toward him. "What are you saying?"

"Perhaps nothing, perhaps a great deal," Miguel replied. "After your father's death your grandparents took care to protect you. But for now, if you will indulge me, I wish to tell you about my own dream, which also occurred one week ago. "

"Oh, man," Erik said.

Alex and Miguel ignored him.

"The dream took place here at Palenque but it was a long time ago. I saw the great center at its zenith. It was called *Cha Kan Pu Tun*, City of the Rains. The buildings were magnificent. The temples were covered in white stucco, and the friezes and murals were painted in brilliant shades of turquoise blue offset by red like cinnabar.

"The citizens looked as if they stepped off the sculptures. Proud Maya faces and colorful clothing looked at home in these surroundings. Avenues and paths were lined with beautiful trees and flowers. The City of the Rains was a majestic and sacred place."

He paused and looked around at the ruined Palenque of the present. He was silent, deeply thoughtful. "Memories are bittersweet, are they not?"

"Look, don Miguel," Erik said. "She's upset and doesn't need to hear a fairy tale."

"Please," Alex said, "I do need to hear this. You probably do too as I'm beginning to suspect our meeting wasn't coincidence either."

Erik exhaled and sat down. He took off his hat and wiped his forehead on his sleeve.

"In my dream, I was a priest, on my way to what is now the Temple of the Cross, to perform a ritual to dedicate a new temple rebuilt over one destroyed in an earthquake.

Alex tensed and moved to the edge of the stone bench.

"I walked across the plaza, past the Temple of the Inscriptions, and stood at the bottom of the steps. I was joined by attendants dressed in white robes which were woven from fibers of trees in the forest and embroidered in beautiful designs. The threads matched the temple frescoes.

Alex closed her eyes and was transported back in time. The pungent aroma of sacred copal incense wafted in the air. White smoke curled from the bowls of incense while drums beat a steady, deep reverberation.

She could imagine the priest and his attendants climbing the steps of the pyramid from her perspective at the top, inside the temple. The muscular body of the priest was adorned with woven cords and wraps in red, green, and blue. He wore a head dress of feathers and leaves which symbolized power. A necklace of jade beads hung around his neck.

"We climbed the steps of the temple," Miguel said, "stopping at each group of steps to recite a portion of the ritual. Seven groups of steps symbolized different aspects of reality. When we reached the top, a young priestess waited in the alcove to assist me with the ceremony.

"Inside the temple, the great World Tree was painted bright blue, red, green, black, yellow and white. Its name meant 'raised-up sky.' The World Tree wasn't an abstract symbol; it represented the union of earth and sky at that moment. The images on the tree were the constellations in the night sky at the time the temple was dedicated. The scene captured the time."

Don Miguel stood. His figure was framed by gray stone pyramids and green jungle. His modern clothes seemed out of place. He placed his white Panama hat on a log and gazed at the horizon.

"From the top of the temple, every word could be heard throughout the plaza as the ornate roof combs acted as acoustic devices. I remember some of the words."

Miguel raised his arms toward the sky in the timeless gesture of invocation. The voice that thundered from his mouth no longer seemed his. The spirit of all the shamans who ever lived seemed to speak through him.

*"Mighty Hunab K'u, Great Lord of Creation,*

*who dwells at the center of the fourfold universe,*
*the heart of the world, where all is one.*

*Bless us Wakah-Chan, Great World Tree Protect*
*us First Father, Shield of the Sun Nourish us First*
*Mother, with Divine Maize*

*Come through the opened portal to our Holy Place*
*Receive the offerings we have prepared for you.*
*Grant us sustenance from the Spirit Realm*

*We are humbled.*
*We are grateful.*
*We honor your presence in our world."*

"I LOOKED at the young woman who had been my assistant. The face was that of a beautiful young woman with red hair. She was accompanied by a blond man and a white dog."

Alex was startled back to ordinary awareness.

"Our meeting was planned, but Rose died before she could prepare you. Our time here in Palenque may help to explain this powerful dream. I have seen your picture, Alexandria, so I recognized you at once." Miguel smiled. "I did not expect you to recognize me. I had hoped to give you a gentler introduction, but it seems your grandmother intervened. It also seems the blond man from my dream is here," he said, looking toward Erik.

Erik scowled at Alexandria.

Alex exhaled, realizing she'd been holding her breath. She stood and turned to look at the Temple of the Foliated Cross. Only the back of the hill and the top of the temple were visible from their vantage point. The cheerful stream cascaded over rocks. A macaw called overhead.

"It's so strange," Alex said, "but in some ways this place feels more familiar to me than my own home. I don't understand what's happening, don Miguel. I can't help feeling angry that I've been kept in the dark. Can you help me?"

He put his arm around her shoulders. "I will do all within my power to help you, Alexandria. Please, sit down. I must ask you a question."

Alex sat on the stone bench under the tall trees and placed her sun hat on a rock. She twisted her damp hair into a ponytail. Her blue-green eyes searched the sharp features of his countenance.

"Did your family give you any idea of our purpose in your dream?"

"No. They said something about a plan that was set in motion a long time ago."

"I see." Miguel smiled at Alex, his expression kind.

"This is getting rich," Erik stood, moving to stand between Alex and don Miguel. "Just what are you trying to pull here?"

Don Miguel's face changed like a summer storm, moving across a landscape. He leveled an icy stare at Erik. When he spoke, his voice was like a dagger. "Because I believe your role in this drama may prove to be central, Senor Anderson, I will be patient with you. But heed me, young man, I may not always be.

"What is unfolding here fits into a larger scheme than you can yet imagine. If you can keep your ego and hormones at bay, you stand to learn a great deal. If you demonstrate strength of character, you may realize the deepest desires of your heart. Protectiveness is noble, but you can help Alexandria most by assisting her with this enigma she's inherited. Have I made myself clear?"

"Perfectly," he nodded, "How about this for clear? Go to hell!" He bolted like a stallion escaping the corral.

Alexandria had watched astonished, as don Miguel, looming larger than life and terrifying, delivered this blistering manifesto. She was appalled by Erik's response. They watched him disappear around a temple.

Miguel shook his head. "Your young man is also confused and surprised."

"He's not my young man."

"We shall see. I first met your grandparents in Boston at an archeological symposium. I believe it was the early sixties. Your father and I were close to the same age and became good friends. They visited me twice in Mexico."

"I wonder why I never knew about this or met you," Alex said.

"After your father's death, we kept in touch through correspondence and phone. They were trying to keep you safe."

"Safe from what?"

"By the way, I sent flowers when I learned of Rose's passing. Did you receive them?"

"What kind of flowers?" Alex's heart raced.

"Roses, of course, lilies, and birds of paradise."

"Those flowers arrived the day I found the envelope. In fact, and this is one more strange thing, the flowers arrived almost at the same time. There was a beautiful card, but it wasn't signed."

"I don't believe in coincidence. Do you?" Miguel smiled, "I wonder what our next surprise will be."

I'm tired of questions and sick of surprises. I need some answers."

# CHAPTER 7
# A GIFT

Alex sat on a large rock, staring at the gray stones of the Temple of Inscriptions surrounded by emerald jungle. Sticky clothes clung to her moist skin and her face ached from sunburn. The air itself seemed damp.

"You look like you need a siesta," Miguel said. "This unfamiliar climate is taxing for you." Except for his modern clothes, Alex saw don Miguel as a Mayan lord on a temple frieze. High cheekbones and a sharp nose endowed his face with a haunting dignity.

She sighed audibly and looked up at him. "I'm miserable, but you look unaffected, Miguel." She wiped her forehead on her sleeve.

"I was born here, Alexandria. Your body is more attuned to colder weather."

"I feel like I'm surrendering to weakness."

"You've been under a great deal of stress, and today's events have only added to the load," Miguel said. " I will take you back to the hotel so you can have a siesta before dinner."

They walked back through the Palenque complex to the parking area. Sparse clouds looked like smoke in a sky that seemed as hot as blue flame. The sun had reached its zenith, and the jungle baked in a tropical oven and birds and monkeys were silent. Alex noticed the Lacondon Maya as they approached the entrance. Small people, barely five-feet tall, their black eyes were bright with intelligence, and their gentle demeanor radiated an openness of heart that touched her.

Both men and women kept their black hair long. Lacondon men dressed in ancestral white-cotton robes and wore simple sandals or went barefoot. Even in this two-thousand-year-old archeological site they seemed anachronistic. Handmade items lay on brightly colored woven blankets that were spread on the ground. The colorful scene beckoned against a backdrop of jungle foliage. One of the men beckoned to don Miguel.

"Excuse me a moment," he said. Don Miguel looked tall standing next to the Lancondon. His modern clothes, walking shoes, and straw hat contrasted with the plain white robe and bare feet. A broad smile illumined his face as the man gave Miguel a necklace made of textured brown seeds from the rain forest. The beads resembled carved coffee beans.

Miguel held the necklace up. "A gift for you, Alexandria."

Alex smiled.

Miguel gestured for her to join them. "This is Chan Ka. He wants to place the beads over your head."

Chan Ka smiled, looking at her out of wise eyes that were childlike in their innocence. She leaned forward to accept the necklace. Everyone smiled.

"Tell him they're beautiful, don Miguel."

Miguel spoke in the Maya language. Chan Ka grinned and nodded. Then his expression became serious. He looked directly into Alexandria's eyes and said a few words in his Mayan dialect.

"He says your cross is a very beautiful Maya symbol and he would like to have the necklace, Alexandria," Miguel translated.

Her eyes widened. She grasped her necklace in a protective gesture. Alex looked at don Miguel for help, but his face was impassive. She could easily make another necklace. Why did his request offend her?

Everyone was still; the moment seemed eternal. Alex wanted to take off the necklace he had given her and throw the beads back at him. She fought the urge to turn and run. As if in response to these strong emotions she heard her father's words.

"Listen to the voice of your heart, Alex. Remember how much you are loved." She sensed his presence and felt a stabbing pang of guilt. She felt ashamed, and her reluctance evaporated.

Alex removed her necklace. Her hands shook as she lifted the cross over Chan Ka's head and a deep sense of rightness stirred within her. She stepped back and saw her treasure against the white fabric of his simple garment.

A chorus of "ah's" emanated from the small group. The ornate silver cross was two inches long, resembling Philodendron vines climbing a tree. The two arms of the cross curved upward and inward. Tiny crystals and pieces of jade, carnelian and turquoise lined the edges. The arms extended up and out from the center of the cross and branched into a stylized letter U.

She recalled the Cross of Palenque she had seen on the temple wall earlier. *This cross belongs with Chan Ka.* Alex looked into the eyes of this outwardly simple man and connected to his inner power. He returned her look with a commanding presence and spoke again in the Yucatec language.

"He will wear your gift with gratitude and honor," Miguel translated. Then he moved to Alex's side and touched her elbow. "Ready for that siesta?" She nodded.

Miguel guided Alex toward an ageless, blue pickup. The vehicle was covered in mud and dust but she thought the truck seemed structurally sound. He opened the passenger door and helped her inside. Alex felt dazed. She had no awareness of don Miguel starting the engine, or riding in the truck, other than a vague sense of bouncing on the road.

She was jolted to alertness when a small, white car swerved on the other side of the road and headed directly toward them. Alex screamed and pitched forward. She braced herself against the dashboard. Don Miguel wrenched the steering wheel to the right and drove into a ditch. The other car did not even slow down. As the white car passed, Alex thought the passenger looked oddly familiar. Although she didn't see the driver but felt a sense of malice.

"Don't worry; we were not harmed. Help will arrive soon."

She wanted to believe him, but that did not prevent tears from filling her eyes. She was frightened, and her heart throbbed in her chest.

Two men suddenly materialized from the brush.

"Where did they come from?" Alex asked.

"They live in the area," Miguel said simply.

The Indian men climbed into the ditch and helped them out of the truck. Alex clamored out of the ditch and collapsed on the ground beside the road. Two vehicles arrived and four men emerged from each one. They laughed and joked in Spanish and Mayan, expressing the good-natured banter of close friends. Alex understood enough to know they were teasing don Miguel about his big city driving.

They easily extracted the truck from the ditch with ropes, and Miguel climbed back in and started the engine. One of the men helped Alex into the truck, and after farewells, they resumed their journey in silence. Alex felt an undercurrent and knew Miguel's quick response had prevented serious injury.

She wondered if the mishap was accidental. *But that's ridiculous, isn't it?*

When they reached the hotel Miguel came around to open the door of the truck. Alex thought he seemed comfortable in any circumstance.

He smiled. "Try to rest, Alexandria, and don't think too much. You are safe here."

Alex returned his smile. "I'm too tired to do anything else right now." She walked to her casita in a trance and checked on the spider, feeling great relief that the plastic cup and eight-legged inhabitant were gone. She took a welcome shower and collapsed on the bed.

CHAPTER 8

# KARMIC NECESSITY

lex rolled over and looked at her watch, realizing she'd slept three hours and the late-afternoon sun now cast long shadows across the room. She stretched and felt hungry. She dressed in a long, goldenrod-colored dress, adding silver jewelry with citrine insets. Her loose mass of red hair softly framed her sunburned face.

Alex looked in the mirror and was pleased with her reflection then shook her head in dismay. *I hate to admit how much I want to see Erik.* She walked through the jungle grounds to the restaurant.

"You look better, Senorita," Miguel said as she approached.

"I feel better too," she said, smiling.

Miguel laughed. "It's a shame to waste such loveliness on an old man."

Alex blushed. "You're hardly an old man."

She thought Miguel was handsome. Silver hair, laced with streaks of black, contrasted with his dark, flashing eyes. His angular Indian features seemed chiseled into his striking countenance. He looked comfortable in slacks and a short-sleeved shirt.

"I feel like a fool for fainting, Miguel. Today was like a dream, almost surreal, and I'm stunned by my response to this place. Palenque seems so familiar somehow. Meeting you after dreaming about you was a shock, and everything to do with my necklace has been unnerving. It's just too many accidents and coincidences, and Mr. Anderson makes me feel like a mindless teenager. But what bothers me most is not knowing what Gran wanted to tell me. Something important is happening that I don't understand."

Don Miguel smiled and gestured dramatically with a wave of his arm and a deep bow. His movements were as agile and graceful as a Flamenco dancer.

"Your *destiny*, Senorita," he said. Then he stood up straight and clicked his heels.

Alex smiled but felt helpless.

A server approached and showed them to a table on the wooden veranda that overlooked the swimming pool and grounds. Sparkling light filtered through tall palm trees, and the angle of the Sun's descent gilded the trees and water with luminescence.

"What would you like to drink?" the waitress asked in Spanish.

"Coca Cola, por favor," Alex said.

"Agua mineral," Miguel said.

Alex gazed at the philodendrons, hibiscus, and tall coconut palms that were filled with the sounds of parrots and macaws. Noisy cicadas competed for mates as classical Spanish guitar music drifted from a radio in the background.

"It's so beautiful, don Miguel, so vital. The temperature and latitude heat up the life force until it explodes in intensity and diversity. Everything teems and boils to express itself, which is quite unlike a Philadelphia winter."

Miguel smiled, and his wise eyes twinkled. "Your thoughts have taken a philosophical turn. Yes, life in the tropics is so intense that there is a danger in taking life for granted. If winter never comes, you can become careless. Speaking of philosophy, did you know your grandmother believed in reincarnation?"

Alex chuckled. "It always comes down to philosophy. Yes, my grandparent's world view influenced mine. I spent so much time with them after my father died, I absorbed a lot. Reincarnation makes sense to me and helped place my father's death in perspective. Gran called it a 'karmic necessity.'"

"What did she mean?" Don Miguel watched Alex intently. His elbows rested on the arms of the chair, and his thumbs and fingers formed a triangle at his chest. His chin perched on the tip of the pyramid.

"That his early death was actually part of the agenda for his life and dealing with that loss was part of the life plans for those closest to him," Alex said.

"I see."

Alex looked into Miguel's eyes, which seemed to emit sparks of light. She pounded her fist on the table, and the silverware jumped. "That's it, meeting you is a karmic necessity."

Miguel laughed, a hearty sound that came from the center of his being. "Each life has a purpose, Alexandria, and yours is being thrust upon you, although in truth you have called it forth. Fate is not an external process. I agree that we have a purpose for meeting, a karmic necessity, if you will."

Alex knitted her forehead. "What's your life purpose, Miguel?"

He smiled, and his face brightened.

"A fair question. My studies have carried me to unexpected vistas and different realms of consciousness. I have devoted my life to studying the ways of the Maya, my ancestors, as the living shamans continue the ancient traditions. I see my purpose as helping them integrate that knowledge with encroaching modern development to reclaim and sustain their heritage. Although I am half Spanish, it is my heritage also. There are prophecies that say the time is at hand."

"No wonder you and my family were friends."

Don Miguel smiled and his profile was outlined by the half-light of the setting sun. "Your grandmother was an amazing and courageous woman. She studied prophecies from many traditions, including the Maya. I admired her and will miss her."

Alex thought he looked strong and wise and felt safe and comforted by his friendship with her father and grandparents.

"Don Miguel, I don't think the incident with the truck was an accident."

He looked at her. "No, I do not believe it was."

Alex thought she detected concern in his kind eyes.

"But why?"

Miguel was silent a moment as if measuring his response. For the moment let me say your grandmother was trying to protect you from things she couldn't control."

Alex frowned. "But now I feel unprepared."

The waitress returned and served large plates filled with beans, rice, tortillas, sliced avocados, and tomatoes. Alex took a bite of beans and rice, closing her eyes to savor the flavor and texture.

"This is wonderful."

Miguel laughed. "Nothing seems to bother your appetite."

Erik approached their table. Freshly showered, he wore long, khaki pants and an olive-green tee shirt. He ignored don Miguel and stared at Alexandria.

"Won't you join us?" Miguel asked, pointing to an empty chair.

Erik didn't answer and continued to stare at Alex.

Alex smiled and again felt like an infatuated teenager. "Sit down please and have something cool to drink. We just started."

Don Miguel ate his dinner and appeared to ignore them. The waitress reappeared to take Erik's order.

"I'll have what she's having," he said, sitting down next to Alex. "How do you feel?"

"Physically, much improved. Psychologically, I'm not sure."

"You look wonderful. I'm sorry I was such a jerk. I don't understand my extreme response to you and this strange situation we find ourselves in."

Alex blushed again and was vaguely aware of her face producing a smile of its own accord. Feeling awkward, she groped for something to redirect the course of conversation and turned to don Miguel in desperation.

"Miguel and I were discussing a troubling experience we had today."

Startled from his trance, Erik wheeled around to look at Miguel. Alex and Erik both focused on don Miguel who had a mouthful of food and a glass of water in his hand. They waited for him to recover. He put his glass down, swallowed, and cleared his throat.

"After you left us, I offered to drive Alexandria back here. We had a mishap."

"What kind of mishap?" Erik asked, this time directing his eyes toward Alex, which she thought might burn a hole in her forehead.

"I was about to tell Alexandria some of the history of her family that might shed light on recent events. I waited for you to join us as I believe you should hear also this. Then we can discuss today's incident."

Erik frowned and sat back in his chair. "This isn't helping my strong reactions."

"Your grandparents were more than they seemed, Alexandria. They were in a vanguard of scientists and workers who were dedicated to holding back the forces of darkness on this planet." Miguel glanced around then looked at each of them. "More than this I can't say now but trust your instincts.

"I didn't have a chance to tell you yet, but my family checked on the white car. Jose Sanchez had rented his automobile to a European. He said the man asked several curious questions and paid generously to use the car. It was Jose's car we encountered today. The man never returned the vehicle and they found the car abandoned.

"Alex and I were forced off the road in what may not have been an accident."

"Did you notify the police?" The volume of Erik's voice increased.

"You're making a scene," Alex said.

"You're right I'm making a scene. Something's rotten in Denmark, and it started to stink when this guy showed up," Erik pointed his thumb sideways and cocked his head at don Miguel.

"That's ridiculous. It started years ago with my grandparents. I don't believe in coincidence and there have been way too many lately. My grandmother sent me here to meet don Miguel. I think I was also meant to meet you, although I'm questioning the wisdom of that at the moment. I would appreciate it if you'd stop making him the enemy and wasting testosterone."

The waitress delivered Erik's dinner. Alex resumed eating beans and tortillas. They glared at each other over their dinner plates.

"Alexandria has inherited this quest, and I am here to help. You can choose to help or hinder, Erik."

Erik looked at both and sat back in his chair and took a deep breath. "I love a good mystery, but I need more facts and less intrigue. I feel helpless and out of control, and I don't like the feeling one bit. It brings out my worst qualities."

"I think it is safe to say we all feel unsure right now. How about a safer topic for the moment?" Don Miguel ventured. "I'm interested in your work in Egypt. Years ago, I encountered the daunting master work of Schwaller de Lubicz. It's wonderful that someone is pursuing this legacy."

Erik stared at Miguel, anger and dinner momentarily forgotten. "You know *Le Temple de l'Homme*?  I've never met anyone outside of our project group who even heard of those books."

Alex was amused by Erik's reaction to this news and struggled to suppress a smile. "What are you two talking about?"

Miguel's expression was unreadable, but Alex thought she detected a brief sparkle of humor in his eyes.

"He was brilliant, if controversial," Erik said. "*The Temple of Man* is a behemoth.  He's the one I mentioned who believed the Sphinx was weathered by water. That makes the big lion thousands of years older than mainstream Egyptologists insist. Researchers John Anthony West and geologist Robert Schock are following in his footsteps.

"The idea behind the project is to prove the thesis geologically, and I think that's been done. It's pretty clear-cut—forgive the pun," Erik grinned, warming to his topic.  "But until we have twelve-thousand-year-old pot shards, it constitutes academic heresy."

"Who does your group think built the Sphinx?" Miguel asked.

"Most of us postulate an earlier mother civilization, called Atlantis usually. We haven't endeared ourselves to the Egyptological establishment."

"Gran was also interested in this topic. She spoke of a psychic who had lots to say on Atlantis. I think it was the same time frame," Alex said.

"Edgar Cayce," Miguel said.

"You know about Edgar Cayce too?" Erik asked, wrinkling his forehead.

Miguel laughed. "Ancient civilizations are also my passion."

Alex watched the interaction between the two men and a thought struck her. "Ancient civilizations were Gran's fascination too. In my dream vision there were temples and pyramids. My father said I had work to do and that you would help me, Miguel. I don't see what I have to do with ancient civilizations."

"Our path will be revealed and we must watch for the signs," Miguel said.

"I believe you," Alex smiled.

"It has been a long day. I will take my leave now and see you in the morning. *Buenas noches*," Miguel said.

"Good night, don Miguel." She kissed him on the cheek. Erik only nodded, but his mood had improved.

Alex yawned. "It's been a long day for me too."

"I'll walk you back," he said.

They walked to her bungalow in silence. The tropical night air was balmy, and a huge full moon rose in the east. When they reached the door, Alex looked up at him.

"I appreciated the company."

"I don't know what's wrong with me. I don't usually overreact this way, but I have this strange need to protect you." His boyish face looked contrite.

He reached for her hand, and his touch was electrifying. She felt a current of energy course throughout her as she stared into his eyes. Erik kissed her, a brief velvet touch on her lips. The smell of his breath aroused her, sending a sudden rush to her solar plexus.

"*Buenas noches, senorita bonita*," he said smiling. "Remember, I'm right next door."

She opened her door and went inside. She leaned against the wooden surface to steady herself. *He thinks he's the one out of control.*

Alex put on a cotton nightgown, sat on the bed, and tried to write postcards. She couldn't concentrate on anything but Erik's kiss and felt exasperated. After attempting a few entries in her journal, she tossed the spiral notebook on the floor.

She stretched out on the bed and was mesmerized by the slowly circling ceiling fan. Alexandria turned out the light and lay on her back in the darkness. Outside insects hummed and a dog barked in the distance. The pungent juxtaposition of tropical flowers and decaying vegetation permeated the night air. Alex's mind was filled with nagging questions as she drifted off to sleep.

# CHAPTER 9

# RAVEN DREAM

Storm clouds gathered in a sickly yellow sky, painting menacing black streaks across the horizon. Thunder rumbled and the air was laden with the pernicious stench of sulfur. A harsh wind blew dry leaves and dust into whirlpools as giant sycamores thrashed in strong currents of wind.

Clothed in a long robe, Alexandria ran across a forbidding landscape, searching for something, and feeling an ominous need. Scanning the horizon, she watched the black clouds become even darker.

Suddenly, a huge raven swooped from the sky, cawed in a threatening voice, and dove toward her. She ducked, and the bird barely missed her. Looking up, a light appeared ahead of her like a beacon. She saw a woman, clothed in purple raiment with a demeanor like a goddess, who held a lantern and beckoned in the darkening gloom.

Alexandria ran faster. She had to reach the goddess before the raven attacked again. She climbed up the side of a mountain. Rocks broke loose and tumbled down the slope, and she stumbled as she exerted a supreme effort to reach the lady.

At last Alex stood in front of the awesome figure. The goddess handed her a silver sword, and she felt the weapon's power enter her body like an electric shock. She whirled to face the evil raven who had grown larger than human size. Her heart pounded, and her lungs ached. As the evil bird swooped toward her, Alexandria swung the heavy sword in a wide arc and severed the raven's head.

The monstrous head fell to the ground, beady black eyes staring open. Foul, green slime oozed from the headless neck. Alexandria stared at the disgusting sight; both her hands were still clenched around the hilt of the sword. She turned to the goddess whose long hair and purple robes blew nearly horizontal in the howling wind. The goddess fixed a severe gaze on Alexandria.

"Do not fail in your appointed task, priestess."

A volcano rumbled deep inside the mountain and erupted in a convulsion. A paroxysm of steam and lava hurtled rocks and sparks skyward as molten lava streamed down the sides of the mountain.

ALEX WOKE SCREAMING. She couldn't comprehend where she was. She heard pounding, and someone shouting her name. Erik kicked the door open, and the wood frame banged against the wall like a cannon blast. He rushed inside and cradled her in his arms, holding her like a child.

"It's all right; it was just a dream," he repeated several times.

Erik held her while her emotion slowly changed from hysterical sobs to quiet tears. She recovered enough to ask for tissues and blew her nose. She looked at him out of red, swollen eyes.

"That's the second time today I've humiliated myself."

"Want to talk about it?" asked.

"I haven't had that dream since childhood," she said. "Parts of it change, but I'm always attacked by a huge black raven. I dreamed a lot about that hideous bird when I was little. Tonight, I killed the raven; I chopped off its ugly head with a magic sword.

He put his arm around her. They sat that way for some time. "My father used to wake me, just like you did. Although kicking in the door was an added element." She smiled and reddened.

"The nightmares stopped after he died, and I always thought the dreams had to do with his death. I think I can sleep now, but I wouldn't mind if you stayed in the other bed."

"I think we'll both worry less," he said. "Lie down, Alex. I'll be over here."

"Thanks," she whispered.

"Go on, under the sheet."

She was asleep again before her head touched the pillow.

# CHAPTER 10

# TRANSFORMATION

Alex woke as the first rays of morning light shone through the window, creating white streaks on the green bedspread. Her sunburned face ached and her head throbbed. Erik still slept soundly in the other bed. The raven's face flashed across her mind, and Alex remembered the stranger at Gran's funeral; she'd told Sheila he looked like a raven.

She sat up too fast and felt as if she had a hangover. She hobbled to the bathroom to take some headache medicine. After a shower, she dressed in cotton shorts and a print camp shirt. She felt reluctant to wake him, so she left a note.

Alexandria walked through the hotel grounds, feeling relieved that the morning air was still somewhat cool. Noisy parrots called overhead from the canopy of trees. Despite the bright morning Alex couldn't shake the dark emotion of her dream.

Don Miguel sat on the restaurant veranda, sipping coffee. *"Buenos dias, Senorita,"* he said, lifting his mug in salute. He stood as she came to the table and helped her into a chair.

"Difficult night?"

"On top of yesterday's unsettling events, I had a nightmare that I had many times as a child."

"Perhaps there is a symbolic connection," Miguel said.

*Ravens and irrational fear.*

The morning sun burnished her hair like polished copper. Her delicate features were drawn, and her fingernails dug into the palms of her clenched fists. Unnamed anxiety gnawed at her abdomen.

She sighed. "The basic elements of the dream are usually the same. I run across a frightening landscape and I'm chased by an evil raven. I meet a goddess-like being who gives me a sword. In the past I always woke screaming when the raven attacked. Last night I killed the bird."

Miguel listened with single-minded attention. Alex shuddered when she described the raven's death. She didn't notice the waitress bringing breakfast.

"I must have screamed. Erik 's casita is next door, he heard me and pounded on the door. I kept screaming, so he actually kicked the door in. He held me like a little girl just like my father did when I had that awful nightmare. When I was ready to sleep again, I asked him to stay in the other bed."

A young waiter brought coffee, and Alex was startled back to the present and awareness of Miguel. She gazed into the depths of his warm, dark eyes. Miguel smiled, and the gesture soothed her raw nerves and aching vulnerability. She wished she could go back to the time before Gran's death.

"Shamans believe dreams are of vital importance," Miguel said. "Their work includes interpreting dream symbols. Your dream is a powerful message."

Alex sipped cinnamon-flavored coffee and picked at her eggs and tortillas. She exhaled and sat back in the chair, pushing her hair away from her face.

"I mean no disrespect, Miguel, but I felt powerless."

"Not at all, you sensed danger and imminent crisis. You found a mighty Spirit Being who gave you a wondrous weapon, and you defeated your enemy. That is an act of great power.

"The sword is an ancient symbol of truth, Alexandria, and represents the ability of the intellect to cut away the non-essential. The language of dreams is symbolic. I believe the volcanic imagery signifies a transformation within you. Fulfilling your appointed task, once you know it, requires courage and strength of will. Your dream suggests that you will be provided with what you need and that you are ready."

"I want to believe you," Alex said.

Erik approached the table. His gray eyes brooded like storm clouds, but wrinkled clothes and unruly blond hair diminished the impact of his annoyance. He looked like a small boy rousted prematurely from his nap.

"Why didn't you wake me?" he asked, pulling up a chair next to her.

"You were sleeping soundly, and I thought you needed the rest."

"You should have wakened me. I worried when I realized you were gone."

"I didn't mean to concern you." She turned toward Miguel, then looked at Erik. "I remembered something else this morning. I saw a strange, sinister man at Gran's funeral. He was tall, wiry, and dressed in black. He made me uncomfortable and reminded me of Poe's Raven. When I went through her things, I saw him in a group picture with Gran and Grandpa that was taken during a scientific conference. Do you think there could be a connection?"

Don Miguel took a deep, audible breath. He clasped his hands and placed his arms on the table. "I do not believe in coincidence, only cause and effect that is not seen.

"Alexandria, a respected shaman who is my relative lives a day's walk from Palenque. I would like to offer help from the Maya way through a technique called the shaman's journey. Its purpose is healing and restoration of power. The practice is part of a congruent body of knowledge that has worked for thousands of years."

"I'm struggling with acceptance here, but it could be a fool's journey," Erik said. "Sounds like it could be dangerous."

"It is a perfectly natural process," Miguel said.

Erik looked toward Alex for confirmation, but she ignored him.

Alexandria evaluated don Miguel. He radiated quiet power and was secure, fearless, and master of any circumstance. By contrast, Erik exuded an immature need to control.

"I want to try," she said.

"Has he cast a spell on you?"

"Excellent, we will leave this morning." Turning to Erik, Miguel said, "I would like you to accompany us as I share your concern about Alexandria's wellbeing, and I think your presence would support her."

"It's a cinch I won't let her go into the jungle alone."

"Good" Miguel said. "Pack two changes of clothing. Bring plenty of water, sunscreen, and insect repellent, and don't forget a hat. Meet me here in one hour."

Alex looked into Erik's gray eyes. "I'm angry, frightened, and confused, just for starters, but my grandmother sent me here to meet don Miguel. If she trusted him I believe we should too."

"I'm trying hard to keep an open mind," Erik said," but I am stretched way beyond anything like a comfort zone. But it's your choice."

"Thank you." Alex realized she was suddenly ravenous and consumed the untouched eggs, beans, and tortillas.

. . .

# CHAPTER 11

# JUNGLE WALK

Alex and Erik joined Miguel at the entrance of the hotel. Miguel wore a wide-brimmed straw hat, long pants, and a long-sleeved shirt. He grasped his curved walking staff carved from Mahogany that looked like a serpent. The bottom was forked like a serpent's tongue, and the staff had been formed in sections that collapsed. A small pack hung from his shoulders.

Francisco Trujillo, don Miguel's grandson and their guide from Palenque, stood with him. Francisco wore jeans, a long sleeve shirt, and a New York Yankee baseball cap. He held a staff of a Balsa wood.

"Francisco will be our guide," Miguel said.

"Wonderful," Alex said.

Erik was silent.

"It is a pleasure to see you again," Francisco said, with a smile that wrinkled the corners of his brown eyes.

"The jungle is magical," he continued, "but can be treacherous to those who do not know her ways. You have dressed well and covered your skin and heads. A walking stick is a good idea for balance, so I brought one for each of you. Try to keep your steps light and your stride narrow to conserve energy."

Francisco handed Alex and Erik each a stick five feet in length and a half-inch in diameter. Alex was surprised by the staff's strength and flexibility.

"We will pass through parts of Palenque that have not been excavated. It is a lesson in humility to see how Earth has consumed the structures built by humans. Let's begin," Francisco said and turned toward the malachite wilderness.

They hiked for two hours in silence through the steamy forest. The path Francisco followed was invisible to Alex, but he proceeded as if it was a paved road. Vines, branches, and thorn bushes caught her clothes. She watched Francisco's gait and tried to imitate his stride, discovering he was right. If her steps were closer together, she could establish a rhythm that allowed her mind to relax and take in her surroundings. But she was grateful when he called a halt.

Two massive Balsa wood trees grew close together and created a clearing in the small space between them. "This is a Chico Zapote tree," he said. "These zig zag machete cuts were made by chicleros as the resin is used to make chewing gum. During the rainy season the sap runs like milk. The modern world's appetite for gum has led the chicle hunters deep into the forests where they discovered many of the ruins."

The forest canopy towered high above them. Birds and monkeys volleyed for their share of the jungle's bounty in the treetops. "These giant trees are Ceibas, the Mayan World Tree, through which it is said souls rise to the heart of heaven," Francisco said. "Drink a small amount of water and rest a few minutes. Eat some of the honey candy, which will restore your energy."

ALEX FELT BETTER when they got underway. Light filtered through the leviathan Ceiba trees, some of which grew to a hundred feet. The width of their trunks and vines made them look like mutants. Nature provided each living thing with an ingenious means of protecting itself. Harmless looking vines grew deadly thorns; others oozed poisonous sap. Insects were cleverly disguised to become invisible in their surroundings. Everywhere the hungry trees and vines consumed the stones of ancient dwellings.

After another two hours, Francisco called a halt for lunch in an inviting spot next to a fresh-water stream. The jungle scintillated with heat. Several large pieces of stone from earlier temples had tumbled into a usable forma-tion. Each of the travelers chose a stone and retrieved food and water from their packs.

The hotel had prepared lunches of thick, salted tortillas, boiled eggs, toma-toes, and limes. Alex mashed a boiled egg inside a tortilla and blended tomato and salt. She rolled the tortilla around the mixture and bit into her delicious creation. She squeezed fresh lime into her water bottle and drank the refreshing contents.

"This is a place of great antiquity," Miguel said. "Maya legends say the first builders came across the ocean from the east. The earliest culture may be much older than archeologists believe."

"My grandfather told me stories of colonists from Atlantis starting over in other places," Alex said.

"Flood myths exist in many cultures," Erik said, forgetting to be annoyed.

"Yes, the Maya also have these stories. One remaining codex of our writing depicts a traveler, crossing the ocean in a boat. The ancient Maya were fascinated with time and looked backward and forward to distant epochs. It is said the shamans could travel in time to see what had come before and to learn what would happen in the future. From these journeys they developed an amazing calendar called *Uinal* that works like interlocking wheels."

Miguel placed a large rock on the ground and placed a smaller one next to it. "One wheel had twenty-day signs; the other wheel had thirteen numbers. As they turned, the cogs connected, and the shamans interpreted these conjunctions. Certain combinations were seen as fortunate while others were potentially dangerous. There is another interconnecting wheel to track larger spans of time.

"Time was depicted as a walker, a god bearing his load, traveling around a great circle. The hours, days, months, and years were all seen as gods bearing the burdens of their place on the great wheel. The Maya used a 365 day solar calendar, and a 260 day sacred calendar based on when Venus rose as morning star right before the Sun. They had special calendars for Venus and the Moon."

"The ancient Egyptian sacred calendar was based on the star Sirius, brightest star in the sky," Erik said. "The helical rising of Sirius in the east before the Sun signaled the annual flooding of the Nile and the start of the new year. They also used solar and lunar calendars. I've read that the Maya calendar ends on the winter solstice in 2012."

"What ends at that time is the fifth sun of the current cycle of the Maya calendar," Miguel said. "Five suns of roughly fifty-two hundred years equal a world period of approximately twenty-six thousand years."

"That's the same as one cycle of the Precession of the Equinoxes," Erik said, his eyes widening.

"That is correct. The Maya were great astronomers and understood the phenomenon of precession as well as the alignment of the center of the galaxy and what is called the ecliptic plane. They conceived this to be like a tree."

"What's precession?" Alex asked.

"I'm no astronomer, but I'll try to explain it the way I understand it," Erik said. "Earth wobbles on her axis as she spins, and if you visualize the axis of the Earth like a stick through the middle of a spinning top, the wobble has two effects. First an imaginary circle is traced in the heavens that changes the Pole Star over time. Second, spring equinox sunrise moves backward against the constellations over time. It takes nearly twenty-six thousand years to make the whole circle."

"Wow," Alex said.

"Well done," Miguel said. "One complete cycle of precession is an enormous time to us, but it was a short cycle to the Maya who created the calendars. A truly grand cycle, a new creation, began more than five-thousand years ago, representing a measure so vast it can only be conceived as multiple big bangs. Scholars differ on the exact date. Some say it was August 13, 3114 BCE, while others believe the date was August 11, 3113 BCE. That makes a difference when the end date will come."

"Why was time so important?" Alex asked.

Miguel laughed. "I believe the shamans understood that time and space are illusions of our ordinary consciousness. The Maya saw the universe as existing in alternating cycles of creation and destruction and created a cosmic clock to predict and prepare for the periodic cataclysms. Maya shamans were masters of time who could transcend the limits of ordinary awareness. Through the calendar, and shamanic travels in other realms, they knew the Spanish would come and welcomed them. This behavior has been seen as naive by some, but the ancient ones saw everything in terms of cycles. They also foresaw the return of their own power toward the end of this great cycle. And so it is that the meaning of the Maya glyphs is now coming to light."

Miguel wiped his palms on his knees. "I have talked too much. We should be on our way."

"Fill your bottles from the stream," Francisco suggested, "and wash your hands and face with this refreshing water."

THEY WALKED FOR HOURS, stopping periodically for short rests. The jungle seemed relentless, and everywhere huge trees had gobbled up stone buildings. Little trace could be seen of human vanity where nature had reclaimed her own. Alex walked in the short-stepped manner Francisco had suggested and lost track of time.

When Alex thought she couldn't go on any farther, a tiny, ordered settlement materialized out of seeming green chaos. Excited children ran from thatched huts, and shy women peeked through doorways. Dogs barked, and chickens clucked at the unfamiliar visitors.

Francisco halted the group at the edge of the huts. Children danced around him as he distributed candy and stones he had collected on their walk. He tossed his baseball hat upward, and three boys raced to snatch the cap from the air. Curious children laughed and pointed at Alex. When don Miguel addressed them, the laughing children ran toward him.

A Lacondon Maya emerged from one of the huts. Dark hair brushed his shoulders. He wore a white robe, and the Cross of Palenque hung from his neck. Erik gaped when he spotted Alex's cross around the man's neck,and shot her a baffled look.

"Chan Ka," Alex gasped.

Francisco bowed his head and spoke to Chan Ka in the Maya language. He pointed at don Miguel; Chan Ka nodded. Francisco then gestured toward Alexandria and spoke again.

Chan Ka looked at Alex. She remembered those powerful eyes and realized he knew she would come. Surrendering the necklace had been an important test.

"How did he get your necklace?" Erik demanded.

"I gave it to him."

"What?"

Chan Ka embraced Miguel and Francisco. He turned and went inside the thatched hut.

"We must follow," Francisco said.

Alex walked behind them. She was nervous, but she trusted Miguel.

"What is this, 'Mother may I?" Erik asked.

"Please try to trust, Erik," Alex said.

They followed Francisco into the simple structure built of mahogany branches that had been tied together in the same manner for millennia. Guano palm leaves formed the thatched roof. Simple furnishings inside included a hammock and a seat made from a felled tree trunk. A wooden table leaned against the wall. Hooks held empty tin cans, rope, and a bow and quiver of arrows. An oil lantern rested on a piece of wood. Three round stones formed the hearth in the center of the earthen floor.

Chan Ka sat back on his legs in a traditional Indian posture. Francisco and Miguel sat on the tree trunk, and Alex followed their example on another trunk. Erik joined her, frowning.

Don Miguel spoke in the Maya language, then opened his pack. He pulled out a beautiful woven blanket and gave it to Chan Ka. Alex wondered if the blanket was offered on her behalf in exchange for the shaman's assistance. She felt she was being tested again.

She remembered the good-luck crystal she always carried in her pack. She had pulled the quartz crystal out of the ground on a Girl Scout camping trip and had carried the shard ever since in a little leather pouch. Alex didn't know what Chan Ka would think, but the crystal was one of her treasures from remembered dreams of the crystal city in what Grandpa thought was Atlantis.

Alex reached inside her pack, remembering the little Girl Scout who had carefully threaded plastic strips through the once-stiff leather to form the pouch. She stood and handed her gift to Chan Ka. His sparkling obsidian eyes seemed to penetrate to her soul.

Chan Ka closed his eyes as he held the pouch, then he slowly opened the flap. Reverently, he removed the clear quartz crystal, holding the shard between his thumb and forefinger so everyone could see. The top was six-sided, and the crystal was the size of his index finger.

The shaman turned the crystal in the sunlight that slanted through narrow openings in the mahogany slats of his dwelling. Alex saw a tiny rainbow flash. Chan Ka looked at Miguel and spoke in a strong voice. Alex feared she had offended him and turned concerned eyes toward Miguel.

Miguel nodded and looked at her. "Chan Ka says you have offered a gift of rare worth; a powerful *zastun*, a stone of light. Before we leave, he will investigate the stone's memories. Chan Ka will do what he can to help," Miguel said.

Alex looked at don Miguel. "What are the Maya words for 'thank you'?"

"*Boh ti ketch*," Miguel said.

Alexandria crossed her hands over her heart, closed her eyes, and bowed her head. "*Boh ti ketch*," she said. She raised her head and smiled at Chan Ka. When their eyes met energy exploded in her heart and solar plexus. A flash of light blinded her momentarily. When her vision cleared, Chan Ka nodded.

"I will tell Chan Ka of your dream," Miguel said. When he finished, Chan Ka was silent. Then he stood and spoke a few words.

"He has agreed to perform the ritual," Miguel translated.

Francisco and Miguel rose as if on cue from some invisible signal. Alex stood on shaky legs and Erik rose in time to steady her.

"Chan Ka seems to be the genuine article," he said, frowning.

"Don Miguel was my father's friend," she said.

"The lineage of Balam still produces true shamans," Francisco said.

The small group left the hut and walked a short distance to a cleared area in a grove of orange and lemon trees. Banana, papaya, avocado, cotton, chili, tomato, and wild tobacco plants grew among the trees. Hives of stingless Maya honeybees buzzed in hives nested in hollow logs.

Don Miguel and Francisco removed woven-cotton hammocks from their packs, expertly unfolding and attaching them to the trees. A shy, Maya woman, who never spoke or made eye contact, quietly strung hammocks for Alex and Erik. Then she carried a container of water for washing, placing the pottery jar behind a tree. They gratefully bathed and changed clothes.

Francisco built a fire at the center of their camping circle. Another woman brought beans, tortillas, peppers, tomatoes, bananas, and mangoes. Hungry after the long hike, they ate without speaking. As a final treat the travelers were served steaming, hot chocolate in special carved bowls.

"Chocolate is a royal gift," Miguel said, inhaling and savoring the rich aroma.

Washed and dressed in clean clothes they stared at the crackling fire, each absorbed in their own thoughts.

"Are there always three stones in the fire circle?" Alex asked, looking into the flames.

Miguel smiled. "Yes, through the hearth we invoke and honor the powers of creation. The three stones represent the three stars in the belt of Orion, the place of creation. We believe souls are symbolically born in the flames of the hearth and ascend to the heart of heaven through the Ceiba tree, which connects to the Milky Way."

"Woman's domain is the hearth at the center," Francisco said. "Man's domain is the field as he is hunter and farmer. Together they create harmony and self-sufficiency. When children are born, the female afterbirth is burned in the hearth, but the male's is placed at the top of a tree to be eaten by birds."

"Robert Bauval, another Egypt researcher," Erik said, "believes that the three main pyramids of Giza are laid out as a precise mirror of the three stars in Orion's belt. The Egyptians saw the Milky Way as a heavenly river and the Nile as the earthly reflection.

"Why is Orion so important?" Alex asked. "Why that part of the sky?"

"I am not certain," Miguel said. "Perhaps because Orion is so large. I have read that Orion is the most-recognized constellation. There are also stories that beings from the stars came to Earth from that part of the sky many thousands of years ago."

"It's also true that the stars of that part of the sky rose with the spring dawn during what is called the pyramid age," Erik said. "Orion has been significant to many cultures. Robert Bauval's most stunning discovery, made through astronomical computer models which move the stars back and forward in time, was that the perfect alignment of Orion's Belt and the arrangement of the pyramids of Giza, occurred only at the spring equinox in 10,500 BCE."

"Isn't that how old alternative scholars claim the Sphinx is?" Alex asked.

"Bingo," Erik said. "That's also the timeframe when Edgar Cayce said the Great Pyramid was built."

"The path of the soul is written in the stars," Alex said, and was surprised by her own voice.

The three men looked at her, and she blushed, grateful for the darkness.

"That is true," Miguel said. "My study of mythology indicates that stories are coded in all world cultures as if they had originated from one source, and they all use constellations as their stage. Star pictures and their stories have always carried a message of the soul's journey. "

"In Egyptian mythology, Orion is connected with the myth of Osiris, god of resurrection," Erik said. "He seemed to show the way to escape the wheel of rebirth."

"It seems all civilizations are telling the same story. I believe there is a great mystery here that relates to birth, death, and rebirth," Miguel said.

"What happens tomorrow?" Alex asked.

"You and I must eat very little during the day," Miguel said, "In the morning I will tell you what to expect and the significance of what will happen tomorrow night."

"I'd like to listen," Erik said.

"Yes, of course," Miguel said.

Francisco banked the fire for the night, and they each relaxed into their hammocks. Alex curled up, staring at twinkling stars visible in the circular space created by the clearing of trees. She identified the Great Bear, the Little Dipper, and the North Star, Polaris at the tip of its handle. Draco's tail wrapped around the celestial north pole—she wished she could see Orion.

Insects hummed in the darkness, and a soft breeze rustled the trees. Alex was grateful for the smoky embers of the fire that kept the creatures of the night at bay.

*I hope I'm doing the right thing.*

CHAPTER 12

# CROSSROAD

fter a breakfast of coffee, tortillas with honey, and sliced mango, Miguel led Alex and Erik to a clearing close to the nearby stream. The three sat on tree trunks as morning light filtered through the jungle trees. Alex felt apprehensive and took several deep breaths to relax, but pride precluded a change of mind.

Miguel's black-and-gray hair was wet and brushed back from his face, accentuating his high cheekbones and hawk-like nose. "The shaman's journey is a practice that is at least fifty-thousand years old," Miguel began.

"It is essentially the same wherever shamans are in the world. Where people do not have sophisticated technology to aid in diagnosis, they use other means. Individuals who can sense, or see, the illnesses of others are valued. These ways of seeing and healing have persisted in indigenous cultures for thousands of years because they work."

"Why is it called a journey?" Alex asked, her brow furrowed into a question. Her red hair was pulled back, and her face had been scrubbed clean in the stream.

Miguel made a cross in the dirt with a rock and drew a circle around the cross.

"Shamans see the world in three levels: upper world, lower world, and this one of ordinary reality. A shaman must learn to travel effortlessly between the three worlds, to climb the Maya world tree, the *Wacha Chan*," he said, gesturing from the bottom to the top of the circle.

Miguel paused and looked at them, his high cheekbones highlighted by sunlight that seemed to convey a way of knowing unfamiliar to the western mind.

"Ancient Maya kings performed this act through ritual sacrifice in the temples and pyramids. The king made the sacrificial ascent for the sake of the people. He was aided in this effort by the priests. Maya shamans still carry on what we call the Great Idea, walking the true path."

"Why was it so bloody?" Alex asked.

"It was not always so," Miguel said. "I believe the height of what archeologists call classic Maya civilization is but a shadow, a faint echo of what went before—those memories are still buried."

"I believe that's true in Egypt also," Erik said.

"In your case, Alexandria, I will first journey on your behalf to the lower world of the spirit realm to obtain a *Nagual*, or guardian spirit. The acquisition of this power animal will strengthen your will. Once you have such a guardian you may journey on your own in the other worlds to seek answers to questions or for teaching and healing."

Time seemed suspended as the three companions sat in silent contemplation. Alex became aware of the calls of birds. The jungle air was already hot and heavy but a welcome breeze moved through the trees, shifting the pattern of sunlight on the ground.

Miguel stood. "I will spend the rest of the day in preparation. Spend time alone in quiet contemplation, Alexandria. Reflect on the questions that are troubling your mind and search your heart for meaning. I will come for you after sundown."

Alex and Erik were quiet after Miguel left. She walked to the water's edge and stared into the stream. Clear water cascaded over rocks that had been sculpted by the water's constant movement. Erik joined her and took her hand in his. She turned to face him.

"Why are you doing this?" Erik said finally. "I have no right to tell you what to do, but it could be dangerous."

She looked into his eyes. "Next to my father and grandfather, I loved and respected my grandmother more than anyone on Earth. She sent me here for a purpose that involves don Miguel. I want to find out what that purpose is."

Erik squeezed her hand, and his gray eyes darkened, his expression becoming serious. "I can't fathom what's happening and I'm off balance by recent events, but in the words of my personal hero, 'The game's afoot, Watson.'"

Alex had to laugh. "You would be a Sherlock Holmes fan, you're anal-retentive enough."

He jerked his hands to his chest as if he'd been shot. "Aye, you wound me to the quick, Lass."

Alex kissed him on the cheek. "I'm glad you're on the case, Sherlock. Would you mind if I spent some time alone?"

Erik returned to the camp site, leaving Alex sitting cross-legged on a blanket near the water. She extracted a spiral notebook and pen from her pack and dated the top of the page. She reflected on Miguel's words, listing clues: dreams, the Cross of Palenque, the mysterious raven, and the mystery of ancient civilizations. Where was the meaning? What was the purpose?

*Why did you send me here, Gran?*

CHAPTER 13

# DOLPHIN

As promised, Miguel came for Alex at dusk and she followed him into the darkening jungle. Animal sounds seemed heightened as they walked through the thick vegetation. They arrived at a cleared place in the forest where Chan Ka's helpers had built a fire and burned copal incense. The new blanket Miguel had brought lay on the ground. Two men played handmade drums, and the deep rhythm reverberated in the darkening evening, accompanied by shaking gourd rattles and chanting.

Chan Ka held Alex's crystal, the stone of light, to his forehead in one hand and shook a gourd rattle in the other; the shaman danced and chanted around the fire. Don Miguel lay on half of the blanket and instructed Alexandria to lie beside him.

"Chan Ka will be the guide for this journey, Alexandria. He must hold the space between the worlds so that I can travel and accomplish tonight's task. It requires a great deal of power to guard the portal and assure that I will return safe and unharmed. A shaman must be able to see his bones and find his way back. Chan Ka is wise in the old ways and possesses this power."

"But you said it wasn't dangerous," Alex said, alarm showing in her voice.

"I said it was a natural process like birth and death. Allow yourself to relax and trust and all will be well."

Her head ached, her throat was tight, and her stomach growled audibly, but Alex breathed rhythmically as don Miguel had instructed, slowly gaining control of her nerves.

The tempo of the drums and rattles increased, allowing Alex to drift in the darkness on the hypnotic sounds, losing ordinary awareness. She didn't know how much time had elapsed when the rhythm of the drums changed, and she felt Miguel move. He knelt beside her and placed cupped hands on her stomach. Miguel blew air into her navel with great force. Then supporting her back, he helped her sit up. He placed his cupped hands on the crown of her head and blew again. Alex imagined whales, spouting water.

"Open your eyes, Alexandria," Miguel said. "I have brought your guardian."

Chan Ka spoke in Maya, and his voice crackled with energy.

"I have brought a small whale, a dolphin," Miguel began. "It appeared four times in different forms. First, I saw the dolphin as a white-marble sculpture, larger than life-size, in a Grecian Garden. Then I came upon a rock garden, where a large, green hedge was pruned in the shape of a dolphin. Next, my attention was drawn upward, where a single dolphin-shaped cloud swam across the sky. Finally, a real dolphin emerged from ocean waters—she was almost dancing. I grabbed the dolphin to my chest and ran back to this place.

"You must honor your power animal by dancing its energy. Help Dolphin experience this world, and she will aid you miraculously when you travel in her domain," Miguel said. He turned and spoke to Chan Ka.

Chan Ka answered, nodding slightly. Alex longed to understand his words.

"He says your *Nagual* is a good omen. Your nature is fiery, and your guardian is a water creature that will balance your spirit. Dolphins and humanity have an ancient kinship. We both came from the sea, but they remained in the oceans.

"These magical creatures sense the energy fields of other beings and always approach those who are ill or pregnant. Dolphins have power to heal through the sounds and energy they emit. Not just one dolphin, but Dolphin, the power of the whole species, comes to your aid—powerful *Nagual*."

Chan Ka's final words were, "Beware of weakness and claim your strength."

Miguel rose and helped Alex to stand. She was lightheaded as he guided her through the forest to their camp. Erik and Francisco were not there.

Alex climbed into her hammock, feeling she had stood at a crossroads and stepped across a threshold into a new reality and been blessed. She closed her eyes and let the warm darkness enfold her like a velvet blanket. Inhaling the smoky scent of the fire, she recalled the dolphins at the National Aquarium who performed with grace and joy despite their captivity.  Alexandria called forth an image of the ocean.

"Dad and Gran, I swear I'll see this through," she whispered to the night. She fell asleep and dreamed of pink-marble temples high on a cliff overlooking the sea.

# CHAPTER 14

# QUETZAL FEATHER

Alexandria woke before daybreak to morning sounds of parrots and macaws searching for breakfast. Her companions were still asleep. She climbed out of her hammock and quietly walked the short distance to the nearby stream and knelt by the water's edge. After drinking three delicious handfuls, she splashed the pure water on her face and neck and ran wet fingers through her tangled hair. She considered submerging her head in the cool water.

Something caught her eye that resembled a green garter snake. A brilliant, chartreuse feather dangled from a bush. The green plume was ten inches long and looked like a decoration from an Art Deco hat.

She picked up the feather, twisting it in her hand. *Maybe Miguel or Francisco could identity the bird who left this magical gift.* Refreshed and ravenous she returned to camp. Miguel and Francisco folded their hammocks and placed them in their packs.

"Look what I found," Alex said, holding out the feather to Francisco.

"A Quetzal feather," Francisco said, taking the feather with a look of awe as if it were made of priceless gems. "That is a great treasure as Quetzals are secret creatures. We hear their song, but rarely does anyone see one."

Francisco handed the feather to Miguel, who lifted it up toward the sun.

"A good sign indeed," Miguel agreed, returning the feather to Alex.

Erik sat up in his hammock and rubbed his tousled blond head. "What does the bird look like?" he asked, squinting, "Must be huge."

"The Quetzal bird is brilliant green with a red chest but is actually quite small.  This feather is from the tail, which can be four times as long as the body," Francisco said.  "But the Quetzal has a great heart."

"Nice going, Watson," Erik said.

Alex grinned. "It's beautiful. I feel honored."

"We will walk to a nearby village today.  My brother, Pablo, will meet us and drive us back to Palenque," Francisco said.

Erik frowned, "Why did we have to walk here?"

"It was part of the journey," Miguel said.

"Can we eat first?" Alex asked, looking worried.  The men laughed.

After breakfast they went to Chan Ka's hut to say goodbye.  Alex showed him the bright-green feather.  He held the Quetzal plume in his hand, turning it slowly to admire its beauty.  He smiled, and his black eyes danced with childlike wonder.  He returned the feather to Alex and spoke to Miguel.

"Chan Ka gazed into the stone of light.  He says you are called to this work. You must become a shaman."

"Can a woman be a shaman?" Alex asked.

"Yes, of course, if she is called and has the heart for the work.  The crystal showed him a vision, Alexandria.  Chan Ka saw the three of us searching for something, digging in the ground.  A tiny Quetzal bird battled a large raven overhead.  The little bird was valiant.  Although challenged severely, the tiny warrior triumphed.  Chan Ka said to guard this feather well; it holds a powerful promise."

Joyful tears welled up in Alex's eyes. "I will."

Chan Ka gestured for her to come forward.  Alex stood in front of him. He started to remove the cross necklace.  She raised her palm.

"No, the cross belongs here," she said, shaking her head.

Chan Ka understood without translation.  Impulsively, she hugged him, then wheeled around and left the hut.

They walked about a mile to a tiny village and followed Francisco to his brother's car.  Alex and Erik were quiet during the return trip.  Francisco, Pablo, and Miguel talked and laughed.  Alex thought of last night's events with a sense of wonder.

When they reached the hotel, Miguel said, "Rest and relax today, tomorrow I will teach you to journey to the lower world."

"I'm ready," she said, "and I have a magic feather to prove it."

CHAPTER 15

# SHAMAN'S JOURNEY

After an early breakfast, the three returned to Alex's casita to begin her exploration. "You must journey first to the lower world," Miguel said, "where you will meet your power animal and experience the shamanic state.

"The lower world represents the emotions and must be entered through a real place where you have been in your life that has power for you. The entrance could be a spring, a cave, or a hollow tree trunk. When I beat the drum, visualize yourself standing at that place. Examine it thoroughly; see the details. This is important.

"Then, enter the opening in your imagination. You will be inside a tunnel that will take you deep inside the Earth. If you see other passageways, do not take them. Move only straight ahead. When you emerge onto a landscape, you will meet your power animal there.

"This is your first journey, Alexandria. Don't expect too much. Look at everything closely and try to remember as much as you can."

Miguel closed the blinds to darken the room. He had brought a drum and copal incense. He lit the fragrant resin and fanned the smoke with a Condor feather.

"Please tie this scarf around your eyes as you need to be in darkness. Signal me by lifting your hand when you are ready to begin."

She did as he instructed and squeezed Erik's hand before she covered her

87

eyes. Breathing deeply to calm herself she visualized her entry point. She had chosen a favorite spot, a secret cove along a stream at the Matthews farm, which she had explored as a child. A wizened Elm tree sheltered the inlet and a trickling waterfall tumbled into the stream. She imagined herself in that spot and pictured herself diving into the center of the waterfall, entering the Earth as don Miguel had instructed. She lifted her hand, signaling Miguel to start drumming.

Don Miguel struck the drum in the quick, staccato beats of the preparatory rhythm, then altered the tempo to a rapid, steady pounding. Alexandria moved through the waterfall and entered the opening. She found herself in a large, tube-like tunnel about eight feet in diameter. The earthen sides of the tunnel were ribbed, stretching out in a gentle downward slope ahead of her. The rich aroma of brown, loamy soil filled her nostrils.

She looked at her clothes and feet and realized she was barefoot, wearing a short skirt, and halter top. Her body was tanned and muscular. Alex felt a primal urge to run and the vibration of the drum gave her speed and momentum. The deep reverberation drove her onward into the fertile womb of the Earth.

Alex ran tirelessly into the tunnel past openings that branched off from the main artery. She did not detour as Miguel had counseled. After what seemed like a few minutes a small circle of light formed ahead in the tunnel, and she ran toward the luminous disk. She emerged from the darkness of the interior passage onto a bright, sunlit seascape. Alex shielded her eyes from the sudden brilliance. Humid, salt air stung her nostrils.

As Alexandria's eyes adjusted, she examined her surroundings. She stood on a golden, sand beach that surrounded a lush, turquoise lagoon. To her left tall, rocky cliffs overlooked the ocean, and a musical waterfall cascaded over the precipice into the lagoon. To her right, a pine forest grew to the edge of the beach.

The blue-green water of the lagoon trembled, and the silvery face of a large, Bottlenose dolphin appeared. Alex thought the creature smiled. Certain the dolphin was female; Alex ran into the water to meet her. Alex spread her arms, and Dolphin came up out of the water on her tail fins and they greeted in a gesture resembling an embrace. Alexandria had never known such spontaneous joy. Dolphin's eyes sparkled with light. She slid back into the water and made a series of clicking sounds. Alex heard a voice inside her head.

"Climb on my back, Child."

Alex didn't hesitate. She clambered on Dolphin's silky, gray back and heard the voice in her thoughts again.

"Do not fear. You will not fall as my desire to carry you will hold you fast. We will journey far you and I."

Dolphin arched her body and leaped into the air like a gymnast and dove under the surface of the waves. The sea water was warm, and Alex could see clearly and was able to breathe. Hundreds of shiny, translucent glass fish swam in precision, turning and twisting in unison like an underwater drill team. A yellow-and-white spotted flatworm posed by a flame-colored sea fan.

Bright-yellow anemone fish, with cobalt-blue bands around their faces, swam among the anemones. The spines of a brilliant-orange sea urchin exploded from the rocks like a fireworks display. Alex saw crabs, jellyfish, starfish, a sea turtle, and a stingray. A shy moray eel poked its head from a crevice on the ocean bottom.

Dolphin swam deep under water into a kelp forest. Sunlight from the water's surface shimmered through the long fronds of dark-green vegetation, creating a haunting, primeval sanctuary. Stones and columns of rock rooted in the ocean bottom looked like the ruins of an ancient temple.

White fire coral, yellow feather stars, brain coral, and red rope sponges protruded from rocky beds in the sand. Gray moonfish with bright-yellow fins and tails surrounded them. Alex laughed at a spiny pufferfish that looked like an aquatic porcupine. Dolphin clicked, and the sound was amplified by the water.

Dolphin turned and swam out to the open sea. Once away from shore, a group of dolphins greeted them with a chorus of effervescent clicks and whistles, swimming around them in circles. Further out, great Orcas surfaced, sprayed, and crashed into the waves. Dolphin turned around toward the beach, racing through the warm water at an astonishing velocity.

Alex had not known such euphoria since childhood. This beautiful being radiated unfathomable happiness. Dolphin turned her lithe body straight up and soared through the air. Circling in the sky, Alex saw the beautiful lagoon from above. Sunlight shimmered on the aquamarine surface, creating dancing prisms of light as gulls and pelicans flew with them.

Impossibly, a glorious rainbow shone in a cloudless sky. Dolphin flew under the fluorescent-colored arch, then banked like a big bird and circled downward in broad spirals, coming gently to rest on the golden beach. Alex slid off Dolphin's back and knelt on the sand in front of her. She looked into the sea creature's magnificent eyes and felt unconditional love. Alex kissed Dolphin's silvery snout.

"Thank you, Dolphin. My heart is full."

Dolphin's eyes twinkled with merriment. "You have a great heart, traveler, but you have scarcely touched its capacity." she communicated telepathically. "Your journeys in this realm will help fill the chalice. I'll be with you as long as our work together requires, so do not forget me while you sojourn in the world of form.

Farewell, little mermaid."

Then Alex heard four loud drumbeats, calling her back to ordinary reality. As quickly as she had appeared, Dolphin vanished into the sea. Alex turned and scanned the gray cliff face for the opening she'd come through. She entered the cave and ran through the tunnel, back the way she had come, matching her pace to the rapid, staccato drumming. When she reached the opening at the other end she came up through the waterfall into her secret place.

Alex felt the drumbeats that assisted her return. Miguel struck the drum hard four more times, signaling the end of the journey. Alexandria became aware of the room, the bed, the kerchief over her eyes, and the fragrance of copal. Inhaling, she removed the blindfold, and looked around in a state of rapture.

"How was your first journey, little mermaid?"

"Are you all right?" Erik asked.

Alex looked at don Miguel. "Why did you call me that?"

Miguel smiled, and his black eyes danced with humor.

"More than all right, I feel wonderful. I don't know if I can find the words," she said. "I was really there. I could feel, touch, and smell."

"Try to tell us what happened," Miguel encouraged.

"Should I take notes? Erik asked.

I don't think I will forget anything. I ran through a tunnel inside the Earth as you said, Miguel, until I saw an opening. I came out onto a beautiful seascape. Then I met Dolphin and went for a thrilling underwater roller coaster ride on her back. I saw incredible sea life and swam with a pod of dolphins in the open ocean. Dolphin flew under a rainbow,"

"A profound first journey. Multiple senses are unusual in the beginning. As Chan Ka said, you have potential as a shaman."

Alex sat up and ran her hands through her hair. "I am grateful for this experience, Miguel. I don't think I'll ever be the same, but what happens now? I don't have the answers I came to Mexico for, just more questions."

Miguel smiled and took her hand.  "We have been reunited, now we must return for a time to our ordinary lives until the next step is revealed."

Alex looked at Miguel and Erik.  She'd met these two men only a week ago, but it seemed she had known them all her life.

"Waiting is not my forte," she said.

CHAPTER 16

# RETURN

Alexandria stared out the oval airplane window as rain streaked across the plastic surface and intermittent lightning briefly illumined the black clouds. She wished she'd taken the aisle seat.

The flight from Mexico City had been delayed and rerouted to avoid a violent spring storm. Alex barely touched her meal, just managing to gobble up the chocolate ice cream before turbulence made eating impossible. She needed to use the restroom, but the seat belt sign was illuminated.

The gray-haired woman in the seat next to her tensed her muscles and gripped both arms of her seat. Her eyes were closed, and her lips mouthed a silent prayer. Alex felt sorry for her. She'd said she was visiting her son's family and this flight was her worst nightmare.

Alex was relieved when they finally approached the airport. The plane bounced and pitched as the pilot descended through dark clouds onto a rainswept runway. Local time was three in the afternoon, but the sky was dark. Breathing a prayer of gratitude as the jet taxied to the gate, Alex looked at her seat mate and saw tears run down her cheek.

"You were brave," Alex said, touching her arm. "I love to fly, and I thought this flight was terrifying. Now you can relax and enjoy your grandchildren." The older woman smiled.

Alex glimpsed Sheila as she emerged into the baggage claim area. Her friend waved a hand decorated with bright-red fingernails and bangle bracelets.

"You look a little green, Kiddo," Sheila teased after they hugged. "I told you not to drink the water."

Alex managed a smile.

"Mumsie's been a handful," Sheila said. "She's called Emma or me twice a day. Thank the Goddess, she connected with Arthur Livingston at the bank. He's been a prince, Allie. They've done lunch a time or two," Sheila flashed a wicked smile, and glanced at Alex out of the corner of her eye. "Don't you love it?" she said in her best Mae West voice.

Alex frowned.

"Seriously though," Shelia said. "I see glimpses of her former self before your father died. I'm praying for some serious magic here."

"I wonder what the connection is. Do you think this banker person is just a gold digger?" Alex asked.

"I don't get that feeling, but it's too soon to say."

As Sheila helped Alex with her bags she spotted her seat mate across the luggage carousel, surrounded by adoring grandchildren. She was radiant; memory of the terrifying flight erased. Alex envied her, she was reeling from the stressful flight and shock of reentry into her own culture. The Philadelphia airport seemed quiet after the tropical intensity of Mexico.

The two friends climbed into Sheila's black SUV and headed out of the airport. Alex stared at rainy streets and manicured lawns, struggling to process her surroundings, while Sheila checked messages on her cell phone. The city seemed antiseptic and quiet compared to the colors and sounds of the jungle.

Alex smiled at her friend who drove and talked enthusiastically. Sheila pushed her chin-length, black hair off her face by making a comb of her fingers. Red talons poked through shiny black strands, sweeping the hair across her head. After terminating her last call, Sheila turned and zeroed in on Alex.

"Well?"

"It's been an incredible week," Alex said. "I thought Mexico was another planet; now home seems alien. I feel like I've been wandering in a dream world. Speaking of dreams, do recall the one I had the night of the funeral?" Alex asked.

"Where you saw your Dad and Rose?"

"Yes, in the dream they introduced me to a man named Miguel Piedra and said he was an old friend. I met him in Mexico, Sheila. He and Gran planned the trip, but she died before she could tell me. I'm angry that she kept secrets from me."

Sheila's eyes widened. "It's hard to drive and listen to this."

Alex grimaced. "I fainted when I met him. I was so embarrassed I blamed it on the heat. My life feels like a B-movie. I also had the raven nightmare I used to have as a child." Alex paused, frowning.

"I know that look. What else?" Sheila asked.

"I met another man; a computer scientist, working in Egypt. His name is Erik Anderson, and I've got a ridiculous crush. I don't think meeting him was an accident either."

"Sounds like a full trip."

Alex sighed. "I have a million questions and not many answers."

Sheila turned the corner of Gran's street. Alex braced herself, but the sight of the real estate sign in Gran's yard felt like a kick in the stomach.

"It's only a house, how can it hurt so much?" Alex asked.

Sheila reached over and took her hand. "So much love was breathed into this house it's alive. You must grieve the loss of your life there, Allie."

When they reached the door, Crystal's barks were strident. Alex's heart started pounding inside her chest. She clutched the wet railing on the porch to steady herself.

"Crystal!" She shouted through the door.

Emma wrenched opened the door, her normally cheery face was contorted by tears, and her starched-white apron was wrinkled from twisting. She pushed loose wisps of gray hair from her face.

"What's wrong?" Alex asked, fighting a rising feeling of panic.

Crystal continued to bark, a high-pitched urgent sound that grated on Alex's nerves. The dog turned her head toward the hall and yipped louder. Alex realized Crystal wanted her to follow and moved in that direction. Crystal padded toward the back of the big house and stopped in front of the library door.

Alex was momentarily paralyzed, but Crystal did not relent. She barked again. Sheila came around her and peered inside. She turned a stricken face toward Alex, whose heart beat so hard she could feel the arteries pounding in her head. Alex forced herself to look into the room. The priceless antique desk and secretary had been overturned and their contents dumped on the floor. Books were strewn across the carpet, or piled in crumpled stacks, as if awaiting the torch of a mad zealot. Alex was so angry she was shaking and dug her fingernails into her palms.

"Call the police, Sheila," Alex said.

Alex left the library and returned to the front of the house where Emma was still rooted in the foyer. "When did this happen?"

Emma struggled to regain her composure. She blew her nose and stuffed the tissue in her apron pocket.

"About an hour ago Crystal and I went to the market. When we returned, the minute she came in the house she went right for the library, barking like a fiend," Emma said, crying again.

"Emma, this is not your fault. Have you looked through the rest of the house?"

"Nothing else seems to be disturbed," Emma said.

"Sheila's calling the police. They'll want to ask you some questions," Alex said, hugging her. Alex walked back to the library in time to overhear Sheila talking to the police dispatcher. She hung up as Alex walked in.

"Philly's finest are on their way. I think sherry is in order," Sheila said.

"Alex nodded. "Another coincidence?"

"They are stacking up," Sheila said.

They adjourned to the kitchen to wait for the police. Sheila poured three glasses of sherry. "Here's to Sherlock Holmes," she said.

"I wish he were here," Alex said, thinking of Erik.

The sherry burned her throat, but the warmth quickly spread into her blood stream, deadening her nerves, and slowing things down. They sat in silence. The telephone rang, jarring her short-lived reverie.

"Hello?" Alex said. Silence was followed by a click, then a dial tone.

"Who was that?" Sheila inquired, directing a scrutinizing look in Alex's direction.

"Hang up," she said.

Sheila frowned. "What's going on, Alex?"

The doorbell rang and jangled her nerves again. Crystal rushed to the foyer. Alex followed the dog to the front door and held her collar as a precaution. When Alex opened the door Crystal wagged her tail. A large, uniformed police officer stood beneath a golf-size, black umbrella.

"I'm Sergeant O'Reilly. Hello there, Crystal," he said, rubbing the dog's head.

"Please, come in, Sergeant. I'm Alexandria Stuart," she said, opening the door wide, and gesturing for him to enter.

Tall and broad, O'Reilly's frame strained the upper limits of police height and weight requirements and the seams of his uniform. His round Irish face was brightened by red cheeks and nose. Streaks of gray at his temples dignified his curly red-blond hair. The sergeant closed his umbrella and tapped it on the porch to dislodge rainwater. He stepped inside and removed his hat. Alex deposited the umbrella in a container by the door.

"I was very sorry to hear about your grandmother's death, Miss Stuart. She was a real fine lady."

Sheila approached the foyer smiling. "How do you do, Captain? I'm Sheila Goldman, friend of the family."

O'Reilly nodded. "It's Sergeant, but thanks for the vote of confidence."

"Names and titles are funny things. I'm thinking of changing mine to Goldwoman."

O'Reilly stared at Sheila, looking puzzled. He started to speak, then seemed to change his mind. Alex stifled what could easily have become a hysterical laugh under the circumstances, which resulted in a strangled coughing noise.

"Let's look at the library," she suggested.

O'Reilly examined locks and windows and took digital photos. "A forensic investigator will be by later to dust for fingerprints, so don't touch anything yet. When did this happen?" he asked.

"This morning," Alex said. "Emma Manchester, my grandmother's housekeeper, discovered this mess when she returned from the market."

"I've known Mrs. Manchester a long time. Anything taken?"

"We aren't sure," Alex said.

"Any ideas about who might be responsible?"

"My grandparents' collections seem intact, as do my grandfather's geodes and minerals. As you may know sergeant, my grandfather was a scientist," Alex said, shaking her head. "It doesn't make sense."

"Could I have a word with Emma?" O'Reilly asked.

"Aye, aye, Captain," Sheila saluted, and went to find Emma.

Alex bristled. "Go easy on her, sergeant, she's frightened."

"Don't worry, Miss Stuart. I've walked this beat for years."

Emma was visibly shaking when they returned. "Hello, Sean."

"Nice to see you, Emma. How's Henry? Haven't seen that husband of yours in a long while. Please give him my regards."

"He's doing well. Thanks for asking."

Emma relaxed, and Alex regretted her concern.

"I just need to ask you a few questions," O'Reilly said.

Alex sat next to Emma, sipping sherry, while he questioned her. O'Reilly took careful notes and nodded frequently as she spoke. After what seemed an eternity, he closed his notebook and rubbed his eyes.

"This was a professional job in terms of entry, but the library looks like vandalism. The destruction almost seems angry. Put the room to rights after the investigator comes and pay close attention to any pattern you see."

"Can I call Henry and the maintenance fellow to upright the furniture?" Emma asked Alex.

"Yes, as soon as the forensic team is finished. Please have them bring boxes for the papers. I'll stay here with you until this mess is straightened out," Alex said.

When Alex showed O'Reilly out, she spotted her mother heading up the walk and cursed the rotten timing. Blanche Stuart looked glamorous in a white-linen suit, carrying a colorful jungle-print umbrella. She tiptoed through small puddles on the sidewalk. O'Reilly nodded to her from under his black umbrella, beating a hasty retreat.

Alex embraced her mother and kissed her on the cheek. "Mother, what a nice surprise," Alex lied. "Your hair looks lovely."

"What was that *policeman* doing here?" Blanche spoke the word with distaste.

"Someone broke into Gran's library," Alex sighed.

"I told you not to go to Mexico. That was very selfish of you, Alexandria. I just knew something dreadful would happen."

Crystal padded into the hall, turning her sites on Blanche.

"Keep that animal away from me. This is a new suit, and I won't have it ruined."

Collaring Crystal Alex turned on her mother. "Gran sent me to Mexico. This would have happened whether I was here or not." Alex wished she was sure.

Chin tilted up, Blanche stepped inside the foyer and stuffed her umbrella in the caddy. "Hello, Sheila dear. Sweet of you to get Alex at the airport; she never asks me."

"You hate the airport," Alex said, temper rising.

"Isn't it dreadful about the library?" Blanche said, ignoring her. "I can't bear to think of criminals being in this house."

Sheila kissed Blanche on the cheek and winked at Alex behind her back.

"Mother," Alex asked, deciding that the best defense was a good offense, "Sheila mentioned that nice man at the bank, Arthur Livingston, isn't it?"

Sheila's eyes became huge, and she shot Alex a conspiratorial look from behind Blanche's back.

"Arthur's been a pillar of strength. I don't know how I would have managed without him since you abandoned me. As it happens, we're having dinner this evening," Blanche said.

Alex was prepared to capitalize on that comment when the doorbell rang again. She gritted her teeth and balled her fists.

Sheila helped Crystal answer the door. The realtor who was handling the sale of the house stepped into the foyer.

"Mrs. Bartholomew, this is a really bad time," Alex said.

"Not to worry, dear. You won't even know I'm here. I just need to clarify a few tiny points before the open house next week."

Inwardly, Alex groaned as Mrs. Bartholomew marched off toward the living room with her mother in tow. Alex and Sheila headed back to the kitchen for coffee and chocolate-chip cookies. They sat at the big wooden table and kicked off their shoes.

"Okay, I know you're upset, but I want details. There's nothing you can do right this minute, and I've waited long enough. Let's hear about don Juan first," Sheila said through a mouthful of cookie. "Vital statistics first."

Alex exhaled. "Tall, blond, and handsome. Add brooding, gray eyes that belong in a Gothic novel. Being around him made me feel sixteen. The bad news is he's anal-retentive and pushy," she frowned.

"Sounds promising," Sheila said, raising and lowering her eyebrows, and pushing her hair out of her face.

The phone rang again.

"I can't believe this day," Alex shouted.

"Hello? Oh, hello, Erik." Alex batted her eyes at Sheila, who mimed Greta Garbo, holding a long cigarette holder.

"There's been an unexpected turn of events," Erik said. "The Egyptian government won't renew our license right now. Seems we've stirred up too much controversy, so we got a fat, bonus check, and yours truly is out of a job. What's up with you?"

"Speaking of interesting, someone broke into my grandparent's library this morning," Alex said.

"Is everyone okay?"

"Yes, no one was home."

Sounds like another coincidence," Erik said in a sarcastic tone.

"My thoughts exactly. It's too soon to know if anything was taken, but it's a big mess with books and papers everywhere."

"I'm afraid my protective streak where you're concerned just went into overdrive, and I think you need the strong, silent scholar's touch. I'll can be on the next flight."

"But you have to look for work." Alex said, pacing around the kitchen with the portable phone, and gesturing as she spoke. Sheila laughed, watching her antics.

"I can't resist a library. Don't start until I arrive, maybe I can see a pattern. I'm in New York and can drive over tomorrow."

"I could probably use the help, but it will be hard to ignore this mess." Alex said.

"One day won't matter. I'll see you tomorrow afternoon."

"Bye," she said, pushing the off button, and tossing the phone on the counter.

"This is better than a soap opera," Sheila howled, grabbing two cookies. "I'm outta here for now, but I'll be by this weekend to meet Blondie and hear what's really going on. You haven't told me the whole story."

Sheila gave Alex a long hug.  "Help is good, Allie."

"He's arrogant, but I can't wait to see him."

# CHAPTER 17

# CATS & DOGS

Erik's call the previous night had rattled her, and Alex was on the verge of chewing her fingernails. She couldn't sit still and when she stood, she paced. Crystal matched her movements, and they nearly collided at every turn.

She felt like a dizzy teenager, spending an impossible hour deciding what to wear. She wanted to look fabulous, but she didn't want him to suspect she'd taken half the morning to accomplish the feat.

Since she designed a signature line of clothing and jewelry, Alex had more options in her closet than some retail stores. After evaluating skirts, jeans, slacks, and shorts, she settled on khaki pants and an aquamarine print shirt. Grappling with a jewelry selection she tried green turquoise that was set in gold, malachite and silver, and the African trade bead necklace. She finally chose an inch-long jade teardrop wrapped in gold-wire trim twisted to look filigreed. Matching earrings dangled from her ears.

Alex stood at the upstairs bathroom mirror, fussing with her makeup to get the colors right. She rubbed and blotted until she achieved a look of no makeup at all. *Perfect.* Satisfied, she galloped down the big spiral staircase with Crystal in pursuit. She went to the kitchen to brew a pot of calming herb tea.

Long after Alex thought she would detonate from a critical mass of anticipation and frustration from staying out of the library, Crystal barked. In a flurry of scraping paws trying to get traction on the wood floor, Crystal arrived at the front door before the bell rang.

Alex was so startled; she was momentarily pinned to the chair by centripetal force as if she was descending the first hill on a roller coaster. Instead of the warm, noncommittal air she'd planned to display she suffered from stage fright. She wiped moist palms on her slacks and took a deep breath.

Crystal sat in front of the door, tail wagging eagerly.

"Some guard dog you turned out to be," she laughed. "You haven't even smelled this guy yet."

Alex opened the huge door, summoning her warmest, most-noncommittal smile. Crystal nearly knocked Alexandria down in her attempt to tackle and lick Erik. Holding aloft a large bouquet of apricot-colored roses and baby's breath, he rubbed Crystal's head with his free hand. He looked comfortable in jeans, loafers, and a white shirt.

"How are you, girl?"

"Not bad, how about you?"

Erik laughed, and Crystal barked a happy greeting.

"Ordinarily, she's such a good judge of character," Alex said, feigning concern.

Crystal licked his hand and wagged her tail double-time. "In my experience, dogs of Crystal's caliber are impeccable judges of character. I'd stake my reputation on it," he smiled.

Alex leaned against the door jamb; arms crossed at the elbows. "I bet you would, Sherlock."

Erik smiled and offered the roses to Alex. A recalcitrant lock of blond hair lay across his forehead. His gray eyes were enhanced by his white shirt, and the smell of his cologne was more compelling than the roses.

Alex thought he looked like a boy who had just picked a handful of wildflowers for his mother's birthday. All semblance of detachment evaporated, and she threw one arm around his neck. She couldn't believe how glad she was to see him.

"They're beautiful."

"You are beautiful; the flowers are merely pleasant. I also have a bottle of respectable champagne in the car."

Crystal pronounced her approval with a short bark.

"There's one other thing," he said, drawing his eyebrows together.

"Hmm?" Alex asked absently, visualizing candlelight and romance.

He disappeared down the front walk and returned with an animal carrier. Crystal growled.

"My cat sitter had an emergency appendectomy, and I couldn't find anyone to take care of Sheba. I hope you don't mind. It was too late to call."

Alex was speechless. Crystal barred the door.

It took her a moment to recover. "As in Queen of Sheba?"

"Yes, I wanted to name her Bastet, after the Egyptian cat goddess, but people had trouble with the spelling."

Alex stared into the cat carrier. Peridot-green eyes peered out of a sleek, black face. A low growl came from inside the carrier and Alex sent a dark glance toward Sheba.

"She doesn't like to travel," he said, "she gets car sick. She's quite affectionate once she gets to know you."

"No doubt," Alex said in a tone as cool as Sheba's eyes, "like a Black Widow spider on her wedding night."

Alex exhaled loudly, then spun around and headed for the spiral staircase. "You and her highness will sleep upstairs," she called over her shoulder. Erik followed, and Crystal brought up the rear. Alex had prepared her favorite guest room. The rose and dark-green room was furnished with Victorian antiques. Print curtains matched the wallpaper, and a small French writing desk overlooked the garden.

She stopped at the door and Erik walked past her without speaking and headed for the window. Placing the cat carrier on the floor he leaned on the window ledge and looked at out Gran's handiwork.

"I'll find a place to board Sheba tomorrow," he said.

Alex immediately felt guilty. "I'm sorry. I'm just overwhelmed right now. Settle in and come downstairs when you've unpacked to survey ground zero."

She turned quickly and took the spiral stairs two at a time, leaving Crystal as sentinel at the guest room door.

# CHAPTER 18
# DINNER

Alex sorted pictures and letters in a small space she had cleared on the library floor. She placed some of the articles in the temporary storage boxes Emma had procured so she could focus on the books.

She glanced up as Erik appeared in the doorway. Crystal padded in behind him and stretched out on the floor. He had changed into worn jeans and a tee shirt, and she thought he looked gorgeous. As he visually surveyed the room a pained look washed across his face.

"Heinous," he said.

Alex nodded. She thought it was an odd word to use but guessed her father and grandfather would both have agreed with the assessment. "Nothing seems missing, not even the geode and mineral collection. This burglar was either very particular, or stupid."

"Or didn't get what he wanted, which means he'll be back."

"That's what Sergeant O'Reilly implied," Alex said, frowning. "Gran only left me her jewelry and the contents of the library. Her jewelry is untouched upstairs."

Erik scowled, "And tickets to Mexico."

"Yes," Alex said, looking up at him. "Are you suggesting there's a connection to the incident in Mexico?"

He moved a stack of papers on the love seat and sat down. "I'm not ready to make that leap, but there are already too many coincidences."

Sheba strolled into the room and jumped onto the love seat next to Erik. She sat up, looking exactly like an Egypt cat deity.

Alex snorted. "White dog and black cat."

"Pardon?"

'There's a White Dog Cafe and a Black Cat gift shop at the place where Helena Blavatsky lived and worked here in Philadelphia. I have some of my jewelry there. I'm beginning to agree about the whole coincidence thing."

Crystal stood and approached, putting her head across Erik's knees. He rubbed her ears with both hands, and her tail swept the carpet in appreciation. She looked at him out of the sides of her big brown eyes.

"Tell me about Duncan Stuart," he said, rubbing Crystal's head.

Alex sat back from the papers she sorted and leaned against a chair. Her hair formed a fiery halo around her pale face. Unconsciously, she stroked the cool jade pendant that hung from her neck as she spoke.

"A tall order. Grandpa's degrees were in physics and chemistry. He was an idealist and visionary first and a scientist second. He was a member of the Manhattan Project during the second world war, the folks who gave us the atomic bomb. Somewhere around here is an eight-millimeter film of the Trinity test in New Mexico. It's eerie to watch the mushroom cloud form. Like Oppenheimer, he grew very disturbed by that episode. He didn't think the end justified the means."

"Seldom does," Erik said, pushing his hair back.

"Most of his research involved energy. His passion was to find alternatives to fossil fuels. He was a fan of Nikola Tesla and believed in free energy."

"An unpopular view in some quarters."

Alex looked at the mess in the library. "Grandpa did original research for Ultrasound, which works by directing an electrical current through a crystal to create sound waves. That's partly how Crystal got her name. Gran said he spent so much time with his crystals she needed one of her own after he died."

"What's the other part?"

"The White Dog Cafe, she said. "Grandpa also had some history with Theosophy.

Erik smiled. "Were all those papers really in those two pieces of furniture?"

Alex laughed. "Gran was a world-class pack rat."

"When did your grandfather die?"

"Four years ago."

She stood and pushed her hair back. "Thinking of the White Dog Cafe has made me realize I'm hungry. Let's check Emma's progress with dinner."

ERIK FOLLOWED her into the kitchen where preparations were underway. "Smells magnificent," he said, lifting his chin and sniffing the air.

Emma blushed and smiled.

"Erik Anderson, this is Emma Manchester, kitchen magician," Alex said fondly. "Her culinary prowess is legendary."

He grinned and extended his hand. "Impressive."

Emma flushed scarlet. She wiped her hands on one of her perennial white aprons, taking care not to dampen the blue-cotton dress underneath. Her kind blue eyes looked up at the tall, young man. Extending her hand, she practically curtsied.

"Pay no attention to Alexandria, Mr. Anderson. "She always exaggerates. It'll be her undoing," Emma said, nodding her head sharply.

Alex and Erik laughed.

"Please call me Erik," he said, approaching the stove and peering into cooking pots with keen interest and an air of authority.

"What's the menu?" Alex inquired.

"Cucumber bisque with fresh dill, spinach crepes, asparagus with ginger sauce and wild rice. Creme Brûlée with fresh raspberries for dessert," Emma answered.

"I don't think Alex exaggerated."

Emma reddened. "Alexandria's a vegetarian, so it's always a challenge."

"Me too," he said.

"I didn't realize that," Alex said, looking surprised.

"Perhaps you would select the wine, Erik?" Emma blurted, gaping at him.

"I would be honored," he smiled.

Alex had never witnessed such a reaction from Emma. She felt amused and faintly annoyed. "Follow me, steward. I'll conduct you to Duncan Stuart's secret cellar. Few venture there and live to tell the tale."

"I have a stout heart where good wine is concerned," he grinned.

Alex opened a door at the back of the kitchen, revealing a small hallway and another door. A flashlight and a rusty coffee can rested on a small wall shelf. She handed him the flashlight and lifted the coffee can, uncovering three, large brass keys. She opened the other door onto a steep staircase.

"Hold onto the railing and watch your head."

Erik bent over to keep from hitting his forehead on the door frame. Alex flipped a switch, and a dim light came on overhead. Dampness muffled the sound of their steps as they descended wooden stairs into a musty cellar. Alex pulled a chain that hung from the ceiling, and a bare bulb blinked on.

A dozen wrought-iron wine racks stood against a stone wall behind an iron gate. A large, brass padlock secured the opening. When Alex inserted the key, the old lock reluctantly succumbed, and the gate creaked like a cheap sound effect in a horror movie.

Alex chuckled. "Grandpa used to let me come with him when I was small. I was frightened, but I thought it was a great adventure. I always held his hand tightly, imagining all sorts of creatures living in the shadows. He didn't let on he knew how scared I was."

Erik smiled.

"He never oiled the gate; it was always part of the game. Grandpa blew the dust off the bottles with great panache and told me why the wine was special. I miss him so much."

"You were lucky to be so loved."

Erik was right beside her, and she could smell his cologne. She felt her color rise and her pulse quicken. For once, she blessed the dim light. His gray eyes reminded her of an unpredictable winter sky. His blond hair had fallen across his forehead again.

"Emma guards this place with her life. She's formed a high opinion of you to grant you access to the family treasure."

"It's mutual; she's a jewel."

Alex nodded. He continued to look in her eyes.

"White or red?" Alex asked with an equanimity she didn't feel.

Instead of answering, he lifted her hand to his mouth and kissed her palm. His breath was warm. Alex closed her eyes and felt a rushing tide of desire rise in her body that she hadn't felt in years. When she opened her eyes, she saw a matching need mirrored in cloudy-gray eyes.

Erik took a deep breath and squeezed her hand. "White, definitely. Let's see what we have here."

His eyes darted over the wine racks, pulling out bottles. He whistled, gasped, moaned, and made other sounds of admiration as he analyzed the labels, and after careful scrutiny, chose a White Bordeaux and a rare-vintage Chardonnay.

"A connoisseur's collection. Your grandfather had exquisite taste," Erik said.

Alex laughed. "Grandpa used to say, 'Life's too short to drink bad wine.' He'd be impressed you appreciated his choices."

"Admirable motto; we'll toast his wisdom this very eve."

Alex rolled her eyes but couldn't help smiling. They replaced the padlock on the old gate and climbed the stairs. Alex walked in front and could feel his eyes on her. Her face was flushed, and she had trouble swallowing. When they returned to the kitchen, she felt Emma's penetrating gaze and thought she detected approval in her blue eyes.

"The first order of the evening is a toast," he said. "Although my champagne pales next to the treasures of your vintner's cellar, it is nevertheless a gesture symbolic of the occasion."

Alex thought Grandpa's Scottish heart would be pleased by this borderline pompous Scandinavian with such unlikely charm. Gran would have adored him and rejoiced at the fire he'd ignited in her granddaughter.

He popped the cork on the champagne bottle with two clever moves of his thumbs, making a joyous sound. Not a drop was spilled as he poured the pinkish liquid into crystal flutes. Effervescent bubbles sparkled in the light.

He faced them and raised his glass. "To beauty," he said to Alex who reddened. "To grace," he said to Emma who beamed. "And to Duncan and Rose, 'Life's too short to drink bad wine.'"

Alex and Emma exchanged glances and giggled like schoolgirls. They lifted their glasses to touch. "Here, here," they said, downing healthy portions.

The telephone rang. Irritated by the interruption, Alex answered the phone in the kitchen.

"Hello?" She heard a click, then the dial tone. Alex frowned and replaced the receiver. "They hung up," she said, a little too quickly.

Erik stared at her, then seemed to decide not to pursue an interrogation. Emma placed her glass on the counter and smoothed her apron.

"You go on into the dining room. Dinner will be ready in two shakes and then I'll be on my way home."

The octagonal shape of the dining room formed the base of the largest turret of the Victorian house. Six large windows admitted the last rays of the sun which shone on a red-and-blue octagonal oriental rug lying under the table.

Emma had placed Erik's roses in a cobalt-blue vase and spread a crocheted white cloth on the antique table. Silver candelabras held glowing blue tapers.

"Emma has a gift for making things special," Alex said.

"Helps that she loves you so much."

"How about a little *Nachtmusik?*" She already felt the effect of the champagne as she inserted the CD into the player.

"Mozart, perfect," Erik said.

Dinner was a blur of music, delicious food, vintage wine, and pleasant conversation. After dessert and coffee, they returned to the library.

"This place sobers me up in a hurry," Alex frowned. "When I dreamed of my father and grandmother, he told me it was time to do the work I came to do. I don't have a clue what that means, but I believe you are part of it," Alex looked at her lap when she spoke.

"I intend to be."

Alexandria felt a long-suppressed desire for union awaken in her heart. "I really can't face any more tonight," she said. "How about an early start tomorrow since it's barely ten now?"

"Eight-thirty?"

"That's early all right," Alex laughed.

They walked to the foot of the staircase. He kissed her softly. "Sleep well."

"You too," she smiled, trying to be light.

She plopped on the bed in her little room on the first floor. *He didn't even try to make a pass at me.*

Alex lay awake, imagining herself lying next to Mr. Anderson in the rose-and-green room, a deliciously scandalous thought. She remembered his kiss on her palm in the wine cellar, shivered at the thought, and imagined kisses in other places. Recalling his gorgeous muscular body in his swimsuit in Mexico, Alex allowed her mind to drift where it would, vowing that tomorrow she'd get more than a good night kiss.

# CHAPTER 19
# SELIG

Alex woke to an overcast sky that was heavy with moisture and the tension that precedes a storm. Her head ached from too much wine, and her back hurt from sleeping in the small bed. Crystal was gone. After showering and dressing in comfortable jeans and a Native American tee shirt from Santa Fe, the aroma of coffee drew her to the kitchen like a magnet.

Alex strolled into the room, ignoring Erik who glanced up from his newspaper. Woven-straw place mats and bright-plaid napkins decorated the table. A plate of hot pecan rolls, a pitcher of orange juice, and a carafe of coffee promised salvation. Alex poured a mug of coffee and walked to the kitchen window. Gulping her first dose of caffeine, she watched Crystal in the garden.

Swallowing the last of the coffee, she turned to look at Erik, who peered tentatively over the top of the newspaper and Ben Franklin spectacles. Sheba, tail arched high in the air, ate from a dish on the floor next to Erik's chair.

"Morning is not my best time," she said.

He held up the carafe. Joining him at the table, she positioned her empty mug under the pitcher. Erik smiled and put the newspaper down, revealing the same Santa Fe tee shirt.

Alex grimaced. "I'll laugh later; right now, my head hurts." She bit into soft dough and crunchy nuts and moaned. "I may live," she said.

"Emma left sandwiches," he said.

Alex nodded. "She has weekends off."

Fortified with coffee and pecan rolls, Alex took a deep breath and looked at Erik. "Shall we?"

She was surprised to see that Erik had already moved boxes filled with papers and documents into the hallway. Stacked four deep, they almost reached the ceiling. When she walked into the library she discovered that Erik had organized the books in stacks. "How long have you been awake?" she asked.

"Two hours. I've arranged these by topic. I woke early and figured I'd get started. I didn't think you would mind. I still can't believe those two pieces of furniture held that stuff," he said, pointing at the boxes and scratching his head.

She sat on the love seat. "You should have called me."

"I owed you one from Mexico," he said.

She blushed. "Thanks. Did you notice any pattern?"

"Not really. In some cases, individual books were pulled off the shelf and tossed into piles. In others, they dumped the whole shelf, or left a row untouched. The stacks of books on the floor are mainly science.

"This library ranges from physics to metaphysics: Eastern philosophy, mythology, atomic energy, chemistry and alchemy," Erik said, shaking his head. "Three shelves on Atlantis, pre-Columbian Mexico, Egyptian, and Peruvian history. Contrast that with solar energy, lasers, and quantum physics."

Alex smiled. "My grandparents shared a passion for knowledge. There used to be a card catalog, but I haven't been able to find it. Grandpa was as organized as Gran was seemingly random. She always knew where everything was though."

"There are twenty books about Edgar Cayce and this collection of Tarot cards," Erik said. "Some of these decks are museum quality."

"I grew up around this stuff," Alex said. "I thought everyone believed in reincarnation and had Tarot readings."

Sheba joined them and perched on the back of the love seat like a gargoyle.

"Why books?" Alex asked.

"Your grandmother obviously thought the books were important."

"Grandpa's notes," Alex said, not hearing him. "Where are Grandpa's notes?"

The front doorbell rang and Crystal jetted off to perform her customary security check. Alex followed her and was surprised to hear her growling.

She left the chain attached and opened the door just enough to peer through the opening.

A tall, thin man with a beak-like nose stood on the porch. Crystal growled again. Alex smothered a gasp and stared into the small-black eyes of the man she had called Raven. Years of fear, triggered by the raven in her childhood nightmare, welled up in her mind. Ever since Gran's funeral, and the nightmare in Mexico, she associated this man with that dream.

A mere line of a mouth was etched between a pencil-thin mustache and a sharp pointed chin. He smiled, and Alex thought the gesture looked unnatural on his face. He appeared to be in his sixties and wore an expensive black-silk suit and bowler hat. He grasped a walking stick and a leather valise in his left hand.

She summoned poise. "Can I help you?"

"Good morning," he said through his forced smile. "I am Rudolph Selig. I was a colleague of Duncan Stuart's, your grandfather, I presume." His deep baritone voice was a startling contrast to his avian demeanor.

"That's right," Alex replied. Her body shook but Crystal, who growled and pulled forward, served as a diversion. She held onto the dog's collar to prevent her from going through the door.

"Your dog seems high strung," Selig said in a blatantly disapproving tone.

Alex had no intention of making this easy. "She doesn't like strangers."

"I'll be brief," he said, not bothering to hide his annoyance. "Your grandfather and I were colleagues, and we had an agreement whereby I would receive his research papers when his wife died. I have come to examine his files and make arrangements to collect them."

"I'm not aware of any such agreement. There was no mention of that in my grandmother's will."

"Your grandmother was certainly aware of the pending legal process and the complaint that has been served. I have a document that clarifies everything."

"Well, it's news to me, Mr. Selig. You'll have to provide our attorney with the documentation. I'm not authorized to negotiate or release anything." Alexandria's heart pounded as she wondered again why Gran had left her the books.

Selig stiffened. "It would be helpful if I could evaluate the quantity of files and records, I will be transferring."

"I'll be happy to put you in touch with our attorney," Alex said.

"I won't take a moment." He tried to smile, and the gesture gave Alex chills. "I'm sure it would be easier on you in the long term," Miss Stuart.

Alex met his stare. There was enmity behind his patronizing smile. "That sounds like a threat, Mr. Selig."

Selig tried to soften his features and form them into another smile. "Not at all. I merely meant it might facilitate the eventual exchange of records."

"You're assuming there will be an exchange of records," she said, fighting to keep revulsion from her voice. He did not reply but held her gaze. They stood that way a moment, then prompted by some inner urging, Alex changed her mind.

"Perhaps it might be good for you to see the library today."

He looked briefly surprised. "You are most astute, Miss Stuart," Selig said, in a voice laced with an undercurrent of sarcasm.

Alex held on to Crystal, whose ears were back, wanting to have her way with the intruder. Alex opened the door just wide enough for Selig to enter. He stepped into the entry hall and removed his hat, revealing sparse graying hair brushed straight back in an attempt to cover his bald head.

Alex shut the big door and spotted Erik, emerging from a concealed spot in the hallway. She surmised he'd been listening. "I'll take Crystal to the kitchen."

He extended his hand to Selig. "I'm Erik Anderson, friend of the family."

Alex smiled, relieved her back was to them.

"How do you do," Selig said, not taking his hand.

"Mr. Selig said he worked with Grandpa," Alex said, returning from the kitchen. "He claims they had an agreement about his research papers. He expects to receive Grandpa's material now that Gran has died," Alex said evenly.

"Really?" Erik asked, as if he was intrigued by the idea.

The three walked silently to the library. When they reached the library door, Selig stared at the boxes. Alex entered the library first and turned around just inside the door. Selig followed, and Alex detected a genuine look of concern on his face.

"Why are those boxes in the hall?" Selig inquired.

"Apparently, you aren't the only one interested in my grandparents' library," Alex said. "Someone broke into the house. Mr. Anderson has offered his assistance to help me restore order; books and papers were everywhere yesterday."

"What was taken?" Selig asked, eyes darting rapidly over the room.

"Perhaps you could speculate, Mr. Selig, since you were so familiar with Duncan's work. What might someone be looking for?" Erik asked.

"I'm afraid my comments would be just that, speculation. My interests are purely scientific, and this appears to be burglary." Selig replied in a flat tone that failed to mask his shock.

Uninvited, Selig perched on the edge of a wing back chair in front of the fireplace and positioned hat, briefcase, and walking stick across his knees. His arms stretched across them, clutching his belongings. Alex noticed his hands, slender fingers with uncommonly long nails for a man, meticulously manicured and filed.

Selig placed his hat and walking stick on the table and opened his valise, removing a large manila envelope. Carefully unfastening the clasp, he extracted the contents and placed the documents on the table. His movements were precise and mechanistic.

"These are copies of correspondence, photographs and research reports that span the years of my association with your grandfather."

He bent the fingers of one hand inward toward the palm, regarding his nails as he spoke. "A copy of our agreement is included. I have waited a long while for this data, Miss Stuart."

Sheba jumped on the coffee table and sat on the stack of papers, facing Selig, and swishing her tail. He winced and sneezed. Selig glared at the cat whose green eyes stared back at him without blinking. Alex was beginning to grow fond of Sheba.

Selig closed his briefcase, placed his hat on his head, and rose from the chair. "I regret troubling you today under these upsetting circumstances. I'll be in touch with your solicitor as you suggested. I'll provide him with additional copies as your feline seems to have appropriated these." He pursed his lips in apparent distaste.

Erik moved to see Selig out.

"Good day, Miss Stuart," he said, tipping his hat and nodding. "I hope you find the villain who desecrated this library."

"So do I."

Alex walked to the library window and looked outside. The air had been heavy all day as a storm approached. When Erik returned, she looked toward him.

"The weather's a great backdrop for a melodrama."

"Meaning the plot thickens?" he said.

"Do you think there's a connection between Selig's visit and the break-in?"

"It's the coincidence thing again, but I don't think we've seen the last of Rudolph." Erik removed Sheba from the table and flipped through Selig's papers.

"Whatever your grandmother left you has generated some keen interest, but he seemed genuinely surprised by the break in, so either his cronies are working against him, or there are more players in the game."

She kept her back to him as she spoke. "Do you remember the stranger I described at the cemetery the day of Gran's funeral?"

"Yes?" he asked. She could almost feel him stiffen.

"You just met him."

"Why didn't you give me a signal? I would have handled things differently."

"Which he would have sensed. I acted like I'd never met him, which is true enough. I knew most of my grandparent's friends and associates, but I never saw that man before the cemetery."

"You're probably right," he said, "though I loathe admitting it. There's a land mine hidden somewhere, and we might step on it."

Alex recalled the raven from her nightmare. She didn't want to remind him of that additional coincidence right now. Better not toss a grenade into the mine field.

Erik joined her at the window and put his arm around her shoulders. She rested her head against him, looking outside. Her skin tingled every placed he touched. He lifted her chin and kissed her.

"We'll get to the bottom of this," he said.

Alex closed her eyes as his lips touched hers. Her body responded with desire, and she turned to face him. Nearly losing her balance, Alex placed a hand on the bookcase behind her to steady herself and heard a noise like a metal lever shifting. Before she had time to react the bookcase pulled away behind her, and she fell backward. Erik tried to catch her, but they tumbled into the opening created by the receding bookcase, landing on the floor in a dark room.

"Are you okay?" he asked, laughing.

"Fine," she said, standing and brushing off her seat. "Speaking of getting to the bottom of things," she laughed. "This is too much. A secret room. I can't believe Gran never told me about any of this. I would be angry, but I know they believe it was for the best."

Erik felt his way in the dark, looking for a light, while their eyes adjusted to the dimness. "I think I found a flashlight," he said, clicking it on. He shined the beam around the room and spotted a lamp on an old wooden desk. Alex turned it on, and the solitary fluorescent desk lamp cast a dim light in the study.

"Eureka," she said. "There's the card catalog and Grandpa's files." The room was about twelve by twenty-feet without windows. The only entrance was a door that masqueraded as a bookcase.

Erik located the switch for the overhead lights and whistled through his teeth as the contents of the room were revealed. Apothecary jars, beakers, tubes, and bottles lined shelves which hung over a worktable with a sink. Dozens of dusty three-ring binders marked with dates and experiment names lined the shelves of another bookcase. Books were neatly stacked into spaces in between. Three large file cabinets flanked the other wall.

He whistled through his teeth. "This was a working laboratory."

"No wonder nothing is missing from the library," Alex mused. What Selig is after must be hidden in here."

"I thought the wine cellar was amazing," he said, pushing his hair back on his head. "Looks like this is where Duncan hid the good stuff. Books on magic, more on alchemy."

Alex pulled open drawers in one of the file cabinets and flipped through manila file folders. "The top drawer has files on crystals," she said. "The next two seem to be energy related." She found a folder labeled ALTERNATE ENERGY CONFERENCE.

"I just remembered something," she said. "The day after Gran's funeral, I found a photo in an old book taken at a conference in 1962. Selig was in the picture with my grandparents."

They looked at each other. "Energy," they said at the same time.

"Maybe if we get this mess cleaned and organized, we'll discover something important," Alex said.

By eight o'clock rain seemed imminent. Exhausted, they stopped to admire their hours of work. The library had been restored to pristine condition. Mahogany shelves were polished, and books dusted. The Queen Anne furniture shined.

A cold front had blown in ahead of the storm, and the temperature dropped from a humid seventy-eight to sixty-two. Selig's visit had cast a pall, and the old house felt damp. Erik built a cheery fire in the stone fireplace in the kitchen.

"Let's order pizza," Alex said.

She phoned for pizza and procured pewter mugs from the pantry. Erik poured foamy root beer while Alex lit beeswax candles in brass sconces on the mantel. She spread a red tablecloth and placed candles on the table. The wet logs hissed and popped in the grate as the smell of burning pine logs filled the room.

"This was my favorite room as a child, especially with a fire. So much has happened in such a short time, but I sense that behind all the seemingly random events I'm supposed to glean a course of action. Right now, it looks like a needle in a haystack."

"I never thought I'd hear myself say this," he sighed. "But I think you should call Miguel. I don't know why I have such a strong reaction to him. Maybe he just represents things I don't understand and can't control."

"Three blockheads are better than one," she smiled.

"Feels more like tumbling down the rabbit hole into Wonderland."

"Speaking of blockheads, my friend Sheila's dying to meet you. How about I ask her to bring breakfast?"

"Perfect. I don't think my brain can handle any more tonight," he laughed.

They cleaned up the dishes and walked to her room. When they reached the doorway, Erik scooped her into his arms and carried her across the threshold. Alex giggled in delight.

He gently placed her on the tiny bed and lay down beside her. His warmth was soothing. Emma would not be back tonight, she realized. Light from the big streetlamp on the far corner shone through the window. Rain streamed down the leaded-glass panes, creating kaleidoscopes of twinkling patterns in the reflected light.

They kissed and wrapped their arms and legs around each other. He kissed her neck and ears, and her body came alive with desire. Sheba jumped on the bed and bumped her head into theirs. Alex was startled, then laughed. Crystal padded into the room and barked.

"Intruder alert," he said. "This will require some planning and orchestration," he said, furrowing his brow.

The phone rang. "I'll probably regret this," Alex said.

"Hello? You have rotten timing, Goldwoman. Come by about ten tomorrow and bring something decadent for breakfast."

"Where were we?" he said, nibbling an ear.

The phone rang again. "Ye Gods," Alex said. "Don Miguel, I was planning to call you in the morning. That's wonderful. news We'll see you Monday afternoon then."

Alex hung up the phone and sat up. She kissed him on the cheek. "He already has his tickets. I guess it's good to have a shaman on the team."

He squeezed her hand and stood. "It isn't time yet."

Alex nodded and smiled. "I want my mind to be totally focused with no distractions, human or animal."

They walked to the door, holding hands.  His lips parted and covered hers, and they shared a long, tantalizing kiss.

"I'll climb to the tower and leave the beautiful princess in the dungeon," he said.

"Good night, sweet prince.  Thanks for everything."

Alex opened the window to hear raindrops on the roof and smell moist air laden with the fragrance of flowers and grass.  She climbed into bed and hugged her pillow, watching the falling rain trace patterns on the glass as she slowly drifted off to sleep.

CHAPTER 20

# PRIESTESS UNA

Priestess Una rose from her sleeping place and walked onto the stone terrace that overlooked the ocean. The dawn mist had nearly evaporated and she shaded her eyes with her hand, squinting into the morning sun. The sea was peaceful, the salty breeze a caress on her face and skin. Behind her gauze curtains rustled gently.

To the west, sea and sky met in a hazy fusion of blue and green. Far below the cliff where she stood gulls and pelicans called as they searched for morning food in the sheltered bay. Una looked fondly at her mother's garden. Lavender clusters of wisteria hung from a trellis, bending their branches like plump bunches of grapes.

Fragrance from large hanging baskets of plumeria, honeysuckle and jasmine filled the air. Round, marble pots brimmed with colorful petunias, impatiens and lilies, and honeybees gathered nectar from the floral bounty.

No one had believed her mother would get anything to grow so high up on this rock, but she had proven them wrong. Breathing in the beauty of her home, the young priestess walked back inside the rose-colored marble dwelling. *How could she leave this place?*

After three-hundred-thirty solar cycles a High Council had been convened. Representatives from all regions in the nation would convene today in the capital city to decide the fate of the great energy stones.

Una sat at her dressing table and applied rose oil and lily water, her favorite fragrances. She dressed in an ivory linen robe and tied the apple-

121

green sash that signified the healer and artisan orders around her waist. A large hood hung down the back of the formal robe required for the Assembly Hall.

She fastened the heavy necklace of gold, which proclaimed her rank as artisan of gems and healer, at the back of her neck. Seven-inches wide, the edges of the necklace reached to her shoulders. Centering the emblem over her heart, she gazed in the glass. The green-jet triangle and blue-lapis crescent filled her with pride.

Una was young for such achievements, and her work with stones and metals had received recognition throughout the island nation. The priestess glanced at the sun clock, which cast a shadow from a metal rod onto a marble disk. Two solar intervals past dawn: the council would convene soon.

A twinge of anxiety grabbed her belly as she thought of the council session. They would discuss the fate of the great crystal, the Tuaoi Stone, which had been used for countless years to generate energy for the country. Zared and his followers wanted to set the range to maximum force to generate more power. *Tuning the vibration too high would be reckless and dangerous.*

Una believed her father was right to fight them as the rebels underestimated the powers of the great crystal. Father said if Zared and his followers have their way with the great stone the land may be too unstable to remain in Poseidia. The enhanced power of the crystal could cause devastating subterranean earthquakes, resulting in volcanic eruptions.

She bristled as she remembered the armed temple guards waiting outside. There had been threats recently and Father insisted they accompany her. She was outraged that a temple needed guards. The wrong people were gaining power, promising unlimited wealth with no restraint on physical gratification.

Una stood inside the doorway, fighting tears. A priestess of the Healing Order did not show tears in public, and she could ill afford such weakness today. *Why couldn't everyone see her father's goodness and dedication?*

For her father's sake, and those who serve the One, she must radiate an implacable aura of serenity. The Priestess breathed and recited the words of a mantra to regain her center. After a few moments she mastered her emotions. A few more breaths, and her body was filled with energy. She felt ready to face them.

She walked outside and nodded to the guards, signaling her readiness. A member of the priest's guard, dressed in the royal-blue-and-gold uniform of his rank, stepped forward. He carried a weapon powered by the crystal, another witness to the sickness of the land. The power of the stone, once used only for the highest spiritual purposes, now fueled implements of destruction.

The guard opened the hatch of an ovoid vehicle that would take her to the Great Assembly Hall. Power was transmitted from the Tuaoi Stone to vehicles such as this with crystalline storage cells. Even this basic form of transportation was threatened by Zared's recklessness.

Una filled her lungs with fresh air before she climbed into the transport. From her home at the pinnacle of the mountain, the guard maneuvered the craft down the winding mountain road past homes and gardens toward the city center. Eclectic homesteads of stone, brick, wood, or adobe were generously adorned by window boxes and terra cotta pots of petunias, daisies, and snap dragons. Roses of every color climbed fences and trellises which were framed by a bright-blue sky. An aching sense of loss threatened her equanimity. Sunny weather contrasted with the bleak feelings that her trained will kept at bay.

The driver slowed his pace as they reached the outer limits of the city. He raised security shields on the clear areas of the car so they could see out but not be seen. Una knew that his actions were for her protection, but the gesture rankled.

The city was designed as concentric circles of land constructed in a large, sheltered bay. Bridges and waterways interconnected in a circular grid pattern. A marketplace, civic and temple complexes were at the center, and residential areas lay in the outer circles.

The amphibious transport craft exited the street and entered a waterway. Una gazed fondly at marble and granite buildings, wondering how many Poseidians carrying out their daily activities suspected a power struggle was being waged at the heart of their government.

The guard stopped in front of the main entrance of the Assembly Hall that faced the sea. He offered his hand and helped her out of the vehicle.

"Shall I accompany you inside, Priestess Una?" he asked.

"No," she said firmly. "If a Priestess of the Healing Orders is not safe to enter the Temple all is indeed lost." Gathering her forces she held her head high.

Feathery, bright-purple blooms of flowering Poinciana trees lined the avenue and filled the space above the street. Regal cypress and cedar trees surrounded the central park. Colorful flags of all the provinces hung limp in an arc around the circular temple complex. The sea breeze had shifted, and the air was cool and deadly calm, holding the threat of a storm.

Constructed of pink granite and alabaster, the massive round structure occupied a city block. Eighty-foot pillars, ornately carved with flowers and vines and inlaid with pearls, shells, coral and semi-precious stones, supported the roof. The Priestess glanced up, reassured to see marvelous paintings of constellations and their stories covering the dark-blue domed ceiling.

Sculptured statues of revered Poseidians graced alcoves girding the central core of the Assembly Hall where the High Council would be held. Una was outwardly composed as she walked along the marble hallway, and her posture erect and commanding. Talking in small groups people scarcely noted her passing.

She turned and entered the magnificent Grand Hall. Designed like an amphitheater, rows of seats extended three-fourths of the way around the room. Tall windows traversed the circumference between the last row of seats and the ceiling. Light filtered into the room from the east.

She moved toward the front of the hall where a large round dais was the focal point. Painted porcelain pots filled with white lilies and golden gladiolas bordered the circular area. Sandalwood incense burned in gold censers, wafting up toward the high ceiling. Two high-back chairs that looked like thrones were positioned behind podiums for the speakers.

Una spotted the young priest Kadir across the room and her stomach fluttered. He was tall and bronze like most who lived in this land with straight black hair that touched his shoulders. She loved the look of his fine aquiline nose. *How handsome he looks in his sky-blue robe.*

She swelled with pride to see the lapis crescent of the healing order around his neck. Una walked toward him in what she hoped was a subtle manner. He saw her and gestured, and she smiled as he approached her.

"Shall we take our seats?" Kadir inquired, extending his arm.

"Yes," she answered, hooking her arm through his.

Choosing seats that afforded a good view of the stage the young couple looked around the room, soaking up the heady feelings of the occasion. The hall filled quickly with people outfitted in their own colors, emblems, and corresponding gemstones. Priests wore violet, musicians rose, and the merchants a deep green. The pale yellow of the visual artists dotted the hall like daffodils. A hushed excitement fell over the Great Hall and people were silent or spoke in whispers.

Una felt a mounting anticipation. "I'm concerned, Kadir."

"Whatever the outcome of this council, Poseidia will never be the same," Kadir said, his handsome features set in an expression of grim determination.

Una watched as the regal form of Hept-supht, Prime Regent of all Poseidia, walked across the stage and approached the speaker's lectern. Tall and dark, he radiated the confident power of a high initiate. He grasped a six-foot brass rod surmounted by a blue sphere with studied familiarity.

The Prime Regent wore full regalia for the most important occasion of state. An equal-armed cross inside a circle hung from a thick-gold chain around his neck. A large diamond shone from the center, and the four arms of the cross were studded with rubies, topaz, pearls, and emeralds.

Hept-supht wore a long white undergarment covered by a vivid-blue outer robe and an orange V-shaped mantle. A simple gold circlet crowned his head. When Hept-supht reached the stage, he positioned himself in a beam of morning light that shone on the dais and augmented his sharp features. He spoke without pretense or posturing.

"Brothers and sisters, a High Council has been convened after long silence. Some of you have traveled far and with short notice. Thank you for your response to this summons.

"We meet today because grave times are upon us, and a sickness has befallen our beloved Poseidia. I pray this disease will not be fatal. There is unrest in our great city as corruption and treachery threaten to rend the fabric of this great land."

The Prime Regent was a skilled speaker. He moved his hands and arms with measured emphasis to strengthen the impact of his voice. Inflections were choreographed to add force to his words. Carefully executed pauses, pitch and modulation resulted from years of rigorous training.

"We are here today to decide a matter of extreme significance," Hept-supht continued. "The fate of our crystalline Tuaoi Stone and that of the priesthood who guard her sacred knowledge are in question."

His voice reverberated through the hall, he paused at certain points to let the significance of his words take effect. The assembled priests, artisans, merchants, and politicians were motionless. The atmosphere in the hall was tense like the stillness before a storm.

"Later today," he continued, "the teaching and healing orders will conclave to decide how to implement the decision you will make this morning. I implore you, consider your vote with utmost discernment and clarity of heart.

"I have asked Hierophant Iltar to officially open this council with an invocation," Hept-supht said.

A murmur passed through the hall as the imposing figure of Iltar approached the podium. Iltar wore a white robe reserved for the most solemn occasions. The sleeves and hem were trimmed in wide bands of gold and violet, and the robe's hood stretched halfway down his back. A gold tassel fastened to the tip of the hood glittered and swung like a pendulum as he walked in deliberate cadence to the dais.

The three-tiered mitered crown he wore emphasized his tall stature and proclaimed his position as High Priest, a religious office equal to the civil role of Prime Regent. His chest plate had twelve divisions, each containing a glyph and gemstone to represent the orders over which he presided. He held an ornately carved staff of cedar inlaid with precious gems and metals and topped with a coiling serpent.

High Priest Iltar opposed Zared's scheme to usurp the power of the stone for purely material uses. Grasping his staff in one hand and a golden censer in the other, he looked into the eyes of the audience. The fine features of his aristocratic face were inscrutable.

The young priestess felt a painful mixture of pride and grief as she watched her father approach his task. Una knew as few others did his uncompromising nature in spiritual principles. He was sometimes accused of rigidity by the younger priests, even Kadir.

Iltar understood the magnitude that what was at stake was nothing less than the very survival of Poseidia. His daughter knew that the depth of the High Priest's concern came from a soul as pure as the snow on Mount Alta. Drawing herself to her full height, Una sent a wave of love and light from her heart to his. She was relieved her mother had not lived to see this dark time.

Hierophant Iltar stood in silence at the center of the round dais for a several moments, gathering power. He raised both arms and looked skyward. When he spoke, his voice was pitched to gain maximum resonance and volume, and the sound boomed and echoed in the hall.

> *Oh Thou, vast and almighty*
> *Infinite and omnipotent One,*
> *Whose everlasting embrace of*
> *Love and Light brings forth*
> *Countless manifest worlds.*
>
> *Purify our hearts to receive Thy Word.*
> *Illumine our minds to know Thy Will*
> *We invoke Thee Invisible One.*
> *May we join Thee in the dance of Eternal life.*

Zared, the outspoken leader of the opposition, stood in his place with both arms crossed across his chest in a haughty stance. A thin veneer of propriety could not conceal the blatant contempt on his face. Zared seemed a stark caricature of his race. His features were sharp and pronounced, and his long, pointed nose bent over a thin mouth that was stretched in a perpetual sneer. He licked his lips habitually, like a reptile.

Cold, greedy eyes devoured others with their stare. He wore the violet hue of the priesthood, but it conferred no dignity. His spirituality had long since been consumed by greed and lust for earthly power. Una knew he hated Iltar.

"Step down old man, you have outlived the wisdom of your hollow words. We don't need a dried-up priest to pray to a useless god."

The audience gasped that Zared would dare to attack the High Priest during an invocation, but Zared had many supporters.

"Your feeble ways no longer serve the will of the people," Zared said, his voice growing louder. "We want the knowledge and power for ourselves. Your days of tyranny are over. We will take what we want."

Many in the hall murmured or voiced disapproval, but a growing number called for Zared to come forward.

"Citizens of Poseidia claim your rights," Zared shouted. "End this repression. The priesthood only wants power for themselves. I say turn the crystal higher so we can have what we want. Stop wasting precious energy healing abominations that should be killed or used as our slaves."

A growing number in the audience applauded. Una watched in horror as hope of a peaceful solution dissolved in Zared's words of hate. Zared approached the stage as if to speak from the podium. He pulled a dagger from his robe. As he lunged toward Iltar, another young priest threw himself in front of the blade, and the crowd erupted in chaos.

"This is sacrilege," a man shouted, "murder in a holy place."
Una battled grief and outrage but remained composed for her father's sake. She would not disgrace him now with weakness. Hept-supht and Iltar slipped out through the rear of the stage behind the curtains. Una knew there was a secret passage underground.

"We must leave at once," Kadir whispered in her ear and pulled her quickly to the door. Struggling with strong feelings, she knew Kadir was right. There was no choice but to leave Poseidia. After this outrage the healers could not safely take time for a conclave.

Outside the sky had turned dark and a chill wind howled. Una and Kadir ran to the side of the building and stood against the wall, hidden from view. Suddenly, a piercing shriek filled the air. Una looked up as the orb of the sun was eclipsed by an enormous, black bird of prey, circling high above. The Condor sensed her gaze and dove. The huge bird landed before them, flapping its wings in a menacing gesture.

"You have no sword, and I am stronger now," sneered the dark, feathered form.

"I have truth, a more powerful weapon," Una shouted.

The Condor screeched as if to laugh. "We shall see." The ugly beast spread its wings to a span of twelve feet and advanced toward them. All was dark now.

The young priestess wanted to scream and run, but Una stood her ground and faced her attacker. Summoning strength from long years of training, the priestess spoke secret words of power and called upon the force of light. Una knew a moment of shimmering incandescence, then silent, leaden blackness.

# CHAPTER 21

# ATLANTIS MEMORIES

Alex screamed and sat up in bed. She was soaked in perspiration and her pulse raced. Crystal was surprised by her sudden movement and barked.

"That's the worst ever," she said. Crystal put her head in Alex's lap, and she hugged the dog a long time. Swinging her legs over the side of the bed she donned a blue-chenille robe and slipped her feet into matching scuffs. She absently ran her fingers through her hair, removing curly red strands from her face as if that would clear her mind of fear.

"I'll make coffee and you can go outside." They padded toward the kitchen and Alex let Crystal out the back door. The sky was the steel-blue color between night and morning, and the day promised to be glorious. Savoring the early morning stillness, Alex breathed fresh air. She lifted and stretched her shoulders, trying to concentrate. She ground hazelnut coffee beans and poured water in the coffee maker.

Alex decided to shower while the coffee brewed. Turning the shower on maximum pulse she enjoyed the intense feeling of the water pelting her skin. She worked up a lather of soap and shampoo as if she could wash off the menace of the black bird that refused to recede from her consciousness.

Dressing in a colorful, print skirt and cobalt-blue blouse she had a vague sense of preparing for battle. Alex brushed her russet hair and forced the wet strands into a barrette. She applied her makeup like war paint. Her jewelry was the final layer of protective coloration, and she chose a gold sunburst necklace with a round cobalt-blue center. Matching gold-and-blue suns dangled from her ears.

Alex stared at the mirror and her awareness shifted. The mirror shimmered like water in a pond that had been disturbed by a pebble. Sparkles seem to fill the air, altering the nature of time itself, and the reflection in the glass changed. She felt the heavy robes she had worn in the dream, and the face of the young priestess Una stared back at her from the glass. Expressive ebony eyes, straight black hair and reddish-brown skin provided a different raiment, but the soul in the mirror was her own.

"What are you trying to tell me?" Alex asked.

The image passed and her familiar reflection returned. Alex felt profoundly moved and strengthened. She realized she'd been given a rare gift.

*Can her power become mine?*

Shaking herself, she returned to the kitchen and prepared a large tray with ceramic mugs, cream and sugar, butter, honey, and yogurt. She filled a large carafe with coffee and ground beans for another pot. Pouring a generous mug of steaming coffee, she stirred in cream and took a big gulp.

"Morning." A cheerful voice boomed behind her. "Smells like hazelnuts in here," Erik said, sniffing.

"Morning yourself," Alex smiled and turned to look at him, trying to stay calm. Wet blond hair crowned a scrubbed boyish face. Erik carried Sheba in one arm and held a can of cat food in his other hand.

"Let's eat in the garden," she said. "Coffee?"

"Wonderful," he said, putting Sheba on the floor and claiming a ceramic mug. Alex smiled inwardly and poured coffee into the mug. Caffeine addiction was common ground but not an ideal basis for a relationship.

Accompanied by an aria of meows, Erik opened the can and emptied cat food into Sheba's bowl. As they sat at the table to enjoy their coffee the doorbell rang. Exchanging martyred looks they both rose to answer the door.

Sheila stood on the porch, grinning like a Cheshire cat in red lipstick. She wore a white jogging suit trimmed in gold. Enormous white-and-gold bangles decorated her ears. Manicured hands clutched a large grocery bag and an insulated carafe.

"What's in there?" Alex demanded, peering into the sack.

Sheila stepped into the foyer, handed Alex the carafe and scooped black hair across her head. "Not before I'm introduced," Sheila said, staring at and extending her liberated hand.

Alex grinned. "Sheila Goldman, meet Erik Anderson."

"Charmed, I'm sure," he said, bending at the waist.  Clasping Sheila's extended arm, he looked into her eyes and gently kissed the back of her hand.

Sheila stood, red fingernails suspended in air, fluttering her eyelids. "Nice," she said, in a voice filled with sultry sarcasm.  "I think Allie's mother may even like you."

"Is that good?" Erik wanted to know.

"I doubt it," Alex said, rolling her eyes. "Let's go outside."

They exited the back door, where Crystal had planted muddy paws on the porch steps.  Sparrows, cardinals, and wrens chirped and called.

"Smells like the Earth's been to the cleaners," Sheila said.

"That's a tufted titmouse," he said, pointing.

"You're joking," Sheila said.

Alex laughed.  "He's an opportunist but accurate.  Gran adored birds, and they all love her garden."

They entered a red-brick patio in the heart of the garden through an arched wooden trellis.  Fragrant crimson roses climbed up the sides and over the top.  A white wrought iron table with four chairs and a red-and-white umbrella marked the center of the bricked area.

Blossoms of multi-colored snapdragons, black-eyed Susans, zinnias, golden yellow bachelor buttons and bright-orange tiger lilies created a background like a Van Gogh canvas.  Ardent honeybees drew nectar from redolent purple and white lilacs.  Damp cedar chips added a woody sent to the fragrance of flowers and wet grass.

They wiped rainwater from the table and chairs.  After claiming her seat, Sheila produced three plastic champagne glasses from the grocery bag. "Mimosas," she proclaimed, unscrewing the carafe, and grinning devilishly.

"We have work to do," Alex objected.

"This is purely medicinal," Sheila said, in her best Jewish-mother voice. "Champagne and orange juice are better for you than chicken soup."

After pouring three glasses of frothy orange fluid, Sheila extracted croissants, strawberries and whipped cream like a magician pulling rabbits from a hat. Alex laughed.

"A toast," Erik said, raising his plastic glass.  "To chicken soup, may I never have it for breakfast."

"Here.  Here." Sheila said.

"What other decadent surprises are lurking in that plain brown wrapper?" he asked.

Sheila raised her eyebrows like Groucho Marx.

"What's the secret word, little boy?"

"I give up," he said, laughing.

"That's it!"

"You two can play games all morning while I eat strawberries," Alex laughed. She selected a succulent red berry and scooped a generous dollop of whipped cream on the tip. Slowly lowering the ripe fruit into her open mouth, she closed her eyes and moaned.

Not to be outdone, Sheila picked a fat strawberry, dipped it in whipped cream and seductively licked white foam from the end.

"Stop, both of you, I'm not a saint," Erik joked.

When Alex couldn't eat another berry, she sat back in her chair and pulled her feet up on the seat. She rested her chin on her knees and wrapped her arms around them. "Can I tell you about a dream?"

"I know that look; this is serious," Sheila said.

"Was there a raven in it?" Erik asked, smiling.

"A condor," Alex frowned.

Erik and Sheila exchanged looks.

"Uh oh," Sheila said.

Erik's face became serious.

"In the dream I lived in a beautiful place overlooking an ocean on an island called Poseidia. I was a priestess, dressed in official robes for an important occasion. My father was High Priest, and his counterpart was called Prime Regent. They were good leaders, wise and honest.

"Political unrest had divided the nation, and I felt a sense of impending crisis. Another man gained influence by appealing to people's greed. A High Council had been called to vote on the fate of a huge crystal that was the power source of the country.

"A power struggle erupted during the council. Zared, a wicked and corrupt priest, incited the crowd," she continued after a period of silence. Alex related the rest of the dream and looked at them.

"Sounds like Atlantis, Allie," Sheila said.

"I agree," Alex said. "When I dressed this morning that priestess stared back at me from the mirror. Alexandria looked at them. "I was once that woman."

"The conflict was about energy?" Erik asked.

Realization dawned. "You're right," Alex said. "Their technology and communication was powered by a giant crystal. Don Miguel will be here tomorrow afternoon, and I'm ready to do whatever it takes to solve this puzzle."

CHAPTER 22

# DON MIGUEL

Crystal rushed to the door after the bell rang. She didn't bark and sat perfectly still until Alex opened the door. Don Miguel stood on the small porch, his handsome brown face illumined by a smile. He wore an elegantly tailored, taupe-colored suit. His white shirt and bright-floral tie were a perfect complement to his graying temples.

Alex hugged him. "Come in," she said.

"It is good to be here. Your grandparents invited me many times, but I regret that I never managed to visit. You look lovely, Alex," he said, his deep voice resonating in the hall.

Alex blushed. She'd absently dressed in a pair of casual, white pants and a pale-blue tunic and asked Emma to French braid her hair. She had donned a necklace and earrings she made from rose-quartz beads.

"The simplest clothing lets the inner beauty shine," Miguel said, as if he'd heard her thoughts. He leaned back on his legs in a timeless Indian posture and placed one hand on Crystal's head and another under her chin.

"Crystal, I've heard about you," he said, looking into her eyes. Afternoon sunlight shone through the leaded glass panes of the front door, creating a magical space of shifting beams of light and floating dust particles around Miguel and Crystal. They remained in that position for several moments locked in silent communion. Alex had never seen Crystal remain so still.

Miguel stood after a few minutes and smiled. Erik approached with his right arm extended.

"I'm glad you're here, don Miguel. I hope you can help Alex."

"Thank you. You and I will both assist Alexandria to find the answers within herself."

"You must be tired," Alex fussed, "I'll show you to your room so you can change, then we'll have something to eat."

Don Miguel smiled indulgently. "Please don't treat me like an old man. My work takes me on many trips, so travel is familiar. But I would enjoy some tea."

ALEX AND ERIK tried to wait patiently for Miguel, but Emma's treats were already displayed with her usual flair, and the aroma of fresh lemon bars and chocolate fudge filled the kitchen.

"Couldn't we just have a taste?" Alex pleaded.

"Absolutely not," Emma scolded. "You should be ashamed for even asking."

"Where your cooking is concerned, we have no shame," Erik laughed.

"That looks more comfortable," Alex said, as Miguel appeared in the doorway in time to prevent an international incident.

"Don Miguel, I'd like you to meet Emma Manchester. You two have talked on the phone," Alex said, looking from one to the other.

"Yes," Miguel said, extending his hand. "It's a great pleasure to meet you, Emma. It is long overdue."

Emma blushed, wiped her hands on her apron, and extended her hand. She wore a yellow-print house dress under her apron, and her silky, gray hair was pulled back in a twist. Kind blue eyes sparkled over reddened cheeks.

"The pleasure is mine, senor Piedra. I feel like I already know you. I'm sorry you couldn't have come under happier circumstances."

He placed his other hand over Emma's and smiled. "Please, call me Miguel."

Erik pulled back a wooden chair. "Have a seat, Miguel. Tea is served, and not a moment too soon."

Miguel grinned.

Relieved, Emma served hot and cold tea with sweets worthy of English royalty. Carrot cake, custard tarts, dark chocolate fudge, lemon bars and Scottish shortbread were symmetrically arranged on a silver tray.

"Ay! A banquet," Miguel said.

"I've been here three days. I've gained five pounds, and my moral fiber has come unraveled," Erik said, patting his mid-section.

Miguel, a consummate diplomat, took a small portion of each delicacy and sampled them, pursing his lips.  He praised their various merits from the point of view of an educated palette and made appreciative sounds of delight.

"You are too kind," Emma beamed.

Erik and Alexandria ate with abandon. When Alexandria paused and pushed her plate forward, Erik turned to her.

# CHAPTER 23

# TURNING POINT

Erik and Alexandria ate with abandon, and when Alex paused and pushed her plate forward, Erik turned to her.

"Tell Miguel about the dream," he said.

"All right, let's go into the library," she said.

Alex felt proud of the restored library. Bookshelves were straightened and organized. The striped burgundy-and-cream love seat and Queen Anne chairs glistened and the polished mahogany reading tables shone. The antique roll top desk and matching secretary looked like museum pieces.

Pictures of Rose and Duncan, Philip, Blanche, and Alex were arranged on the tables and mantel. A mauve-and-blue Oriental rug lay between the chairs and couch in front of the fireplace. Afternoon light shone through diamond-shaped panes of large leaded glass windows, brightening fuchsia roses and white lilacs that Emma had placed in crystal vases.

An unabridged dictionary with yellowed pages and a worn leather cover lay open on a three-legged stand. A globe of the world rested in a walnut cradle in front of one of the bookcases. Don Miguel smelled the dictionary and tenderly ran his hand over the pages. He gently spun the globe, which rattled in its cradle.

"A wonderful room, Alexandria," Miguel said, glancing around the library. "This place smells like old books, my favorite aroma, dust, and wisdom. I can feel Duncan and Rose in this room."

Alexandria's eyes filled with tears. "I miss them so much."

Don Miguel smiled, compassion in his eyes. "It's natural, but they are close by. You can be with them while your body sleeps, and you have already experienced this. They sense us when we think of them, so it's important to send strong and loving thoughts. Our strong emotions are painful for them otherwise."

Alex nodded, wiping moisture from under her eyes. She didn't trust herself to speak. After a pause she took a deep breath and asked, "How about a quick tour of Dr. Frankenstein's laboratory?" She worried what he might think of her grandfather's secret life.

Miguel cast her an appraising look and she winced internally.

"That's not what I think," she sighed. "It's all just so unsettling. Too many coincidences, surprises, and mysteries."

"Your grandfather was a remarkable man. There is nothing to be ashamed of. Let's have a look."

Duncan's secret room had been transformed by Alex's scrutiny. Sparkling bottles and beakers lined clean shelves. Books and binders had been dusted and placed upright. Cleaned fluorescent lights brightened the dungeon-like feeling of the dark room. Miguel scanned the hidden laboratory, absorbing the contents.

"Were you aware of professor Stuart's secret life?" Erik asked.

Miguel chuckled. "Duncan Stuart was a visionary and an iconoclast and a staunch guardian of what he saw as his mission. He planted seeds where he thought they might germinate one day. I recall enigmatic statements he made about unlimited energy, controversial research that could have troublesome consequences. He certainly believed he was onto something transformative."

"Unlimited energy," Alex said.

"There's that word again," Erik said.

Alex had a sudden intuition and picked up the conference photograph of her grandparents and Selig, pointing at the Raven. "This is the man I saw at the cemetery. He was here yesterday, demanding Grandpa's research papers,"

Don Miguel scrutinized the picture. "Curious, I believe I have seen this man before."

The three emerged from Duncan's private study.

"Tell Miguel about the dream."

"Right," she said, unconsciously pushing her hair behind her ears, forgetting that the unruly strands were already pulled tight into a braid. Alex related the dream in detail as Miguel listened with rapt attention, trying to capture the details of the island country and the characters she recalled. When she finished, she sat back on the love seat, exhaling.

"What do you think?" Erik asked.

"The images are vivid, and the people in your dream have names and personalities. Because of these details, it strikes me as a memory of a past life rather than dream symbolism," Miguel said.

Alex nodded. "I agree. I want to continue the shamanic training, don Miguel. I need to get stronger and understand what's happening to us."

"We have two options," Miguel said. "I can teach you the next major tool of the shaman, the journey to the upper world. Or we can try hypnotic regression to investigate the significance of your dream," Miguel said.

"What do you suggest?" Alex asked, brow furrowed in a question.

"The purpose of a journey to the upper world is to seek a teacher. The journey should serve to further increase your power. I think that would be the best choice for the next step. Then we will work with regression."

"Let's get started then," Alex said with a firm nod. "What do we need?"

"You'll need a comfortable place to lie down and something to cover your eyes," Miguel said. "It's best to have the room dark."

"I still feel concerned," Erik asked.

"This is no different than the nightly journey the spirit takes during sleep. We die each night, but the breath calls the spirit back to finish its task in this dimension," don Miguel said gently.

"Can I help her?" Erik asked.

"I can't promise success, but if you lie next to her while she journeys you may get impressions. I have no objection if Alex doesn't," Miguel said.

"I like the idea," Alex said.

"The preparations are basically the same as for the lower world. I brought a recorder instead of my drum. Do you have earphones?" Miguel asked.

"Yes, and another set of earphones with an adaptor so Erik can listen too."

"Good. That will help him concentrate," Miguel said. "As you know this physical dimension seems solid but is formed of atoms separated by immense distances. Solidity is an illusion and shamans believe the other worlds are as real as this one. You must respect that to work in the other realms.

"Choose a place from which to ascend; preferably a high place like a mountain," Miguel continued. "As with your journey to the lower world, it must be a place you know in this reality. Select a place that special meaning. This will be the doorway between the dimensions and will aid your return."

"I know just the spot," Alex said.

# CHAPTER 24

# UPPER WORLD

Carrying a sleeping bag into the library Alex spread it out on the floor in front of the love seat where Miguel and Erik sat. They looked like night and day to her. Erik's blond Scandinavian looks, and Miguel's dark and mysterious Maya features formed a striking contrast.

She tossed pillows and a blanket on top of the sleeping bag and procured scarves to cover their eyes. Kicking off her shoes, she removed her necklace and earrings and placed them in a dish on the coffee table.

"I'm ready," she said.

"Please sit down first while I explain the technique for reaching the upper world," Miguel said. "You went through a pool of water to reach the lower world, which is the home of the feeling nature where healing occurs.

"To reach the upper world you must pierce a barrier that surrounds the outer layer of Earth itself. This barrier is like a membrane that separates the dimensions of the middle world of ordinary awareness from the upper world, which is the mental realm of thoughts and ideas.

"State your purpose mentally as you begin this process. Have you selected a place to ascend?" Miguel said, leaning back in his chair.

"Yes," she said.

Alex had picked a spot in a national park where she had ventured off the footpath one day. Following where her curiosity led, she had been rewarded with a primordial grove of elderly pines. The old trees grew in a circle and formed a sacred space whose center was a fragrant carpet of pine needles.

Streaks of light danced through evergreen boughs as they swayed in a soft breeze. She knelt on the ground and scooped up a handful of brown needles, watching them float back to earth through her opened fingers.

A boulder stood at the heart of the circle like a stone altar in a green cathedral. The large rock was surrounded by a random configuration of smaller stones and pebbles that had tumbled down the mountain ages ago before the trees grew around them. The roots of the ancient trees grew deep inside the earth, finding strength and sustenance, and the branches climbed toward the Sun in search of illumination.

"Once you can picture yourself in the place you've chosen, imagine smoke rising in the air, as if from a fire," don Miguel continued.

"See yourself rising on a current of air. The smoke, or mist, helps your visualization. Feel yourself becoming weightless. As you lift off the ground, mentally accelerate—then fly," he said.

Alex and Erik lay next to each other on the sleeping bag and covered themselves with the blanket. They connected the earphones and plugged in the player. The final step was to cover their eyes.

"Raise your hand when you want me to begin the drumming recording," Miguel said.

When she felt ready, she squeezed Erik's hand and lifted her fingers to signal don Miguel. She heard the primal, driving beat of the drum pounding in her ears. The sound seemed to come from inside her head and fill the whole world. Her body grew relaxed and heavy. Then her awareness shifted, and she no longer felt her body.

Visualizing the grove of pines, she entered the circle in her mind's eyes. Alex visualized herself walking into her magical green circle and felt the presence of the trees like conscious beings. She climbed onto the rock altar, spread her arms wide and mentally signaled Dolphin, who appeared in moments.

Dolphin swam through the air, moving downward in graceful measure coming to rest beside her. As she had been taught, Alex imagined smoke that began as a swirling mist. White plumes circled around her. She willed the smoke to spin faster and rise into the sky until she was surrounded by a whirling white column.

She rose into the air, spinning slowly at first. Alexandria raised her arms above her head like a diver. She gained momentum as she felt a release from gravity. Dolphin was beside right her. She felt the exhilaration of flight, speed, and freedom.

Ahead of her was the membrane Miguel had described that separated the middle world from the upper world.  Pointing her arms, she aimed and pierced the barrier.  Suddenly, she moved through space.  Blackness, bejeweled with myriad, sparkling stars surrounded her.  She looked down and saw Earth, big and blue beneath her, and nearly panicked.

"Dolphin!  I'm going to fall."

She jerked around and was relieved to see Dolphin right beside her. Dolphin swam in a circle and came underneath.

"You will go where your mind directs but ride on me for a while."

~

# CHAPTER 25
# SLEIGH RIDE

Alex clung to Dolphin like a vise clamp, fingers digging into her pliant skin. Dolphin made a clicking sound that resembled a chuckle. Relieved to be on Dolphin's back, Alexandria felt drawn in a specific direction.

"That way," Alex said, pointing to the right. Dolphin moved so fast the stars looked like strings of light flowing past them. They traveled so far Alex thought they must be at the edge of the galaxy, perhaps the end of the universe. She fought a rising fear that she might never return to ordinary consciousness.

"Breathe, child."

Alexandria exhaled like air expelled from a balloon.

"What was your intention, Alexandria?" Dolphin asked telepathically.

"To learn the reason for recent events. To understand my purpose."

Alex tried to calm herself. She imagined her mind as a still mountain lake, perfectly reflecting the image of a snow-capped mountain. She deepened her breathing and willed the desire for knowledge of her purpose to permeate her being.

*I am safe. All is well.*

She saw a green planet about the size of earth. Dolphin slowed her speed and reoriented her position. They closed in on the lovely green-and-white orb, descending through the planet's atmosphere into clouds. They floated through solid whiteness until Dolphin landed in a snow-covered field.

Crystal flakes fell softly, but the distant skylines were cloudless. An orange sun, three times the size of Earth's, hovered near one horizon, looking like an enormous half circle. Fading golden-yellow and pink light illumined the horizon around the sinking solar orb.

Skeletal winter trees looked like black sea fans against the pastel backdrop. Two full moons, one blue, the other starkly white, rose in the sky on the opposite horizon from the mammoth sun.

Alex leaped from Dolphin's back, suddenly overcome with the desire to make a snow angel. She fell on her back in the field, arms spread wide. Moving her arms up and down and her legs back and forth, she squealed with delight. Dolphin made a circle around her and pushed up a big ball of wet snow with her snout.

Alex squealed, "I don't feel cold! Let's build a snow dolphin."

Dolphin whistled and pushed up mounds of snow. Alex sculpted what she thought was a masterpiece. Dolphin rolled over in the powdery white snow amidst a cacophony of clicks and whistles. Alex scooped up a handful of snow and took a mouthful. It tasted cold and pure, like ice from a mountain stream.

"I haven't eaten snow in thirty years,"

"That's a pity, dear. You're too young to be so old," chimed the kind voice in Alex's thoughts.

Alex was startled by movement at a distance. Something advanced toward them across the meadow, and she thought she heard tinkling bells. Out of the gathering darkness Alex could barely make out a grand sleigh pulled by the largest white stallion she had ever seen. He appeared to be ten-feet tall from head to hoof.

The proud steed and his alabaster sleigh stopped in front of them. The stallion whinnied in a loud voice and tossed his silvery mane. Steam jetted out of his nostrils and filled the air around his head.

Without hesitation Alex climbed into the sleigh. Dolphin was already in motion, gliding along the top of the frosty surface like an aquatic snow mobile. Alex covered herself with a thick rose-colored blanket and brushed her hand across its exquisite softness. Snowflakes felt wet on her face, but the air was not cold.

The magnificent horse turned the sled, whinnied, and raced across the field. Alex felt her hair blowing in the wind. Her breath made white wisps when she exhaled, but she felt snug inside the soft blanket. The sun was no longer visible, just a lingering golden-orange light beneath the receding cloud cover at the edge of the horizon. Twin full moons cast their light on the field, transforming the snow into a kaleidoscope of iridescent crystals.

They approached a chain of hills, and Alex noticed lights in the direction the sleigh was headed. Fixing her gaze on the source of the lights she saw a colossal white castle built into the side of a mountain. Triangular flags flew from numerous tall turrets and spires. Bright moonlight reflected off the castle, turning the stone to a shining fortress of abalone. The inviting scent of burning wood reached her nostrils.

The stallion slowed his pace to a high-stepping trot, kicking up a flurry of snow. He stopped in front of a cave-like opening at the foot of the castle mountain. The white horse bobbed his powerful head and neighed, and the sleigh trembled.

"Thank you for a thrilling ride," Alex said, jumping to the ground.

She curtsied instinctively. The great horse snorted, reared on his hind legs, and galloped off.

# CHAPTER 26

# THEA & DREAM WALKER

lex shook her head in wonder. She entered the opening in the side of the hill where Dolphin waited inside in a warm dry cavern. Rock walls emitted an unseen source of light. A seat, resembling a wooden porch swing, hung from a rock ceiling at the rear of the chamber.

A flax-colored robe with a large hood and deep pockets lay on the seat. Comfortable-looking boots of soft honey-colored material like fine-tooled leather lay beside the robe. Alex removed her wet outer clothes, slipped the robe over her head, and sat on the swing. She kicked off her shoes and pulled on the cozy slippers.

"I feel like Goldilocks."

Dolphin clicked, a merry sound, then leaped onto the swing, sprawling her huge body across Alex's lap. The swing rocked precariously, and Dolphin squealed and clicked in what was unmistakably laughter. Alex giggled like a child.

The swing jerked like a Ferris Wheel seat and shot straight up inside the cavern. Alex thought they'd been fired from a rocket and was certain they would crash into the roof of the cavern overhead. Suddenly, the strange craft came to rest with a thud in a wide chamber with a white-marble floor.

At the end of a long corridor of the same white marble a doorway stood ajar. Dazzling light escaped into the hall. Alex walked the length of the corridor with Dolphin gliding beside her. The wooden door was twelve-feet high, six-feet across and as thick as the length of her hand. A copper door ring, larger than her head, hung at eye level.  She stood at the partially opened doorway, heart pounding and legs shaking.  For the second time in her life, she thought she might faint.

"I'm afraid, Dolphin."

"Remember to breathe, Alexandria," Dolphin signaled mentally.

Alex recalled the brave priestess from her dream and breathed the same way.  Reluctantly, her pounding heart slowed. She pushed the door open wider and peeked inside.  A fire roared and crackled in a monstrous stone fireplace, reaching twenty feet from floor to ceiling.  Dancing firelight was reflected in scores of diamond-shaped windowpanes.

She entered the room and gasped at the sight of two luminous beings seated on enormous carved-wooden thrones.  Here was the majestic purple-clad lady from her childhood dreams.  The magnificent goddess was seven-feet tall and radiated awesome power.

Shocking violet eyes that were full of compassion peered from a face the color of Russian amber.  Her purple-velvet gown was trimmed in silver brocade, and she wore a double strand of large pearls with a rectangular amethyst at her throat.  A piece of rose quartz rested over her heart, and a white crystal was set into her waist band.

The lady wore a splendid coronet of silver filigree worked to look like lilies.  The crown was studded with diamonds, pearls, amethyst, and topaz.  Eight silver points, surmounted by pearls the size of acorns, rose from the ornate band.  A large Alexandrite was positioned in the center of her brow.  Long curls of pewter-colored hair swept up through the silver crown, cascading down her shoulders like a fountain.

In her right hand the goddess grasped the sword.  Alex remembered its weight and felt the force of the blow that had severed the raven's head.  The glinting steel blade issued from the mouth of a gold dragon with blood-red ruby eyes. The hilt of the sword rested on the arm of the lady's throne.

Next to the magnificent goddess sat a Titan.  Silvery-white braids, woven with pieces of leather, beads and feathers hung to his waist on either side of a snow-white beard.  A silver diadem circled his head, which contained a large white crystal that rested at the center of his brow.

His reddish skin, hawk-like nose, and high cheekbones contrasted dramat-ically with electric ice-blue eyes, shining from an ageless face.  The giant wore a tunic and pants of supple white buckskin.  A beautiful turquoise necklace was barely visible beneath his long, silver beard.

A colossal red lion, with a three-foot mane, sat between the wondrous beings.  The crimson beast stared at Alex and Dolphin as if poised to pounce, and Alex reminded herself to breathe.

"Greetings, Dolphin," Lion said in a booming baritone.  "You are always welcome here."

"Well met old friend," Dolphin replied mentally.

~

THE WOMAN SMILED.  "I AM THEA," she said, in a voice like wind through a canyon.  Turning to the man, she said, "This is Dream Walker.  We have waited a long time for you, Priestess of Atlantis."

Alex sensed that nothing could be hidden from these beings, and she felt her soul laid bare in their presence. "I have come," she replied simply.

"It is well," Dream Walker said, in a kind voice like a babbling brook in spring.  "Kneel candidate and receive the initiation of the Third Eye."

Alexandria knelt on the floor and Dolphin floated beside her.  Thea rose and her towering presence filled the room.  She placed a hand on the top of Alexandria's head and raised the sword on high.  When she spoke, her voice encompassed Alex's awareness.

> *Time grows short and the hour approaches.*
> *A call to arms for the Spiritual Warrior.*
> *The day of reckoning is upon us.*
>
> *Be not faint of heart.*
> *Fail not in your duty.*
> *Fear not the darkness.*
>
> *Your sword is wisdom.*
> *Your shield is love.*
> *Your armor is truth.*
>
> *Be valiant, Server of the Light.*
> *Yours could be the heart that tips the balance.*
> *Yours the choice that saves the world.*
>
> *Choose Love.*
> *Choose Truth.*
> *Choose Power.*

In the potent silence that followed Thea touched the hilt of her sword to Alexandria's forehead. Light exploded inside her head as billions of particles from the shattered obstructions of her mistaken beliefs and outworn habits were blown to the far reaches of space. Only brilliant light remained.

"Rise," Thea said.

"The time has come to reclaim your power, Alexandria. You can no longer afford the luxury of the curious seeker. You must be about your business."

"What is my business? I came here to learn my purpose."

The goddess replied in a booming voice that rattled the windowpanes, and the world seem to shake to its foundation. Alex raised her hands and covered her ears.

*Remember what was forgotten.*
*Unearth what was buried.*
*Shatter long-held falsehoods.*
*Vanquish an ancient enemy.*
*Rejoice at finding what you feared was lost forever.*

Inexplicable tears of recognition that seemed to originate from an exhaustless spring of grace and healing flowed down Alexandria's cheeks .

Dream Walker spoke in a gentle but powerful voice. "An old enemy stalks you. He is alive again seeking false power. He has not learned his lesson and still he lusts for power. He does not know the source of his obsession and does not remember his prior bond with you. He knows the knowledge he seeks and will stop at nothing to obtain it. He is not alone, and there are others who have also returned to play out their roles in this ages-old drama. These players on the stage will be revealed as once again the legions of darkness mount their attack on the forces of light.

"Know that you and your companions belong to a larger group of servers, each having a part to play," Thea said, "you already possess the key to open the necessary door, but you have yet to find the lock. Do not give in to fear. You will need courage, but you are supported. Align yourself with the angelic realms. We cannot intervene unless we are invoked.

"The time has come for the portals between the worlds to reopen. Many who lived before will respond to their own remembrances, and you will assist them in reclaiming their history and inheritance. This is your purpose, a millennial promise about to be fulfilled. You have been reunited with others who share this destiny," Dream Walker said.

As he spoke a vision flashed through Alexandria's mind of the Great Pyramid. She saw hieroglyphics and understood their message. Inside a chamber she saw a vessel that looked like the Arc of the Covenant. In her hand she held a silver key that would unlock the mysterious container. Somehow, she knew the contents were protected by an electromagnetic field and only one who resonated with the exact frequency could enter. The hieroglyphics held the secret.

"I have a gift for you," Dream Walker continued. "Open your hand."

Alexandria did as she was instructed, and Dream Walker placed three stones in her palm. They looked like green peas made of jade. She stared at them.

"What an unusual color," she said.

"These small orbs are ancient," Dream Walker said. "They belonged to you in a distant epoch. Make them into a ring for your right hand. These stones will evoke memories, and the ring will be a strong talisman. Three green orbs, one for each member of your quest."

"Thank you, Dream Walker, and my deepest gratitude to you, Thea. Your presence has always made a difference in my life. I will draw comfort from the knowledge of your existence here and my ability to contact you.

"I will do whatever is necessary to accomplish this quest. I vow to be worthy of your trust," Alex said in a strong voice.

"Farewell, Alexandria," Thea said. Her unlikely coloring made her exquisitely beautiful, like a rare flower.

"Remember your warrior nature," Dream Walker said. His blue eyes looked like flames. "Call upon that focus of will and summon the fire in your belly. You will find the answers to everything you seek within you."

He handed her a small woven pouch on a cord. "Keep the stones in here, close to your heart, until the ring is ready."

"Come onto the terrace, Child," Dolphin said mentally.

Alex followed her outside where a black swan, ten times ordinary size, sat on the large balcony. A seat was fastened around her, and a rope ladder hung from the seat to the floor of the balcony. Alex climbed up the ladder and into the seat. Her dry, folded clothes lay beside her. She pulled the ladder up and inside the seat.

Swan gracefully lifted off the balcony, revealing a wingspan of thirty feet. As soon as they were airborne the swan picked up speed. Dolphin sailed alongside as stars blurred into bright streams of light. When Swan slowed, beautiful, blue Earth came into view.

"This is your stop, dear," Dolphin signaled. You must go back through on your own power, but I'll be with you."

Alex took off the comfortable robe and boots and put on her own clothing, being careful to place the pouch next to her heart. She stood at the edge of the seat, looking down at earth. Feeling a new strength, she dove out of the seat as if from a diving board.

"Concentrate on your destination," Dolphin said. "Picture yourself landing gently on the rock and you will control your speed and direction."

Alex felt the penetration of the membrane like diving through a waterfall. She entered Earth's atmosphere and approached the surface. As she closed in on the circle of evergreens, she slowed her speed and turned around to descend feet first, coasting to a standing stop on the rock altar.

Dolphin clicked. "Well done, Alexandria. Until next time."

Alex felt exhilarated. She threw her arms around the wonderful sea creature. "Thank you for everything."

Alex became aware as the tempo of the drums changed, signaling her return to ordinary awareness. She jumped from the rock and walked out of the circle of conifers. Alex was aware of lying on the floor and felt the sleeping bag around her. After a few more moments the drumming in her ears stopped. She lay motionless on the floor, unwilling to move. She felt Erik stir and sit up beside her.

"Are you okay?" he asked softly.

She nodded and pulled the scarf from her eyes, blinking. Erik and Miguel stared at her. Reluctantly, she sat up. Her body felt heavy, but her mind was on fire. She touched the place where the pouch had been, feeling silly to expect the jade beads to be there. Still, she felt a painful loss.

"I don't know where to begin," she said. "I feel as if I was gone a week instead of an hour. I feel so emotional and need some time to think," Alex said.

"It's important to process the experience. You won't forget anything," Miguel said. "Now seems like the right time to give you something I brought with me."

Don Miguel reached into his shirt pocket and pulled out a small, woven pouch. He handed it to Alexandria, who had stopped breathing. Her hand shook visibly as she accepted the small bag.  She exhaled and opened the draw string, pouring the jade beads into her hand. Alex touched the bright-green stones with a sense of disbelief.

"I can hardly believe they're real."

Erik looked puzzled.

"These ancient stones were found at Palenque.  The color of the jade is quite rare," Miguel said and put his arm around her shoulder.  "These beads have been in my family for generations, but I believe they belonged to you in another life.  When I saw your handiwork of the Cross of Palenque, I realized they should be yours.  I hope this gift will replace the necklace you gave to Chan Ka," Miguel said.

"I was given these beads in my journey," she said, looking at Erik.

A torrent of pent-up feeling exploded from a place deep within her.  The sudden emotion shattered the well of unshed tears still dammed up inside the broken heart of a twelve-year-old girl.  That young heart had mended enough to function but had never mourned the loss the child endured.

Alexandria wept while Erik embraced her.  She allowed herself to be comforted and to accept the release of her long-buried grief.  She suffered the tears to flow and permitted the aching sobs to cleanse her spirit. Erik's arms felt strong and safe, and the smell of his skin soothed her.  Alex didn't even resist when he stroked her hair.  She clutched the priceless heirlooms tight in her fist, vowing never to be separated from them or the two people they represented.  She wasn't alone anymore.

When Alex recovered her equilibrium, she stared at the wonderful contrasting men in her life. Ebony eyes radiated warmth and affection. Steel-gray eyes emanated concern and protectiveness.

"Had enough for one day?" Miguel asked.

"I certainly have," Erik said.  His face was drawn with concern.

"Thank you, Miguel. Alex rubbed her nose on her sleeve and used the shirttail of her blouse to wipe beneath her eyes.  She felt a little dizzy.

"I'll walk upstairs with you," she sniffed.  "There's a heart-shaped locket in my room that belonged to Gran.  I want to put these stones inside the locket until I can make a ring.

CHAPTER 27

# ROMANCE

Miguel and Erik followed Alexandria up the spiral staircase where four large bedrooms occupied the second story of the Victorian house. Miguel's room, decorated in Wedgwood blue with peach accents, was at the end of the hall next to green-and-rose room where Erik stayed.

"I didn't realize you had an upstairs room," he said, looking at Alex.

"I moved downstairs after my father died. This is Gran and Grandpa's room," Alex said, changing the subject.

Rose and Duncan's room was across the hall from Miguel's. A deep-turquoise and white color scheme imparted a distinct flair. Tiny white roses dotted the fabric of the curtains and chairs, and a priceless, walnut four-poster bed stood between two leaded-glass windows.

"Grandpa called Gran his bride for the forty years of their marriage," Alex said smiling. "He said she was the most pure and beautiful creature he had ever known, a perfect white rose, and always kept fragrant reminders of her namesake in their room."

"That's beautiful," Erik said, staring into their room.

"Buenas noches," Miguel said as he approached his door. As he turned to enter the room he laughed out loud. He motioned for Alex and Erik to join him in the doorway. Crystal was curled up on the carpet beside the bed. She opened one eye but showed no sign of moving. Sheba was sprawled across Miguel's bed like Cleopatra on her barge. She glanced up, then turned away.

Erik guffawed, "You're no one until you've been ignored by a cat."

"Apparently I won't be sleeping alone tonight," Miguel chuckled. "I'm a lonely old man," he said in mock anguish, "and I welcome feminine companionship."

Hand over heart and acting stricken, Erik backed from the room. Alex shook her head, rolled her eyes, and walked toward her childhood bedroom. The lavender room was a girl's dream and looked as if it had plucked from the pages of a fairy tale. Gran had created the fantasy bedroom in shades of purple for her only grandchild when Alex was three-years old.

A white canopy bed framed against a deep-violet carpet was the centerpiece. Matching white dressers, desk and shelves lined the lavender walls. A white cedar hope chest stood at the end of the bed, and a magical seat was built into a large bay window overlooking the garden. Alex had spent countless childhood hours stretched out on the curved window seat, gazing at the stars.

Shelves were crammed with dolls, yearbooks, mementos, and photographs of young Alex with her parents. Thumbtacks held curled and yellowed pages of Alex's childish artwork on a bulletin board.

Erik picked up a pink satin jewelry box and opened the lid. A tiny ballerina popped up inside. He wound the key on the side and set the music box back on the dresser. The dancer twirled as the little box played Skater's Waltz.

"My sister had one of these," he said.

Alex looked at him. "That was a birthday present the year I turned twelve. A cultured pearl necklace was tucked inside. Grandpa told me how pearls were formed and said we should be thankful for our imperfections because overcoming them strengthens and improves our value like precious gems." She smiled. "I was thrilled. My birthday is December 18th. My family always tried to make it special since it's so close to Christmas. Within months Dad died and my world changed forever."

He frowned. "Mine is January 1st and was always lost in a haze of Christmas and New Year celebrations. Birthday memories are mostly of adults with hangovers. Erik looked in her eyes. "My father actually died of alcoholism, and I don't think my mother has ever recovered."

"How sad," Alex said. "Are you close to her?"

"Let's just say we look at things differently."

"We that have in common too. We'll start a new tradition this year and celebrate for two weeks," Alex said.

Erik looked thoughtful.

She opened drawers and looked inside boxes. "Thank heavens, I found it," she said, removing an antique, heart-shaped locket and silver chain from a black velvet box.

Alex sat on the window seat and removed the pouch from her blouse pocket. She opened the locket, placing the necklace beside her. Pulling the pouch apart, she carefully poured the jade beads into the locket.

"Perfect," she said, relieved. "Will you help me with the clasp?"

He joined her at the window. The padded upholstery seat circled the inside of the turreted bay window, and a circular purple carpet covered the hardwood floor. A round white table stood at the center of the large turret, and frilly white-lace curtains, tied with lavender sashes, draped across the windows.

Alex handed him the necklace and turned around, so her back was toward him. He kissed her neck, and his breath felt warm. She gasped in surprise and shivered as goose bumps spread over her skin. Erik lifted the necklace over her head and fastened the clasp. Alex put both hands around the heart-shaped locket. *What an incredible gift these jade beads are.* It seemed fated, predestined. She stared out the window into a clear night sky. A silver crescent moon hung against a starry background.

"I always expected Peter Pan to show up here," Alex said, grabbing a white stuffed bear and hugging it to her chest. "I always felt like a child in this room and needed to leave to grow up."

She looked up at him, wanting to touch his face and run her fingers through his blond hair. She needed to feel his arms around her. Erik removed the white bear from her grasp, depositing the stuffed toy on the window seat. He took her hands and pulled her to her feet.

"I believe it's time to bring some grownup passion into this little girl's room," he said, tilting her chin up.

She regarded those mesmerizing gray eyes, and her own eyes gave assent. They kissed, and his lips were moist and she loved the smell of his breath. Erik's strong arms circled her waist and pulled her close. She put her arms around his neck.

He loosened his grip, took her hand, and led her toward the canopy bed. He sat on the white bedspread and held both her hands. Erik took an unhurried look at her from her hair to her feet. He pulled her close and dropped her hands. She sensed that he intended to undress her, and the idea inflamed her.

He opened her blouse like a Christmas present. Every place his hands touched felt hot. When all the buttons were unfastened, he pulled the blouse off her shoulders and down her arms. The blouse fell silently to the floor, and the fabric pooled at her feet.

Erik pulled her close so that she stood between his legs. He unclasped and removed her bra. She felt aroused and vulnerable simultaneously. Alexandria shuddered with the intensity of the sensation that was both pleasure and anticipation.

He sat back and looked at her. "You are so beautiful," he said, his voice husky. "Let your hair down."

She unfastened the barrette that contained her mass of long hair, and red curls cascaded onto her shoulders. While he watched, she removed her jeans. He pulled her on top of him. Hungry mouths shared kisses. He rolled her over on her side and unceremoniously removed his own clothes.

Alex remembered the beautiful body she had first noticed in Mexico. His waist was narrow, and a generous amount of hair covered his broad chest. She thought she would ignite from the fire inside her, and the pressure was unbearable. He climbed back on the bed and lay next to her. They kissed and eagerly explored each other's bodies with their hands. They rolled, limbs tangled together, craving everything now.

"You feel wonderful," Erik whispered.

They moved together in perfect rhythm until their pace increased and they exploded together like a shooting star. They collapsed breathless on the bed and clung to each other in a silent embrace. He moved to her side, and they lay on their backs holding hands, bodies touching from foot to shoulder. Erik turned his head and looked at her. Profound openness showed in his gray eyes. Shields had been torn away by intimacy, and Alex knew that vulnerable look was in her eyes too. She longed to feel this close forever.

"You're a lot different to take to bed than my bear," she sighed, feeling content. "Hotter, for one thing."

"And you're a lot different to take to bed than my baseball glove," he laughed. His face grew serious. "I've looked for you a long time, Alexandria Stuart. Don't get any ideas about wandering off."

She nestled close to him and rested her head on his shoulder. She kissed his neck for emphasis. "You'd just find me."

"Roll over," he said, turning so her back faced him. He put his arm around her waist and held her close.

"I'm glad we waited."

Erik kissed her shoulder.

She sighed. "Miguel is in Dad's childhood room. When he reached his teens, he moved downstairs because he liked the independence. After he died

I felt closer to him somehow when I slept downstairs. Gran understood, but she kept the lavender room. I think she always hoped I'd move back upstairs, especially after Grandpa died."

He held her and let her talk. Alexandria fell asleep feeling safe and protected for the first time since her father's death. She knew he would still be there in the morning, and the realization filled her with a sense of peace she hadn't felt in a long time.

$$\sim$$

ALEX WOKE as early morning light filtered in the bay window from the garden, making the windowpanes sparkle. For a moment, she was transported to her childhood. She recalled blissful summer mornings when she slept in this room while visiting her grandparents. She looked around the room at photographs, dolls, blue ribbons and drawings, reflections of her past.

She knew she would no longer be alone, and that whatever they would have to face in their quest, they would do it together with the added strength and wisdom of Miguel.

Erik lay sleeping beside her. His boyish, blond hair was tousled and begged to be touched. She cuddled up next to his warmth, touching his body with hers wherever possible. Every point of contact felt like an electric charge. Memory of last night's lovemaking reawakened her desire, and she closed her eyes and imagined.

Alex drifted back to sleep and was awakened later by the exquisite sensation of Erik kissing her neck. She moaned with pleasure and opened her eyes. He pretended not to notice and continued to gently kiss her ear and neck.

"I want to make love with you again," he whispered, "slowly this time."

"We should go downstairs, it must be nine o'clock already," Alex said, struggling to concentrate while he continued kissing her. A few moments later she couldn't remember her objection. She surrendered to the urge to kiss him, to touch his firm muscles and smell his skin. For the moment nothing else mattered.

CHAPTER 28
# MUSIC

Showered and dressed in yesterday's clothes, Alex and Erik descended the spiral stairs. She was apprehensive about facing Miguel, but the voice she heard in the kitchen eclipsed that concern.

"Good morning, Alexandria," Blanche Stuart said, in a voice as stinging as dry ice. Her mother stood next to Emma at the kitchen sink. Her blond hair was brushed into a French twist that accentuated her aquiline features. Sporty coral slacks and matching top coordinated with white-and-coral jewelry.

"I understand you slept in your old room." Blanche said, brushing her hand over her head, smoothing stray strands of blond hair. "Rose would be pleased."

She didn't look at her daughter when she spoke, for which Alexandria was grateful. Alex turned a shade of red ordinarily reserved for fire engines.

"Good morning, Mrs. Stuart," Erik beamed, "what a pleasant surprise. I'm delighted to meet you." Erik's charming demeanor didn't help Alex's embarrassment. Crystal barked, sensing the tension.

Miguel pretended to be absorbed in the newspaper. Sheba, proclaiming mistreatment in pitiful meows, approached, and rubbed his legs.

"Pay no attention to her highness," Emma laughed, whisking gray hairs from her face with a soapy hand. "She's been fed." Emma turned back to the sink, sloshing dishes through soapy water.

"Coffee?" Erik asked. Alex tried to become invisible in one of the chairs at the big table and lifted her mug in response. Miguel looked dapper in a blue Madras shirt. His salt-and-pepper hair was neatly combed. He folded his newspaper and directed an appraising look at the couple. Inscrutable black eyes sparkled like shards of obsidian.

"Emma is up to her usual standards and the apple pancakes are positively decadent," he said, handing the platter to Erik.

"I'm ravenous," Erik smiled, patting his stomach.

"Did you sleep well?" Miguel inquired.

"Like an innocent babe," he replied, flashing his best boyish grin. "Must be the cool nights."

"What happens on hot nights?" Blanche asked.

Alex wanted to glare and respond but decided to ignore her mother instead. She accepted the pancake platter and riveted her attention on her plate. She felt as if a scarlet letter A was emblazoned on her forehead and an invisible megaphone, proclaiming, "I slept with Erik."

"I also had a marvelous rest," Miguel said. "As content as if my beloved Sophia were still alive and by my side. There's a lot of love in this wonderful old house. Of course, I did have two beautiful female companions in my room," Miguel said dryly.

Blanche flashed him an indignant look.

Emma laughed out loud. Alex looked at Miguel after he'd delivered his barb and might have been able to keep a straight face if she hadn't seen her mother's expression.

"It's nothing to worry about, Mrs. Stuart," Erik said. "Crystal and Sheba chose to abandon their regular sleeping partners to be with don Miguel. There was no impropriety, and I was only a little jealous," he explained in his most appealing tone.

Blanche had the good sense to realize she'd been out maneuvered, and the air was cleared.

"Do you feel ready to try regression, Alex?" Miguel asked. "You had a remarkable journey yesterday, but this process should not be rushed."

Alex was relieved to focus on something else. "Yes, let's not waste time." She lifted the silver locket from her shirt and looked at Miguel.

"These beads give me a sense of destiny, as if there's a larger purpose to our meeting, and I'm ready to know what it is. Alex smiled, "These pieces of jade remind me of peas; three peas in a pod. Can you imagine a more unlikely trio than us?"

Miguel chortled. "There is a similar expression in Spanish, *'parecerse como dos gotas de agua,'* like two drops of water. We are the three drips," he chuckled. "Forgive me, I've amused myself.

"As we're proving, there are no coincidences," Miguel said. "Peas that grow within the same pod have a close relationship but drops of water partake of a larger reality. When you place those drops into the same container they merge."

He lifted a spoonful of coffee from his mug and allowed some of the liquid to flow back into the cup. "It's a deeper metaphor for our spiritual relationship."

"I like that," Alex said smiling. "Three drips it is."

"Like water off a duck's back. I always go with the flow. How about three drips in the fountain?" Erik quipped.

Alex pretended to glare and Miguel scowled, but his dark eyes twinkled.

"I've never been hypnotized," Alex said, furrowing her brow.

Blanche huffed and stood to get more coffee. "And now does not seem like a good time to start. I don't like it. What are your credentials Mr. Piedra?"

"Will she prance around the room like a poodle and beg for dog biscuits?" Erik chimed in, gray eyes twinkling with mischief under raised eyebrows. He petted Sheba, who had reclaimed her territory in his lap. His other hand grasped his coffee mug aloft between gulps.

"A trained pet would be a welcome contrast to that cat," Blanche sniffed.

"I appreciate your concern Mother, but this is my decision, but her eyes widened as the implication of Erik's question registered. Miguel leaned his head back and laughed.

"My apologies" he said, "I admit that is an amusing image, but frivolity is for charlatans. Even in Mexico we have PhDs, Mrs. Stuart."

"Very well," she said, "but you know my feelings." Blanche turned and left the room.

"Yes, you've been very clear," Alex said.

Miguel placed his hand on top of Alex's. His presence radiated a quiet power his casual clothes could not mask, and his confidence reassured her. "We'll work with a technique called hypnotic regression. It's an effective means of remembering forgotten incidents or dreams."

"There's nothing mysterious or frightening about hypnosis," Miguel said, smiling. "It's a state of focused concentration. Your body relaxes, your mind concentrates, and your memory comes into clear focus."

Alex was reassured by his kind, honest eyes. She trusted him and felt herself relax.

"The subconscious mind stores our experiences in photographic detail,"

Miguel continued. "People can return to the scene of a crime while in a hypnotic trance and recall the license number of a fleeing car. They may have no conscious memory of seeing the license number, but they see the numbers or letters clearly while hypnotized.

"I didn't realize that" Erik said. "That sort of information could be useful to an attorney."

"Regression data has been admitted as evidence in some legal cases," Miguel said. "I'd like to record the session if you don't mind," he said, looking at Alex.

"I think that's a good idea. Okay, I'm ready. Let's work in the living room," Alex replied. "The electronic stuff is there, and the couch is bigger."

Alex carried her dishes to the sink. "Can we get started?" she asked. "I don't want any more time to think about it."

"Certainly," Miguel said, standing.

"Enjoy your games, boys and girls," Blanche said as they left the kitchen.

Alex emitted a muffled sound like a growl. *She never quits. It breaks my heart because she wasn't always like this.*

THE LIVING ROOM beckoned like a French country cottage. Morning sunlight flashed a beam of radiance onto a white, baby grand piano. A white-brick fireplace anchored the corner of the room next to the piano. A colorful still life hung above the mantel. The setting for this journey was a stark contrast to her experience in Mexico.

Huge sunflowers burst from a blue-and-white ceramic vase. Juicy-looking peaches, apples, and cherries, piled in a hammered, copper bowl, begged to be picked from the canvas. A couch of generous length with numerous pillows faced the fireplace. Blue-and-yellow floral print fabric covered the couch and comfortable chairs and ottomans that stood on either side. A white, crocheted Afghan was folded on an arm of the couch.

Floor-to-ceiling windows were covered by blue tie-back curtains with valences, and sheer white curtains hung over the windows beneath. One wall was devoted to electronics and an elaborate stereo system. Shelves of videos, DVDs, and audio tapes, along with a collection of phonograph records, surrounded the electronic equipment.

An antique phonograph player stood next to the shelves. The beautiful piece of oak furniture still played 78 RPM records, and a valuable collection of the old black disks was carefully stored in a wooden box on the bottom shelf.

"Glenn Miller, Tommy Dorsey Mario Lanza. I could spend a week listening to these," Erik said, delicately examining the black disks.

"Before your time, aren't they Erik?" Miguel asked.

"I love the music from this era."

"What a charming room," Miguel said, turning around and taking it in, "so different from the library but equally inviting."

Erik glanced at Alex as he slid onto the piano bench. "Do you mind? This is an exquisite instrument." He lifted the keyboard cover and played a few chords, running his fingers over the keys creating a harmonic background.

"You play the piano?" Alex asked, stunned. "No one has touched that piano since my father died."

"What a shame," Erik said. "It's still in tune."

Flustered, but trying to concentrate, Alex spoke to Miguel. "We have two recorder options and plenty of blank tapes."

"Perhaps Erik should choose since he'll be overseeing the recording."

Busying herself, and struggling not to imagine her father sitting at the piano, Alex arranged pillows, placing two where her head would be. She kicked off her shoes, plopped on the couch, fluffed, and punched the pillows to get them right, and threw the white Afghan over her legs. Her arms lay across her stomach, on top of the Afghan.

Erik's random chording was gently transformed into the melody of a song. The tune was familiar, but Alex couldn't identify the title.

Miguel looked up and walked toward the piano. "That's a wonderful old song. How about starting over?"

"By all means," Erik said, commencing an introduction that spanned the keyboard with trills and flourishes.

Miguel sang the old song *I'll Be Seeing You* in a pure and vibrant tenor. Erik accompanied him as if they'd rehearsed for days. Alex was transported by the beauty of their music that touched her soul and carried her spirit to a higher realm. They were a constant surprise to her. *Who knew he could play?*

As Miguel's triumphant voice reached the final chorus, a crystal-clear soprano joined in harmony. Blanche's lilting voice provided the perfect counterpoint to Miguel's tenor. Alex sat up in shock and stared at her mother. She hadn't heard her sing since her father had played at their last Christmas together. Blanche stood in the foyer, eyes closed, and chin raised. Her face was transfigured as if enchanted by the music.

Alex was sure that her heart could not contain the joy. A magic spell had been cast. Erik repeated the last verse, and the rich voices raised to a crescendo. The final words were filled with bittersweet emotion. The last notes graced the air like a benediction from sacred temple bells.

Emma stood next to Blanche, crying and clapping, a standing ovation of one. "I've never heard anything so beautiful. You couldn't have known, but that song was a favorite of Duncan and Rose," Emma spoke through tears.

Alex pulled back the Afghan and leaped from the couch. She ran to her mother, throwing her arms around her, "Oh, God, I forgot how much I love to hear you sing."

Miguel approached and took Blanche's hand. "Thank you for joining us. What a joy to sing with you."

Blanche was white and shaking; her eyes were wet. "Alexandria's father was a gifted pianist," she said with difficulty. "This house was filled with music once, perhaps it can be again. Thank you," she said, looking at Erik. Blanche squeezed her daughter's hand and walked back to the kitchen.

"I'm a sight, aren't I?" Emma said, sniffing and pulling a tissue from her apron pocket. "Make no mistake; you worked a miracle today," Emma turned and walked toward the kitchen.

Alex gaped at Miguel. "Emma's right, that was a miracle of major proportions. I could hardly believe the beauty of your duet when I heard my mother's voice. Mother hasn't sung a note since my father died. You two reached inside her and brought the music back."

"Music is healing, Alexandria, and Erik has a magic touch. This magnificent instrument has been silent too long. Your mother's exquisite voice needs to be used, even if it's in an empty room," Miguel said.

"I wish they were all here," Alex said, her voice cracking.

"What makes you think they're not?" Miguel smiled.

"I'm selfish. I want to see their faces and touch them, not just imagine them in some vague hereafter."

"My dear Alexandria, the veil between the seen and unseen worlds is quite thin. Communication between the living and the so-called dead is a natural phenomenon. If you will still your mind and open your heart, you will feel their presence. You've already met them in dreams and have heard your father's voice," Miguel said looking into her eyes.

"You're right," she said, feeling chastised. "And I'm grateful for you and Erik."

# CHAPTER 29

# HYPNOTIC REGRESSION

Alex walked back to the couch and collapsed like a rag doll. "I keep forgetting. I'm sorry to be so self-centered but it all feels like too much. This is proving to be quite a day."

"Are you sure you want to do the regression now?" Erik asked, sounding concerned. He rubbed the spot between his eyebrows as if his head ached.

Crystal's fluffy white form trotted into the living room and settled in front of Alex on the floor. Alex sighed.

"I'm better now that Crystal's here. I'm nervous, and my emotional reserve tank could use some fuel, but I want to do this now. What else could happen?"

"Don't ask," Erik said, pushing blond hair from his forehead.

Miguel sat in a comfortable chair by the fireplace, placed his feet on the ottoman, and positioned tablet and pen on his lap. "I cannot predict if you will be able to access a prior life during the first attempt, Alex. Just relax and we'll see what happens," Miguel said.

Erik put on his glasses and took charge of recording. He pulled up a chair next to the coffee table and readied a small arsenal of blank cassettes and extra batteries.

Alex reached under the afghan and pulled a kerchief from her jeans pocket. She tied it over her eyes and placed her head on the pillows, shifting position until she felt comfortable.

"Close your eyes and breathe easily," Don Miguel said in a soothing voice.

"Don't listen to any sound but my voice.  Pay attention to your breath.  Each time you exhale, feel the tension leave your body.  When you inhale, imagine breathing in peace and serenity.  Know that any exterior sound will only deepen your trance."

"Begin at the top of your head and allow your muscles to relax progressively.  Feel that calming sensation move slowly from your face and neck, down your body to the tips of your toes.  Your whole body feels relaxed and peaceful."

Alex experienced the progressive relaxation and felt herself becoming stone-like, starting at her head and moving down her body.  Her breathing slowed, and her only sensation was heaviness.  She experienced her breath as coolness moving in and out of her nostrils, lulling her into deeper stillness.  Her breath made a soft sound like a tropical breeze.

"Excellent.  You're doing very well.  See yourself enveloped in a warm golden light.  This light makes you feel safe, tranquil, and relaxed.  Let every breath take you into a deeper state of relaxation."

Alex lost the sense of heaviness and her head seemed to float above and separate from the rest of her body.  She felt buoyant, as if she was suspended in salt water.  A fleeting thought passed through her mind that this was better than Nitrous Oxide in the dentist's office.

"I will count backward from ten to one," Don Miguel said, in the same reassuring tone. "With each number you will go deeper.  Concentrate only on my voice.  Ten.  Nine.  Eight."

Alex's body ceased to exist.  She became a faint breath moving in and out in a warm safe place, feeling content to float in this tranquil womb.  Everything slowed and Miguel's voice was as soothing as a bubble bath.

"Three.  Two.  One.  Imagine a place or time in your life where you were supremely happy.  Visualize yourself there.  Continue to relax and breathe."

Alex found it difficult to respond and there was a long silence.

"Can you tell me where you are?" Miguel asked.

"I'm home.  It's Christmas!" she squealed.  "I got a new sled, and Daddy and I are going outside to try it.  It snowed a lot last night, and the hill in the back yard is white.  Gran called it a white Christmas."

"How old are you, Alexandria?"

She paused to consider the answer.  "I'm eight years old."

"Look down at your clothes and shoes.  What are you wearing?"

She looked at her feet, then her legs and arms.

"Mom made me wear leggings and boots that match my coat. I don't like them. They're heavy and hard to walk in.  She made a string for my mittens, so I won't lose them, and she's tying a scarf around my neck because it's cold," Alex said, feeling impatient.

"What is happening now?" Don Miguel encouraged.

"This is fun." Alex giggled in a childlike voice. "I rode down the big hill in the back yard, the one that goes all the way to the fence. I got snow all over me. Daddy laughed and said I looked like an Eskimo. He threw a snowball at me, and some of the snow went down my collar," she laughed. "It made me shiver."

"Stanley's barking at the snow," she giggled again. "I'm going to pull the sled back to the top."

"Alexandria," Miguel said in a kind, firm voice, "go back a little farther. Can you recall your first day at school?"

Alex was quiet for a few moments. She didn't want to leave this scene; she felt so happy. She tried to resist, but her awareness shifted. "I don't like Sister Mary Catherine, she's mean," Alex said crossing her arms and extending her lower lip in a pout.

"What else?" Miguel probed.

"I met two friends today, Sarah and Elizabeth Anne. Sister won't let us talk. Elizabeth Anne says she's got lots of dolls. We walked home from school together. They're nice."

"Good. I'll count to three, and I want you to go even farther back in your memory, to the source of your recent dream. You are calm and completely safe," Miguel said. "Continue to relax and focus on your breath. One. Two. Three."

Miguel's voice sounded far and remote and Alex felt bathed in balmy darkness. She floated in comfort and silence for several minutes, just wanting to drift.

Alex was jarred by a wrenching wave of nausea. Her arms reached for something to steady herself. She gagged and choked, as if vomiting.

"You are safe," Miguel said. "You are not in any danger. Relax, breathe, and tell me what's happening," Miguel said in a calm voice.

The voice that spoke through Alex had a different quality, confident and in command. "The sky is dark and full of storm clouds. We travel on a personal transport ship that tosses on a rough sea. I came on deck to get fresh air, but I feel no better. Nothing is left in my stomach." She gagged again.

"Go forward in time until you feel better," Miguel directed.

Alex breathed and became calmer. She was quiet for several moments.

"How are you feeling now?" Miguel prompted.

"I feel better, just weak. Three days have passed. I am still on the ship, but today the salt breeze is refreshing."

"Why are you on a ship, Alexandria?"

"I am Una Alana, Priestess of the Healing Order," she said in a strong voice. "We sail west from our homeland of Poseidia to the land known as Yu Ka Tan to begin a new life. Others sail on other ships to different lands. We carry the history of our land to be safeguarded for a future time and to start new lives."

The timbre of her voice projected an aura of confidence and authority, as if accustomed to royal stature and authority.

"Why did you leave?" don Miguel asked.

"Political circumstances forced our departure. Power shifted to different philosophical views, and it was not safe to remain. Some have foreseen a catastrophe and we must start over elsewhere and preserve our knowledge and history." A hint of condescension lay beneath the surface of her words.

"The land itself is in peril from unscrupulous people. All life is endangered through selfish plans to abuse our sacred energy source," she said.

"What is that?" Miguel asked.

"The Tuaoi stone," she answered, as if surprised that he didn't know. "It is a large, crystalline stone that focuses and concentrates the energy of the Sun and stars to provide power for our country."

"Can you describe your ship?" Don Miguel asked.

"The shape is long and cylindrical, tapered at the front and back. The ship is a multi-purpose vessel capable of flight, as well as travel on and below the surface of the water. The frame is constructed of lightweight curved metal bars and covered with layers of animal skins. The motive power is electrochemical force."

"Do you recognize anyone from your present lifetime?" Miguel inquired.

She wrinkled her brow. "You are here. Your name is Iltar. You are High Priest and my father. Erik is also here and in this time is the priest Kadir." In her hypnotic state, Alex felt no surprise at that recognition. It seemed a mere statement of fact.

"What do we look like?" Miguel wanted to know.

"The people of our country have straight, black hair and bronze or coppery skin. You are considered handsome, Father. Your skin is reddish-bronze, and you have blue-black straight hair that reaches your shoulders. You usually dress in the white-and-purple robe of your office.

"A gold band circles your head and covers your forehead. A large blue jewel shines in the center of the band. Called Sky Stone, it aids understanding and opens the inner eye. You wear the thick gold chain necklace with a round pendant of Azurite and Malachite I made for you. I designed it to reflect your love of the Earth.

"We left everything behind, and I don't know if I will be able to continue my work. There may not be sufficient gems or minerals, and we may be unable to make metals."

"What do you look like, Una?"

"My robe is made of sand-colored linen that was dyed using herbs, by making a tea. My hair is long and black like yours, twisted in a braid of four strands that hangs to my waist. I wear a large pendant with a light-green, oval stone in the center called Sun Stone.

"My skin is darker than yours. I look more like my mother who died several years ago." She paused. "She was Rose, Alexandria's grandmother in your time."

"What period of history you live in?" Miguel asked.

She paused. "Thirteen thousand years before your time."

"How do you measure time?" Miguel asked.

"In increments of solar cycles and the Grand Cycle of stellar ages. Each age is measured by the apparent movement of the rising Sun on the spring day of equal light and dark as it moves westward in the sky through the constellations. A Grand Cycle is one complete passage through thirteen-star pictures, lasting almost twenty-six thousand solar orbits.

"Our history spans two-hundred thousand solar orbits. Two prior catastrophes devastated our land. Forty-thousand orbits earlier than this time the surface of Earth shifted due to cosmic pressures from other planets and stars. An immense catastrophe resulted that changed our vast continent into a group of islands.

"A similar devastation occurred twenty-six thousand years from your time," Una's voice replied, like a teacher instructing a pupil. "Zared's scheme will likely trigger another more catastrophic inundation."

SHE INHALED SHARPLY. "Dolphins! What a glorious sight. Many of them jump in the air and splash into the water. Their voices are musical. This is a fortuitous omen for our new beginning. I am grieved by this journey, but the dolphins ease my heart." She paused.

"Go forward in time five years," Miguel prodded. "Where are you now? Tell me what you see."

Breathing audibly, Alexandria deepened her trance. Her consciousness floated through time and space five years into the future. Peacefully drifting above earthly concerns, Alex resisted returning to awareness of Una.

"We have accomplished a great deal," Una's voice said. "The people welcomed us, and we built a strong community. Work on the new temple progresses and a hall of records has been constructed to contain and safe-guard the histories as we prepare for a visit from Hept-supht from another of the colonies. He will travel over land and ocean in a transport vessel.

"I am now married to Kadir, and we have a beautiful daughter. Her name is Mirari, which means miracle. She paused. "Mirari is Blanche, my own mother in the current lifetime," Una's strong voice proclaimed.

"Things in Poseidia continue to decline. Zared's crystal scheme caused subterranean earthquakes, volcanoes, and violent weather distortions. We fear the island will soon be completely destroyed."

"Una, I want you to move ahead to the end of this lifetime. Where are you? Who is with you?" Miguel encouraged.

"After three-hundred solar cycles on this good Earth my body and mind are weary of the rejuvenation temple where we use the secrets of the stones to prolong life.

"Kadir is with me and holds my hand. My children and grandchildren are gathered to say farewell. We will meet again." Her voice sounded tired.

"It is peaceful, and I do not suffer. My time has simply come. I tell Kadir, my dearest love, that he will join me soon. We can never be parted for long as ours is a timeless bond."

There was a long silence, and her breathing became shallow and irregular. Alexandria's body grew completely still, and her voice was quiet when she spoke again.

"The spirit has departed the body. I float above, looking at my family. Kadir bowed his head beside me. I do not want them to feel sorrow as I am free of the burden of that aged body. I feel no pain, only lightness and joy after a long and fruitful life. Seeds were sown for the future that will flower many lifetimes from now. I am content."

Alexandria was silent and felt a sense of surpassing peace. After a few moments of silence her body became rigid, and a different voice spoke through her mouth. The sound bellowed from her throat with the potency of a lion's roar.

*"Priestess, you served well in that epoch, and you now are called upon*
*again to serve the Great Plan. A prophecy was encoded in the*

*design of my ancient architecture. Hear and understand. The time of the Initiates is at hand.*

*'When great Ra ascends in the sign of the Water Bearer and smiles on the face of the Lion, the portals will open to the children of Earth again. The long watch of the sentinel will come to an end, and the unending night of sleep will give way to the morning of remembrance.*

*The eternal wheel of the ages will turn again toward light. Those who slumbered will awaken. Those who prepared will come forward to uncover the long-guarded secrets. Isis will joyfully draw back her veil to the opened eye of Horus. Osiris is jubilant. Seth is vanquished.*

*I, Thoth, in the dim mists of great Atlantis, conceived a plan to hold fast the initiatory energies of Earth during the cycle of cleansing. Sacred Science was protected for those who would honor the Divine Heart and tread the path of enlightenment.*

*"I constructed a vessel to safeguard the eternal flame, and the light has never flickered through eons in darkness. The secrets were safe from the cleansing flood and chilling ice of purification. I proclaimed an aegis, and it was so. The message has ever been declared in stone for those who passed the inner trials.*

*"Priestess of Light, thy destiny is upon thee. The resurrection of Osiris is at hand. Claim the joy that remembrance will bring. Come greet the dawn in ecstasy, daughter of Isis. Horus has risen before thee. Great Sirius rises with Ra."*

Alex inhaled sharply and deeply three times, and her breathing slowed again.

"What is happening now?" Miguel asked quietly.

Una's voice answered. "Master Thoth spoke from his dimension where he dwells in the stars of Arcturus. It is time for me to proceed on my way. The Priestess must heed his message."

"Thank you for your time with us, Una. Fix the state of peace and freedom you described in your mind," Miguel said. "Bring that feeling back with you as the consciousness of Alexandria slowly returns to this time," Miguel instructed.

"I will count slowly from one to ten, and you will return to ordinary consciousness one step at a time. When you awaken, you will feel rested and refreshed. You will remember everything you have experienced, and nothing will disturb you. You will feel wonderful, better than before," Miguel said.

He counted to ten in a slow deliberate manner as she eased back to ordinary awareness. Alex climbed toward light on the surface of her consciousness as if rising from the bottom of the ocean.

"Open your eyes," Miguel directed.

Alex opened her eyes to see Erik on the edge of the couch smiling. Tears glistened in his eyes. Miguel stood behind him; his face was radiant. She sat up and gave Erik a fierce hug, feeling a flow of energy between their hearts like liquid fire.

The three stared at one another in stunned silence. Alex exhaled. "I don't know who I am, or which world is more real. It's like I'm straddling two realities."

"That is an accurate description. Time exists only in the third dimension. You've experienced that truth beyond an intellectual abstraction," Miguel said, handing Alex a glass of water.

"I've always taken past lives for granted, but I never thought too much about prior relationships. Una communicated to me that Gran was my mother and my own mother was my child in that lifetime.

"I feel like I reclaimed a part of myself. Una was strong and didn't have my weaknesses." Alex sat cross-legged on the sofa. "I want to hear her voice. I am blown away by Thoth. Did you get that recorded?" she asked, astounded.

"You sounded like another person when Una spoke," Erik said. "Your demeanor was different, almost imperial," he smiled. "The voice of Thoth felt like it was amplified through a speaker. It seemed impossible that sound could come from you."

"Don't be too hard on yourself," Miguel said. "Your ability to travel in the spirit realms is profound. Una's training as a priestess in that lifetime prepared her to live in alignment with truth. Her knowledge, which is your memory, will be accessible to you now."

"You mentioned a hall or chamber of records, history, and knowledge. I've read other mentions of that," Erik said.

"As have I," Miguel added.

"When Una answered the questions, the information came as knowledge,"

Alex said. "Like describing something from a history book or personal experience. Those events were real to her.

Alex knitted her brow. "I need a phone."

"Now?" Erik asked in disbelief.

"I need to call a friend of Gran's, Lela Blackstone and invite her to dinner. I didn't pay too much attention before, but she and Gran talked about this stuff all the time. They were in the A.R.E. together, the *Association for Research & Enlightenment*, the Edgar Cayce organization."

Shaking his head, he handed her the phone, and she punched in the numbers with her thumb. Lela's raspy voice echoed in the receiver, "Hello?"

"Lela, this is Alexandria."

"Alexandria, hello darling. I feel guilty. I've meant to call you for a week. I don't know what happens to the time," Lela croaked.

Alex smiled. "I wouldn't bother you, but I've had some unusual dreams recently along with an amazing past-life regression. I'd like your thoughts."

"That's up my alley all right," Lela said. "I still have some of your grandmother's books. Shall I bring them by later?"

"Perfect. Some friends are visiting I want you to meet. Come for dinner, and don't argue. Six o'clock, Emma will do something wonderful," Alex said.

"Sounds like my kind of an outing, dear. I'll see you in a little while," Lela said.

Alex clicked off the phone and looked at Miguel and Erik. "I don't know if I can stand up." Erik helped her to her feet. Alex lifted her chin.

"This priestess needs a nap," she said, proceeding toward the spiral stairs. When she reached the steps, she turned to see them staring at each other and laughing.

"Well?" she said to Erik, her eyes full of meaning.

"Duty calls," he said, nodding and winking at Miguel.

Don Miguel guffawed.

CHAPTER 30

# LELA BLACKSTONE

Alex and Crystal stood behind Emma as she opened the front door of the Stuart house dressed in a fresh blue dress and clean apron. She had brushed her gray hair in a tight, prim bun. Fireflies twinkled in the twilight of a warm spring evening, and fading light cast long shadows across the darkening yard.

"Lela Blackstone, you are a sight for sore eyes. I've been meaning to call," Emma said.

Lela Blackstone's infectious laugh echoed down the hall. "As I told Alex, I don't know what happens to the time," she cackled. The two women embraced, then Lela wrapped Alex in a bear hug. "You look like something is agreeing with you, young lady."

Alex blushed and Emma smiled. Lela Blackstone was in her mid seventies with coarse black, yellowish-gray-and-white hair like the fur of a calico cat. The wiry multicolored mane grew around a full black face and her generous mouth had permanent laugh lines. Brown eyes, the color of strong dark tea, were usually warm and stimulating like a cup of Earl Gray, but they could sting like iodine if she was provoked.

She looked equipped for any eventuality in khaki slacks, a plaid shirt and mountain hiking boots. Her shoulder bag resembled a backpack. A gold Egyptian cartouche hung from a chain around her neck, and she carried a large canvas bag filled with books.

Crystal greeted Lela enthusiastically. "Crystal, how are you, doll-face? I've missed you." Lela rubbed behind her white ears and shook Crystal's head back and forth. She followed Emma into the library, patting Crystal on the head and talking to her as she walked. She frowned when she entered the room.

"This place looks as sterile as a hospital—it's not natural," she huffed, "your grandmother would be uneasy." She deposited the bag of books on the floor. "These are Rose's. I don't know where you'd like them under the circumstances."

Emma looked worried, and Alex stifled a giggle. "We couldn't help it," Alex shrugged. "Someone broke into the library and emptied the roll top desk, secretary, and bookshelves onto the floor. We sorted through everything to see what was missing and organized all the papers from her will," Alex said, gesturing around the room.

Lela sniffed and looked hard at Alex while she spoke, as if assessing what she wasn't saying. Miguel and Erik stood to meet Gran's friend.

"I'd like you to meet two special people," Alex said, changing the subject. Don Miguel Piedra, this is Lela Blackstone," Alex said. "You must know each other by reputation."

"Don Miguel, I feel as if I already know you."

"It is a great pleasure to finally meet you, Lela. I've heard so much about you." Miguel said. He extended his hand and leaned toward her. His black eyes shone. Small wrinkles at the corners of his eyes made his smile seem warmer.

Lela nodded and smiled, "I agree, it's wonderful to meet you too," she said, her eyes returning a warm smile. Growing serious she said. "I'm glad you're here, Miguel. Rose grew very worried near the end."

Alex looked from one to the other, then zeroed in on Lela, her hands forming fists. "Are you in on the secret too? Why didn't anyone bother to tell me?"

"Rose believed she was an observer and researcher. She didn't understand she was also a participant," Lela said. "Things really got stirred up after one of Duncan's later discoveries."

"What discovery?" Alex asked.

"I don't know, but I believe it was something he worked on before he died," Emma said.

"Don't worry, Em, it will all get sorted out," Lela said, squeezing her hand.

"And you, young man," Lela said, "must be the something that's agreeing with my baby girl." Her expressive eyes appeared to double in size as she directed a look of evaluation and then approval toward Erik.

Erik grinned. "I sincerely hope so."

Alex fired a glance around the room, daring anyone to mention her love life. Erik's expression waxed cherubic and Miguel was as stone-faced as Mount Rushmore. Emma vanished into the kitchen, and Lela simply grinned like a Cheshire cat.

Sheba jumped onto the arm of the chair next to where Lela stood. She meowed three times with inflections that sounded like words. Lela laughed. "Who might this be, looking like an Egyptian goddess?"

"Sheba," Erik said.

Lela rubbed her head and scratched behind her ears. Sheba leaned against her and continued to make expressive sounds. "Sheba, my queen and darling," Lela said, "I understand your concern, but you might as well get used to it. Alexandria is going to be part of your life now. Once things settle down, you'll get more attention than ever. I can tell that you're capable of charm, and now's the time to show it."

Sheba looked up at her, meowed in a subdued tone and jumped off the chair. "She actually talked to you," Erik said. "I've never seen her act like that."

"Cat's think I'm one of them. I believe it's from an Egyptian lifetime when the lions came from Sirius," Lela chuckled. "Enough preliminaries, tell me about these dreams and regressions."

Alex laughed in spite of herself. "I can never stay annoyed with you. This dream had a different feeling, not the 'Alice in Wonderland' quality that many have." People and objects had more substance. I was inside the experience center stage, not viewing it on a screen.

"Usually when I dream, impossible things happen," Alex said. "Cars fly, roads lead nowhere, scenes change suddenly, animals talk, dead people live, and it all seems plausible. When you wake up, the dream seems 'curiouser and curiouser,' as Alice so aptly said."

Alex sat cross-legged on the love seat. She had changed into a tan skirt and peach cotton top with green turquoise and gold jewelry. The stones matched the color of her eyes that sparkled expressively as she related the dream. Her red hair was partially pulled back from her face, revealing the chiseled lines of her jaw and cheekbones.

"I lived in a large seacoast city named Poseidia. The name of the island country was also Poseidia. I had a sense of a political storm brewing, a crisis building."

"Did you say Poseidia?" Lela asked.

"Yes, I was a priestess, and my father was High Priest. My name was Una, and he was called Iltar. The people in the dream looked like American Indians dressed in ancient Egyptian-type clothing."

"I see," Lela said, nodding. Her face was intent, her brow knitted in concentration as if working out the solution to a puzzle. She grasped the arms of her chair.

"A high council had been convened to decide the fate of a giant crystal known as the Tuaoi Stone. The crystal provided the major power source of the land, and there was a controversy building about its use. Alex described the dream in detail.

"This same story is related in some of the Cayce readings," Lela said.

"The dream felt like a past life, so Miguel suggested we try hypnotic regression. We recorded it, and I'd like to play it for you.

"Are you kidding? Crank that puppy up," Lela laughed.

Erik pushed play on the recorder and sat back and held Alex's hand. As she listened to the recording, she experienced the feelings of surprise, love, loss, and gratefulness that seemed more disconnected while she was hypnotized.

Erik put his arm around her, and his touch was comforting. The bond that existed between them in the past was returning to conscious awareness.

When the recording was finished, Erik turned off the recorder. Alex looked at Lela and waited for her to speak. Tears ran down Lela's cheeks, and she pulled a handkerchief from the pocket of her plaid shirt.

"I'm overcome," Lela said. "Are any of the names familiar to you?"

"Not consciously," Alex said.

Lela sat back in her chair, brown eyes wide and intense. She ran her fingers through her calico hair and stared at Alex.

"Alexandria, the first thing you must know is that your grandmother only wanted to keep you safe. As this mystery unfolds, and all the players move on the game board, you must remember that."

"Safe from what, Lela?"

"This may be a bombshell, and I don't want to rush this discussion, but it may save time for juicier topics. According to Edgar Cayce, Poseidia was the last vestige of once-glorious Atlantis. Just as you described, the original continent was broken up into islands in stages over thousands of years. The misuse of the Tuaoi Stone, the great crystal you described, caused the final destruction of the island about thirteen thousand years ago." Lela paused.

"You're saying the information in my dream and regression matches information in Edgar Cayce's trance readings? Alex asked, surprised.

"That's exactly what I'm saying."

Alex walked to the library window.  She stood with arms folded and looked outside. Feeling the eyes of the others on her, she turned to look at them. Lela rose and joined her at the window, putting her strong arms around Alex's shoulders.

"I've been in the A.R.E. , Cayce's organization to protect the legacy of the readings, for thirty years.  Some members would give both arms and a leg for this experience."

"But what does it mean?" Alex asked, exasperated.

Lela shook her head.  "I'm not an expert on the Atlantis aspect of the work, but Edgar Cayce said America as a country is the reincarnation of Atlantis. He said many souls from that time have reincarnated now.  Those who caused devastation and those who worked for good have returned to play out their dramas and try to re-establish equilibrium.  Cayce said we'd face another challenge to our survival and have another chance to get it right."

# CHAPTER 31

# MORE SECRETS

Emma appeared in the doorway. "I hate to interrupt, but can you continue your discussion over dinner?"

They adjourned to the dining room where Emma had created a Mexican theme for dinner in honor of Miguel. Heaping platters of vegetable enchiladas wrapped in blue corn tortillas and covered with cream sauce were surrounded by concentric circles of avocados, tomatoes, cucumbers and *pico de gallo.* Generous bowls of black beans, corn masa, guacamole and corn chips rounded out the bounty.

Don Miguel assisted Lela with her chair. "Emma, this is so beautiful," he said.

"Alexandria, did you know that your grandparents had readings from Edgar Cayce?" Lela asked.

"No," she said, surprised again. "Gran never mentioned it."

"Around 1939, Duncan developed serious health challenges from a crippling disease akin to arthritis. He worked his way through a cavalcade of medical doctors and not one of them could help him.

"Rose had heard of Cayce and some of the remarkable successes his trance remedies had achieved. She persuaded Duncan to get a reading," Lela laughed conspiratorially, her face alight with humor. "That was no small accomplishment. Even with all his metaphysical beliefs, Duncan Stuart was a show-me-the-evidence scientist—no hocus pocus. "

"Duncan was skeptical about some psychic who barely had an eighth grade education telling him anything important in a trance." Lela cackled. "Well, you know your grandmother could be persuasive. She told him there was nothing to lose and everything to gain, and eventually he agreed just to please her. We became friends later through a Cayce study group."

"You said trance remedies? What happened during the readings?" Erik asked, eyebrows raised. "I only have a vague awareness of Cayce, but I've heard others mention him."

"Edgar Cayce had a rare gift. He was given a hypnotic suggestion, generally by his wife in the earlier years, and he went into a deep hypnotic trance. He never remembered a word he said when he came out of it."

Lela laughed, an endearing cackling sound. "We didn't have individual tape recorders in those days. A stenographer transcribed every word and typed them up. Mr. Cayce did fourteen-thousand readings over the course of his lifetime, and they're all in three-ring binders in the association's library in Virginia Beach. Those black binders take up two whole walls."

"Gran talked about the potential for healing humanity that Cayce's work represented. I wonder why she never told me about the readings," Alex frowned.

"Duncan's health reading indicated a weakness in his thyroid or pituitary and recommended a homeopathic remedy. Duncan was skeptical, but Rose had it made up anyway and cajoled him into trying it. His symptoms were completely gone in a month.

"Duncan ordered a health reading post haste for Rose. They both had what they call life readings in 1940. Those readings talked about past lifetimes in Atlantis and Egypt and the story of the Hall of Records where many things were hidden at the time of the fall of Atlantis.

"It was a stretch for their beliefs in those days, but after Duncan's healing, they were more receptive. His reading talked about crystals and power sources and said he was a priest who had worked on the Tuaoi stone in Atlantis. Your grandfather was obsessed with energy sources so that resonated. That reading was the beginning of his conscious fascination with crystals and involvement with the A.R.E.," Lela nodded.

Alex and Erik looked at each other. "Energy," she said.

"Free energy," he said. "Some would want to suppress that knowledge."

"Speaking of recorders, recently they put all those readings onto a little phonograph record that you play in a computer. A CD is it called? All fourteen-thousand readings fit on one little disk. Land sakes alive, I can't fathom such a thing."

Erik laughed in delight.

"How would we get the disk, Lela?" Alex asked, nearly falling off the edge of her seat.

"I can give you the phone number in Virginia Beach," Lela said.

"You said everything was transcribed. Did the person who had the reading get a copy?" Alex asked, struggling to contain her excitement.

"Yes, in fact I read your grandparents' readings. It's been decades, but I'll wager those reports are here somewhere. As you know, Rose never threw anything away. If Duncan had anything to do with it, they were neatly cataloged and filed. Rose might have held onto them, but they would have been lost in one of her ubiquitous stacks," Lela smiled. "Those two were mighty different. I can't believe she's gone."

No one spoke. Alex keenly felt the loss but couldn't wait to get into the secret room and search the file cabinets. She felt she was finally on the trail of Gran's intention. "I've got to find those readings," she said.

Lela's laugh burst forth full force. "The game's afoot, Watson," she chortled.

"I like this lady," Erik grinned.

"It's been a full evening, and I'm an old woman," Lela croaked, her warm eyes bright with mischief.

"You are barely in your prime," Miguel smiled.

"I do love that Latin charm. Help me up, Miguel." He rose to assist Lela.

"I need to talk to Emma before I leave, so I'll let myself out. Keep me informed, young lady. Your Grandmother expected to live to see this through," Lela said, looking sadly at don Miguel. "While Duncan was alive, he seemed able to keep the wolves at bay."

"I'm not happy about the way this has happened, but I won't let her down." Alex gave Lela a big hug.

"I'm certain our paths will cross again soon, Lela," Miguel said. "Until then, vaya con Dios."

That goes for me as well," Erik smiled.

"Elementary," Lela quipped and walked down the hall toward the kitchen.

Alex, and don Miguel looked at one another as Lela Blackstone's sturdy footsteps echoed down the hall toward the kitchen. The grandfather clock ticked in the foyer and chimed the quarter hour.

"Can anticipation be fatal?" Alex said, crossing her arms in frustration.

# CHAPTER 32

# EDGAR CAYCE READINGS

"I can't wait to search those files now that I know what might be in there," Alex said. "I wouldn't mind if Emma or Lela knew about the secret room, but I'm wondering now what's safe. I'm beginning to get a glimpse of Gran's concern."

"Perhaps one can search, and two can stand guard," Miguel suggested. "If anyone returns while you're inside, we'll pretend you went to the bathroom."

"I'll create a diversion, if necessary," Erik said. He rubbed his hands together and blew into his palms as if he was about to roll a pair of dice. He put his ear to the bookcase as if he were listening to the tumblers in a lock.

Alex rolled her eyes. He smiled wickedly and pushed the place on the bookcase that looked like an ordinary whorl in the wood. The wall receded into the darkened room and Alex entered and turned on the lights.

"Close the bookcase and I'll knock on the wall when I'm ready," she said. Once the eerie ingress to the secret room became a blank wall, Alex headed straight for the antiquated Army-green file cabinet. The heavy drawer creaked when she finally wrenched it out of the ponderous metal cabinet.

Alex craned her neck to see inside the drawer. She combed through faded manila folders, eagerly scanning the curled and yellowed typewritten labels. Some came loose from the folders and fell to the floor.

The top drawer contained folders labeled atomic energy, crystals, energy sources, lasers, navigation, propulsion systems, solar power, and ultrasound.

She closed the top drawer and pulled the second drawer open. About halfway back in the drawer she spotted a file whose tattered label read 'E.C. - 1940.'

She pulled the file out of the drawer and adrenalin rushed through her body, and her stomach churned. Her hands were damp as her eyes drank in the faded and yellowed documents. The folder contained five readings given to the Stuarts by Edgar Cayce. Each bore an identification number that rendered the document anonymous for research purposes and protected the identity of the client. She was holding health and life readings for Duncan and Rose along with a life reading for her father.

Alex was momentarily paralyzed and held her breath. She wanted to read every word right there and controlled the urge with difficulty. She took another look in the drawer and noticed a plump folder behind the one she had just removed. The label said 'E.C. Data.' Inside was correspondence and excerpts from Cayce readings. Alex removed the thick folders and pushed the drawer closed.

She felt a surge of anger. *Why hadn't Gran told her any of this while she was alive?* That would have made things simpler. Then she remembered Selig and wondered what he was really after and if he was working alone. She felt grateful for her new companions.

Clutching the folders like priceless treasures, Alex went to the spot where the bookcase opened and tapped on the wall. Nothing happened. She wondered if they had company in the library or just didn't hear her rapping. She waited a few minutes and knocked harder. This time she heard the mechanism engage and watched as the wall opened and the bookcase swung into the secret room. She turned off the light and stepped into the library. Erik pushed the lock, and the entrance to Duncan's hermitage became an ordinary bookcase again.

"Coast is clear, but we had a near miss when Lela left," Erik said, waving her into the room. His eyes were eager. "Emma came to the doorway to see if we wanted anything just as you knocked the first time. Miguel and I acted as if we didn't hear anything. I held my breath and prayed you wouldn't knock louder. We told Emma we were fine, and she went back to the kitchen."

"Find anything?" Miguel inquired, eying the file folders she carried. Alex stood dazed in front of the bookcase, clutching the folders to her chest. Her cheeks were flushed.

"Five readings, including a life reading for my dad. I also found this file called 'E.C. Data,' which looks like correspondence between Grandpa and the Association for Research & Enlightenment in Virginia Beach. He seems to have visited there."

"Well?" Erik asked, motioning for her to sit next to him on the love seat.

"Sorry," Alex apologized, sitting beside Erik. "It appears Grandpa requested additional information from the A.R.E. that pertained to his reading. There are excerpts from other readings, along with newspaper clippings and letters. From a quick glance it seems most of the information relates to crystals," Alex said.

She opened the file that contained the Stuart's readings. "Let's divide and conquer," Alex suggested, "you take Grandpa's readings, and Miguel, here are Gran's. I want to read my father's." Alexandria's eyes raced over the pages, and her silent reading was punctuated by nods and hums. Alex looked up when she finished.

Don Miguel took his regular seat in front of the fireplace and scanned the pages in his hands.

"These are all identified by a reading number," Erik said. "I think we should make a note of the ones that seem significant. We might need to reference them later."

"Great idea," Miguel said. "If you tell me the numbers I'll keep track."

"Listen to this," Erik said, leaning forward and placing his elbows on his knees. "It's from reading number 813-1, Miguel. Alex, this sounds just like your regression."

'Before that we find the entity was in the Atlantean land, when there was much turmoil and strife from the rejections by many of those laws and tenets of One; when the upheavals began that made for the egress of many from that city of the Poseidon land, or in Poseidia.

The entity dwelt among those where there was the storage of the motivative forces in nature for the great crystals that so condensed the lights, the forms, the activities, as to guide not only the ship upon the bosom of the sea but in the air and in many of those now known conveniences for man as in the transmission of the body, as in the transmission of the voice, as in the recording of those activities in what is soon to become a practical thing in so creating the vibrations as to make for television -- as it is termed in the present.'

"The syntax and phrasing are difficult to follow, especially in my second language, but the information is startling," Miguel said.

"This one is about the Tuaoi stone; the information is from the correspondence file," Alex said, eyes bright with excitement. "I can't believe I'm seeing this in print. My dream and regression experiences seemed real, but it's spooky to have them corroborated this way." She shook her head as if to ward off doubt.

"The session conductor asked a question while Edgar Cayce was in trance," Alex continued. "Reading number 2072-10, Miguel.

Question: 'Going back to the Atlantean incarnation -- what was the Tuaoi stone? What shape or form was it?'

Answer: 'It was in the form of a six-sided figure, in which the light appeared as the means of communication between infinity and the finite; or the means whereby there were the communications with those forces from the outside.

'It was set as a crystal. It was in those periods where there was the directing of aeroplanes or means of travel; though these in that time would travel in the air or on the water, or under the water, just the same. Yet the force from which these were directed was in this central power station, or Tuaoi stone, which was as the beam upon which it acted. In the beginning it was the source from which there was the spiritual and mental contact.'"

Alex stopped reading and looked at them. "The principle of ultrasound technology works by directing an electrical current through a crystal to create sound waves. Seems like the principle of the Tuaoi stone. Did Grandpa invent or remember?"

"When did Duncan die?" Erik asked.

"Four years ago. He collected his minerals and crystals, his rock pile Gran called it, over a forty-year span," Alex said.

"What does Philip's life reading say?" Miguel asked.

Alex felt an inexplicable familiarity with her father's reading.

'The entity then was not only one skilled in aircraft and in watercraft, as an aviator and a navigator, but made great strides in keeping in touch with other lands through the forces of nature in the experience.

'Hence those things of nature that have to do with communications become a part of the entity's experience. The imaginations of tales of travel, the activities, that have to do with strange lands, strange people, strange customs, become a portion of the innate forces. And from those very influences there may arise later in this experience those activities that may bring again renown to the entity in this experience.'

"What number is that, Alexandria?" Miguel asked.

"Sorry, I was captured—number 3253-2."

"That is remarkable, considering your father's distinguished career as a pilot during the Korean war," Miguel said. "Your grandparents said he was one of the youngest pilots in that conflict since most had flown in World War II."

"Dad used to say all he ever wanted to do was fly. Funny that he became a Navy pilot, flying planes that took off and landed on ships. Aircraft and watercraft, like the reading said. I still don't understand how he survived a war and crashed during a routine flight."

"There could be many reasons. Some karmic, some mundane. Perhaps because it was just his time," Miguel said kindly.

"How old was your father at the time of the reading?" Erik asked.

Alex glanced at the date typed at the top of the page. "Ten," Alex replied. "I wonder if he ever knew about this reading. No one ever mentioned any of this until Lela told us," she frowned. "How about Gran's reading, don Miguel?"

"According to this, Rose also went with Iltar to the Yucatan," Miguel said.

'The entity was among those that chose to enter as leaders in what is now called Yucatan. The entity aided in establishing the temple through which there was hoped to be the appearance again of the children of the Law of One, as they listened to the oracles that came through the stones, the crystals, that were prepared for communications in what ye now know as radio. For ye may tune again to things afar off, if ye set thyself in order and attune to the infinite.

'The entity was among those that interpreted the messages that were received through the crystals and the fires that were to be the eternal fires of nature and made for helpful forces in the experience of groups during that period.'

"Number?" Erik asked.

"Right, this one is number 3253-2," Miguel said as he made a note.

"The language is arduous, but the content is stunning," Erik sighed. "That sounds like the regression too." He leaned back on the love seat, placing one foot across the opposite knee and cupping his hands around the back of his head.

"The Atlanteans read messages from the crystals. That reminds me of Chan Ka and the stones of light," Alex said.

"What do you make of it, Miguel?" Erik asked.

Miguel rose from his chair by the fireplace and walked to the leaded glass window. He looked out at Rose's Garden, softly illuminated by moonlight. "If you accept the premise of this material, it certainly explains my connection with Rose and her love of Mexico. Our collective past is coming into focus, and I'm eager to see what we find in the computer disk when we search for the names. We need to know the purpose underlying these messages," Miguel said.

"What about the danger? I don't understand why there is such risk," Alex said.

Miguel turned to face them. "Have either of you ever heard the term Illuminati?"

"Yes," Erik said, "but I always it was a myth."

"Doesn't that mean 'enlightened' or something?" Alex asked.

You are both partly correct," Miguel said, "there was a historical group by the name that no longer exists, but in this time the term is often used loosely to refer to a dark or shadowy power cartel who affect global policies, particularly related to oil and banking. Sometimes they have been tied to the Freemasons and legends of the Knights Templar."

"I don't think it's the same thing," Alex said. "One is about guarding hidden knowledge and the other is about wealth and power."

The men looked at her. "I don't pretend to be an expert," Miguel said, "but it stands to reason that if Cayce was correct, the dark forces from Atlantis, if also reincarnated, would try to wield power from behind the scenes."

"So, what's in the Hall of Records might upset the apple cart?" Alex asked.

"I'd say that's an understatement of epic proportions," Erik replied.

"Excuse me," Emma said from the hall. "I don't mean to interrupt." Emma's body was illuminated from behind and her wispy hair looked otherworldly framed by the hall light. Her form darkened the doorway, and she seemed to speak from another dimension.

"Lela just phoned. A friend of hers has the computer disk you want and will loan it to you for a couple days. She'll drop by in the morning," Emma said. "I'll be heading home now."

"Fabulous, thank you," Alex said.

"I'll order the CD tomorrow, but meanwhile, we can start searching in the morning," Erik said, rubbing his hands together and raising his eyebrows.

"Shall we call it an evening then?" Miguel said.

Alex looked at him. "That doesn't seem like you."

"I am tired," Miguel smiled, "and I want to dream about this."

"I feel like I'm on fire. I'll read the folders upstairs and see what else I can learn." Alex leaned over the table and scooped up the files like a college student hoisting textbooks on her way to the library. "This technical stuff will be a sedative," she laughed.

"See you at breakfast," Erik said, rising as Miguel left the room.

ALEX PHONED Sheila and invited her to the CD-ROM session in the morning, then headed up the stairs, clutching the files. Once inside the bedroom, Alex removed her clothes, tossing them in a pile on the floor in an uncharacteristic gesture and donning an emerald-green night shirt. The silky fabric clung to the curves of her body. Unfastening her barrette, she shook her red hair loose.

Erik lost no time in stripping down to his cotton boxer shorts. He stretched out on the bed and smiled his approval from a supine position. Leaning on one elbow he said in a theatrical tone, "You are so beautiful, like a precious emerald. Your night gown shimmers like the facets of a rare jewel."

Alex laughed. "Aren't we poetic? Does an ulterior motive lie behind those fancy words, Mr. Anderson?"

"I think I'm too tired," he said, rolling on his side to look at her. "Come here, and we'll discuss my plight."

She joined him on the bed. He kissed her, and they embraced, tangling their limbs together. Erik ran his hands over the curves of her body and caressed her through the smooth fabric. She felt his telltale response as he pulled her to him.

"Pity you're too tired," she teased, kissing his neck. "I hoped you'd rise to the occasion."

"Funny," he whispered into her ear, "All of a sudden, I'm feeling inspired."

They made love with the fervor of long-separated lovers, each eager to please the other. Afterwards they held each other close, and Alex felt love flowing between their open hearts. She looked at his face and ran her fingertips over his mouth. He kissed her palm. She touched his cheeks and eyes, marveling at the magic of their union. Tenderness engulfed her, and she responded with a gentle kiss.

"I'm spent," he sighed.

"I still can't relax. Will it bother you if I read?" Alex asked.

"Tell me everything in the morning," he said, rolling over and punching the feather pillow to achieve just the right shape and indentation for his head. Erik turned out the light on his side of the bed and settled into the covers with his back to her. In minutes she heard his rhythmic breathing and envied his ability to shut his brain off as quickly as his computer.

Alex attacked the contents of the folders. She felt close to her father and grandparents as her eyes devoured the material. She still couldn't understand why her grandmother had never shared this information and wondered if her mother knew. The files contained numerous excerpts from other readings, mostly scientific in nature. All were numbered in the same way and most of the information applied to crystals. Some readings referred to television, then an infant technology, and hinted at other revolutionary discoveries on the horizon.

She learned that the Tuaoi Stone was originally under the control of the Atlantean priesthood as her dream had shown and was used to commune with what the sleeping Cayce called 'the forces of light' for spiritual guidance. She wondered who or what were the forces of light.

The priests focused the rays of the Sun and stars through the great stone to amplify stellar energy. This allowed them to regenerate their bodies, so they lived hundreds of years. Over a period of thousands of years, the stone's capability to capture and store stellar energy was modified for more mundane purposes such as transportation to distant parts of the island realm.

The energy of the crystal, later called the Firestone, was directed through polished granite spheres positioned at remote locations, or on ships and planes, to capture the energy and distribute it locally.

As the fame of Atlantis spread, the capital city of Poseidia became a target for invasion., and an aspect of the great crystal was modified to be used as a defensive weapon. Called the death ray, the device was like a laser. The weapon was meant to be used only as a last resort if the city was attacked. The ultimate test of the weapon emerged in an unexpected manner. Outlying mountainous regions of the large island reported increasing attacks on wildlife and people from wild beasts roaming the wilderness areas.

A heated controversy arose between those who followed the spiritual leaders and those who were focused on materialistic values regarding the use of the death ray to eliminate the animals. Political turmoil resulted as the citizens aligned on opposing sides of the issue. Alex shivered as she remembered the council session in her dream and the powerful manipulation of Zared as he swayed the Atlanteans to turn the crystal to a higher setting.

The stone was tuned to its highest setting and directed at the animals. The high frequencies resulted in earthquakes that caused the complete destruction of the land. Many people left before the earthquakes and underground volcanoes created the final cataclysm that caused the island paradise to sink beneath the ocean waves.

She thought of her grandfather's work on the atomic bomb and thought of Selig. Unlimited free energy and weapons. Was Selig after weapon technology? Surely he wasn't acting alone. She felt a growing unease with the implications of what she was discovering, feeling that she needed to learn more and quickly.

When she finished the last page, she squinted at the red numbers of the digital clock—2:20 AM. Her head ached, and she crawled out of bed to take some pain medication and realized she was stiff. She was so absorbed she hadn't moved while she read. Alex swallowed the pills with a glass of water and stretched her muscles in exaggerated feline movements. She turned off her table lamp and nestled into Erik's back, putting her arm around his waist. She smiled as he responded to her touch with a soft moan. Alex dozed off as the pain in her head subsided.

# CHAPTER 33

# MIRA - HEALING TEMPLE

igh Priestess Mira approached the Temple of Healing and squinted as she gazed east. The brilliant representative of the great god Ra climbed from the horizon, once again victorious over darkness, and heralding a new day in the land of Khem. The pyramidal shape of the temple eclipsed the lush grove of palm trees that grew along the river behind the building. Chilly morning air was filled with cries of heron, and the compelling aroma of baking bread escaped from brick ovens.

In half a moon cycle, the festival of the beneficent star Sirius would celebrate her rising with Ra on the most propitious day of the year. Droves of people requested rites of purification in preparation for the new year celebration.

The priestess sighed, weary from many long days of healing work in the temple. Today another endless stream of supplicants would present themselves, and she prayed that an early start might give her an advantage. Mira entered the empty temple and breathed deeply as the blessed stillness caressed her.

This healing temple culminated the preparatory work in six initiatory temples that flanked the River Nile. The current of the longest river in the world flowed south to north as the energy of enlightenment was intended to do once the serpent fire awakened in the body.

The fiery energy lay coiled like a slumbering serpent at the base of the spine, waiting to emerge from latency. Each temple along the river focused on one spiritual center in the body and the work of unfoldment required to raise the light along the spine. The initiates worked through expressions of survival, procreation, power, love, speech, wisdom, and immortality.

Mira walked around the circular hall that surrounded the dome of the central healing chamber. She passed the seven stations that encircled the main chamber. Fine beeswax candles, cradled by golden sconces and covered with translucent alabaster globes, hung on the wall outside the seven rooms. Seven hallways bordered the rooms like spokes on a wheel and opened to the outside to admit light.

Within the seven rooms around the circle, the initiates fine-tuned the energies they mastered in the preparatory temples and completed advanced training. Seven symbols carved into the stone above each doorway repre-sented the work of that stage: a red coiled serpent, orange cockerel, yellow scarab beetle, green equal armed cross, blue gateway, violet hawk with wings spread, and over the seventh doorway was the brilliant white crown of mastery.

Each room's furnishings corresponded to the color and energy of the center to be aligned. Corresponding gems, incense, and metals were utilized to intensify a particular vibration. Gold jars inlaid with precious gems and metals, bowls of precious oils, vials of healing flower essences and carved alabaster lamps graced the initiatory chambers. Mira recalled her rigorous training to become a priestess in this sacred healing temple. Her progression through the initiatory rites of purification and consecration had been swift, and she was installed as High Priestess at the young age of thirty-eight summers.

The priestess removed clean linen towels from storage and spread a fresh white cloth on the large rectangular altar in the central chamber. Carved from a single block of pink granite, the rectangular altar was free of orna-mentation but had been polished to a high gloss.

She organized incense and bowls of fragrant oils, arranging crystals and sacred gemstones on the altar cloth around them. The stones were used to focus sunlight during the rituals to amplify healing energies. Mira configured a seven-pointed star of candles in the colors of the rainbow. When she was satisfied, she lighted a globule of frankincense resin, and the smoky aroma filled the sacred space.

The High Priestess tied back woven wool rugs that covered the windows during the night. Each rug was a work of art, hand-loomed from threads of vivid colors, depicting scenes from temple life. White gauze curtains, covering the windows underneath, responded to the chill morning breeze that gained admittance to the temple. Cool air drifted through the openings and caused graceful plumes of white incense to dance around the room.

Although temple attendants would soon arrive to perform the routine tasks, the High Priestess carried clean towels into the baths. She experienced these tasks as a meditation. She removed jars of bath oils and cleansing herbs from overnight storage and poured them into alabaster bowls in the bathing rooms.

Attendants would light fragrant oil lamps and place fresh flowers from the garden into glazed pottery vases. They would stoke the fires, banked just hours ago when laundry workers left, adding dung and coals. Water for tea and bathing flowed into the temple through masonry viaducts from nearby irrigation canals. Pottery jugs of water would soon warm on the fire.

Mira finished her preparations in time to have tea. She walked out to the temple garden to gather additional herbs and flowers and plucked sprigs of fresh mint, chamomile, and lemon grass. She selected delicate lotus blossoms from the pool to place in a green alabaster bowl on the altar.

Three cheerful temple cats greeted her. They enjoyed regal status as sacred symbols and kept the temple free of rodents. The cats followed her into the kitchen, and she gave them water while she waited for hers to boil. When she poured boiling liquid over the fresh herbs, their wonderful aroma was released. Closing her eyes, she inhaled their essence.

She returned to the garden and sat under a large date palm; the dark-green fronds were framed by an azure sky. She sipped tea and nibbled bread and honey. When she finished, she walked around the garden, admiring the varieties of cactus and touching them lovingly. Some were small and fragile; others were spiked and forbidding. Delicate flowers of brilliant orange, fuchsia and gold burst from spiny crevices. Other plants crawled along the ground like beached sea serpents. Birds of paradise, calla lilies and bromeliads bloomed. The magical white blossoms of the night-flowering cactus, which opened only in moonlight or starlight, had withdrawn their petals for the day.

Breathing deeply the priestess went to pay homage at the shrine of eternal fire, burning in the holy of holies at the heart of the temple. Mira cleansed and anointed herself and donned ritual robes and a copper breast plate. The ceremonial piece was formed of three pyramids. Two white crystalline triangles pointed downward and looked like wings beside the green triangle pointing upward in the center.

She wore the diadem of her personal emblem on her forehead; a seven-pointed star, symbolizing the seven spiritual centers. Each point of the star was set with a gemstone in one of the seven colors of the rainbow. Ruby, amber, topaz, peridot, lapis, indigo-tourmaline, and amethyst. A clear, faceted quartz crystal shone from the center of the star.

Mira left the preparatory alcove to join the other priests and priestesses in meditation. Facing east, she welcomed the new day.

> *"Bless us fading stars and growing light and all the healing deities that we may perform our work with skill and wisdom. May your light guide our minds, hearts, and hands so that those who are imprisoned by illness may be restored. We give thanks as we begin. May we help bring more joy to the world."*

She rose and entered the central healing room. The chamber's circular shape represented a sphere of pure white light whose protective essence would envelop the healers and the one being healed. The center of the ceiling was a retractable dome like an astronomical observatory. When the cover was opened, sunlight shone through a large crystal onto the table beneath.

White light, refracted by the crystal, was transformed into the seven hues of the visible spectrum and a rainbow enveloped the person's body with red at the head and violet at the feet. The first supplicant of the day lay on the healing table. A white linen robe of the finest material covered a disfigured body. Much of the work of the temple dealt with these tragic beings, angelic spirits who watched the Earth with fascination and desire for physical sensation. These souls projected curious thoughts into materiality, inhabiting the bodies of plants and animals.

In the beginning, they had been able to move between the physical dimension and the unseen realms with ease, but they grew careless, driven by desire, and became imprisoned in physical forms. Many of these unfortunate souls sought release from their physical chains. Some had tails, feathers, or claws, incongruous mixtures of human and animal characteristics.

To prepare for today's ceremony, the candidate fasted three days, eating nothing and drinking only fresh water and teas of medicinal herbs to cleanse the system. Temple attendants treated each supplicant with love and respect regardless of appearance. They were bathed and massaged with fragrant healing oils and ointments to facilitate the removal of poisons from muscles and organs.

Incense and candles burned and three healers took their positions and formed a triangle. The High Priestess stood at the head. She selected gemstones according to their color and energy properties and placed them on the patient's body over areas that needed strengthening and purification. Gently, she placed rose quartz over the heart, malachite on the throat, amethyst on the eyes, dark lapis over the joints and a white crystal on the brow.

A temple musician struck gongs and a lyre tuned to the frequencies of colors and energy centers in the body. The healers chanted tones corresponding to the seven energy centers. They looked at the color that aligned with that center, and the light of the Kundalini fire was raised along the spine.

The healers focused their minds to draw solar energy through the great crystal. They acted as transformers and modified the amplified power of the Sun like lightning rods before the energy entered the one on the table. The rainbow of light shimmered with power as the potent energy in the room increased. The gems on the patient's body seemed on fire from within as the stones worked in conjunction with the refracted light of the crystal, harmonizing and strengthening the energy currents.

When the High Priestess signaled the conclusion of the healing session, grateful tears flowed from the sightless eyes of the supplicant. His spine was straightened, and his skin looked more natural. He was still blind, but the opaque material that covered his eyes had cleared.

"Your desire for light was strong," the Priestess said.

The man placed his palms together and bowed. She touched his arm, and he eagerly clasped her hands. He looked up toward the light as tears ran down his cheeks. The Priestess smiled as humble tears glistened in her eyes. Such moments made the work fulfilling.

At the end of the long procession of suffering people, the priestess left the pyramid of healing and emerged into a darkening evening. Her eyes were drawn up to a sky full of stars. She hailed Orion and his companion, wondrous Sirius, brightest star in heaven and great benefactor of the land of Khem. Her heart lifted, and she smiled and whispered a prayer of gratitude. Mira gazed at the Lyre, her favorite constellation, and at its brightest star, bluish-white Vega, the star that anchored the poles of the earth.

Orange Arcturus twinkled from its place in the Herdsman, and she admired the imposing form of the Dragon. Her consciousness shifted, and she was startled as an unseen force lifted her from the ground. The priestess rose into a star-studded night until she was above the earth. The circle of the

Zodiac was visible around her, and Mira stared in awe as the star pictures metamorphosed into living beings.

Recognizing them, she saluted each in turn. She smiled at the Virgin and gazed past her to the Scales. She greeted the forbidding-looking Scorpion. The ominous form of giant Serpent Bearer had one foot in the circle and the other on the Scorpion's claw. Towering above the circle, the patron of healers moved to stand between Scorpion and Archer. The other constellations shifted as their starry companion took a more central role on the belt of the ecliptic.

Leviathan serpents of stars writhed in the arms of the patron of healers. Mira was transfixed as Serpent Bearer closed his eyes, and the giant snakes coiled around him. His body became the central pillar of a fiery caduceus.

The priestess shielded her eyes from the blinding light. When she looked again, she stood in front of the Great Pyramid. Bright Vega, brightest star in the Lyre, shone down into the opening on the north side. Mira turned east to face the river and saw that the ground in front of the Great Lion was open. Workers filled underground chambers with artifacts and tablets as they prepared for the dedication of the master initiation temple and final sealing the record chambers.

Her own resting place was being prepared in an underground chamber. Nine honored individuals would be entombed in the burial chambers with records and artifacts as gratitude for their work. Mira held a star clock she had designed to include with the other buried treasures. Like a sun dial, the clock was divided into thirteen sections like the constellations of the ecliptic. Serpent Bearer stood in the circle between the Scorpion and the Archer.

She had designed a carving of two star maps with her own likeness between them. One chart showed the night sky in her time, and the other showed the positions of the stars thirteen thousand years in the future. The coded message of the monuments was written in stone, stars, and legends.

Mira knew that far into the future, on the other side of the darkness, she would once again hold the star clock, gaze upon her own ancient remains, and remember this time of sadness. Storm clouds approached, harbingers of the long night. As a wall of gloom gathered on the plateau, a shadow crossed the face of the Lion. Two huge doors slammed shut over the storage chambers. Serpent Bearer's incandescent form burned within the flames of the caduceus, and his voice reached her from the fire.

> *"As the mill of heaven grinds the wheel of cosmic ages, light will*
> *slumber through the cycle of darkness. At the appointed time,*

dawn will bring the morning of remembrance, and a new humanity
will be born."

He was consumed in the flames as his voice faded into silence.

"Don't leave!" she cried.  Her voice seemed to echo to the ends of the solar system.

# CHAPTER 34
# CD-ROM

Alexandria became aware of a dim voice, calling from a vast distance across light years. She couldn't make out the words. She focused to comprehend the meaning, but it was an immense effort to respond. Someone shook her arm.

"Alex, wake up. You're shouting."

She felt another nudge. Alexandria slowly opened her eyes, feeling disoriented. Tears rolled down her face.

"Nightmare?" Erik asked, concern showing on his face.

"Another unbelievable dream," she said, sitting up in bed and blinking. Alex rubbed the spot between her eyes with her thumb and index finger, trying to clear her mind. She snatched a tissue from the bedside table and blew her nose.

"This was Egypt, a long time ago," she said.

"Why were you shouting?" asked.

"Constellations came to life like Frosty the Snowman," she said with a sardonic grimace. Erik's confused look made her smile. "Sorry. I need to start at the beginning, but before I can do that, I need to write the dream down and etch the details in my brain. I'll read my notes at breakfast so Miguel, Lela, and Sheila can hear too."

"Fair enough. I'll bring coffee after I shower," he smiled.

"Thanks," she said.

Alex recorded the details of her dream in a spiral notebook. The first part of the experience felt real, but the second part seemed surreal. She knew the symbols were significant but couldn't decipher any meaning. The image of the Serpent Bearer was burned into her awareness as if she'd been marked with a branding iron. She felt an excruciating sense of loss, as if everything that mattered had been buried in those storage chambers.

Erik brought coffee and handed her a mug of steaming brew. She drank the hot liquid as she poured the words of her dream onto paper. When she finished, she showered and dressed in a pastel-print sun dress. She twisted her wet hair like a rope and secured the unruly curls to the top of her head with a metal barrette. The doorbell rang as Alex galloped down the spiral stairs.

"Coming," she shouted.

Lela and Sheila stood together on the porch. Lela's tricolor hair was awry, and she wore wrinkled khaki walking shorts and an oversized white camp shirt. Sheila wore a long, red dress and gold earrings, and her straight-black hair was brushed back in a clip. She held a computer printer in her arms.

"I had another dream," Alex announced without prelude, hugging each of them, and turning toward the kitchen. The two women followed Alexandria toward the kitchen and found Erik setting up his computer on the round wooden table. Don Miguel fed Sheba, and Crystal watched with interest.

"Why don't you put the printer here," Erik said. "Thanks for schlepping."

"Only a slight extra charge," Sheila said.

"Coffee?" Alex asked, lifting a carafe. Four hands went up like school children, and she poured coffee into ceramic mugs. Alex gobbled raspberry scones, washing the sweet pastries down with coffee and cold milk. Fortified, she washed her hands and poured another mug of coffee.

Alex stood in front of the sink and was framed by a halo of sunlight behind her. Once he had connected the printer, he looked toward her expectantly. She recounted every detail of her dream experience, glancing up from her notebook when she finished to assess their reactions.

"I've studied dream symbols for years," Lela said. "That was no ordinary dream, young lady. The Una dream was certainly Atlantis, and I think your regression proved that. This sounds like a lifetime in ancient Egypt combined with some sort of prophecy. As you know, the Cayce information refers to a hall of records underneath Giza."

"I seem to recall Gran mentioning something like that, but I never thought the record hall was an actual place. I thought it was a metaphor," Alex said.

"Cayce said both information and artifacts are buried under the Sphinx and in Mexico. I didn't realize people might be buried there too," Lela said in a breathless tone.

Miguel stood and joined Alex at the kitchen window. He looked at her, then turned to face the others. "I also had a dream last night."

Flashing back to the dream he had shared at Palenque; Alex nearly dropped her coffee mug. "I think I should sit down for this."

Miguel smiled. "On its own, my dream is not as startling as yours, but in combination the symbology seems significant.

"You are all probably aware of legendary Quetzalcoatl, or Kukulkan in Maya myth. Thought to be a wise teacher, his image to both groups is the Feathered Serpent. Last night in my dream a large rattle snake grew wings, and then flew toward the east as the Sun set in the west."

"Endings, beginnings, and regeneration," Lela said.

"The symbolism alone is powerful, but the two dreams together pack a wallop," Sheila said. "To me, serpents always represent wisdom."

"Yes," Miguel said.

"I read an article about Serpent Bearer in an astrology magazine recently," Sheila continued. "Ophiuchus, Greek for Serpent Bearer, is a thirteenth zodiac sign, reaching into the ecliptic between Scorpio and Sagittarius, the Scorpion, and the Archer. You've plugged into some cutting-edge stuff."

"The legend of a hall of records exists in several mystery schools," Miguel observed, black eyes dancing. "Khem is the ancient name of Egypt, and the Khem were the Pleiades."

"Right, and our word alchemy comes from Khem," Erik said.

"This is too much for me to take in," Alex said.

"Serpent Bearer is the same archetype as Quetzalcoatl and also Asclepius in Greek mythology," Miguel said. "His cult was always connected with serpents. Asclepius was such a great healer he could resurrect people who had died. When Asclepius tried to revive Orion from a fatal scorpion sting, Hades persuaded Zeus to kill him. He didn't like the implications of an empty underworld."

"Orion again, and resurrection," Alex said, frowning.

"But what is the message, and what's the connection between serpents and the crystal?" Lela asked.

"The right use of force?" Sheila asked.

"Serpents can be seen as icons of ancient wisdom. Hermes gave Asclepius the caduceus in recognition of his skill," Miguel continued. "Asclepius was placed in the sky as a constellation to honor his achievements. He stands next to the Scorpion, on the opposite side of the sky from Orion, to prevent further trouble. The two constellations are never visible at the same time."

"So, one is rebirth and the other immortality?" Alex asked.

"In your dream, you said Vega anchored the poles of the earth," Erik said. "Vega was the pole star twelve thousand years ago."

"Did Egypt even exist then?" Alex asked in disbelief. "Maybe there's also a relationship between Vega and the Pleiades." She stood and began to pace.

"I have astronomy software that moves the stars backward and forward in time. Robert Bauval, who perceived the relationship between the pyramids and the belt of Orion, used an early version of this kind of software. Bauval, and his co-author, Graham Hancock, believe that the Giza monuments mark not just an idea but a precise moment in time," Erik commented.

"On the spring equinox sunrise in 10,500 BCE, the three pyramids of Giza perfectly mirrored the three stars in Orion's belt. Also at that epoch, during the astrological age of Leo, the Sphinx looked due east at the sign Leo. Some researchers believe the Sphinx was originally a lion," Erik said.

"I saw it as a lioness in my dream," Alex said.

"According to Cayce, the Great Pyramid was built between 10,400 BCE and 10,300 BCE," Lela said.

"If the Sphinx looks due east at the equinox, and he saw a lion in the sky during the age of Leo, he will see the Water Bearer, the constellation of Aquarius, rise at the dawn of the age of Aquarius," Sheila said.

"Will the Moon be in the seventh house?" Erik quipped.

Sheila continued undaunted. "Those two constellations are one-hundred-eighty degrees opposite each other. If Orion was on the southern horizon in 10,500 BCE, your friend the Serpent Bearer would be north with Scorpio. Orion is aligned with Taurus, the Bull. The four points of the astrological fixed cross."

"All the cultures I have studied use the movements of the stars and planets to create a reference point, a star clock, if you will," Miguel said. "Star pictures are turned into creatures and planets into gods. Stories are created and remembered through myth and legend."

"So, we're decoding a message that's thirteen thousand years old?" Lela asked. "We don't even know if we have the puzzle pieces."

"Why go to all that trouble?" Alex asked. "Wouldn't it have been easier to bury a scroll in a cave?"

"Difficult to say, but the fixed cross has always held deep symbology and scrolls decay," Sheila said.

"And didn't Thoth say something like that during the regression?" Erik asked.

"Wait a minute," Lela said. "The lion, bull, human, and eagle. Aren't those like the animals from Ezekiel's vision in the Bible?"

"Like a prophecy?" Alex asked.

"Like a promise," Emma said quietly from the corner by the fireplace where she had been standing unnoticed. They all turned to stare at her. "Timing is everything. Rose used to say we were coming to the close of a great cycle and that the stakes were high. She often worried about choices she made in your regard, Alexandria."

Alex stood and took Emma's hand. "I know she did what she thought was best."

"Many traditions predicted the time period around the year 2000 of the Current Era would be significant," Miguel said. "The fifth sun of the Maya calendar, the Hindu Kali Yuga, and the close of the age of Pisces conjoin. There is also a great conjunction of the winter solstice Sun in 2012 with the center of the galaxy. Is it possible the constellation of the Serpent Bearer returning to the zodiac could signal the revelation of hidden knowledge."

"I wonder where Serpent Bearer is in relation to the Galactic Center?" Erik mused.

"If Giza is a coded astronomical message, a star clock, something should trigger the alarm," Alex said, shaking her head.

"And something that big should be easy to see," Erik said.

"How about we fire up that CD thing and see what the readings have to say," Lela suggested.

"We can check out the astronomy later," Erik said, donning his reading glasses.

He installed the program onto his laptop to run the CD-ROM, and Alex thought he looked professorial in his wire-rimmed glasses. She felt the urge to ruffle his hair but scooted a chair next to him instead as she wanted to see everything first-hand.

The others moved their chairs around the table to see the screen. When he started to run the program, the computer whirred and clicked as the processor read the disk. The main screen came up and the word SONAR flashed on the screen.

"Okay folks, we're live. Give me a word or phrase to search."

"Atlantis," Alex said.

Erik typed Atlantis on the keyboard. The computer continued to hum and click as it searched. A dialog box appeared on the screen, showing the search process. After a few seconds another box appeared.

"Atlantis, thirteen-hundred-ninety-three occurrences in nine-hundred-seventy-three documents," he laughed.

"Oh, my stars," Sheila said.

"I had no idea," Lela said. "No wonder people marvel at the consistency of the information. Considering the number of references and the time span, it's unbelievable."

"Try Poseidia," Miguel suggested.

Erik keyed in the word, and a few moments later the screen reported sixty-two occurrences in fifty documents.

"How about Yucatan?" Alex asked.

"One hundred-forty-six occurrences in one-hundred-twenty-four documents," Erik reported.

"This could take forever," Sheila sighed.

"How about Tuaoi stone?" Lela asked.

Erik typed the words.

SONAR reported fifteen references in seven documents.

"That's more like it," Alex said and scanned the references as they appeared in sequence on the screen. "These references are all in Grandpa's files. I read last night that Cayce called the crystal a Firestone. He described the stone as a large cylindrical opalescent crystal with six facets used in the Atlantean sacred temple.

"The crystal was an unlimited energy source. Eventually they used the power as a weapon. They set the frequency too high, which caused massive earthquakes. What I read was very similar to the dream about Atlantis."

"What next?" Erik asked.

"Shall we try 'Iltar'?" Miguel asked. "I am curious to see if the High Priest appears in the readings."

"Four references in one document. That's promising, let's have a look."

The name Iltar appeared highlighted in a sentence. Erik scanned the screen. "Let me print this. I think Miguel should read it, but let's keep a list of the reading numbers for reference later. This one is number 5750-001."

"I volunteer to track the reading numbers," Lela said.

Three sheets emerged from the printer. Erik handed them to Miguel, and his bright eyes raced over the pages. His clear and beautiful voice filled the room.

'Then, with the leavings of the civilization in Atlantis (in Poseidia, more specific) Iltar - with a group of followers that had been of the household of Atlan, the followers of the worship of the One, with some ten individuals - left this land of Poseidia and came westward, entering what would now be a portion of Yucatan. And there began, with the activities of the peoples there, the development into a civilization that rose much in the same manner as that which had been in the Atlantean land.'

Alex put her coffee mug on the table and gaped at don Miguel. "I have chills," she said. "Don Miguel, I really believe you were Iltar. I can almost see it, like my dream and regression."

"What else does it say?" Sheila asked.

The first temples that were erected by Iltar and his followers were destroyed at the period of change physically in the contours of the land. That now being found, and a portion already discovered that has laid in waste for many centuries, was then a combination of those peoples from Mu, Oz, and Atlantis.

In which pyramid or temple are the records mentioned in the readings given through this channel on Atlantis, in April 1932?

'As given, that temple was destroyed at the time there was the last destruction in Atlantis. Yet as time draws nigh when changes are to come about, there may be the opening of those three places where the records are one, to those that are the initiates in the knowledge of the One God.

'The temple by Iltar will then rise again. Also, there will be the opening of the temple or in Egypt, and those records that were put into the heart of the Atlantean land may also be found there - that have been kept, for those that are of that group. The records are one!'

Don Miguel's silver and black head bowed. He held the papers in his hands and continued to stare at the printed words. His brow furrowed and his lips pursed. He seemed deep in thought, transported to another time.

"Just imagine. Reading about your own past life this way," Lela said. "I guess we get an idea of how folks felt who had readings when Mr. Cayce was alive."

"My goose bumps have goose bumps," Alex said. "I just remembered something else. In my Atlantis dream, your staff had a serpent on top. And the walking stick you used in Palenque looked like a snake too."

"I have it with me in fact," Miguel said.

"You are a serpent bearer, Miguel," Alex whispered.

"And wisdom is what you carry," Lela said.

"Want to take a break?" Erik asked.

"No, let us continue. We are just beginning to understand," Miguel said.

"Okay, let's see," he said, squinting at the screen, this is an excerpt from 486-1."

"Got it, Lela said."

"Hence we find the entity then, Ax-Ten-tna, as would be said in the present, was the first to set the records that are yet to be discovered, or yet to be had of those activities in the Atlantean land, and for the preservation of the data, that as yet to be found from the chambers of the way between the Sphinx and the pyramid of records.'

"We're supposed to find the records," Alex said with an intense shiver of recognition. "We were there when they were buried. This is our purpose, reclaiming the ancient wisdom."

The group sat in stunned silence as the implications of Alex's revelation sank in. Their reverie was shattered by pounding at the front door.

# CHAPTER 35

# OBSESSION

Crystal growled, alarming Alex, and raced past her toward the front of the house. She opened the front door to see Rudolph Selig accompanied by Officer O'Reilly and another uniformed officer. She noticed Selig's obsessive grooming, as if extreme fastidiousness would somehow free him from moral degradation.

"Sorry to trouble you, Miss Stuart, but we have a search warrant," O'Reilly said, cocking his head toward Selig with unconcealed distaste. "I'll oversee the search, and we'll do our best not to disrupt your house."

Alex took the envelope O'Reilly handed her. She removed the thick document and unfolded the pages and pretended to read the search warrant, but the words blurred.

"I told you earlier, this is a waste of time. My grandmother donated everything to the university," Alex said with forced bravado, silently blessing Grandpa's foresight for creating the secret room.

Selig glared at Alex. Malice dripped like icicles from frigid, beady eyes. "It's futile to resist the inevitable, Miss Stuart."

Inwardly she recoiled, but she held his gaze.

"Wait out here, Selig," O'Reilly ordered.

Selig waited on the porch, looking like a vulture perched on a tree branch, waiting for prey to become carrion. He didn't have the courage to hunt and kill himself, leaving the dirty work for others so his talon-like fingernails remained pristine.

Crystal stood inside the door; eyes riveted on Selig. A low growl echoed in her throat. Alex stood beside her and held her collar  Selig lit a pencil thin cigar and placed his lips around its plastic tip.

"Your dog is an excellent judge of character," O'Reilly said, scowling.

Alex looked at O'Reilly. "I'm glad you're here." She was sure the police could hear the thunder of her heart as they searched the house. She stopped breathing while they searched the library, terrified they would accidentally trip the mechanism to the secret room.

Selig was desperate for Grandpa's files, that much was clear. Alex felt her stomach turn as she recalled the Cayce files that she she'd taken upstairs last night. She breathed a silent prayer of thanks that she had stuffed them under the bedspread so Emma wouldn't notice.

Don Miguel joined Alex and Crystal at the door.

"Don't let him upset you," Miguel said, placing his strong arm around her shoulder. She relaxed a little as Miguel moved behind her and rubbed the muscles in her neck and shoulders with his powerful hands. She hadn't realized she was so tense.

"Call upon your strength, Alexandria. Fill your being with power. Selig acts out his role in this drama and we have yet to see what that is," Miguel said.

Alex breathed deeply and felt a shift like an opening. She sensed an overshadowing presence. Calmness, peace, and strength washed into her consciousness. Crystal relaxed but did not reduce her vigilance. The search lasted thirty minutes but seemed like hours to Alex.

"We're finished," O'Reilly said, walking toward the front door. "We didn't find anything resembling the material he's looking for. Mr. Anderson said the computer belongs to him."

Alex nodded. "I don't think my grandfather computerized anything."

"Hello, Miss Goldwoman," O'Reilly said as Sheila joined them in the foyer.

"Hello yourself, O'Reilly," Sheila smiled. Miguel's eyebrows furrowed in amused curiosity.

O'Reilly opened the leaded glass front door.

"What did you find?" Selig demanded.

"Absolutely nothing," O'Reilly said.

"This is not over, Miss Stuart," Selig said. Anger revealed a slight Eastern European accent. "I know you have the records in your possession. I can feel it. If necessary, I'll confiscate the contents of this library and tear each book apart page by page until I find what I'm looking for."

Alex felt like he'd thrown acid in her face. "I told you, my grandmother donated everything to the university," she lied. "Perhaps you can find what you're looking for there."

Selig glared at her then directed a look of intense disdain toward Miguel. "Duncan Stuart ventured far afield. He seemed to have difficulty discerning significance and had to have a strange attraction to outworn relics."

"That's enough, Selig" O'Reilly ordered. "We'll be in touch if there's anything else, Miss Stuart. Thanks for your cooperation." He pulled the big door shut as he left.

I will make you a cup of strong herb tea," Miguel said.

"Who was that nasty-looking man?" Lela wanted to know when they walked into the kitchen. "There's something familiar and decidedly unpleasant about him. I think I may have seen him at an A.R.E. event."

"Alex collapsed into a chair and rubbed her temples with her thumbs. She realized she had a pounding headache. "His name is Rudolph Selig, and he claims he has the rights to Grandpa's research data. There was no mention of him in the will, but he trumped up a phony document and managed to get a search warrant."

"You said the good guys and the bad guys are back, Lela," Erik said.

"I can't imagine him at the A.R.E. except as a spy," Sheila said.

"The plot thickens?" Miguel said.

"That's beneath you, Miguel," Lela said chuckling.

"Let's get back to work," Alex sighed. "I want to get my mind off that awful man. Try searching the word 'capstone.'"

Erik keyed in the word and when the first of four references came up, he scanned the screen. "This is interesting. Number 440-5, Lela. This one also references another reading number.

'As to describing the manner of construction of the stone, we find it was a large cylindrical glass (as would be termed today), cut with facets in such a manner that the capstone on top of same made for the centralizing of the power or force that concentrated between the end of the cylinder and the capstone itself.

"As indicated, [See 996-12] the records of the manners of construction of same are in three places in the earth, as it stands today: In the sunken portions of Atlantis, or Poseidia, where a portion of the temples may yet be discovered, under the slime of ages of sea water -- near what is known as Bimini, off the coast of Florida. And in the temple records that were in Egypt, where the entity later acted in cooperation with others in preserving the records that came from the land where these had been kept. Also, the records that were carried to what is now Yucatan in America where these stones (that they know so little about) are now during the last few months - being uncovered.'

"What's the date of that reading?" Sheila asked.

"December 20, 1933," Alex sighed.

"Selig could know about this if he spent time with Duncan. And if he hung around the A.R.E., he knows what's supposed to be buried there too," Sheila said.

"Knowledge of the crystal as a power source is buried with the records," Erik said, removing his glasses and rubbing his eyes. "A volatile irony to be sure, knowledge of free energy buried in the Middle East. That information could certainly upset the balance of power."

"Free unlimited energy and powerful weaponry, a deadly combination in the wrong hands," Alex said.

"Enough to kill for?" Lela asked.

"I'm beginning to wonder if Rose's death was completely natural," Emma said in a voice like a whisper, her eyes brimming with tears."

Alexandria wheeled around and looked at Emma, her eyes huge. "You're saying someone could have killed Gran over this?" Alex felt anger building toward rage. Miguel stood and took hold of Alexandria's hands. She was so upset she wanted to shake them loose. Erik rose and stood behind her.

"Emma is right," Lela said, "I have wondered this myself, and we must face how much is at stake. Rose knew the risks involved. She and Duncan both knew. If he was alive, he was able to protect you both because he bargained with his knowledge."

Alex wanted to scream or throw something. Her body shook as she battled with this latest possibility. The others were silent, waiting to see what she would do. After a few moments she struggled to compose herself and looked at each of them.

"The only way I know how to deal with this is to fight. Since I still don't know what or who we're fighting we need more knowledge. Let's keep working, I'll have to deal with grief later." She returned to her chair and stared at the computer as if her brain could penetrate the screen.

Miguel sighed deeply. "Remember how happy she was in your dream. She may be able to help you more from the other side."

Alex fought to bury her anger and mobilize her will to learn whatever she could.

"What was that other name? Hep something?" Erik asked.

"H-e-p-t-s-u-p-h-t," Alex spelled.

"Fifteen references in six different documents." Erik printed the Hept-supht references, and Alex read the materials.

"There's a fair amount about the construction of the Great Pyramid," she said, "and more about the records. The syntax is even more unwieldy than usual."

"Number please?" Lela asked.

"This one is reading 378-16, Erik said.

"In the record chambers there were more ceremonies than in calling the peoples at the finishing of that called the pyramid. For, here those that were trained in the Temple of Sacrifice as well as in the Temple Beautiful were about the sealing of the record chambers. For, these were to be kept as had been given by the priests in Atlantis or Poseidia (Temple), when these records of the race, of the developments, of the laws pertaining to One were put in their chambers and to be opened only when there was the returning of those into materiality, or to earth's experience, when the change was imminent in the earth; which change, we see, begins in '58 and ends with the changes wrought in the upheavals and the shifting of the poles, as begins then the reign in '98, as time is counted in the present, of those influences that have been given by many in the records that have been kept by those sojourners in this land of the Semitic peoples.'"

"The syntax seems worse," Sheila said.

"Patience," Erik said, raising his index finger. "Listen to this question. What does the sealed room contain?"

'Answer: A record of Atlantis from the beginnings of those periods when the Spirit took form or began the encasements in that land, and the developments of the peoples throughout their sojourn, with the record of the first destruction and the changes that took place in the land, with the record of the soujournings of the peoples in the varied activities in other lands, and a record of the meet-ings of all the nations or lands for the activities in the destructions that became necessary with the final destruction of Atlantis and the buildings of the pyramid of initiation, with who, what, where, would come the opening of the records that are as copies from the sunken Atlantis; for with the change, the temple must rise again.

'This in position lies, as the sun rises from the waters, the line of the shadow or light falls between the paws of the Sphinx, that was later set as the sentinel or guard, and which may not be entered from the connecting chambers from the

Sphinx's right paw until the time has been fulfilled when the changes must be active in this sphere of man's experience. Between the Sphinx and the river.

'Am I the one to receive directions as to where the sealed room is and how to find it?

'Answer: One of the two. Two, with a guide. Hept-supht, El-ka, and Atlan. These will appear.'

"The same records in three places," Alex said, aquamarine eyes on fire. "A connecting chamber from the Sphinx's right paw. We know Hept-supht connected with Cayce when he was alive. Who are El-Ka and Atlan? Didn't the Iltar reading talk about the house of Atlan?"

"Alexandria," Miguel said, grasping her hand, "if your dream is correct, your former incarnation as High Priestess may lie buried in the Record Chamber in Egypt."

"But the man who was Hept-supht died in nineteen fifty-four," Alex said.

"That was more than sixty years ago. Plus, souls can assist from other dimensions," Miguel said.

"So that soul could have returned?" she wondered.

"We might find the star clock you described," Erik said, whistling through his teeth.

"The star charts you described would prove their antiquity," Sheila said.

"We are at the center of the fulfillment of the prophecy," Lela said in awe.

"Try record chamber," Alex said, captured by the need for answers.

"Right. Here's another good one; number 5748-6," he replied.

"Got it," Lela said.

'With the storehouse, or record house where the records are still to be uncovered, there is a chamber or passage from the right forepaw to this entrance of the record chamber, or record tomb. This may not be entered without an understanding, for those that were left as guards may not be passed until after a period of their regeneration in the Mount, or the fifth root race begins.'

"Those who were left as guards," Alex said, frowning.

"What's the fifth root race?" asked.

"The next evolutionary step for humanity," Lela said.

"I agree," Miguel said. "The doctrine of root races is common to eastern, western and indigenous traditions."

"Don't the Hindus use a symbol like a caduceus to represent the energy flowing through the body?" Alex asked.

"Yes," Miguel said. "Ida and Pingala are twin currents of what is called Kundalini that circle in alternating serpentine fashion around the spine."

"I think Serpent Bearer has something to do with the fifth root race, something about immortality. Like Moses raised the serpent of brass in the wilderness," Sheila said.

"The Sanskrit word Kundalini means sleeping serpent. The Eastern mystery schools speak of raising the serpent energy, like raising the light in your dream, along the spine. Enlightenment and the ability to regenerate the body, immortality is the result," don Miguel said.

I'm detecting the glimmer of a pattern here," Erik said. "Limitless energy, powerful weapons, and immortality. Selig is probably not acting alone."

"Or he's in competition with someone else," Lela said. The group became silent, each pondering their own thoughts. Alexandria walked to the kitchen window and stared outside for several moments. She turned to face her companions, looking fierce.

"When do we leave for Egypt?"

CHAPTER 36

# FLIGHT INTO EGYPT

Alexandria sat on her suitcase in the foyer of Gran's house, resting elbows on knees and cupping her chin in her palms. Afternoon sunlight pierced the leaded panes of cut glass, creating patterns of light on motley pieces of luggage that had been marshaled at the entry. Crystal sat at Alex's feet, looking forlorn. Two months had flown by as preparations were made for the trip.

*We're going to Egypt.* Alex reviewed her checklist for the hundredth time: pants, long skirts, sun hat, water bottles, flashlight, film, digital camera, journal, protein bars and sunscreen. She'd carefully wrapped and packed the Quetzal feather as a symbol of guidance and providence.

Satisfied, she relaxed and extended her right hand toward the light. Alex twisted her hand, admiring the ring she had made as part of her preparation. The three, precious jade beads were arranged inside a sterling triangle. An ornate silver snake coiled around the green orbs like a serpent in the sun.

She had also found an exquisite, apple-green peridot shaped like a pyramid. She was delighted with the radiant central star. She had bartered with a friend and procured two triangular diamonds. The finished gold amulet reproduced the image of the three pyramidal stones from her dream. The green triangle pointed up, and two diamonds looked like wings on either side.

When she had placed the finished necklace around her throat, she felt a curious rush of familiarity. She touched her breastbone where the talisman

223

rested beneath her shirt and smiled, remembering the Cross of Palenque on Chan Ka's neck in Chiapas.

"Ready?" Erik queried from the hall, hands on hips and feet apart. He wore long khaki pants and hiking boots. A beige vest, with a dozen pockets in various sizes and combinations of snaps, flaps, and Velcro, covered a white cotton camp shirt. Alex thought he looked like a movie poster of Indiana Jones.

"As ready as I can be, considering the whirlwind preparations," she replied, brushing russet hair from her forehead.

"I can't wait to get back to Egypt," he said. "Mohammed will meet us at the airport. I hope we'll have a chance to put this pricey camera to the test."

Alex smiled. His excitement was contagious. Outside a horn signaled Sheila's arrival. "This is it. Where's Miguel?"

"Here," Miguel said, appearing behind Erik. He looked distinguished in dark brown slacks, woven leather belt and white shirt. Silver hair showed at his temples under the brim of his white Panama hat. His black eyes danced.

Emma and Crystal followed them onto the porch. Alex hugged Emma. "Be careful," Emma pleaded. "Come back in one piece. Your mother is beside herself with worry." Emma's forehead wrinkled, and her blue eyes clouded.

Alex dropped to her knees and put her arms around the fluffy white dog she adored. "Don't worry, you two. I'll be home soon with exotic presents." Crystal attempted to wag her tail, but her brown eyes looked sad.

"We have to do this, Emma."

Sheila, dressed in khaki with matching hat, stood next to her SUV like a scout master. The three questers piled into the vehicle like children heading off to camp. Erik crammed luggage into every available space, then climbed in front with Sheila. Alex sat in back with Miguel and felt a pang of guilt when she looked at Emma and Crystal on the porch.

As Erik and Sheila chatted in the front seat, Alex became lost in her own thoughts, recalling her trip to Mexico. Sheila drove the two hours to Kennedy airport and dropped the travelers outside the international check-in location. She administered a fierce hug to each of them.

"Always a bridesmaid, never a bride. You better call before you rewrite the history of the world," she admonished. Moist eyes belied her stern words.

"Don't worry," Alex promised. She gave Sheila's hands an affectionate squeeze and kissed her on the cheek.

~

THEY ENTERED the terminal and joined hundreds of other travelers in the large open area for international flights. Finding the Egypt Air counter, they entered the line that was marked off by cords and stanchions. A long line of mostly Egyptian families waited for seat assignments on the booked flight. A few small groups of American tourists gathered, their English standing out in a chorus of Arabic. Alex was unaccustomed to seeing so many women wearing scarves and veils. The men and children mostly wore Western clothes.

After administrative machinations, travelers finally funneled to the departure lounge to await boarding. Once onboard the travelers walked down narrow aisles of the huge plane like an ant colony on the move. Passengers squeezed into tight rows of bright-gold upholstered seats, preparing for the overnight flight. Attendants distributed plastic packs of earphones, travel slippers, and ear plugs, offering pillows and blankets to the travelers.

Alex glanced at Miguel, who looked serene in the window seat. He stared into the darkness, watching the ground crew stow luggage into the bowels of the huge plane. He seemed unaffected by the press of humanity. Erik had taken a generous dose of Valerian Root and was already asleep in the aisle seat. Alex felt like the occupant of a tin of salted fish sandwiched between them and squirmed like a child resisting a nap.

The pilots finally taxied the plane to the end of the runway and revved the powerful engines. When they accelerated for takeoff, the plane labored on the runway like a gigantic duck-billed platypus, lumbering down the beach in an attempt to fly.

The engines thundered, and the overhead luggage carriers shook and rattled. At the point she was certain they would abort takeoff, the behemoth was airborne. The pilot banked the plane in a wide arc, revealing a million diamond lights of the Manhattan night skyline. Alex leaned across Miguel to look.

"It's breathtaking," he said.

Alex sighed, crossed her arms, and sat back in her seat. She stared at the map on the bulkhead that would electronically plot the progress of the transatlantic flight. The computer flashed periodic weather reports. She glanced at her watch and did a quick calculation. Six A.M. in Cairo and they were scheduled to arrive at five the next afternoon.

Miguel looked at her, his eyes twinkling with affection. The corners of his mouth turned up slightly. "I suggest you take measures to relax and use this time to advantage. Otherwise, it will be an unpleasant night."

Alex blushed. "You're right." She kicked off her shoes and pulled on the royal-blue acrylic slippers that reminded her of baby booties. She positioned a blindfold and ear plugs, readying her CD player with relaxing music. She inserted a favorite CD of electronically generated thunderstorm sounds designed to synchronize the hemispheres of the brain.

Alex willed herself to relax. Breathing deeply, she allowed the sounds of the synthesized rainfall to lull her consciousness into an altered state. With each intake of breath, the cramped discomfort of her third-dimensional surroundings melted away. She drifted into a dark, dreamy calmness and imagined the vast waters of the Atlantic Ocean far beneath her.

ALEXANDRIA ENTERED the realm of dreams and found herself at the intersection of four paths amid a large forest. She stood at the crossroads of an impossible juncture. Each quadrant of the wood expressed the quintessence of one of the four seasons.

Scarlet tulips and buttery daffodils danced in the spring wood. Chartreuse new leaves burst from trees and bushes. Fragrant pink cherry blossoms, white apple trees, goldenrod, vivid fuchsia quince and rose azalea proclaimed their awakening from winter sleep.

The trees of the summer wood were heavy with the weight of fully grown leaves, and insects hummed in hot, heavy air. An ibis bird fed in the shallow waters of a pool. A fiery canopy of towering golden oaks, yellow elms and red maples crowned the autumn quadrant. Pine and spruce trees provided a green contrast to the glory of the flaming trees.

A white mantle blanketed the winter realm as large snow flakes fell onto a crystal carpet that covered the forest floor and stillness pervaded the slumbering woodland. Alex gazed at the archetypal representations of spring, summer, fall, and winter, the simultaneous expression of birth, death, and resurrection. A path led into each seasonal landscape from her vantage point at the center of the wheel of four directions.

She chose the autumn path. The trail curved beneath vibrant trees and ran along a rippling stream. Sunlight filtered through red and gold leaves, creating sparkling diamonds of light on cascading water. Dry leaves cracked beneath her feet as she walked, and the pungent aroma of decay reached her nostrils.

Brilliant leaves drifted slowly to the ground as tall trees released their magnificent raiment and covered the ground in a gentle, maternal gesture. A patchwork quilt of crimson and amber prepared earth for the long winter night.

Alex inhaled and filled her lungs and diaphragm. A sapphire sky was dotted with wispy white clouds. Industrious squirrels chirped as they gathered nuts. Noisy birds flew in formation high overhead, rehearsing their southern flight. Alexandria's perceived the exquisite interplay and balance of the annual cycle of light and dark.

Alex walked along the edge of the cheerful brook until she caught the scent of burning wood. The path took a sharp turn and she spied an ivy-covered cottage nestled at the edge of the stream. An inviting plume of white smoke rose in a welcoming spiral from a stone chimney. She smelled fresh bread and realized she was ravenous.

Alex approached the small wood and stone cottage. Orange marigolds, deep crimson, white and purple chrysanthemums surrounded the house and walk. Blue and yellow pansies spilled from window boxes. A grove of old apple trees grew behind the cottage. Their branches bowed to ground, laden with a heavy crop of round, red fruit. Her mouth watered, and she ached to pluck one.

The door opened, and a man emerged from the small cottage wearing a gray hermit's robe. Brilliant blue eyes smiled at her. Her own eyes filled with tears of joyful recognition.

"Ra Ta," she said.

He extended his arms. She ran to him, and they embraced. "It is a long while since our work in the temple, young Mira," he smiled as he motioned her inside.

Overcome with wonder and emotion, Alexandria stepped into the welcome warmth of the cabin. She sat in a wooden chair where a place was set in front of a stone fireplace. A cheery fire of pine logs burned and crackled, and the aroma of the smoke was like incense. A woven flax cloth and a pottery vase of fall flowers cheered the simple carved table. Beeswax candles burned on either side of the flowers.

A black cat, sleek as a panther, slept by the fire with her tail wrapped around her. When Alex sat at the table, the cat opened her eyes. She stretched, sat up and assumed a posture like an Egyptian cat deity, her regal demeanor contrasting with the simple surroundings. The cat meowed a greeting.

Ra Ta laughed. "Forgive Bastet. She seldom has visitors, and I'm afraid she tires of my company."

The hermit served her a pottery mug of hot, spiced cider and a plate piled high with warm baked bread, honey, cheese, and cold sliced apples. She bit into a cold piece of apple and a slice of cheese. The sweet juice filled her mouth, and the tart cheese made her pucker.

"Delicious," Alex said, savoring the food.

Ra Ta smiled and watched her eat. When she finished, she sat back in a rocking chair in front of the fire. Bastet jumped into her lap. Alex stroked the shiny fur of the elegant feline, and Bastet purred in response. Alex felt a pang of guilt, realizing that she had never petted Sheba. She looked into Ra Ta's startling blue eyes. He seemed to read her thoughts.

"If you're ready," he said, "we must take a journey. Someone waits for you."

"Of course," Alex said without reservation. "Should I lie down?"

"No. Close your eyes. I will be your guide."

Alex did as he instructed. She cradled her arms around the soft body of Bastet and willed herself to relax. With a swiftness that astounded her, they rose into space. A luminous temple shone like a magnificent beacon against the darkness of the starry background. Alexandria stood next to Ra Ta at the entrance.

"Where are we?" she asked.

"Shambhala, dwelling place of the spiritual masters of wisdom that exists on the etheric plane. All spiritual traditions have saints, and this is their spiritual abode," Ra Ta replied.

They entered the city of light and walked into a grand foyer. The enormous space was filled with beings of light. She could not distinguish physical features, but she was aware of their individualities. Alex recognized Thea and Dream Walker and experienced their power. They nodded and extended a silent greeting.

One being's light burned brighter than the others, and she was drawn to his intense fire like a moth to a flame. She approached the radiance of his presence and felt impelled to genuflect.

"Do not kneel, Priestess of the Light," he communicated. There were no words. The communication took place through thoughts.

"You have known me in many guises in many lifetimes. You experience me now as Thoth, as I appeared in Egypt and Atlantis."

An aura of love, power and authority emanated from him like brilliant sunlight. In her mind's eye, she envisioned a handsome man with dark auburn hair and eyes like pale translucent amber. Alex sensed a compassionate smile.

"It is a momentous time," Thoth continued. "Humanity is poised to enter a new dimension, an expanded universe. This is the moment of your collective initiation. The great being whose body is the Earth prepares for another initiation and humanity is swept along in this process. Human consciousness can choose a higher ground or remain in denial about what needs to change. You must surrender judgment and learn compassion. Move into your hearts and reclaim the stars.

"The universe is a vast, multi-dimensional reality. Earth has been isolated because the realm of the third dimension is the laboratory of choice. There are no rewards or punishments, only consequences as humanity learns through endless repetition not to repeat unpleasantness. Souls have a right to the outcome of their choices no matter how painful those consequences are from a human point of view."

Alex saw the blue planet from space and thought how conflict was invisible and unity a reality from this perspective.

"In this classroom," Thoth continued, "you have studied the lessons of the heart. Look closely at the words "earth" and "heart." The last letter of "earth" is the first letter of "heart." Using the same letters, we have "terah," or "terra." "Terra" is Earth with an opened heart, a fourth-dimensional sphere, the next evolutionary step for humanity.

"A path of return has always existed for those whose aspiration drew them inward and upward to a more actualized state. They listened with the heart and heard the music of the celestial spheres, feeling the harmonies of the divine symphony.

"I drew the constellations in the sky in a distant epoch. The star pictures portray the blueprint of humanity's unfoldment. The story endured throughout the ages through myth and legend. Teachers and way showers were sent as guides.

"The pattern of completion is encoded in humanity's DNA. The number and kind of linkages determines the level of expression. Compassion opens the heart and forms new linkages in the helix. Existence is holographic, and as individual units expand their capacity for divine expression, the projection of the whole expands.

As Thoth's words echoed in her mind, Alex saw the stars as if she were inside a cosmic planetarium, viewing the starry canopy from inside the celestial bowl. The ancient depiction of the star pictures was revealed to her in their true significance. She grasped the stories they were intended to tell and felt the power of the stars themselves.

"The Orion nebula is a galactic birthplace of stars, a place of generation," Thoth said. "Orion, the great hunter, with brilliant Sirius behind him in the stars of his hunting dog, stretches his bow and aims his arrow across the sky.

"See how he pursues the seven sisters of the Pleiades, who appear to flee before him, as he chases them into manifestation. Just as your body's maturation is tied to secretions from the endocrine glands, your spiritual development is related to the movement of life force in your chakras, the centers of spiritual force.

"Across the celestial bowl, Serpent Bearer holds the key to the doctrine of immortality. He is the image of Horus Bedehty, who rose to heaven on falcon wings, overcoming death and avenging his father Osiris. The serpent coils up and around to mastery when the energy reaches the crown above his head. The constellation marks the ascension point, doorway to the next evolutionary step."

Thoth placed his hand on her head. Knowledge and memory filled her consciousness.

"It is your privilege to perform a service for humankind. You and your companions must perform the ancient ritual of the soul's journey through the Duat as did the initiates of old in the Great Pyramid. This structure was built under my direction as a temple and school ten thousand years before I took the final stages of initiation with John in the same temple," Thoth said. "I was called Yeshuah then."

"The long-awaited alignment of stars has culminated. As it is above, so it will be below. You are messengers, sent to carry the ancient message to this time, and the message will awaken your fellow travelers." Alex had a vision of robed initiates in different chambers of the pyramids.

"The upward-pointing triangle of the pyramid represents fire. The pyramid of records is deep in the earth, under a canal, representing the downward triangle of water. Fire from the sky and water from the Earth must be balanced. Awaken the energies that have been quiescent for millennia and anchor the timeless symbol of union of opposites."

Alex imagined the great pyramid, interlocking with another pyramid pointing deep inside the earth, and forming a colossal hexagram.

"Your genetic patterns were encoded into the monument thirteen thousand years ago. The ritual will activate the pattern in your chakras and form new linkages in your DNA helix. If you are successful, you will trigger the next root race within yourselves. The Hall of Records was protected by Atlantean technology. After the ritual you will be able to pass those left as guards at the portal of the record chambers as they will recognize your genetic signatures. Many were prepared for this opportunity, but only three face the challenge today."

Thoth taught her the ritual of the journey through the Duat in the twelve hours of night. As Thoth's message permeated her consciousness, Alex saw the celestial sphere surrounding Earth.  Soaring through space, she viewed the Milky Way above the spiraling arms of the galaxy.

She climbed higher so that her perspective included the family of galaxies orbiting the colossal black hole that magnetized the super-galactic center. Her awareness touched the vast Oneness that encompasses all that is.  She was enfolded with a profound love so unconditional she thought her heart would break.  Joy pierced her soul like a sword.  Transcendent love filled her being, then radiated back in reciprocity to the universe of which she was both a tiny cell and everything at once.

Thoth's voice echoed in her consciousness like a triumphant chord at the close of a majestic symphony.

"Let the plan of Love and Light work out, and may it seal the door where evil dwells."

# CHAPTER 37

# GIZA

Alex woke on the plane with a brutal headache. She'd slept for seven hours. When she removed her blindfold, bright light assaulted her eyes like sharp Persian daggers.

"How do you feel?" Miguel inquired.

"Sick to my stomach," she said, rubbing her temples. "I'll be right back."

When she emerged from the cramped lavatory, flight attendants distributed bottled water, soft drinks, and cookies. "I think everyone on the plane's been in there five times," she said.

Erik smirked. "Full flight."

Alex drank a bottle of water and swallowed three aspirin. Rubbing her temples, she looked at Miguel and Erik.

"I'm beginning to recognize that expression," Erik said. "Another dream?"

She nodded. "More like a journey. I found myself at a crossroads in a wooded area. Four paths led in different directions; each pathway embodied one of the four seasons."

"Cool."

"Which path did you choose?" Miguel asked.

Alex smiled. "Autumn."

"Matches her hair," Erik said, eyes twinkling.

"I met a hermit named Ra Ta, who I recognized from Egypt. He took me to a place called Shambhala."

Miguel's dark eyes widened.

"Everything was made of light," Alex said, her eyes dancing. "An incredible being of light, who said he was Thoth, spoke to me telepathically." Her cheeks reddened. "He told me we are to perform a special ritual in the Great Pyramid, honoring what he called the twelve hours of night, and he will be our guide. We are to stay in the pyramid from sundown to sunrise, reenacting an ancient rite of initiation. If we are successful, the ritual will alter our DNA."

"Regeneration in the mount?" Erik asked.

"Fifth root race?" Miguel added.

"Exactly," Alex said.

"What if we're not successful?" asked.

"Thoth said the Hall of Records is protected by Atlantean technology. I don't know what that means, but he also said the code was programmed thirteen thousand years ago to recognize those with altered DNA because of the ritual. I guess you could say we have an appointment. If we're not successful, it could be fatal."

"That's good motivation," Erik said.

"Thoth said many were trained and prepared for this assignment, sort of as back up. Evidentially, we're the ones who showed up."

"How do we manage to be alone in the pyramid?" Miguel asked.

"Money can buy anything in Egypt, Mohammed will make the arrangements."

"Thoth said we must follow the journey of what he called the great Neter, like a god who represents the soul, in his barque, like a boat I think, through the underworld. He said each hour has a name, a guide, a gate, and a guardian," Alex said.

"That sounds like the 'Book of the Dead,'" Miguel said.

"Actually, the name is the *Book of Coming Forth into Light,*" Erik said. "The idea connotes morning twilight and implies what rises with the Sun. The words were written on papyrus rolls and placed near the deceased's mummy."

Alex pushed her red curls away from her face. "Thoth said the ritual depicted the Sun's apparent movement around the Earth and the cycle of the seasons. He said the soul undertakes a similar cyclical journey through successive incarnations until final liberation is attained.

"He told me the Sun had four aspects to the Egyptians: Ra Khepher, the scarab beetle at dawn, Re at noon, and Atum in the evening. At night, while traversing the Duat, the name was Iwf, which meant flesh."

"So earthly existence is the underworld?" Miguel said. "I read Thoth was in charge of the journey even though Anubis was guide and Osiris was lord of the underworld."

"Thoth said there was a choice of two ways for the soul to leave the pyramid," Alex said. "South toward Orion to be reborn in the physical, or north toward final liberation and eternal life."

"Resurrection or ascension," Erik said.

"After long silence, the initiates are returning to the temple," Miguel said in a hushed tone.

CHAPTER 38

# MOHAMMED

et-lagged travelers disembarked from the plane and rode on buses to the arriving terminal in the crowded Cairo airport. Hundreds of people waited in ticket lines, at baggage claim, or greeted arriving passengers. Alex was amused by a slogan in Arabic letters printed next to a six-foot bottle of Coca Cola above the ticket counter. The familiar symbol of the universal solvent was a welcome anchor in the unfamiliar sea of Moslem culture.

A handsome Arab man, dressed in jeans and jogging shoes, approached with arms wide. "Erik," he said, grinning.

"Mohammed, my friend it's good to see you." The two men embraced.

"How was the flight?"

"The best kind, uneventful."

"You must be Miguel," Mohammed said.

"A pleasure to meet you," Miguel said, shaking his hand.

"This is Alexandria Stuart," Erik said.

"I knew your grandparents from Virginia Beach, Alexandria. They were wonderful people. I am sorry for your loss."

She looked surprised. "Thank you." Before Alex could respond to that shock, Mohammed continued.

"I suggest you cover your fiery hair to avoid attracting too much attention," Mohammed said and turned toward baggage claim.

"You knew my grandparents?"

"Yes, I have made many trips to Virginia. I have lectured often about Egypt at the A.R.E."

Erik touched her arm and shot her a glance that said, "Later."

Alex shoved her red hair inside her sun hat and put on her sunglasses on to hide her confusion. After claiming their luggage and clearing customs, Mohammed led them out of the airport to a white passenger van. The driver bowed and presented Alex with an exquisite pink rose tied with a white ribbon.

"Thank you," she said, blushing. The driver helped her into the van and gave each of them a bottle of water.

"Drink plenty of water, even if you don't feel thirsty," Mohammed instructed.

When they were underway, Mohammed relaxed and looked at Alex for the first time. "This is a Moslem country. We live with religious fundamentalists and political terrorists. Young men carry assault rifles at archeological sites. My behavior is for your protection, so please do your best to blend in."

"She will," Erik said.

Alex chose the diplomacy of silence as Erik obviously loved Mohammed even though it was annoying that he spoke for her.

"Things are heating up," Mohammed said. "International teams have produced anomalous readings using different technologies. A rectangular chamber has been located in front of the Sphinx. The antiquities department digs in secret and covers up whatever they find. Naturally, I have sources.

"The existence of multiple chambers has been confirmed, but they have not breached the portal," Mohammed said enigmatically. "Of course, officially the report is that nothing is ever discovered, just a series of failed projects."

"Those who were left as guards may not be passed until a period of their regeneration in the mount," Alex said softly.

Mohammed directed an appraising look at Alexandria, and she held his gaze. When he looked away, she turned her attention outside the false calm of the van to the teeming streets of Cairo. The kaleidoscopic crowd of vehicles, humanity and animals ignored traffic signals but moved without collision in an inexplicable cadence. Carts bound for market rolled along the road's edge, overflowing with green produce. Mules were dwarfed by the size of their heavy loads and hundreds of people walked or rode bicycles.

Women in long black robes and scarves balanced baskets or pottery vessels on their heads and moved through the crowds with ancient grace. Older men wore *galabias,* traditional long cotton caftans and woven scarves circled their heads. A growing number of young men and boys wore western clothing.

The driver turned and the panorama of the Nile opened before them. Something deep in her heart opened in response. She knew she was home. The river was wide and strong but still a narrow ribbon of fertility, reaching life-giving tendrils of moisture into the parched sand of the all-pervasive desert. Sailboats cruised along the river. For thousands of years Egyptian civilizations had lived in spiritual reciprocity with the annual cycle of the river's life-giving flood and the archetypal gods who embodied that relationship.

They drove over a large bridge. "We have crossed the Nile and entered the city of Giza on the western bank where deceased pharaohs resided before their resurrection," Mohammed said.

The streets of Giza were less crowded and were lined with shops selling papyrus, essential oils and perfumes, gold jewelry, hand-blown glass artifacts and clothing. The driver pulled off the main road and drove through a large wrought-iron gate that looked like black lace against the vivid-blue desert sky. Alex thought she'd stepped into a scene from the Arabian Nights. The oasis of the Moorish Mena House hotel sprawled across a twenty-acre complex. Fifty-foot palm trees, their trunks wrapped in white cloth, formed perfect rows along paved drives. Flowerpots, brimming with red, yellow, and pink hibiscus lined emerald lawns.

"Enjoy dinner and get plenty of rest," Mohammed said. "Tomorrow we will be busy as I have made the necessary arrangements."

The travelers checked into spacious rooms with balconies overlooking lush, manicured grounds. Tall palms provided relief from the unforgiving sun.

Alex walked outside and discovered their room had a view of the pyramids. She stood in the shadow of the greatest monuments in the world and experienced the same haunting sense of familiarity she'd known at Palenque, coupled with an aching sadness.

"I can't believe I'm in Egypt," she said.

Mingled smells of automobile exhaust, cooking odors, and flowers reached her nostrils. She tried to absorb the grandeur of the sand-colored pyramids framed by tall palms against the bright blue sky. Alex closed her eyes and a very different image flashed before her imagination.

⌒

The Great Pyramid stood amidst a verdant garden oasis, painted brilliant white and crowned with a glistening gold capstone. Thousands stood in silence. Many wept. Several robed figures stood below the north entry. She opened her eyes, and the fleeting vision passed. Erik joined her on the balcony. They held hands and watched the angle of the sinking sun cast angular shadows on the huge stone structures.

"This is home," he said.

"Yes, we've come home together to fulfill our ancient promise," she said, looking at him with eyes like fiery opals. She frowned. "I don't want you to go crazy, but I felt someone watching us in the airport."

"You don't think Selig and his cronies, whoever they might be, will let us waltz into the hall of records without a fight, do you?" he said, glowering at her.

"Did you tell Miguel?

"I didn't have to. I have told Mohammed and he knows about Selig, his people will be watching."

CHAPTER 39

# LIONESS

Alex woke cradled in Erik's arms. They were scheduled to meet Miguel and Mohammed for breakfast at six AM. Mohammed promised sunrise on the Giza plateau was worth the effort. She felt like a child on Christmas morning as she'd dreamed of visiting Egypt her whole life.

Alex gently extricated herself from Erik's embrace and put on the clothes she had laid out the night before. When she brushed her teeth, Erik wandered into the bathroom looking sleepy and disheveled.

"What ungodly hour is it and in what time zone?"

"You're the morning person," she said, mouth filled with toothpaste.

Erik scowled. After they dressed, they walked through the dark hotel grounds to the restaurant. Without the Sun, the dry desert air was cool. Palm trees looked like ghostly wraiths, and the aroma of baking bread beckoned.

Don Miguel and Mohammed were already in the restaurant, drinking strong Egyptian tea and laughing. Both wore khaki pants and shirts.

"Good morning," Mohammed said, his face brightened by a broad smile.

"We need caffeine," Erik said.

Mohammed laughed. "When you are ready, we'll take my favorite approach to the Giza plateau, from the east through Mena Village. You will thank me when you see sunrise on the face of the Sphinx."

"I had difficulty sleeping last night," Miguel said, "so I did some research about where we might draw inspiration for our ritual in the Pyramid.

"That's great," Erik said.

"Let's meet later, and learn what you found," Alex added.

The group finished breakfast and followed Mohammed out of the hotel and boarded the white van. Camel drivers in caftans and colorful head wraps readied brightly decorated camels to hawk rides to captive tourists on the street. The van driver came to an abrupt halt, and the three travelers emerged from the vehicle and fell in step behind Mohammed. They walked between buildings, bazaars, and private homes, emerging onto an open space.

The first rays of sunlight deepened the creases on the stone face of the great Sphinx. The three pyramids loomed like shadowy stone mountains in the background as the companions stared at the last remaining wonder of the ancient world.

"The resurrection of Re-Khepher, smiling on the face of the great Sphinx," Mohammed said, gesturing toward the rising sun. "Always an awesome sight."

Alex was rooted to the spot as the fleeting vision she had seen from the hotel balcony returned with Technicolor intensity. She felt transported to another dimension and was overtaken by what she imagined.

Thousands stood in reverent silence on the Giza plateau in predawn darkness. The High Priest intoned the sacred sounds chosen for this profound occasion. With heavy heart and deep purpose, he sealed the record chambers for the last time, safeguarding the knowledge for long eons.

Lord Thoth conceived a mighty plan to mark the time forever. The precise moment of the ceremony was coded by the stars into the stone monuments and silent sentinels would carry the message through time.

The leonine form of the great Sphinx gazed east into the sky at its starry likeness. The multitude looked east and waited to glimpse the rebirth of the golden orb of day over the Nile. As the Sun rose on the spring day of equal light and dark, Re-Khepher smiled on the countenance of the lioness. The faces of the faithful were illumined.

To the south at the moment of sunrise, the stars of Orion's girdle were mirrored on the ground by the awesome white pyramids whose gold capstones glistened in the dawning light.

To the west, the Water Bearer waited in darkness for the wheel of ages to bring his time of ascension, when the Sphinx would welcome him. To the north, the giant Serpent in the Sky, mastered by the healer and tamer, held the prophecy.

"Thirteen thousand years from now the plan will unfold on the other side of the darkness," the High Priest said. "The long watch of the sentinel will end, and the long night of ages will give way to the morning of remembrance. Isis will deliver the keys to unlock the buried treasures and open the gateway to the stars. The time will come for humanity to return home."

The High Priest intoned a series of chants. Alexandria felt the vibration from his powerful voice inside her head. A stone slab moved shut at the base of the lion's right shoulder.

"Alex?" Erik asked.

Tears of remembered grief mingled with hope streamed down her face. She looked at Erik and Miguel. "I had a vision of the sealing ceremony. I saw thousands of people gathered here and heard and saw a great ceremony. That's the moment the alignment of pyramids represents."

"Ah," Miguel said, a smile of understanding spreading across his face.

"Maybe the opening is coded too," she said, wiping her nose on her sleeve.

"What is she saying?" Mohammed asked, staring at Alex.

"I'll explain later," Erik said.

Mohammed frowned and nodded. "Follow me, please," He walked toward a vantage point in front of the Sphinx. "This area is closed to the public because of repair work on the monument. We'll get as close as we can.

"You can see the famous stela of Tutmosis IV, who lived around fourteen hundred BCE," Mohammed continued. "Ancient Egyptians believed the land was ruled by the gods. One day after hunting, Tutmosis fell asleep in front of the Sphinx, which was covered in sand to its neck. The Sphinx spoke to Tutmosis in a dream and promised if he cleared away the sands, he would become king of all Egypt."

"Did that happen?" Alex asked.

"Yes, and there is the stela to prove it," Mohammed said smiling.

"The Sphinx temple was built from limestone blocks removed from solid bedrock in the Sphinx enclosure when the statue was carved from the living rock," Mohammed said. "The blocks weigh two-hundred tons each. How the ancient Egyptians accomplished this feat is a mystery. Modern technology cannot match this achievement.

"The architecture of the Sphinx and Valley temples are unlike anything else in Egypt, except the Osirian temple in Abydos. Mammoth blocks are devoid of any decoration or markings. The Osirian is now below the water level. Flood waters and silt have covered the temple over the centuries, perhaps millennia."

Alex noticed the magnitude of restoration. Her eyes were drawn to the right shoulder of the Sphinx where scaffolding covered recent repair activity. Cold chills enveloped her. *Between the Sphinx and the river.*

Miguel followed the direction of her gaze. "What is happening there?" he asked Mohammed.

"That area is constantly being repaired," Mohammed said. "For some reason it is unstable." Mohammed discreetly pointed out the spot where the antiquities department entered in secret.

Alex looked at them. "Those who were left as guards," she whispered.

"Let us proceed to the pyramids," Mohammed said.

The three friends followed Mohammed up the sixteen-hundred-foot causeway toward the pyramid of Khufu. The path was set at an angle of fourteen degrees from due east.

"Bauval and Hancock believe the half-buried position of the constellation Leo on the celestial horizon represents the half-buried body of the statue viewed from the same perspective," Erik said. "Another clue to the as 'above so below' message of the whole area."

Alex nodded. She found it hard to concentrate, the notes of the High Priest's chant still echoed in her ears.

"Forgive me," Mohammed said, "I feel compelled to provide tourist information."

Miguel laughed. "I am delighted. Visiting Egypt has always been a dream and to have such a guide is a rare gift."

"Excellent," Mohammed grinned and warmed to his topic. "The Great Pyramid covers thirteen acres of land and is oriented to the cardinal directions. The pyramids sit at the base of the Nile delta and the center of the world's land masses. The corners are perfect right angles—it is an extraordinary achievement. Modern buildings do not match this accuracy."

They followed Mohammed around the base of the geometric marvel which gave mute testimony to the wisdom of the ancients.

"The structure is estimated to weigh six-million tons and contain two-point-three million limestone blocks. The three pyramids were originally covered with white limestone casing stones, weighing ten tons each and polished like mirrors. As you see, some of these stones remain on the second pyramid. Imagine the awesome spectacle of these giant diamonds shining in the desert, visible for miles. Tragically, they were removed to rebuild Cairo after an earthquake.

"What is called the King's Chamber is constructed of red Aswan granite, obtained five-hundred miles to the south. The sarcophagus was carved from a single block of red granite. Controversy rages how this was accomplished with stone age tools."

Alex stared at the massive structures. "Photographs can't prepare you for the colossal scale," she said, shaking her head.

"A message we left to ourselves," Miguel said.

Mohammed's expression became serious. He stared into Erik's eyes. "The arrangements are made for your overnight stay. Do not enter the subterranean chamber under any circumstances."

"We won't." Erik said.

Mohammed frowned. "Good."

He turned and walked toward the van. They climbed into the white vehicle and rode to the rise above the Giza plateau. Street vendors descended like a swarm of locusts. Timeless leathery-brown faces sculpted by the harsh desert climate peered from cotton head wraps. Long, cotton *galabias* in pastel colors brushed the sandy ground as they walked.

Even enterprising young children, learning the ways of their world early, peddled post cards, small stone scarabs or cheap scarves with cord so tourists could masquerade as Arab sheiks, bartering for stone scarabs like a native, feigning outrage at the asking price and countering with an outrageous figure of their own.

A young Egyptian boy pushed articles at Alex. "I give you good deal lady. How much you pay?" Round, brown eyes betrayed hunger for American dollars to feed his family.

Alex shook her head. "Not today." She couldn't help feeling frustrated and guilty. Poverty engendered no respect for what the great monuments represented.

The travelers stood on the rise, overlooking the expanse of sandy plains containing the pyramids. Riders with colorful robes draped across horses or camels galloped across the vista like sheiks from the Arabian Nights, kicking up sand in their wake. Tied head wraps blew in the wind.

Alex almost expected to see a magic carpet rise from behind the pyramids and soar skyward. When she could speak without being overheard, Alex turned to Miguel and Erik.

"I saw the Sphinx as she was created," Alex said.

"She?" Erik asked, raising his eyebrows.

"The original statue was a tawny lioness crowned with a reflective orb with a cobra at the top of her forehead. Her eyes were bright blue. "In my vision, she looked east as a bright star hovered on the horizon. I knew in a matter of days Sirius would rise, blazing white, just ahead of the sun. Then the floods would come."

"You've described the goddess Sekhmet, the powerful," Erik said.

"The lioness smiled," Alex said. "Her fiery blue eyes were beautiful and terrible. When she opened her jaws and roared, the ground trembled. I believe the sound of the lion's roar later became the name of the god Ra."

Erik laughed out loud. "That's perfect, the hieroglyphs are phonetic."

"I read the Egyptians loved puns," Miguel said. "Maya language is also filled with puns and homophones."

"When Sekhmet roared, a stone slab closed at the base of her right shoulder. The voice of the lion closed the entrance, but what sound opens the door?"

Alex looked at them. "I know this seems illogical, but the star I saw wasn't Sirius but one that rose before Sirius."

"That would be Procyon," Erik said. "The name means 'before the dog.' Sirius is called the dog star."

"We have work to do," Alex said.

# CHAPTER 40
## STARS & STONES

Erik hunched over his computer at the makeshift desk in their hotel room, frowning at the colored lines and dots of the Sky Globe program. His reading glasses were perched precariously on the bridge of his nose. Don Miguel poured over reference books that were spread across the round table. Outside the air-conditioned room the blazing desert sun climbed in the sky.

"That completes the report to home base," Alex said, placing the telephone receiver in its cradle. "Everyone sends regards."

She sat cross legged on one of the double beds and removed the elastic band from the red braid at the nape of her neck. She twisted the strands in the braid tighter and replaced the band, then pushed a few stray hairs from her face.

"Shall we discuss the plan before we have lunch?" she asked, blue-green eyes sparkling with excitement. "Certainly," Miguel said, with a formal nod and a twinkle in his black eyes. "According to your instructions, we must spend the night in the Great Pyramid, preparing to enter the hall of records."

"Without being vaporized," Erik said, looking up from the computer.

"We're supposed to honor the ancient rites of initiation," Alex said, "but Thoth said will be doing something unique. We will experience a group initiation."

"I've scanned the Cayce readings CD for further clues," Erik said. "I spotted a couple of intriguing references to the entrance of the Great Pyramid and an alignment to Polaris."

"There is a reference in this book to Procyon," Miguel said, "Procyon sounded the advance warning of the annual inundation. As Erik said, 'before the dog,' when Sirius rose ahead of the sun, the flood was upon them."

"I think astronomy is the key to this puzzle," Alex said, placing her index finger on her mouth. "Sheila and Lela conducted some research of their own, and it turns out we're in Giza at an important time for ancient Egypt."

"There are no coincidences," Miguel said.

"Sheila said the annual flood came when the Sun was in the sign of Leo, and the Sun moves into Leo in a few days," Alex said. "Sheila also said the Moon will be full tomorrow night. Among the stars, stones, and legends, the ancient wisdom dwells," she said in a dramatic poem tone.

"My, aren't we waxing poetic?" Erik smiled.

"*Touché,*" she said.

"Since the construction of the Aswan dam, Egypt no longer has effects of the annual flood, I'll check the computer for other possible alignments," Erik said.

"Speaking of waxing, Sheila said the fixed star Sirius is roughly at 14 degrees of Cancer in the Tropical Zodiac. Since the Sun is still in the sign of Cancer, she said the Moon will be 180 degrees across the sky in Capricorn from Sirius as it waxes towards full."

Erik pushed his glasses upward with his middle finger. "I'll check the time."

The telephone rang, interrupting their comments.

"That's odd," Erik said.

"Hello," Alex said.

A man's voice spoke through the receiver in halting English. "Am I addressing Alexandria Stuart?"

"You are. Who is this?"

"One moment please."

After a pause, a woman spoke in flawless English. "Alexandria, please excuse the subterfuge, but it is necessary. I speak on behalf of her grace, Sekhmet Mantu, and the people of the faith."

Alex felt cold chills of confirmation spread over her skin. She imagined the face of the lioness she had seen, feeling the keen gaze of ice blue eyes and the discernment of a pure heart.

"The time has come for the ancient ones to fulfill the prophecies. Our spiritual warriors will watch over you. Be brave, my sister."

"Thank you," Alex whispered.

"Goodbye for now," the woman said.

Alex heard the dial tone. "Who was that?" Erik demanded.

A knock at the door preempted further discussion. Erik opened the door and Mohammed entered. The scowl on his face threatened like a desert sandstorm.

"I believe your pursuer is in Cairo. More guards will be required, but my people will keep a close watch on his activities."

Erik frowned. "We expected this."

"Are you certain you want to go through with your overnight stay?" Mohammed asked.

The three men looked at Alexandria and she met their stares. "This is our purpose."

"I don't like it, but I agree," Erik said.

"Initiates took lifetimes preparing for these rituals, and many did not survive the tests and trials," Miguel said.

"I believe we will be guided and protected," Alex said.

"I can't explain my feeling," Mohammed said, "but I believe that you will be. Your lunch has been arranged. I will be back after lunch to hear the results of your research."

"Erik, you know this better than I do," Miguel said," but it occurs to me if we are spending the night in the Great Pyramid we might imagine that we are journeying through the twelve hours of night as is described in the *Amduat* and the Book of Gates."

"That is similar to what Thoth said," Alex agreed.

"That's a fantastic idea, Miguel," Erik said. "The god Aker was portrayed as a solar disk on the horizon flanked by two lions back-to-back. The lions were named Yesterday and Tomorrow."

"Twelve hours and twelve gates?" Alex asked.

"Exactly, Erik said, getting into the idea. "And you will love this, Alex, in the Book of Gates each portal had a guardian and a star goddess. The one making the journey through the Underworld had to know the name of each star goddess to pass."

"I do love that."

"Why don't we divide the twelve hours among us and each write something for each one? We might each choose a god or goddess." Miguel suggested. "We can regroup in a couple hours this afternoon to compare and rehearse."

# CHAPTER 41

# TWELVE HOURS OF NIGHT

After spending three hours researching online and drafting prayers to say at the beginning of each hour during the night in the Great Pyramid they came back together with Mohammed in Miguel's room.

"I have my prayers ready for your reaction, and I am eager to hear yours," Miguel said.

"Me too," Alex said.

"Me three," Mohammed said with a smile.

They each shared what they had written and offered a few suggestions and agreed on the sequence, who would speak, and the flow of the night's events. Alexandria walked to the window and stared through the glass at the Great Pyramid as the afternoon sun created a haze on the horizon.

Mohamed listened intently as they each shared the short prayers they had written based on ancient Egyptian texts they had read.

"I think our speeches are wonderful, but something about the sequence is not quite right," she said.

"What do you mean?" Erik asked.

She turned to look at them. "Thoth told me in my vision that we are to learn the lessons of the heart."

Alex walked back to where they sat and pointed at the diagram. "You said an ancient name for the King's chamber was the Chamber of the open tomb, and the Queen's chamber was called the Chamber of the second birth. The

Queen's chamber is directly under the apex, and that feels like the center, the heart, of the pyramid to me.

"I think we should perform our meditation in the King's chamber at midnight and enter the Queens chamber afterward."

"She makes a good point," Mohammed said. "The heart was the most important thing to the ancient Egyptians. The heart lived on Ma'at, the principle of truth and divine justice."

Alex noted that Mohammed spoke of her in the third person, and she smiled inwardly.

"The stellar alignments of Bauval and Hancock also discuss a link from the star Sirius to the Queen's chamber," Erik said.

When Alex spoke again, she was transformed as if the spirits of Una and Mira were united in her consciousness. Her voice was filled with ageless wisdom.

"The shafts from the Queens chamber are not open to the outside," Alex said. "Perhaps they represent the final integration of the energies of initiation. The niche on the eastern wall might have five steps to symbolize the completion of the fifth root race, the regeneration in the mount that Cayce mentioned."

Miguel stared at her, probing her expression.

"When the astronomical alignment was right, I think something may have opened in that shaft and starlight shone down and was refracted through a crystal, illuminating the dark chamber," she said.

Miguel smiled. "In Egyptian temples, and later in the temple of Solomon, the holy of holies resided at the innermost center and the darkest and highest place of the sanctuary. Thoth replaced the left eye of Horus, the full moon, which represents the perfect reflection of divinity. That act restores the feminine to a world that sadly needs her—most fitting my dear."

Alexandria's eyes filled with tears, and her own heart was filled with awe and humility. She walked outside on the deck to look at the pyramids. The shaded balcony protected her from the full force of the desert sun as the stone structure seemed to shimmer in the midday heat.

"I'll be back around six to collect you," Mohammed said.

After he left, Alex looked at her beloved companions and related the exchange from the phone call. When she finished, Erik took off his glasses and rubbed his temples.

"I've read about the Ammonites in a book by sir Jonathan Cott. Historically, we call them Ammonites, followers of Amun, the hidden god of ancient

Egypt. There are legends that they still act as guardians and that they have a force of lethal warriors, like Ninjas.

"If this is true, then we will be well protected," Miguel said.

"I think they have been waiting for this night a long time, Alex said.

They spent the next two hours rehearsing their speeches and then slept to prepare for their twelve-hour vigil.

# CHAPTER 42

# TWO WITH A GUIDE

Miguel phoned and woke Alex at 5:15 as the late afternoon sun cast long shadows on the lawn outside their hotel room. She showered and dressed in comfortable clothes, gathering the items they had chosen for their overnight stay in the Great Pyramid. Alex and Erik met Miguel in the Mena House lobby and waited for Mohammed. Her stomach growled from hunger and apprehension.

"Final check," Erik said. "Flashlight? Batteries? Blanket, emergency energy bars, water, candles, and flowers?" Alex held up the items as Erik named them and put them in her backpack.

He wore a Don Miguel wore a brightly colored woven belt and a white headband. He carried his carved wooden staff that was shaped like a serpent with a forked tip, signifying snake defense.

"How did you get that staff into your suitcase," Alex asked.

Miguel smiled, "It is jointed. As you know, this is not the first time I have traveled incognito but never before with such purpose."

Mohammed arrived shortly before 5:30 and drove them to the Giza plateau, passing through security check points. The three companions climbed out of the van and followed him to the north side of the Great Pyramid. The Sphinx was in shadow, and the descending sun hung huge and orange between the three pyramids, gilding the edges of the sand-colored monuments. Alex shaded her eyes with her hand, remembering the reflective disc on the head of the goddess Sekhmet she had seen in her vision.

"You will be undisturbed between sunset and sunrise as you asked, Erik," Mohammed said, his jaw set in a firm line. "I will wait in the van until morning. Be on guard."

"Thank you, my friend," Erik said.

Alex gasped as she thought she caught a fleeting glimpse of someone moving across the plateau.

"What is it?" Erik asked, frowning.

"Just an overactive imagination, I admit I'm feeling nervous."

Mohammed frowned, "I warn you again to be careful. There are many eyes in the desert tonight and not all of them are friendly."

"You have my word," Erik said, grasping his arm. The men stared at each other and Mohammed nodded.

Alexandria gazed up at the artificial mountain of two and a half million limestone blocks, looming like Everest. "I feel like an ant contemplating the ascent of a camel," she said.

"A 500-foot camel," Erik replied.

Mohammed led the way as they clambered up the steps chiseled into the ten-ton stones on the north side of the Great Pyramid. They climbed toward Chalif al-Mamun's point of entry, which had been forced open in the ninth century, and stopped outside the place known as Mamun's Hole. Alex shielded her eyes and looked up toward the gabled stones of the original entrance at the 19th course of masonry.

"It is now seven o'clock and time to recite our first invocation. Will you join hands with us, Mohammed?" Miguel asked.

"Very well."

Alex trembled in anticipation of what would face them during the next twelve hours as they joined hands with Mohammed and spoke the words of the first prayer.

> *"As we enter the first gate, guarded by the Lion named Yesterday, we come to fulfill a promise made ages ago on the other side of the great wheel of stars. As Ra Atum, the setting sun, sinks in the west at the first hour of night, may our journey through the underworld and the twelve hours of night be blessed, protected, and guided by deities of both darkness and light.*

Mohammed closed and locked the gate at the entrance. "Armed guards have been posted at critical points," he said, leveling a fierce stare at each of them. Alex knew that concern and affection lay beneath his scowl.

"We are blessed and grateful to have you as our friend," Miguel said.

"*En Shallah*, I will see you unharmed at dawn," Mohammed said as he whirled around and headed down the northern face of the pyramid.

"Showtime, Erik said.

Alex smiled at Miguel, then looked at Erik. "I love you both. We have come this far, and whatever happens tonight, never forget that."

They stepped further inside the dim cavern formed of limestone blocks. Alex touched the large stones and ran her hand across their scarred surface. They seemed like living presences.

"How long have these stones stood in silent testimony of their makers genius?" she asked.

They rested quietly for an hour. Miguel's face was transformed by concentration and dedication. His voice was strong, but the stone passage absorbed the sound as he spoke the second prayer at 8 PM and Alex and Erik joined their voices to his.

> *At the second hour of night we call upon Nephthys, lady of the temple,*
> *goddess of night and daughter of earth and sky. As we go from*
> *daylight to darkness, we leave behind toiling, dancing, and feasting,*
> *and enter the stillness of deep inner work. Guide us Nephthys as*
> *our eyes adjust to the darkness, opening to the inner eye that we*
> *may see the path ahead and walk with confidence.*

They advanced horizontally through the artificial tunnel that had been created with boiling vinegar by Mamun and his workers until they reached the junction that marked the entry to the ascending passage and access to the off-limits subterranean chamber. The route toward the original entrance was barred by a steel door. On the western side, elephantine-sized granite plugs marked the junction of the descending passage.

"How could anyone believe this awesome structure was built as a tomb?" Alex asked. "It seems as arrogant as believing Earth is the center of the solar system."

"Ignorance and hubris," Erik said.

When they reached the ascending passage, the gate of ascent, Alex made herself comfortable and tried to relax while they rested. At nine o'clock

Miguel positioned himself at the juncture of passages and recited the next speech.

> *At the third hour of night we ask the blessing of Amun, the hidden one,*
> *as we stand at the bottom of the Grand Gallery and prepare to*
> *ascend the Hall of Truth in Light. Grant us your great but unseen*
> *power as we proceed on our journey this night.*

"There's no chance I would ignore Mohammed's warning and go toward the subterranean chamber," Alex said, shivering.

The three travelers stooped over, bending at the waist and entering the ascending passage, which was less than four feet square and stretched 129 feet upward and at a 26-degree incline. They progressed upward in an ape-like fashion through the cramped space toward the bottom of the Grand Gallery.

Alex recoiled as a dark form scurried into the corner. She recalled the majestic vision of the pyramid covered with gleaming white stones and crowned with a shimmering gold capstone.

"How can they let this happen to this incredible monument?" she asked.

"If the officials cared, we wouldn't be here," Erik said. "It's a perverse paradox, but the politics have actually protected the secrets."

"Please, try to calm yourself, Alexandria, and conserve your energy," Miguel said.

"I'm sorry," she blushed and tried to slow her breathing.

When they emerged from the ascending passage, Alex felt dizzy. She leaned against the wall to catch her breath and steady herself. At this point a choice of ways presented themselves. Straight ahead lay the horizontal route to the Queen's Chamber. Behind a steel covered door was the second access to the subterranean chamber; a nearly perpendicular passage that dropped toward the base of the structure. They took the steps that led to the bottom of the Grand Gallery. The breathtaking vista from the foot of the architectural masterpiece spread upward before them.

"Magnificent," Miguel said. "I have seen pictures, but I never imagined such beauty."

"The gallery is 157 feet in length and 28 feet high, with seven courses of limestone masonry," Erik said.

"I don't think I can make the climb," Alex said, sitting on the floor. "I feel sick, frightened, and overwhelmed."

"You must," Miguel said in a gentle but firm voice.

"We have about a half hour until the next prayer," Erik said, handing her a water bottle. "We'll rest here until then."

Alex extracted a protein bar from her pack and peeled back the foil wrapper. She washed down the chewy peanut butter bar with a generous swallow of water. *I have to get ahold of myself.*

"No ornamentation or inscription speaks of the intent or significance of this masterful achievement," Miguel said.

"Which is out of character with other Egyptian monuments," Erik said.

Alex closed her eyes and tried to gain control of her uneasiness. She breathed deeply and called up the memory of the priestess Una, recalling her courage and power. A few minutes before ten o'clock, Alex and Erik stood beside Miguel and gazed upon the ascent. At ten PM Erik spoke in a strong voice.

> *At the fourth hour of night as we ascend the Grand Gallery, the magnificent Hall of Truth in Light, we call upon the goddess Neith, spinner and weaver of destiny. Inspire us that our steps will be sure and the threads of our choices and actions become woven into patterns of beauty.*

Alex sighed and looked once more at the long gallery. They began the arduous ascent, and she clung to hand railings and wooden slats that had been inserted into the limestone ledges. They climbed the wooden ramp that lay over polished ancient stones. Alex recalled the Stations of the Cross from her Catholic childhood, the reenactment of the crucifixion of Christ, and the memory strengthened her resolve. She sent a silent message to Gran.

They moved slowly and reached the top at 10:45 PM where Alex turned to look back. Her chest hurt from the rapid pounding of her heart, and she was soaked in perspiration. Removing the water bottle from her pack, she swallowed a generous helping.

They rested for several minutes, and at 11:00 o'clock, the fifth hour of night, Alex gathered herself and spoke.

> *At the fifth hour of night we approach the King's Chamber and invoke the goddess Nut. As you swallow the sun each evening for its nightly passage through the starry vault of your body, we ask that we are likewise guided by the stars and protected by your grace. We prepare to enter the chamber of sacrificial fire where we will reach for your starlight to ignite a flame.*

The three friends clambered onto the limestone ledge known as the big step, leaning against the stone wall of the pyramid.

"We should rest here for the next hour before the King's Chamber," Miguel said.

"I agree," Erik said.

"Thank you," Alex said, closing her eyes and falling asleep.

"It is time," Miguel said, looking at his watch, it is shortly before midnight."

Alex felt stiff from sleeping on the stone surface but rose for the next phase. They stood and faced the opening that led into the King's Chamber.

They stooped and crawled inside a low passage where the substance of the pyramid changed from alluvial limestone to igneous granite. When they entered the antechamber, they were able to stand. Three deep grooves had been carved into the walls. Alex glanced above her head and noticed a pair of granite leaves had been set into the grooves.

"What are these?" she asked.

"The mainstream theory is that three huge portcullis stones were lowered to protect the chamber, which was a common practice in Egyptian burials," Erik said. "How that happened in this tight space has been the subject of heated controversy as no trace of the stones has ever been found."

"Seems like a lot of effort if there's no purpose," Alex said.

"Grist for the mill for pyramid scholars and cranks alike," Erik said.

"We are at the threshold of the chamber of the open tomb," Miguel said. They bent over and negotiated the final short passage between the antechamber and the King's Chamber. They had timed their approach to enter right before midnight. Once inside the chamber, Alex drew a deep breath.

"The room feels like it's vibrating," she said.

"Some have compared the feeling to being inside a hydroelectric power plant," Erik said. "There is an acoustical resonance that causes sound to echo above your head and also be heard throughout the pyramid."

"The ancient Maya builders also possessed such knowledge," Miguel said.

They gathered around the empty black sarcophagus and stared into the empty coffer. Alex touched the surface of the cool stone.

"I have read that the coffer has the same ratio proportions as the Ark of the covenant," Miguel said.

"Another controversy," Erik said.

"The opening we crawled through isn't large enough to accommodate this container," Alex said.

Erik smiled. "Exactly, that's one of several mysteries. How the Egyptians carved a single block with such precision using only Stone Age tools is unexplained. Modern drilling tools can barely manage the job and are still unable to produce such sharp corners. The rest of the pyramid, as far as anyone knows, is constructed of limestone. This chamber is built from red Aswan granite that was quarried 500 miles to the south."

"Granite is an igneous rock," Miguel said. "Therefore, this chamber must represent trial by fire."

Erik pointed to the five courses of masonry that formed the walls. "There are exactly 100 blocks in this room. The nine monoliths in the ceiling weigh 50 tons each, perhaps even more."

"What's this?" Alex asked, pointing to an opening on the southern wall.

"One of the infamous air shafts," Erik grind.

"With the infamous astronomical alignments?" she asked.

"Precisely."

"This place is incredible, even if Egyptologists are right about the date. Whether this monument has stood for 5,000 years or 13,000 years, it's magnificent and powerful," Alex said.

THEY SELECTED a spot near the center of the room to prepare for their ritual. They placed a white votive candle in the center, arranging Lotus blossoms and papyrus leaves around the candle. Miguel grasped his shaman's staff. Alex pulled her necklace from under her shirt and lovingly touched the three interconnected triangles.

The three initiates sat on the floor and joined hands, positioning themselves in a triangle, embodying the archetypal trinity of Osiris, Isis, and Horus, father, mother, and divine child. They lit the candle and closed their eyes, beginning their meditation. Alex felt the pulsing vibration of the pyramid's energy as the mammoth structure seemed to respond to their ritual. Each of them entered a place of silence and power to enact their appointed role as messengers from the past to the future.

Alex felt a sudden rise of powerful energy. Fiery astral light stirred into wakefulness in the granite chamber, stimulating the energy centers at the base of their spines. Alex rocked back and forth as the potency of the force uncoiled. She experienced a jolt of power as the unbridled energy rose into her solar plexus. Her heart chakra opened in an exquisite and piercing sensation of oneness. The fiery wheel of the throat center spun as the word of life prepared to emerge. At exactly midnight, when the Sun was at the nadir, all three spoke as they had rehearsed.

> *At the sixth hour of night we invoke Osiris, lord of the underworld and ultimate transformation as we light this flame in the chamber of sacrificial fire, the chamber of the open tomb. Grant us power of purpose as we fulfill our ancient oath. May our lives be like candles in the darkness, flames burning bright, radiating light to others.*

Brilliant white incandescent light exploded inside Alexandria's head, pulsing like a heartbeat of light at her brow. Molten consciousness streamed into the crown of her head, burning her awareness. Energy moved up and down her spine, forming a caduceus of spiraling light. She opened her eyes and saw light emerging from the black sarcophagus. Swirling incandescence moved in two streams of twisting light. The current spun faster around each other until they merged.

The twirling lights became a giant black serpent twenty feet in length, slithering from the crypt. Alex tried to scream but could make no sound. She wanted to run, but her body seemed to have turned to stone. The serpent Apophosis, nemesis of Osiris, approached. The huge snake advanced across the chamber and stopped in front of her, coiled like a king cobra ready to strike.

"I am death and immortality," the serpent said in a rasping voice, "adversary and redemption. To survive, you must embrace me."

The chamber's resonant quality caused the sound to reverberate above her head. The serpent's forked tongue licked the air like a red flame and faceted jewel-like eyes bore into her skull. The chamber seemed to wreak with menace.

"Summon your power," Don Miguel communicated telepathically. "This is your purpose, Alexandria."

His presence strengthened her, and she breathed to still her heart, calling upon the memory of Mira and Una. She thought of Dolphin and sent a silent message to her. "I claim your power for my own, serpent," she said to the black form.

"That is well," the snake hissed. Alex thought the serpent smiled. "Journey with me, priestess."

The snake uncoiled and arched its back. Alex willed herself to move but was frozen to the spot. Her consciousness left her physical body, and her astral form climbed on to the back of the serpent Apophsis. Her spirit left her body and rose through the ceiling of the King's chamber, out of the apex of the pyramid and into an indigo sky bright with stars. Billions of suns burned across light years like diamonds in the darkness.

Feeling disoriented, Alex looked for familiar constellations and recognized the belt of Orion and the bright star Sirius in the constellation of Canis Major. The luminous Milky Way stretched across the celestial canopy. A bright star on the opposite side of the great celestial river in the sky seemed to form an equilateral triangle with Sirius and the brightest star in Orion in his right shoulder.

"What is that star, Serpent?" she asked.

"Procyon, the star of Horus," the Serpent replied telepathically. "Orion the hunter, masters the energy symbolized by his club, but that is not enough for salvation. The ultimate victory of the divine son, Horus, results from raising and utilizing those energies throughout his being. Horus becomes the Serpent Bearer as he claimed my power for his own."

Alexandria searched the skies for the zodiacal constellations. Above the Water Bearer a small group of stars formed the astral shape of a dolphin. As she watched, her friend emerged from the twinkling configuration.

"Dolphin!"

"Pay close attention to what you see, little traveler," Dolphin said telepathically.

The giant serpent climbed higher in gentle undulating movements, moving toward the circumpolar constellations. Alex saw a multi-dimensional cube formed by shining alpha stars. The snake stopped at the constellation of Cepheus, the King. Alex was amazed to realize that three of the central stars were in the same positions as the chambers inside the Great Pyramid.

"This is the destination of the soul," the serpent said, the eternal castle in the sky. The work in the pyramid on Earth prepares the soul for immortality. The chambers are gateways to other dimensions."

The serpent flattened its form, and Alex stepped off. She stood at the place of Polaris, on the axis of the world, and gazed upon the silvery garment of the Galaxy. The great snake moved to take its place in the constellation of the serpent bearer. Rasalhague, brightest star in the head of the snake charmer, shone like a beacon.

Alex noticed the constellation of Serpent Bearer stood between the Scorpion and the Archer, directly across the sky from Orion and Taurus, the Bull. The Lion and the Water Bearer formed the other arms of a great cross in the sky. She understood the processional wheel of ages had turned, fulfilling a cyclic destiny. Sirius outshone all the other stars and as Alex watched, the shining one became an enormous cow with a brilliant blue-white star between her horns. The sacred cow opened her mouth, and the sound of her bellowing filled the skies. The faint echo of Miguel's voice called Alexandria's spirit back to the King's Chamber.

~

THE THREE MESSENGERS became a mystical caduceus. Erik and Alexandria were the male and female currents, spiraling around the central pillar of the shaman. Spiritual lightning electrified their cells, and Alexandria could see inside their bodies and perceive the double helix of their DNA. The spiral strands shifted and formed new linkages and connections of a spontaneous genetic mutation. When Alexandria opened her eyes, the chamber seemed illuminated, and a halo of light surrounded the heads of her companions. She felt a sense of blissful oneness—the same emotion seemed to be reflected on the faces of her companions.

"We were with you," Erik said, we experienced everything."

After a few moments of silence and gratitude, they gathered their belongings and left the King's Chamber in a state of reverence. It was nearly 1:00 AM as they crawled through the low passage and antechamber and emerged at the great step overlooking the Grand Gallery. They leaned against the wall and drank more water.

"Let us rest again," Miguel said.

After a short time the three stood and Erik spoke,

> *At the seventh hour of night we have fulfilled our purpose and stand*
> *poised at the top of the Grand Gallery. We again call upon the*
> *power of gods and goddesses to empower us to complete our work.*
> *We call upon Anubis, the god who counts the hearts, to guide us*
> *onward through the night to our next step.*

Alex and Erik followed Miguel down the long ramp, holding on to the rails. When they reached the foot of the Grand Gallery, she glanced at the sealed entrance to the narrow shaft, leading to the grotto, the subterranean chamber. They turned and proceeded once more in ape like fashion along the cramped horizontal route to the Queen's Chamber, which had been left unlocked, an expanse of 127 feet in length and only less than four feet high. The floor dropped abruptly two feet at the opening into the chamber, which

Thoth had called the Chamber of the Second Birth. They entered the room and stood.

Miguel looked around the room and said, "The King's Chamber is a place of fire and radiance, while this chamber is like a cool lake or mirror that is intended for the perfect reflection of divine essence."

"That is true," Alex said, smiling.

"The chamber is constructed of plaster over limestone walls and appears to have been left intentionally unfinished," Erik said.

"Regeneration in the mount?" Alex asked. "There are five steps in the niche, and five courses of masonry in the walls of the King's chamber."

"And five levels in the relieving chambers of the King's chamber," Miguel added.

"The shafts are also on the north and south walls. The niche is just south of the center line on the eastern wall," Erik said.

"East for rebirth, or the birthing of a new creation?" Alex suggested.

They rested awhile to prepare for their next ritual. Alex placed a mirror on the floor as she'd seen in her vision and arranged a crystal and a Lotus blossom on the reflecting surface.

"The flower of life," Miguel said.

At 2:00 AM they took their places. Erik and Miguel stood on the northern and southern walls in front of the shafts. Alex stood near the Niche, symbolic mother of humanity's next evolutionary unfoldment, that had been represented in ancient times by the child Horus. The shaman raised his staff on high toward the apex of the Great Pyramid, which was now directly overhead, and Alexandria spoke,

> *At the eighth hour of night we humbly enter the Queen's Chamber,*
> *chamber of the second birth, at the heart of the Great Pyramid. We*
> *call upon goddess Ma'at that like you, we may always choose love*
> *and wisdom. We pray that when our time comes to be judged, and*
> *our hearts are weighed on your golden scale of truth, they will be*
> *found to be as light as your white feather of justice.*

The three initiates had returned to the temple in fulfillment of their ancient promise. They drew energy from the stars that passed through them and the ancient temple of initiation into the Earth. They had become a living chalice of liquid flame. In a loud voice they chanted, "Amen," the name of the ancient hidden deity of many traditions. Their chant echoed three times in the chamber.

Terra responded to the ancient call and reciprocal energy moved back up the pathways and out the shafts of the great temple. A blinding flash of light rushed from the top of their heads out of the apex of the pyramid like the wings of a white phoenix. Their ritual initiated a chain reaction, and the pyramid became a lightning rod for the planet.

A slow tremor began in the walls and floor of the chamber. They felt the vibration as stone scraped against stone, allowing a small unknown door high up in the shaft to open. A thin ray of pale light entered the chamber and shone on the crystal and a prism of rainbow colors erupted and were reflected in the mirror. A spectrum of crystal starlight shone on Alexandria's face. She was transformed into a priestess and raised her arms as Miguel spoke the words they had chosen and spoke in a loud voice.

> *At the ninth hour of night, we call upon god Thoth, scribe of the gods.*
> *May we strive to see truly with the eye of the heart as you proclaim*
> *us speakers of truth. Time passes, days stretch into years, and years*
> *into lifetimes. May we live again and again to serve truth and*
> *justice for millions of years.*

The three initiates stood in silence for several minutes. As a shimmering rainbow of light bathed the chamber in a delicate iridescence. They collected their belongings in silence and crawled back along the horizontal passage. When they arrived at the bottom of the Grand Gallery they waited in silence until it was time for the next prayer. Erik stood tall and spoke,

> *At the tenth hour of night as dawn comes and stars fade, we honor*
> *goddess Isis. May we remember our blessings and know that true*
> *joy does not dim with time. May your magic bless us and enhance*
> *our lives so that we might bring happiness to others that their*
> *burdens might be lessened, and their sorrows healed.*

After several minutes Miguel looked at them. "Our work here is complete."

They climbed down the lower portion of the Grand Gallery and returned to the junction of Mamun's entry of the Ascending Passage. At the eleventh hour of night, Alex spoke,

> *We come forth in a triumphant spirit, thanking all who guarded,*
> *guided, and inspired us on our journey from darkness to light,*

*fulfilling our long-ago vow. We invoke Seshat, mistress of the house of books and recorder of deeds. We ask that this night be recorded in the halls of eternity. Having our hearts renewed our spirits are also strengthened.*

They made their way back toward the entrance and waited. At 6:00 AM they heard Mohammed's keys unlock the gate. Alex, Miguel, and Erik emerged at morning twilight, coming forth into day in the tradition of millennia.

A brilliant star hovered on the eastern horizon, rising in a moment of dazzling transcendence before the Sun. At the twelfth and final hour of night the three pilgrims stood outside Mamun's entrance,

"You look like Moses descending from Mount Sinai," Mohammed whispered, his eyes wide.

They joined hands and spoke the words of their final ritual prayer in unison. Their voices rang like trumpets as the Sun rose in brilliant light to bless the ancient land.

*"We greet the brilliant resurrection of Ra Khefer who fills the morning with radiant joy. We greet the day in a spirit of anticipation. As the solar boat sails on the great ocean of the sky, we stand forth on Earth, breathing the fragrance of flowers. We will drink fresh water, bathe in the great river, and be cooled by gentle breezes under swaying palm trees. We rejoice that the ancient land is blessed, and our oath has been fulfilled.*

# CHAPTER 43

# MOONRISE

Alex heard water running in the shower and rubbed her eyes, looking at her watch she realized it was 3:00 in the afternoon. She decided to phone Miguel and when he answered she announced, "I'm hungry."

Miguel's laugh echoed in the receiver, "Let's have an early dinner as there is much to discuss."

Alex and Erik met Miguel and Mohammed by the swimming pool. They circled around an umbrella table in the shade of tall palm trees, gaining relief from the intense heat. Sunlight sparkled on the surface of the water. Mohammed opened a paper sack, brimming with fried falafel cakes that were wrapped in warm Egyptian bread.

"That smells delicious," Alex said.

Miguel and Mohammed drank iced tea, and Alex and Erik each ordered a beer. Alex bit into one of the sandwiches and moaned. Savory flavor filled her mouth, but her pleasure was short lived.

"We had problems during the night," Mohammed said, his face was strained from the effort to suppress his emotions. "One of my men is dead."

"What happened? Erik asked, his eyes widening with concern.

"There was a struggle at the entrance to the pyramid as someone wanted to join your slumber party," Mohammed said. "We apprehended the killer, but I do not believe he acted alone."

"I am so sorry," Alex said her voice filled with sorrow.

Mohammed looked at her. "Thank you on behalf of all those who serve in silence and in secret, giving their lives for the ancient ones." Their eyes remained locked for several moments.

"Our next move becomes more urgent," Miguel said.

"You realize the danger," Mohammed said in a tight voice.

"The priceless knowledge that is buried in those chambers belongs to the world, not special interests," Erik said.

"Many more will be killed in the name of greed if we do not succeed. I believe that we will be protected," Miguel said.

"It is like a curse to live to see such time, and yet it seems to have been ordained. *Maktub*, we say in Arabic, 'it is written.'"

"But we still need the key to unlock the door," Alex said.

"If the sound of a lion's roar closed the hall of records, what sound opens the way?" Erik asked.

"I've been thinking," Alex said and shrugged her shoulders.

"Uh oh," Erik commented.

Don Miguel's black eyes sparkled like beads of jet.

"Cats are nocturnal," she said, why choose a lion as a solar symbol? In astrology the Sun rules Leo, but that seems too simple somehow."

"Lions roar at sunset to rouse themselves for the nightly hunt," Mohammed said.

So the lion's roar could signal the onset of the long night," Alex said.

"That makes sense for entering a cycle of darkness, Erik said.

"Look at this diagram of the Zodiac of Dendera," Miguel said, placing a book open on the table in front of them. "The figure representing Thoth is placed between Virgo and Libra, the autumn equinox. You saw the ceremony that sealed the hall of records in your vision at dawn on the spring equinox, the beginning of a cycle of light. Could the opening be signified by the autumn equinox?"

"Good question, Alex said, "if so we're a couple of months early."

"Perhaps we're missing the obvious," Erik said, "you said the Sphinx was a lioness, like Sekhmet. If this temple was dedicated to Isis and masterminded by Thoth, there must also be a lunar connection since he is a moon god."

"That is correct, Thoth was a lunar deity, Mohammed said, "the Sun was considered to be the right eye of Re, and the Moon was the left eye of Horus. Thoth was responsible for replacing the eye of Horace after he lost it to Set in their famous battle."

"And, the full moon rises in the east tomorrow night, directly opposite the setting sun," Erik added.

"So, the Sphinx will gaze at the full Moon after the Sun sets behind the statue," Don Miguel said. "Sheila also told you the Moon will oppose Sirius as she waxes towards fullness at this time of year. I sense a powerful significance about the lioness being aligned between the star Sirius, the Sun and Moon."

"Not sunset, but moon rise," Alex said, smiling.

"Sometimes Isis as Sirius wore a crown showing the phases of the moon. But more often she was depicted as a cow with a large star between her horns," Mohammed said.

"Isis, a cow?" Alex asked, looking from Erik to Miguel. You said you could see what happened during my vision in the pyramid.

"Yes," Erik said.

Miguel's eyes sparkled with curiosity.

"That would explain my vision. Don't laugh, but what is the sound of a sacred cow," she asked.

Erik and Miguel smiled in recognition and replied together, "Moo, and Mu was the legendary motherland in the Pacific that was also an origin culture," Miguel said. "How clever."

"Cattle are ancient symbols of substance and nurturing as they are the only mammal to produce milk continually," Miguel said. "That could represent a powerful vibration and vowel sound indeed.

"Egyptian vowel sounds were sacred and unwritten," Mohammed said. "Hieroglyphs were consonants, homophones, and symbols."

"Eureka," Miguel said, "how exquisitely simple, subtle, and profound."

"And how exquisitely Egyptian," Erik said. He crossed his arms over his chest, pretending to pout. "But now I can't say Open, Sesame."

Alex pretended to glare at him.

"You may be right, but I still believe this enterprise is madness," Mohammed said.

"Lunacy, to be precise," Erik said.

"Sirius business, Alex said, biting into a falafel sandwich. "I don't mean to seem rude or unconcerned, Mohammed. I feel devastated by your loss and intend to vindicate their sacrifice.

"It's why we are here, Erik said.

"We have to try, even if we die trying," Alex said.

"We have dedicated ourselves to bring the morning of remembrance, 'Miguel added. "Strange that such a short time ago we had not even met and yet we've known each other for thousands of years."

CHAPTER 44

# GUARDIAN

A brisk breeze blew across the Giza necropolis as they approached the Sphinx. The night air was chilly, and Alex was glad for the protection of a hooded sweatshirt. Her only jewelry was a clear quartz crystal wrapped in a silver wire that was tucked beneath her shirt.

The leonine enigma of the Sphinx crouched in the bedrock, guarding her secrets with the tenacity of a lioness protecting newborn cubs. Alexandria pondered the inscrutable features of the great feline as the silent watcher gazed east. The stone sentinel had waited millennia for this night.

"*Sciere. Velle. Audere. Tacere*, Miguel said as he faced the giant statue, you are the embodiment of the four powers of the Sphinx."

"Latin, Erik said, what do the words mean?"

"To know, to will, to dare, and to keep silent," Miguel answered.

"That is my sentiment," Alex said. "Thousands witnessed a sealing of this holy place, but tonight only three of us return on behalf of many."

"Three who come in the name of many to honor our vow," Miguel said. "We will open the portal of memory, walk through the gates of yesterday, and approach the portal of tomorrow."

Alexandria did not trust herself to speak. She nodded, giving silent thanks to those who watched this night.

∼

Night is the province of the feline. As the silver orb of the Moon rose in the eastern sky, pale moonlight stole across the body of the Sphinx like a predatory creature of the night, transforming the great solar symbol into a magnificent nocturnal cat. Starlight could not compete with the brilliance of the full lunar disc. Sekhmet, the powerful, protector of the high priestess' scrolls, gazed into the argent eye of Horus.

"In ancient times, at the full moon, silver light would have been reflected from the orb crowning her head and the uraeus cobra on her brow," Alex said.

"That would have been an awesome spectacle," Miguel said.

"At the time of the equinoxes, Sekhmet was aligned with sunrise and moonrise," Erik said, "so it would be golden light at dawn and silver light as the Moon rose."

Alexandra removed her hat and shook her hair loose. Her fiery mane was rendered monochrome in the ghostly moonlight, and the desert looked like a lunar landscape. Alex turned and followed the direction of the Sphinx's eastern gaze, imagining that the lioness smiled as the Moon touched the cusp of Aquarius. The promise of a new epoch, when both eyes of Horus Sun and Moon, might look upon a world of balanced polarities.

"Is it time?" she asked.

Miguel nodded and they joined hands.

> *"Tonight, we call upon the Lioness, the Cobra, and the Jackal. May*
> *their power strengthen and assist us as we invoke the intercession*
> *of Thoth, Ra, and Isis and endeavor to fulfill our promise."*

They walked around to the south side of the Sphinx and approached the right shoulder. A canvas tarp covered the point of forced entry they had noticed earlier. They touched the place on the stone as Mohammed had instructed them, and a faint quiver seemed to move through the body of the great statue. A limestone slab scraped across the bedrock, revealing a nearly square aperture roughly three feet on each side. Musty air escaped from the opening.

"This seems too easy," Erik said.

"Remain focused and alert," Miguel said.

Alexandria's heart raced and she felt dizzy. "We're not even inside yet, and I can't think about what might be down there."

"I've heard stories of alligators, snakes, and demons," Erik said, wiggling his eyebrows.

Erik and Miguel shone flashlights into opaque blackness. They climbed into the opening that had been masked by the fire box on the side of the Sphinx, pausing to allow their eyes to adjust to the darkness.

They crawled through a horizontal passage five feet beneath the bedrock for a distance of fifty feet and emerged in the underground chamber that was between the Sphinx's paws. They stood and Erik shone his halogen lantern around the cavity. The smooth walls of the rectangular room were carved from solid limestone bedrock, similar to the Sphinx enclosure.

"Mohammed said that they recently cleared rubble from the passageway into this room, but they haven't been able to move beyond this point," Erik said.

"It's difficult to tell the dimensions of this room in the dark," Alex said.

"Roughly twelve by fifteen meters, according to Mohammed's source," Erik said.

"Scan slowly over the eastern wall with your light Erik," Miguel said.

The light revealed the faint outline of what could be a door that was barely discernible on the eastern wall. They moved closer to get a better look, and Erik shone the lantern on the edges of the outline. The door was constructed of the same limestone and was devoid of any ornamentation or carving.

"Time to test your theory, Alex," Erik smiled.

Alex was grateful that the darkness masked her uncertainty. *What if their chant didn't work?* She breathed, gathered her power, and called upon Thoth and Isis.

The three faced west where Sirius, mother of the universe and benefactor of Egypt, occupied the sky. Invoking her power and blessing, they intoned the sound Mu three times in a long powerful note, holding the vowel at a low pitch. Alex felt the vibration reverberating inside her skull.

Then they turned toward the eastern door, where the Full Moon continued her ascent, and chanted the tone three more times. The stone door vibrated and resonated with their chant like a hollow obelisk ringing.

A crack appeared, and the door opened inward, slowly scraping against the floor. Limestone dust fell around the opening and a blast of cool damp air washed across their faces.

"We have passed the first test," Miguel said.

"Thank goodness," Alex whispered. Her knees shook from the intense effort of the chant, and she took a deep breath.

"Good work, Watson," Erik said.

Miguel shone his light into the dark opening. "There appears to be a narrow descending passage that continues into the bedrock."

"Can you see anything inside Miguel?"

"I'll go in first," Erik said, "Alex, follow me."

They entered on hands and knees and progressed on the smooth moist stone into the cramped space that was sloping downward at an angle. Their head lanterns cast dim streaks of light on the stone blocks as they navigated the musty passage. They moved at a slow pace on the slippery stones, gradually probing deep into the bedrock beneath the water table. Moisture seeped onto the rocks from an underground water source.

"Could anything live in here?" Alex asked.

"I don't think we want to know," Erik said.

Alex willed herself to be calm, and after what seemed to be an interminable length of time, they emerged into a larger space. Their darting head light beams displayed a narrow stone bridge that spanned an underground channel of water.

"I imagine we are under the remains of the Sphinx Temple," Miguel said. "I believe we have progressed about another twenty meters."

"This was probably at ground level at one time," Erik said, "seems like the remains of a canal, maybe even a boat dock." He shone his light on the ceiling, revealing what appeared to be a recent excavation from above.

"I hear noises in the water," Alex said, wanting to cringe.

"Snakes, rats, or crocodiles," Erik said. "Nothing to worry about."

Miguel struck a match and ignited a preparation of copal incense. The flash of light disclosed an ample space that had been carved into the limestone bedrock.

"There is little margin for error on this bridge," he said. "Remember, we were part of the original plan to protect this sanctuary, and we must prove worthy to pass the guardians who were left in place."

Erik went first as they crawled on hands and knees across the slippery stone expanse. Tensing her muscles, Alex concentrated on each movement as they advanced for twenty feet.

"Damn!" Erik shouted. "The bridge ends." His words were followed by a loud splash and Alex's scream.

Don Miguel stood on the narrow channel, shining his lantern on the water. He began a chant in the Maya language. Erik's head poked above the surface of the water and he clutched the bridge. Alex grabbed his arm and helped him gain purchase to climb back onto the stone walkway.

"I'm afraid I lost my flashlight in a disagreement with a crocodile," he said.

"That is not funny," Alex said.

Miguel's lantern exposed a distance of more than twelve feet without a bridge.

"I guess we could swim; I'm already wet," Erik said.

"We are facing the second test," Miguel said.

"I think we should chant again," Alex said.

"We have nothing to lose but collapsing the rest of the bridge," Erik said.

Alexandria centered herself and balanced on the narrow stone causeway. They intoned the same notes as before. When the stone bridge vibrated beneath her feet, she faltered. As they finished their chanting, a loud scraping sound wrenched across the ceiling above their heads, and Alex feared the stone bridge would indeed collapse. Miguel shone his light in the direction of the sound, and they watched as an enormous block of limestone descended into the open space, completing the bridge.

"The second challenge has been met," Miguel said.

THEY CONTINUED AT A SLOWER SPACE, and within twenty feet they came to the other side of the water in an area where they could stand.

Miguel shone his lantern in front of them and the beam of light revealed the startling site of a circular alcove with three doors. Two enormous stone serpents, carved to look like giant menacing cobras with hoods spread, reared between the doors. The black basalt statues appeared to be at least twelve feet tall.

"Holy cow," Erik said.

"What a funny thing to say," Alex said, startled from her state of shock. "I hope Sirius is amused."

When they stepped off the bridge, the circular space was illuminated. A light source of unknown technology illuminated what seemed to be large glass globes in metal sconces that stretched several feet down the wall. In the light, statues of two granite cheetahs were revealed in the center of the alcove, crouching back-to-back on large granite blocks with a large orb between them, looking like a pair of sphinxes.

They had been painted in their natural colors and were at least three times normal size. One looked east toward the doors, and the other gazed west as if on the alert. The cheetahs were crowned with reflective orbs and uraeus serpents emerged from the tops of their foreheads. Vivid blue eyes probed the three intruders.

"This is just like my vision," Alex whispered, "but these are cheetahs not lionesses. They must be scale models of the Sphinx in her original form."

"These cheetahs represent the ancient Egyptian goddess Mafdet, as indicated by the spots on their coats that represented stars," Erik said, "but why two?" Erik asked.

"One to protect the past, and another to wait for the dawn of the future," Miguel said. "These cats are also reminiscent of the ancient Egyptian depiction of the God Aker, guardian of sunrise and sunset, yesterday and tomorrow, with two lions back to back," Miguel said.

"Something about these felines reminds me of the Cherubim on the Ark of the Covenant," Erik said, "a potent and often lethal energy field was connected with those guardians."

"The third challenge presents itself," Miguel said.

"And do those serpents look Mayan to you Miguel?" Erik asked.

"Perhaps the Mayan ones looked Atlantean," Alex said.

"I agree that is likely," Miguel said.

Alexandria noticed that a design of three triangles fashioned like her ring was emblazoned above the middle door. The center triangle was white, the left blue, and the right one red. The tops of the door frames were carved with designs that looked like writing.

"This is the moment of truth. Door #1, door #2, or door number 3?" Erik asked.

"Three doorways and three of us," Alex said. "I imagine we only get one guess."

"I believe all three pieces of the code must be present to pass the guardians," Miguel said.

"As the serpent Apophis said in the Great Pyramid, 'adversary or redemption,' to survive we must embrace what he represents. I believe we should walk through the doorways together," Erik said. "Then the center doorway should be yours, Miguel. Do we choose the same or opposite polarity, Alex?"

Alexandria stared at the design. After reflecting she said, "I'll take blue for water, you take red for fire."

"Agreed, take a photo first."

Removing her camera, Alex photographed the amazing sight. When the camera flashed in the semi-darkness, the huge black serpents slowly opened their eyes, revealing cabochon rubies and blue sapphires, matching the triangles above the doors. The jeweled eyes of the serpents scanned the area like electronic motion sensors, and the snakes opened their mouths, emitting energy fields like red fangs of laser light. "

"Damn!" Erik said.

"Those who were left as guards," Alex whispered.

"May not be passed until their regeneration in the mount, or until the fifth root race begins," Miguel finished the quote from the Edgar Cayce readings.

"I believe these ancient machines are scanning our DNA," Alex said. "And they're like the serpents who spit fire from the Book of the Dead."

"This is a perfect blend of Atlantean technology and Egyptian mysticism, that was programmed 13,000 years ago," Erik said, shaking his head. "I wish I could remember more as the stakes feel really high. This is the ultimate moment of truth."

"There is no room for fear or hesitation," Miguel said. "Our initiation in the Great Pyramid has prepared us to meet this challenge."

"What if we are to say some sort of opening words or password?" Alex asked, feeling a sense of heightened anxiety.

"Let's join hands and center ourselves before we chant again," Erik said.

Miguel led them as they chanted the seven notes of the musical scale, visualizing a rainbow of light moving upward through their spiritual centers. Alex feared her legs might not move her body forward, but summoning every reserve of strength and courage, she willed herself to approach the entrance. Scarlet arrows of light flashed around them as they advanced toward the doors, and a high-pitched whine stabbed their ears. Everything, including the serpent statues, was bathed in intense red light.

They walked slowly, keeping pace with each other. The intense sound from the serpents was shrill and painful and the flashing lights made it difficult to focus. With every step the sound seemed to grow louder.

They finally passed through the three doorways unharmed and entered another chamber. When they crossed the threshold, the next room became illuminated by the same unseen light source. On the opposite wall were mirrored panels painted with life-sized murals with gilded frames, figures dressed in costumes from another time. The figures in the panels wore long white robes and gold and silver diadems on their heads. Their own reflections were superimposed on the glass paintings as if they were dressed in that ancient clothing.

Alex recognized the clothing from her visions and regressions. Each of them more the pendants and head pieces she had seen. "This seems impossible," Alex said.

"We are seeing ourselves as we were the days the chambers were sealed," Miguel said in a hushed voice.

Alex approached the glass and touched her own reflection. "I have seen this face in a mirror before, she is the priestess, Una."

"I wonder if these designs above the doorways are names and dates," Erik wondered. "The writing is unlike anything I've ever seen, block capital letters, Celtic runes, and some sort of homogenized computer code. The language seems strongly symbolic."

"I will turn off the flash," Alex said, and took a few photos. "Shall we travel through the looking glass, gentleman?"

Opening the doorways of their own likenesses, each one entered a catacomb of alcoves and chambers that were inlaid with alabaster, marble, and other semi-precious stones. Crystal orbs, resting in carved stone sconces, blinked on as they passed, powered by the legacy of an unknown and vastly ancient technology.

"This place is in pristine condition as if it has been hermetically sealed," Erik said.

"I believe the legend of these chambers must be the origin of that expression as the Egyptian Thoth became the Greek Hermes," Miguel said. "As a teacher of hidden wisdom he held the secrets."

They walked through a time capsule that was organized like a museum or a library of priceless treasures that was arranged in attractive displays. "

"The floor plan here seemed similar to the Sphinx Temple," Miguel said.

With a rush of chills, a sense of familiarity washed over Alexandria. "I think I will remember where everything will be," she said. "I believe my former incarnation could have been mistress of records, and was involved with gathering and organizing these contents in conjunction with the Atlantean Thoth," she said, blushing and smiling. "As you shepherded the records in the Yucatan, Miguel."

Paintings, sculptures, and pottery adorned a room that seemed like an art gallery. Musical instruments that resembled lyres, harps, and flutes filled another hall. Alex examined a display of jewelry, gemstones, and crystals, that were delicately arranged on silk and linen clothes. She reached for a necklace insert with stones and beads of lapis, carnelian, turquoise, and Onyx.

"This is exquisite," she said, admiring the delicate artistry.

Clothing, cooking utensils, children's toys, and woven blankets were spread across chairs and tables as if left only yesterday. Erik picked up a tiny toy that resembled a miniature airplane. Miguel removed the stopper from an alabaster vial, closing his eyes and inhaling the aroma.

"Rose oil," he said with a sense of wonder.

"This seems to be the technology and transportation area," Alex said as she continued walking. Models of aircraft like dirigibles and watercraft were displayed next to shelves of exotic looking equipment and machines.

"This place could keep Egyptologist busy for another thirteen thousand years," Erik said. "Nothing in my life has prepared me for this."

"But something in a past life did," Alex smiled. Erik squeezed her hand and returned her smile.

The history of humanity was depicted in paintings, carvings, and maps of Earth as the landmasses shifted and evolved through earthquakes and volcanic upheavals. The progressive destruction of Atlantis was shown through a series of maps. Aerial views depicted the first continent, then a group of islands, and the final large island that Edgar Cayce has called Poseidia.

"From the looks of this, humanoids have been on this planet for a very long time," Erik said.

While Erik entered a room and poured over ancient maps, Alex discovered another room that seemed like an astronomical observatory where bright stars were painted on a domed indigo ceiling. On the floor a circular map of Earth was painted with locations that reflected a global pattern of astronomical monuments in relation to the stars above. Circular walls were covered with paintings, conveying ancient timelines. The cardinal directions were represented by star groups that would have held those places twelve thousand years ago. A picture of the Earth's globe and axis pointed to a circle of stars.

Alex shouted, "Erik, come here." Both men rushed to join her.

"A cosmic mirror, "" Erik whistled through his teeth.

Miguel stared at a circular representation of stars and constellations. "What does this represent?" he asked.

Erik moved in to get a closer look. "Brilliant." Alex and Miguel stared at him.

"This circle denotes one complete rotation of a precession of the equinoxes. Those are various stars the imaginary pole points to as it wobbles through the 26,000-year cycle. Here is Polaris in Ursa Minor and here is the constellation we now call Cepheus," he said.

"This one is larger than the others," Alex said.

Erik studied the picture for a few moments. "This is Vega, which was the pole star 13,000 years ago, and these astronomical references provide exact dating."

"So, Vega was the pole star when this was painted, just like in my dream," she said, her eyes widening in surprise.

"Look at this," Erik said, paintings of constellations that describe the night sky at that time. The written characters beneath them must be both Atlantean and ancient Egyptian."

"A Rosetta stone of stars," she said.

"As you said Alex, astronomy is the key to the puzzle," Miguel said.

"Sirius has a prominent role," Erik said, pointing to a large star in the center of another painting.

"This looks like my dream too," Alex said. "Can you imagine the worth in wealth and wisdom that this place represents? What if this knowledge falls into the wrong hands?"

"That was the point, right? Only those who were ready could get in, Miguel said.

"What about now? The barn door is open," Erik added.

"Then we must lock the door when we leave, Miguel said.

ALEX PHOTOGRAPHED without flash as they explored the chambers. A beautiful carved and painted relief of the city of Poseidia, the Atlantean temple and the great crystal, the Tuaoi stone was placed center stage in one of the rooms. Many people were depicted in murals, showing different racial characteristics and clothing from ancient millennia.

Some looked unfamiliar as if they might not have come from Earth. The Atlanteans looked like American Indians, the red race, as Cayce had described. Some beings were quite tall and looked thin and pale, while others were short and more dark skinned. They approached an unusual display behind the relief panel. Thirteen green crystal cylinders were suspended in cases that looked like clear plastic.

"The Emerald Tablets of Thoth," Miguel said. "I always assumed they were legendary. Imagine what knowledge of sacred science is contained in these crystals."

"The technology that destroyed Atlantis. My grandfather must have had a hand in this in that lifetime," Alex smiled.

"This is what Selig wants. Knowledge of free energy that would destroy the current balance of power, or place that power in his hands," Erik said.

"A time bomb and a time capsule," Miguel said.

Alexandria moved on, then she came to a sudden stop, staring straight ahead.

"What is it?" Erik asked.

"The burial chambers," she whispered.

They walked down a generous hallway that branched into seven smaller halls. Alexandria approached a door where a seven-pointed star set with gemstones glittered above the arched opening. Erik and Miguel followed her into the sepulcher.

"Sleeping Beauty," Erik said softly.

Alex stared at the painted likeness of the beautiful woman lying in state. She wore a crown with a seven-pointed star that was inlaid with seven gemstones in the colors of the spectrum.

"Rainbow star," she said.

"Like the goddess Seshat," Miguel said.

Treasured artifacts were arranged with loving care. Alabaster jars to hold oils and unguents. Small painted portraits were accompanied by woven scarves and golden sandals. A depiction of the seven-rayed healing temple was painted on one wall.

Alexandria gently touched the sarcophagus, weeping tears of joy and relief. "We have returned at last."

"Alex, look at this," Erik said.

Shaken she walked toward the direction he pointed. Placed among other articles on a gilded table was the small star clock from her dream. The star chart from her dream hung on the wall.

"It's really here." She held the clock in her hands, feeling deep gratitude for the evidence that consciousness transcends lifetimes.

Miguel placed his arm around her shoulder. "The legend promised that we may each remove one artifact."

Her expression was pained; she shook her head, fighting tears. "The star clock is too obvious." She chose a pure white crystal orb and tenderly placed the sphere in her pocket. "Perhaps this is a stone of light with a story to tell," she said.

Erik chose a beautifully cast gold coin, inscribed with the same unknown characters. Miguel selected a small translucent alabaster urn that could fit in his palm.

"For incense. We have accomplished what we came to do. The angels of heaven must guide the rest of the unfoldment."

Their reverie was interrupted by the piercing whine of the black serpents and a scream of agony. They ran back toward the sound and into the antechamber.

Alex gaped at the lifeless form of Selig. His crumpled body lay on the floor of the alcove, hands clutching his ears. Blood oozed from his eyes and nose and the acrid stench of charred flesh filled the room. The intruder's death had stopped the whine of the serpents.

"He followed us," she said, feeling sick.

Miguel bent over Selig and felt for a pulse. "He is dead."

"The technology still works after all this time," Erik said.

"Yes, too bad about Mr. Selig, a voice said from the darkness. He was always impatient and lacked caution.

Alex froze.

After what seemed an eternity a man emerged into the light, careful to stay out of the range of the serpents. Looking like a phantom, he stepped from dark shadows into the pale light that was emitted by the sconces. He was tall and powerfully built, wearing a black wet suit and a mask. He approached them, pointing a gun at Alex's chest. She could feel Erik tense beside her.

"Don't overreact, Mr. Anderson. "I want your deaths to look like an accident. You three have been very useful so far, much more than Selig in fact. We had to intervene more than once, and it appears I will need your help again tonight. I wish to see these chambers for myself before they are destroyed and you along with the evidence. In order to do that I will need to leave a tiny device inside that will leave no trace."

"Why destroy this place?" Alex asked.

"Mankind is not ready for this knowledge, and archaeology is of no interest to me," the man said in a tone of disgust. "The human race is a herd of ignorant sheep. Power is better kept in the hands of the shepherds. Better that all trace of this is obliterated.

"Who are these shepherds?" Miguel asked in a calm voice.

"Although it is of no concern of yours, I suppose it doesn't matter that you know. Let us say that those who wield true power from behind the scenes constitute an aristocracy that spans countless millennia. My superiors come from an ancient lineage that has been known in many guises, spanning many civilizations and epics. Always this bloodline has controlled wealth, energy, and politics. They are stewards of earth's resources and monitor the population and purity of the race, making corrections and adjustments where necessary. Their high purpose is to maintain a quality of life for those who are most qualified to rule."

"But why destroy this priceless legacy?" Alex asked, gesturing to the feline statues and black serpent sentinels.

"It is a pity, really, as some of my colleagues would certainly enjoy these trinkets, but the risk is too great."

"What happens after you eliminate the threat?" Erik asked.

"An astute question. The time has come for another global conflict, precipitated over oil. This will occur and we will move into a greater position of control. We also have technology to create crises in weather patterns, so the expected climate changes will decimate the disturbing rise in world population. Conveniently, ancient prophecy, much of which was generated by our brotherhood, will be fulfilled and we will then be in charge. Always unseen, of course. It will seem as if Armageddon has arrived right on schedule." He laughed in a menacing tone.

"Clever and well planned," Miguel said, stealthily moving closer to the man so slowly that no one noticed. "What of the damage to the Earth caused by these climate changes and disasters?

"We have prepared for this and will remain underground for a period. When the time is right a new order will emerge on the surface of the planet."

"But it makes no sense. You already have enormous power and wealth." Alex said.

"Silence! We know best." He waved his gun. "Enough talking. Go ahead, Miss Stuart, please lead the way. You passed, and as a perfect genetic specimen, so shall I. My superiors will want a report."

Alex did not believe the man could pass the serpents, so she slowly turned around and faced the opening. She approached the doorways in a deliberate cadence. She took a few steps, then heard a groan and the sound of metal hitting stone. She wheeled around to see the man fall to the ground unconscious.

"Fancy footwork, Miguel," Erik said, stooping to pick up the gun.

"He was much too sure of himself," Miguel said.

"I am beyond ready to get out of here as soon as my heart gets back in my chest," Alex said.

"Not so quickly," a female voice said from the darkness. Three more black-suited figures emerged from the shadows. "We will not be as patient or arrogant as our companion."

What happened next occurred so swiftly that Alex would never recall the sequence. Two figures emerged like a flash from the water. Water dripped from tight white wet suits, revealing that one was male and one female. Their heads were wrapped in white scarves and all that was visible were their eyes— vivid green eyes. These were the mythical ninjas. They seemed to sail through the air, aiming flying feet at the black-suited attackers. In unison they pivoted and toppled the woman with the gun.

Then the woman's feet kicked a knife from one of the other assailants hands, and the man's heels connected with the head of the other, knocking him to the ground. Shots erupted from the darkened bridge and rang out in the hollow chamber followed by screams and silence. The men and women turned green eyes like cats toward Alex and bowed. As quickly as they had appeared, they picked up the unconscious attackers and disappeared back into the darkness.

"Is anyone injured"? Miguel asked.

Alex shook her head but trembled.

Erik grabbed Alex"s arm. "We need to get out of here." He pulled Alexandria toward the bridge.

"Get down," he ordered, snapping her out of shock. They crawled back across the long stone bridge. Out of breath, they struggled up the sloped surface of the passage to the cavity beneath the paws of the Sphinx. Three dead bodies littered the room.

"Selig's work or his companions," Erik said.

Alex recoiled but managed to keep moving. They negotiated the horizontal route back to the Sphinx's shoulder. Mohammed's furious face appeared in the opening.

"Hurry. They came for me as soon as they discovered they had followed you. We don't have much time before the authorities learn what has happened here."

"More valiant lives have been sacrificed," Alex said.

"We will honor their memory through what we accomplished tonight and our continuing quest for the truth." Miguel said.

They ran across the sand toward Mohammed's van. Alex barely had time to jump onto the seat before the driver speed off in the direction of the Cairo airport.

"I have collected your belongings from the hotel. Your new tickets are waiting at the airport," Mohammed said. His expression was grim. "I have been quite busy for the past hour." Looking at Erik's arm Mohammed noticed that he was bleeding."

"It's only a scratch. Thank you, my friend," Erik said we recognize the true price of your support. Did you lose any more men tonight?"

"No, Allah be praised."

Miguel removed the alabaster urn from his pocket. "Protect this treasure Mohammed and use it as you see fit."

Mohammed accepted the small vase with trembling hands. "Then the legends are true."

"Beyond anything you can imagine." Erik said, handing him the gold coin. Mohammed turned the coin examining the inscriptions.

"I will send the pictures we took in the chambers," Alex said.

Mohammed nodded and looked at each of them. "I'm sorry I doubted you. We need to proceed carefully with this profound discovery as these are dangerous times and there are those who are beyond greedy. "

Hands still shaking, Alex removed her silver necklace and pried the silver wire loose from around the quartz crystal and inserted the white orb from the Hall of Records in its place. Twisting the silver wire around the priceless treasure she placed the chain outside her shirt.

"Sherlock Holmes always claimed the safest place to hide something was in plain sight."

"Elementary," Erik said.

The van driver handed Erik a headscarf and he pulled up his sleeve. Alex wrapped the cloth around the wound, relieved to see it was a shallow cut. They were quiet on the trip to the airport, wondering if they were being followed.

Alexandria's heart still pounded as she stared at the Full Moon, now high in the sky. She wrapped her fingers around the crystal ball, wondering what secrets the tiny orb contained.

# CHAPTER 45

# QUEEN OF SHEBA

Mohammed herded them through the Cairo airport, ushering the three beleaguered travelers to the front of the line for the 2:00 AM flight to New York. The airline officials stamped their tickets and passports, returning them as if they were infected with plague. Alex cried when Mohammed hugged her.

"Thank you for everything; I hope we can return under better circumstances one day."

He looked deep into her eyes "My thanks to you, priestess of Seshat."

With fierce hugs Erik and Miguel made silent farewells to their Arab comrade. They boarded the plane and claimed their seats in the first row of coach behind the bulkhead. The night flight was only half full, and after take-off, Alex stretched across the empty seats in the middle section, staring at the ceiling of the plane.

Erik opened his computer and began transferring images from their cameras. He worked on a draft email that would be ready to send when they arrived in New York.

"I intend to launch a few missiles on the Internet," Erik said.

Alex listened to Erik's fingers clicking on the keyboard of his computer, struggling to get comfortable. When she finally relaxed and fell asleep, troubled dreams filled her mind with images of robed initiates, deception, and betrayal.

WHEN THEY LANDED at JFK early the next morning Alex phoned Sheila, leaving a message to contact Lela, take the train, and meet them at the Warwick hotel later in the afternoon. Disconnecting her phone, she looked at Erik. "Quite a night's work. How does you're your arm feel?"

"Sore, but that's the least of it. Mohammed lost dear friends. Things will be in an uproar as some of these images leak out."

"Atlantean technology reincarnated," Miguel said. "It's for the best that those who oppose us realize we have learned the truth. After claiming their luggage they moved through Customs and Immigration like robots. Once outside they hailed a cab and made their way into the city and the charming Warwick hotel in Manhattan. Alex showered and collapsed on the bed, falling into a deep sleep. Erik sent several emails to his contacts, starting a groundswell of controversy.

Hours later Sheila and Lela phoned from the lobby. "I made reservations at my favorite Ethiopian restaurant," Lela said.

"Fabulous," Alex said, physically refreshed and hungry after her long nap, but feeling deeply changed and humbled by her experiences.

After a manic cross-town trek with a seasoned New York cabbie at the helm, the motley group descended on the Queen of Sheba restaurant. A colorful mural, depicting the legend of Solomon and the Queen of Sheba, covered an entire wall. The Ark of the Covenant was prominent in the painted scene and Alex pointed to the cherubim.

"Dwellers on the threshold," she said.

Erik tried to a smile but their experience had taken a toll.

They sat around a cozy table that was covered with a brightly colored woven cloth and warmed by candlelight. A smiling African woman brought a circular woven basket that was brimming with Ethiopian delights arranged on warm bread. Alex tore off a piece of the bread and scooped a serving of spicy salad. Her eyes rolled backward in pleasure.

"This is heavenly," she said.

Lela practically cackled. "Lord, I love to watch you eat child. Did you hear that Mandisa?" She called across the room to the owner, and the woman beamed her pleasure.

"Have you seen the New York Times?" Sheila asked, shoving a copy at Alex.

She looked through the pages and buried at the back of the first section was an article Sheila had marked.  Alex read the headline aloud, *Bodies found beneath Sphinx: Mummy's curse or foul play?"*

"The game's a foot Watson," Lela chuckled.

"Beyond your wildest dreams,"Erik said. "I checked the Internet before we left the hotel and the few seeds we planted are already sprouting. The Web is as busy as a convention of spiders. I spoke to Mohammed and the honchos in the Egyptian antiquities department are publicly denying everything, hurling hyperbole at the international media. Privately they're threatening to charge us with murder unless we tell them how we got in there."

The three travelers shared their experiences over dinner and when Alex told them about discovering Seshat's tomb, she grasped the necklace, holding the crystal aloft. "There were dozens of these in different sizes and degrees of clarity."

"This came from the Hall of Records?" Lela whispered. "May I touch it?"

Alex smiled, removing the necklace, and placing it around Lela's neck.

"I talked to Emma. There's an offer pending on Gran's house." She paused for a dramatic effect waiting until they all looked at her. "Mom is engaged to Arthur Livingston from the bank."

"You're kidding," Sheila said eyes bulging, "That was fast.

"Thank God Almighty free at last," Lela laughed,

Miguel and Erik laughed.

"What are you three planning for an encore?"  Sheila asked.

"We've done what we can for now in Egypt," Miguel said. "Now it's up to others to pick up the torch."

"According to a friend of mine, divers have identified anomalous findings in the Gulf Stream of Bimini," Lela said. "Anomalous, I love that word."

"What do you think?" Alex smiled. "Shall we return to Atlantis?"

# EPILOG

Erik put his arm around Alexandria's shoulder as he joined her on the sofa. She smiled up at him as they snuggled in front of the crackling fire and twinkling lights on the tall Christmas tree. Twenty years ago they had decided to buy Gran's home.

Alex held the faceted ruby Erik had given her for her birthday, feeling the energy of the stone and already imagining what she might design.

"Well, it was a big day," she said. "It's wonderful to have Jason home from college."

"Yes, Erik agreed, smiling, "It's hard to believe he'll graduate next June with a degree in archeology; I guess the fruit didn't fall too far from the tree."

Alex smiled.

"It was wonderful to talk to both Miguel and Mohammed," he said.

"Yes, and I was happy we could prepare a feast for Sheila—so many memories. I miss Emma and Lela so much. It's amazing to think how much time has passed and that all we discovered in Egypt is still mostly hidden.

"Mohammed said things are bubbling beneath the surface, but no one else has been able to enter the hall of records. He told me about a man who lives on the Giza Plateau who dug down in his own property, which is forbidden, and discovered a tunnel that looked like it would go clear to the Nile. Of course the Department of Antiquities swooped in and shut it down. He also mentioned reports of a strange staircase in an off limits area of the Plateau that reaches far underground."

"It would be wonderful to go back and go inside the Step Pyramid and see the restoration of the Serapeum," Alex said. "Maybe we could take a graduation trip with Jason next year?"

"What a great idea, maybe Miguel could meet us. I'd love to see the caves that Andrew Collins has discovered at Giza and learn more about the chamber they've found behind the original entrance to the Great Pyramid."

"So many things are happening. As modern researchers continue to chip away at the naive belief of the age of pyramids and Sphinx," Alex said. "But it seems our work did not yield the transformation we hoped for. Did we fail or succeed?"

They sat in silence for a time, each lost in their own thoughts.

"Miguel said on the phone that the time has not yet reached the point that humanity is ready to forsake war and embrace the peace that is possible. We did our part and kept our promise, and we have to be grateful that we accomplished our purpose. Now it's up to others, and perhaps our son will have a role to carry the torch into the future."

"You're right, even though it's difficult to accept. Merry Christmas my love. We have a lot to be thankful for."

# Acknowledgments

A wise teacher once said, "The spiritual path is the solitary work we cannot do alone," and the same is true of the writing life. I'd like to thank my family for years of love and support. Thanks to my husband Ted who unselfishly offers both editorial and astrological advice that always improves my efforts. He also provides encouragement when faith in myself falters.

Many thanks to the Edgar Cayce organization, the A.R.E., the Association for Research and Enlightenment, for their guardianship of the Edgar Cayce source material. Cayce's trance readings have inspired me for decades, and I feel I have recovered many memories from my own prior lives from the research that informed this story.

Enormous thanks to my publisher Satiama Publishing for their ongoing faith and support of my work. Special thanks to author and teacher Theresa Crater who read the original book in 2005 and made excellent suggestions that have been incorporated into the second edition.

My gratitude goes to all the readers for your support and encouragement over the years, many of you have expressed delight that a second edition is forthcoming. My immense gratitude goes to friends, students, and clients for giving life deeper meaning and purpose.

If you enjoyed this book please considered writing a short review on Amazon or Goodreads. It means a great deal and would be deeply appreciated.

Thank you
Julie Loar

# ABOUT THE AUTHOR

**Julie Loar** is the multiple national award-winning author of *Symbol & Synchronicity: Learning the Soul's Language in Dreams Waking Life*, the two-volume *Sky Lore Anthology*, *Goddesses For Every Day*, *The Hidden Power of Everyday Things* and *Tarot and Dream Interpretation*. She is also the co-creator of the board game *Quintangled*. Her work has been translated into several languages, and her popular Astrology column appeared in *Atlantis Rising* magazine for two decades. She is featured on SatiamaPublishing.com. Julie has led eighteen sacred journeys to Egypt and is a frequent speaker and presenter.

After a near death experience in Mexico in 1966, she pursued what has become her lifelong interest in dreams, symbols, angels, space travel and ancient Egypt through an intensive thirty-year study of metaphysics. Focusing on symbols, mythology, Astrology, Astronomy, Tarot, Qabalah, dreams, and shamanism, Julie has been a spiritual practitioner and teacher since 1972. She has spoken internationally on women's issues, leadership, motivation, mythology and symbolism.

http://www.JulieLoar.com

# ALSO BY JULIE LOAR

### As Julie Loar

*Symbol & Synchronicity: Learning the Soul's Language in Dreams and Waking Life*, Satiama Publishing, Palmer Lake, CO 2021

*As Above, So Below: Sun, Moon & Stars*, Satiama Publishing, Palmer Lake, CO, 2023

*Ancient Sky Watchers & Mythic Themes*, Satiama Publishing, Palmer Lake, CO, 2023

*Quintangled: A Game of Strategy, Chance & Destiny*, Satiama Publishing, Palmer Lake, CO, 2018

*Goddesses for Every Day: Exploring the Wisdom & Power of the Divine Feminine Around the World*, New World Library, Novato, CA, 2008, 2011

*Atlantis Rising Magazine* articles from 2000-2019

*Astrology & Tarot: Linking the Archetypes* course 2000, 2019

*Occult Symbology & the Metaphysics of Number* course 2000, 2019

### With Ted Denmark, PhD

Denmark, Ted, Ph.D. & Julie Loar, *The Star Table Trance Missions*, Volume 1, the *Five Star Series*, BookBaby, ebook 2015, print edition awaiting publication.

__________*Star Family Excursions*, Volume 2, the *Five Star Series*, BookBaby, ebook 2016, print edition awaiting publication.

__________*Star World Ascension*, Volume 3, the *Five Star Series*, BookBaby, ebook 2018, print edition awaiting publication.

__________*Star Time Convergence*, Volume 4, the *Five Star Series*, BookBaby, ebook 2019, print edition awaiting publication.

___________ *Star Light Reflections*, Volume 5, the *Five Star Series*, BookBaby, ebook 2020, print edition awaiting publication.

### As Julie Gillentine

*Tarot and Dream Interpretation*, Llewellyn Publications, St. Paul, MN, 2003

*The Hidden Power of Everyday Things: A Complete Personology Guide to Your Lifestyle Every Day of the Year*, Simon and Schuster, New York, NY, 2000

*Messengers: Among the Stars, Stones, and Legends the Ancient Wisdom Dwells*, Archive Press, Boulder, CO, 1997

# ALSO BY SATIAMA

**Other Publications and Works Available From Satiama Publishing**

**Non-Fiction Books**

*A Speckled Stone* by Karen Stuth

*Ancient Sky Watchers & Mythic Themes (A Sky Lore Anthology Volume One)* by Julie Loar

*As Above, So Below: Sun, Moon & Stars (Sky Lore Anthology Volume Two)* by Julie Loar

*Artist Shaman Healer Sage* by Katherine Skaggs

*How the Trees Got Their Voices Coloring Book* by Susan Andra Lion

*How the Trees Got Their Voices* by Susan Andra Lion

*The Essence of Sound: Full Spectrum Vibrational Healing for the Meridians, Chakras, Auric Field & Figure Eight Energies* by Evelyn Mulders

*Symbol and Synchronicity: Learning the Soul's Language in Dreams and Waking Life* by Julie Loar

*The Truths of Tula* by Dianna Cates Dunn

*The Way of the Simple Soul (The Way Series Book One)* by Catherine Grace Landry

*The Way of the Lightkeeper: Your Inner Journey to Spiritual Liberation (The Way Series Book Two)* by Catherine Grace Landry

*The Way of the Grace-filled Heart: Travel the Unbroken Path of Light and Love* (The Way Series Book Three) by Catherine Grace Landry

*The Way of the Inner Path: A Guided Journal to Your Innermost Beliefs and Stories* by Catherine Grace Landry

*Three Awakenings: A Spiritual Memoir* by Theresa Crater

**Fiction Books**

*My Uncle Owes Me a Favor* by Morrigan Milligan

*Jewels of Kidron* by Susan Miner

*The Invisible Riptide* by Carron Montgomery

*Magic on the Mountainside* by Nancy Godbout Juka

**E-books**

*The Way of the Simple Soul* (The Way Series Book One) by Catherine Grace Landry

*The Way of the Lightkeeper:  Your Inner Journey to Spiritual Liberation* (The Way Series Book 2) by Catherine Grace Landry

*The Way of the Grace-filled Heart:  Travel the Unbroken Path of Light and Love* (The Way Series Book Three) by Catherine Grace Landry

*Symbol and Synchronicity: Learning the Soul's Language in Dreams and Waking Life* by Julie Loar

*How the Trees Got Their Voices* by Susan Andra Lion

*Jewels of Kidron* by Susan Miner

*The Essence of Herbs: A Meridian Approach to Physical and Emotional Well-being Using Nature's Wisdom* by Evelyn Mulders

*The Essence of Sound: Full Spectrum Vibrational Healing for the Meridians, Chakras, Auric Field & Figure Eight Energies* by Evelyn Mulders

*Three Awakenings: A Spiritual Memoir* by Theresa Crater

**Audio Books on CD**

*Children's Spirit Animal Stories* Vol I by Dr. Steven D. Farmer

*Children's Spirit Animal Stories* Vol II by Dr. Steven D. Farmer

**Card and Tarot Decks**

*Children's Spirit Animal Cards* by Dr. Steven D. Farmer with Jesseca Camacho

*Cosmic Cat Wisdom Deck* by Randy Crutcher and Barbara J. Horn

*Divine Dog Wisdom Deck* by Randy Crutcher and Barbara J. Horn

*The Wisdom of Tula* by Karen Stuth, Art by Dianna Cates Dunn
*Masters of Light Wisdom Oracle* by Katherine Skaggs
*Mythical Goddess Tarot 10th Anniversary Edition* by Katherine Skaggs
*Whispering Herbs Healing Card: Essential Wisdom from Mother Earth* by Evelyn Mulders

**Games**

*Quintangled: A Game of Strategy, Chance & Destiny* by Julie Loar, Susan Andra Lion, and Karen Stuth

**Meditation and Music CDs**
*Come Walk With Me: Four Meditation Journeys to Becoming Your Higher Self* by Eva Black Tail Swan
*Safe Passage* by Trina Brunk

**All titles and products are available at your local bookstore, at SatiamaPublishing.com, at Amazon.com, Alibris.com, Faire.com, and on Etsy.com**

https://satiamapublishing.com/

www.ingramcontent.com/pod-product-compliance
Lightning Source LLC
Chambersburg PA
CBHW070521310726
48976CB00002BA/499